NO ONE IS SAFE

OTHER TITLES BY ELLIE MARNEY

The *None Shall Sleep* Sequence

None Shall Sleep

Some Shall Break

All Shall Mourn

The Circus Hearts Series

Circus Hearts 1: All the Little Bones

Circus Hearts 2: All Fall Down

Circus Hearts 3: All Aces

The Every Series

Every Breath

Every Word

Every Move

No Limits

Stand-Alone Titles

The Killing Code

White Night

"Missing Persons" *in Begin, End, Begin: A #LoveOzYA Anthology*

NO ONE IS SAFE

A Novel

ELLIE MARNEY

Published by Thomas & Mercer, Seattle

www.apub.com

EU product safety contact:
Amazon Media EU S. à r.l.
38, avenue John F. Kennedy, L-1855 Luxembourg
amazonpublishing-gpsr@amazon.com

ISBN-13: 9781662533143 (paperback)
ISBN-13: 9781662533136 (digital)

Cover design by Joanne O'Neill
Cover image: © Richard Nixon / ArcAngel Images; © shayes17 / Getty

Printed in the United States of America

For everyone who keeps their demon on a short leash

Macbeth: Canst thou not minister to a mind diseas'd,
Pluck from the memory a rooted sorrow,
Raze out the written troubles of the brain,
And with some sweet oblivious antidote
Cleanse the stuff'd bosom of that perilous stuff
Which weighs upon the heart?
Doctor: Therein the patient
Must minister to himself.
—William Shakespeare, *Macbeth*

The good and bad cannot be kept apart,
But there is some commingling.
—Euripides, cited by Plutarch

Prologue

October 1987, Saturday

Waking up after being knocked unconscious is like being reborn, and equally painful. It is not, Simon decides, an experience that improves on repetition.

Oh, his head. His vision is spinning, so he closes his eyes. That's unfortunately worse. The hurt is intense. He breathes through it, controls the urge to throw up, opens his eyes again.

Everything is blurred, fractured shapes of black, brown, and gray, which gradually resolve. This is a room; he's somewhere inside. There's the edge of a ceiling where it meets a wall. Buttresses are black; the wall is tarry brown, with gray metal shelving. Left of the empty shelving, a stack of white plastic thirty-gallon drums. For a moment, in his debilitated state, the stack seems like a modernist sculpture made from larger-than-life Tic Tacs.

The air is icy, and he's lying on a hard, cold floor—feels like concrete. This room is industrial—maybe a warehouse? There's some natural light from a small high window on the wall past the drum stack, which helps him get his bearings. He can hear a pattering sound: rain on a tin roof. It's raining outside. The room is gloomy but not completely dark; it's still daytime.

The last thing Simon recalls is walking into his apartment, closing the door and turning around . . . then Claude Ameche's ugly sneer. Okay, he's got it now. Or rather, he knows how they got him.

A long tacky-wet line on his cheek itches. One of his nostrils is blocked with what smells like blood. He swallows—definitely blood. He brings his hand up to touch his nose; it doesn't feel broken.

This is what you get for being caught out and knocked unconscious. Nomi warned him, even said the words *Be careful*, and he didn't give her advice enough consideration. She's going to be pissed. She'll give him that look—thin lips closed in a line, mink-brown eyes boring into his, a direct admonition. He almost wishes she were here right now, so he could say "What?" as if he didn't know, and she could blink at him in that way she does, like she's waiting for his brain to catch up to his mouth . . .

Dammit, his brain is rattling in his skull. And Nomi's not here, but that's a good thing—she'll know he's been taken; she'll figure it out. Unless Eric Lamonte's men have followed their mob boss's orders and simply shot her and left her in a dumpster somewhere, which is a possibility Simon doesn't want to think about.

It's freezing in here. He swipes a hand down his front: Henley, pilled knit vest, coat. He's still in his work clothes. His brown trousers are scuffed and dirty at the knees. There's dark blood on his coat lapel—goddammit, that stain's going to be impossible to get out.

A soft voice says, "Are you okay, mister?" and Simon startles, looks to the right.

Background: more brown wall, a hanging bulb, a door, the top of another white drum. Foreground: a girl's face, very dark-brown skin, black hair in short braids framing her eyes, plump cheeks, wide mouth. She's wearing blue jeans and a yellow T-shirt with a Care Bear on it and a multicolored nylon windbreaker. She's hugging herself for warmth and looking at him with concern.

Although he has never met her before, Simon knows this girl.

"You're—" His throat is rough. He clears it. "You're Brittany Jackson."

"Uh-huh." The girl nods.

"Your mom is Solange Jackson. She's been looking for you."

"You know my mom?" the girl asks, hopeful.

"Yes." He sits up carefully, winces. "Don't suppose you have any aspirin?"

Brittany bites her lip. "Sorry."

Simon rubs the back of his neck with a cold hand. His head is splitting. A rumble of thunder from outside makes his teeth vibrate, which doesn't help. He looks at Brittany, crouched on her haunches nearby. The intention was to find this girl and rescue her, not get himself laid up in what he assumes is a locked room *with* her.

"This . . . isn't quite going the way I anticipated," he admits.

Brittany just stares at him. "Uh-huh."

"My name is Simon Noone." Which is not true, but he's not getting into that now. "Brittany, your mom hired a woman I work with, Nomi Pace, to help find you, and . . . Actually, forget that for a minute. Do you know where we are?"

"We're in a room in a big building." Brittany sketches toward the air behind her with one hand. "The men out there, they put me in here, and the door is locked."

"Yeah, I got that."

"We can't get out. I didn't see anything when they put me in here, but when they open the door to bring food in, the other side looks like a big, like, factory or something? A big room, bigger than a house."

"Okay." He needs to get up. He's bracing for it. "Give me one second."

He rolls to the left. *Oh fuck.*

"When they brought you in, I was scared," Brittany says. "I thought you were dead."

He's not dead, he just *wants* to be dead. Head like a supernova, black fuzzy sparklers in his vision. His stomach is sliding around, and his rib cage is too small. On hands and knees, he pants and tries not to vomit. Concentrates on what he can feel: crumbs on the buffed concrete floor, cold air on his face. Pulsing pain in his left cheekbone and eyeball, maybe some swelling around the zygomatic arch. His breathing is occluded; he presses his thumb against his nostril, clears his blocked nose onto the floor, wipes his face with the sleeve of his coat.

Ai-ai-ai, this is wool, his landlady, Sofia Rosa, would tut. *You should take better care of your clothes.*

But he can smell now: the scent of rust and perishing wood, like mulch under a tree in spring; the acerbic tang of ammonia; the stink of food scraps. There's probably a bucket in here that Brittany's using for a toilet and a trash can. Or maybe it's the smell of the street outside.

"Are you okay?" Brittany repeats, somewhere in the upper atmosphere.

"Fine." Simon grunts, pushes himself back, clambers dizzily up to standing.

Perspective is good. The room is eight feet wide by twelve long, and the walls are eight feet high. If he calls the window north, there are drums and shelving against the east wall, the door to the south, a narrow wooden desk and more shelving at the west.

The window: Holding the desk, then the upper edge of a drum, he totters his way toward it. It's small, placed six and a half feet up the wall—he can just see over the bottom sill. They're at ground level. Rain dashes itself against the glass, seeps into a water stain under the sill. There's the damp brick wall of a fence, then another building about twelve feet away, a cramped alley between them.

Where the hell *are* they? Are they still in Manhattan? He can't hear traffic, only the whistling of the wind and rain. He hopes they're still in the West Village—it's ridiculous to be getting a rush of longing for the filthy, disreputable streets that he knows, but Simon's been cut loose from his personal geography before. He hates this feeling of disorientation, like he's a snipped thread.

He pulls his coat tighter against the chill, tries to concentrate. Hard to tell what time it is because of the storm, but he can't have been out that long; it's probably still midafternoon. This is an industrial building, a warehouse. Nomi followed Lamonte's flunky to a warehouse off West Nineteenth Street last night. So what's the likelihood this is the same place?

"I climbed up to that window," Brittany says, "but it's blocked off."

Simon angles to see, and she's right; the window is covered with wire mesh on the outside.

Lightning cracks like a flash grenade outside: Bright light suddenly spears through the window, jags into him like a glass knife to the eye. He hisses, presses his hands against the wall, tries to breathe. This is worse than his regular headaches.

His teeth are clenched, his shoulders bunched. The doctor would be telling him to let his muscles relax. Flores's deep voice always had a calming burr: *You tense up; you hurt. Let go. I know it sounds counterintuitive, but just try it.*

Simon relaxes, lets go. Lets his chin hang down to his chest. The pain in his temples subsides to a dull throb.

Brittany again. "Head's hurting, huh?"

"You have no idea." He turns around, props himself against the wall.

She's standing up. She's surprisingly tall for a seven-year-old, but her mother is a tall woman. "Yeah, I think they beat you up pretty good."

Simon huffs air. There's a certain comedy in it, he'll admit. Then Brittany grins, and he sees a dark gap—she's missing two of her bottom baby teeth. He winces at how, in these circumstances, she might have lost them.

"I've got a bottle of water, if you're thirsty," Brittany offers, "and some gum, if you—"

She stills, eyes flicking. Then he hears it, too, over the noise of the rain.

He quiets his own voice. "Is that them?"

Brittany nods. The whites of her eyes show stark against the brown of her skin.

"How many?"

"Four," she whispers. "That's all I seen."

Something like mercury—cool and calm and alien—is easing into his veins. "They have weapons, Brittany?"

She nods again. "Usually."

The sounds are clear to both of them now: the clump of heavy boots, the clipped echo of arriving voices. Simon can smell cigarette smoke. A door is rolled open, farther away, the rumble distinct from the low growl of thunder outside.

Brittany steps closer. She grips the sleeve of his coat with both her small hands. "Simon . . . What are we gonna do?"

Lightning cracks out the window behind them once more. Simon looks around the room, at the size and shape of the space, the objects it holds, the cold light in the air, the little girl by his side. Considers the ripe-bursting pain in his head, the quicksilver under his skin. How is he supposed to answer?

We can get out, but I'll need to slaughter some people first. If I remember how to do that. If my new conscience allows. And once I let the beast out of the box, will he want to go back in?

He can't say any of that. For Christ's sake, she's only seven.

"Don't worry." He pats Brittany's shoulder awkwardly. "I've got a plan."

Chapter One

September 1987, Friday
One week earlier

Simon wakes before his 2:30 a.m. alarm and lies under the covers, assessing his headache and listening to the night noises inside the building: the furtive scratchings of mice, the gurgle of pipes, the pad of feet as residents on the floors below make somnambulant visits to the bathroom or the kitchen. The tenement itself makes its own sounds; constructed in the nineteenth century, it shifts and creaks on its foundations like an old oak.

More noise comes from outside: the rumble of vehicles on the cobblestones, the chuckle of voices near Royale Veal. At distance, the thump of bass from one of the clubs. This is the Meatpacking District; it's never really quiet. He doesn't mind it. It reminds him of Guatemala, the village of Piedras Negras where he last lived, that sense of community, of everyone living in each other's pockets.

His digital alarm clock beeps once, and he silences it. Onward.

Throwing back the blankets, he stalks naked to the bathroom, flicks on the light. The bathroom is the apartment's weakest feature: Water-stained walls are high and glaring, and the bath, toilet, and upright sink are all crammed close together. Behind the mirrored door of the cabinet above the sink, a box of Vicodin; he washes one down with water from the faucet. This morning's headache is low grade, so he wants to get on top of it before it escalates. Once the pain becomes unmanageable, there's nothing he can do but bomb himself on medication and lie in a cool dark room, praying for the sweet release of death. And he can't die today; he has work.

Simon boils espresso coffee in the apartment's galley kitchen while he hunts for clothes, drinks it as he pulls them on. Checks himself in the mirror by the door. It's good to remind himself of who he is in the day-to-day: a white man in his mid-twenties with a longish face, blue eyes, the structure of the bones under the skin sharply delineated. A fairly standard configuration for a face. He looks normal. Eyes and cheekbones are perhaps too striking, but he's stuck with them. The groove in his skull, just above his left ear, is also nonstandard but is covered by his brown hair. He rubs two fingers over the ridged white scar where his neck meets his shoulder on the right: still there. He's still him, whoever that is.

He pulls his collar over the scar, tugs down his sleeves at the wrist. Today's outfit is boots, khaki trousers, and a gray hooded sweatshirt over a waffle weave long-sleeve Henley. No coat—he won't need one inside the cutting room. The clothes look right. His first day at Gennaro's Meats, he could tell his clothes were wrong, too neat, the lines and textures too formal. He had to rummage through a dozen thrift store bins to find what he needed, but he's got it now. His doctor, Richard Flores, had told him that New York City—that America generally—would be about blending in, which has been correct. The clothes are important. His mismatched socks, both brown but of different lengths and patterns, complete the look.

Final check: His hair isn't too tidy, and his pupils aren't too pinned. Simon lights a cigarette and is out the door by ten to three.

On Gansevoort Street, his boots thud on the cracked concrete sidewalk, the sound joining the rest of the night music. Truck horns are honking, and two cab drivers are leaning on their car doors, listening to talk radio. It's cold without a coat; Simon shoves the hand not holding his cigarette into his armpit, skirts a pile of crushed cardboard boxes near the curb. Cheap workers' cars are moored in random spots in and around the sagged chain-wire fencing of Edison ParkFast. As Simon crosses Washington Street near Centaur Packaging, he sees a young white transvestite bum a light from a Black hooker, both of them walking toward the johns waiting for them on the remains of the West Side Highway.

"It was always like this with the sexy ladies." Sofia Rosa has been regaling him with stories of the district from the last twenty years, spilling the kind of insider details that only an outsider immigrant can observe. "The wharf is right there, yes? And oh, the blood! I would come out in the street each morning to buy vegetables—blood would be steaming in the drains. Cats and dogs would come to lap. Even cattle waiting for slaughter would lick it off the stones."

Cannibal cows seem very plausible at 3:00 a.m., when streetlamps show clumps of men in their butcher uniforms, white coats glowing, spattered with gore. Simon's in the thick of it now. Men everywhere—coughing, talking, smoking, walking back from their break. Carcasses hang in a row near the entrance to Gennaro's, beneath the overhang. The air has the chilled, greasy smell of refrigerated fat.

He tosses his cigarette butt and slips inside the staff door with two other workers, grabs a white vinyl apron from the line of hooks on the right-hand wall.

"Noone?" Mike Nell, the shift supervisor, chews a toothpick as he marks off the roster sheet. "You're on breakdown."

"Really?" He's only been on knives for two weeks. Before that he was on packing. But one of the men on the boning line somehow sliced through his abductor pollicis transversus, taking off most of his left thumb, and Simon was slotted into his spot. Since then, he's experienced a rapid promotion.

"You up for it?" Nell squints. "Your prep lines seem okay, and you can drop a shoulder and cut a steak."

"I'm up for it."

"Wonderful. Then I don't have to find another hire." Nell's eyebrows rise. He's a glowering Scotsman with a bulldog's barrel chest and a thick mustache; this is as overjoyed as he gets.

Simon grabs gloves, hairnet, white coat. More gear—boning knife, breaking knife, honing steel, all in the scabbard on the butcher's belt. Something about putting on chain mail gloves is strangely sensual, the cold heaviness against his skin like the muscular coils of a snake.

"Tell me something, Noone." Mike Nell catches his eye. "Most new fellas don't last a week. The smells, the noise, the blood—and it's heavy work. But you seem to be in your element. How's that, eh?"

Simon fixes a baffled look onto his face, shrugs.

"I'm not complaining. Just to say, if you can avoid cutting your dick off, you'll do all right here. Understand? Okay, off you go."

A final stamp of his boots on the rubber mesh mats and Simon's through the doors, onto the floor of the slaughterhouse, with a feeling of relief. For eight hours, the duration of his shift, he can lose himself in the scream of the electric saw, the way a razor-sharp blade slides over bone, yellow fat parting neatly, steel separating flesh.

He's not sure what it means, that he loves this job so much. But it can't be unusual. Other people love their jobs. It's normal.

The 3:00 a.m. shift finishes at 11:00; it's always a shock, emerging from the cold, dim cutting room into glaring midday sun. On his way back home, Simon smokes a cigarette. He buys milk and a pack of Pall Malls from the deli grocery near the corner of Washington. He's already eaten his big meal of the day in the break room at work—a corned beef sandwich, slabs of warm pink meat with dollops of relish squashed between thick slices of white bread, washed down with a mug of bitter, overbrewed coffee—and he can get something for dinner later.

Streets are empty now the trucks have trundled off to deliver their loads: The district is like a ghost town by midday. At his tenement, Simon takes the front stairs and walks through the tall, narrow entrance, whistling. He always feels good after work. In the ground-floor hall, he knocks twice at the second door on the left. Sofia Rosa might be sleeping. No, the door is opening.

"Simón?" The old lady rubs her eye with a knuckle, fishes in her apron for a cigarette.

"Auntie, I brought you something." She is not his auntie, not in the slightest. But she pronounces his name in the Spanish way, and she is the only person he speaks that language with, the only person who reminds him of home. What he thinks of as home.

He gives her the paper-wrapped parcel from his pocket—a pound of pork sausage, a half pound of brisket. Nothing that Gennaro's will miss. He already has more steak in his fridge upstairs than he needs.

"Ah, good boy," Sofia Rosa says. "You will have coffee, yes?"

He makes the correct amount of mild protest at the offer. She gives him a little cup of Mexican coffee; he drinks it in the doorway, burning his tongue, before thanking her and returning the cup, heading upstairs.

The building narrows as it ascends. Irregular street patterns in the Meatpacking District are the result of the clash between the Greenwich Village system, the Commissioners' Plan of 1811, and the demands of heavy industrialization after the Civil War—Simon has looked it up—which is why all the apartment blocks are oddly shaped. This one is like a wedge of cake. There are six small apartments at ground level, four midsize ones on the second floor, three larger ones at the top.

The ground-floor tenants are all elderly. On the second floor, residents include a gruff woman in her mid-twenties who dresses in all black, a bicycle courier who is probably a drug dealer, and two more meatpacking workers. Simon shares the third floor with a middle-aged nurse and her disabled adult son. The last third-floor apartment is locked and infrequently occupied; Sofia Rosa keeps it for people sent her way by Felipe Brava, people just off the boat. Simon stayed there briefly six weeks ago, when he first arrived in Manhattan—when *he* was just off the boat—before he found the meatpacking job and decided to stay.

Inside his own room, he dumps his keys and groceries, strips out of his boots and clothes. He takes a hot shower, standing in the old claw-foot tub under the spray, scrubbing particularly at his nails. Then he gets back into bed, sets the alarm for two hours, and does a breathing exercise to force himself back to sleep.

At one thirty in the afternoon, Simon jerks up, enveloped in blankets, and slaps the alarm off. He's sweating.

He scrubs his face with his hands. He doesn't always dream when he sleeps, but it's almost always the same dream. And that was a bad one.

Untangling himself awkwardly from the blankets and pulling on a pair of jeans, he assembles a fresh pot of espresso, takes another Vicodin as the coffee brews. Then he sits on a chair by one of the long windows, bare feet up on the sill, sipping coffee and smoking until his sweat dries. The apartment is warm; golden afternoon light spills through the parted curtains. Outside, a radiant slice of street. Downstairs, one of the other meat workers is playing rock music at low volume. After a while, Simon feels better.

He rubs the muscles behind his neck with his free hand, working out the stiffness there. The dreams always throw him off balance. He doesn't know what they mean, doesn't know how to make them stop . . . He only knows they're exhausting.

The dreams are merely one symptom of his condition, though. It's been five years since Simon was found washed up on the riverbank in Guatemala, five years since he was hauled onto the back of a pineapple truck and taken to Richard Flores's village clinic in Piedras Negras to have his skull pieced back together. No name, no home, no identity—no memories except the ones he's made since he regained consciousness. He's lived with memory loss for half a decade, and it's never gotten easier, with the dreams and the headaches and the snippets of hazy recall.

He's a ghost of a person, spat out by the river, his only North Star a handful of clues pointing him toward a possible point of origin in America.

Still, he wonders if this quest was a mistake. Coming here to track himself down has introduced more complications—he's had to find work, avoid immigration, manage a new style of life. But while there are many things he's figuring out about living in the United States, none of those mysteries have so far held a candle to the mystery inside his own head.

This is why Dr. Flores pushed him, encouraged him to go.

"So many years of your life in a country not your own . . . It's not right." Flores stood in the kitchen of the clinic house, near the concrete counter with the kerosene stove. Out the window, in the gathering afternoon dark, a woman in a long skirt with a bundle of palm leaf kindling walked along the red-dirt lane. Inside, a gecko clung to the wall, watching the doctor pour measures of cusha corn spirit into two small glasses. "You should go to America—find out who you are."

"I don't know that country." Simon was wary. He had a routine in Piedras Negras; he had a life. He'd spent the day labeling equipment in the clinic room next door and studying medical textbooks. His knowledge of human anatomy had come very easily and was by then almost equal to the doctor's. Whether Flores's suspicions—that Simon had some medical training in his background—were correct or not, it had certainly made him a better assistant at the clinic.

"Going to America is worth a try," Flores had insisted. "Maybe you will see familiar things. Maybe your memory will come back. Maybe your soul will remember."

"I don't have money. I would need papers, passage—"

"I have money. Forget the money." The doctor clunked the glasses onto the table. "If you find out you are a rich man, return to Piedras Negras and pay me back."

"But—"

"No, listen." Flores sat down with a sigh. The gecko eyed the mosquitoes zooming around the light bulb under the tin roof. "I understand it will be difficult. America is not what you're used to.

But there is a deep part of you, something inside, that you do not yet understand. You know it is there, yes?"

Simon was forced to glance away. Yes, he knew.

"You must continue to interrogate it. To resolve it." Flores passed him a glass. "Anyway, I didn't put you back together after that trip down the river so you could sit around here at the clinic, or in the village."

Why *did* Flores put him back together? Simon still isn't sure.

He stubs out his cigarette in the glass ashtray on the sill. It's time to scrape off the residue of the dream and get to work—his other work. Uncovering the clues to his missing identity is slow going and involves a bit of effort, but he keeps digging.

One day, he will get some relief. One day, he will *remember*.

From the top of his dresser, Simon collects a phone book, the top hardcover notebook from a stack, and an old orange cigar box. He transfers everything to the little breakfast table near the window by the kitchen. The notebook contains page after page of jottings in his own spiky handwriting. He has a full collection of notebooks: They contain timelines of dates, accounts of his existing memories and his experience in the river, accounts of his dreams, notes from Dr. Flores, details about his migraines, and the steps he's already taken to explore his lost past.

This latest notebook has journaled info that starts from when Simon arrived in America, with a list of investigative options. His most recent dead end involved a trip to the Municipal Archives on Chambers Street. He wanted to look up American death notices from 1982 to see if any US citizens had been reported deceased in Guatemala during his time frame, but the population of the United States is too enormous. He'll have to narrow things down; he's been trying to figure out how to do that. By accent? America is vast, and there are many types of English spoken here. Perhaps he could scour a detailed map for recognizable place-names? Or test himself with regional foods—some of the junk food in the USA is very location specific. What he really needs to do is check the newspapers from five years ago for missing person reports. But again, this is a massive job, a task that must be broken down into parts. He can start with the southern states, the ones nearest Mexico, and even that will take weeks.

Today he has only three hours before offices close. What can he do in the immediate term? Consulting the phone book, Simon creates a list of places to make inquiries. He'll have to go down to the grocery to use the pay phone.

He tears out the notebook list and stuffs it into his jeans, packs everything up. Pulls on a black shirt, his boots, his peacoat. Cigarettes in his left coat pocket, keys and cash in his right, gold-rimmed sunglasses on his head. These clothes are more *him* than the clothes he wears to Gennaro's. When looking for items at Goodwill, he usually goes by touch, feeling for textures he knows: cashmere, linen, silk, wool, leather. He doesn't overthink it. Everyone has their own style, right? Once again, it's normal.

The rock music has stopped playing downstairs. As soon as he gets out the door, he hears a ruckus. Someone on the second floor is speaking loudly.

"—not paying her to come up here and make *trouble*—"

A softer voice interrupts. Can't hear the words. Simon turns his key in the lock, walks to the top of the dark-painted stairs.

"Don't give me that bullshit!" Male, rough voiced. "It makes problems for *me*, and then *I'm* the one getting it in the ass because Miss Solange can't do what she's told!"

Someone is being vulgar and disturbing the peace in this building. In *his* building. Sofia Rosa would not like it, and Simon does not like it. He goes down each step to the second floor at a measured pace, assessing the territory.

One level down, in the dirty-yellow bifurcated hall, the gruff young woman in black clothes stands in the open doorway of her apartment. Her arms are up, hands clenched on the jambs, barring entry. Another, taller figure stands in shadow behind her.

"Malcolm, you're being unreasonable," the gruff young woman says. "Solange is still doing her job."

A middle-aged man in black trousers and a pimp's polyester shirt—Malcolm, presumably—stands in front of her, shouting. "If she were doing her *job*, she wouldn't be up here seeing *you*!" Face contorted, Malcolm takes a lumbering step across the linoleum toward the young woman in the doorway. "You dumb bitch—"

"Hello, friend." Simon finds himself suddenly at Malcolm's side, although he can't remember moving—how did that happen? His vision grays a little at the edges. He straightens his shoulders, and it feels like an uncoiling. "You're being very loud."

Malcolm grimaces at the interruption. "I don't give a flying *fuck* about—"

Simon bumps Malcolm hard backward. People aren't used to being manhandled by strangers, and it slows their reaction time. Malcolm also reacts slowly. His mouth makes a dumbfounded "oh" between his jowls as Simon pushes him inexorably toward the second-floor balcony. There's an electric familiarity here; Simon doesn't know why, but he feels very alive in this moment. Something inside him is stretching, flexing, released from confinement.

Malcolm's facial expression cycles from fury to frustration to fear. "Hey—"

"You're in my building, and I don't like you." Simon keeps his tone friendly. "Nobody likes you."

"What the fuck are you—" Malcolm is bent back against the banister. The wood creaks. "Jesus Christ, man."

"You should go." Simon keeps his gaze lasered on Malcolm's eyes, which are a darting, muddy hazel.

"Don't hurt him," the young woman says behind them, in a voice that suggests she doesn't care either way.

Simon smiles.

"Okay, okay, Jesus," Malcolm whimpers.

Simon releases him. Malcolm stands, takes a breath. Looks at the young woman.

"*Don't*," Simon warns darkly.

Malcolm closes his mouth, backs up. He moves to the stairwell, jogs down to the ground floor, polyester shirt flapping.

Simon looks over the banister to check that Malcolm strides out the narrow door. He hasn't done anything like that before. Not in America. A terrifying thrill of exultation bubbles up inside, leaving him peculiarly charged as he turns around.

"Great," the young woman says, shaking her head, which apparently means that nothing is great. "Thanks a lot."

Simon blinks. "He was being a problem."

"There was no problem, and it was none of your business." The young woman is rail thin, in tight black jeans and boots and a knee-length black cardigan. The gray T-shirt underneath—so she doesn't wear only black after all—reads *Ladies and Gentlemen, The Fabulous Stains*. Her long brown hair is shaved in an arc over her right ear, the remainder pulled back in a straggly ponytail from a stern, plain face.

Simon squints. "I don't—"

"I better go talk to him." The taller figure in the apartment entrance sighs.

She hoists a shoulder bag, steps forward into the hall. She's a Black woman, very attractive, maybe early thirties, wearing purple pants and a white T-shirt. Her coat is in the crook of her elbow.

Simon's neighbor turns to her and frowns. "You want me to come along?"

"He'll be pissed that Boy Wonder here had him on the rail, but he'll calm down."

"Then check in with me later so I know you're okay."

"Will do. Thanks." The tall woman eyes Simon, walks past him for the stairs, heads down.

He's just deflected a potentially nasty incident with an aggressive man, but neither of these women seems appreciative, or even relieved. This is confusing.

Simon looks back at the young woman. "I thought—"

"There was no *thought*, you didn't *think*, you just acted." She has a faint accent, which becomes more pronounced when she's clearly angry like this. She throws up her hands. "But it's over now, it's done, so thank you very much and goodbye."

She pivots into the entrance of her apartment, collects a tote bag from a hook on the wall, and a beanie, which she tugs over her hair. Shouldering the tote bag, she backs out, pulls the door shut after herself.

For the first time, Simon sees a small blue card stuck with clear tape to one side of the door. The card reads **N. Pace, Private Inquiries**, and a phone number.

A few things are coming clearer now. "You're a private investigator."

"Yes. Congratulations for noticing." She yanks her keys out of her jeans pocket, turns her back on him to lock up.

"That woman, Miss Solange, is your client."

She glares over her shoulder. "Look, we don't know each other—"

"We live in the same building."

"And we still don't know each other. Excuse me, I have to go." She walks around him to the stairs.

Simon hesitates, but the words *private investigator* are ringing in his head.

He's spent six weeks trying to figure things out on his own, getting nowhere. Could the solution really be this simple?

It's worth a try.

Chapter Two

September 1987, Friday

Simon catches up with the gruff young woman halfway down the staircase.

"Look, I apologize," he says.

"Don't follow me." Her expression has moved from stern to stony. "Fine, you've apologized. Now you can leave."

"I'm going out as well." Simon thinks of a good excuse. He gestures toward the narrow front door as they reach the small lobby area. "And I don't want to let you walk out there on your own, in case that loud guy is still around."

The young woman stops, blocking the door to face him, high spots of red on her cheeks. She has dark-brown eyes, glossy and sharp, like a little carnivore. "Oh, so you want to protect me from a situation *you* caused. Very chivalrous."

"I didn't mean to—" Maybe she is too canny for excuses. He needs to reassess. "Look, I'm sorry. Can we please start over? I'm Simon Noone. I live almost directly above you."

He sticks out his hand. She glares at it. But then she unclenches her jaw, takes his hand and shakes.

"Nomi Pace." She's still very stiff cheeked. "I'm sorry if my client's associate disrupted your activities. I'll ensure there's no more disturbances."

Professionalism restored, Nomi Pace turns and walks outside.

"Great." Simon follows the clip of her boots out the door, down the concrete steps. It's a nice afternoon, and surprisingly warm. He tugs his sunglasses out of his hair and slides them on. "I'd like to go back to the part about you being a private investigator."

Nomi sighs. "You and every other person I meet."

"I wondered if you could tell me—"

Still striding, she cuts him off with a raised hand. "First of all, you should know that I don't give advice for free."

"Fine." They are heading along Gansevoort, away from Hudson Street. Passing the Florent Diner, he sidesteps a fire hydrant. "I'm not really looking for advice—more like . . . suggestions."

"Right." Nomi keeps walking. "Why are you following me, again?"

"I'm not following you. I'm going to the pay phone outside the grocery store."

"Uh-huh."

She already thinks he's annoying; he might as well shoot his shot. "How would you trace someone if all you had was a name and a location?"

Her mouth twists. "Don't tell me—you met someone at a club, and you lost their number."

"No. This is . . . kind of a hypothetical."

"Sure." An eyeroll.

"So how would you do it?"

"You have a name and a location, but nothing else?" Nomi frowns. She's still stomping along, but he can see she's intrigued despite herself.

"Only a first name." They're nearly at the deli grocery near the corner of Gansevoort and Washington.

"Just a *first* name?" She stops in the street to gape. Recovers and turns around, continues walking. Looks like she's going to the grocery too. "Well, that's crazy. It can't be done."

It's not her tone; it's the way she pulls the shutters down: *It can't be done.* He's been at this for weeks, and she's giving up so easy? To hell with that.

Frustration firms his voice. "I want it done."

Nomi looks at him and frowns, pulls the door handle of the grocery store to go inside. Oh well, he's come this far. He catches the door and follows behind her.

It's about as crowded as it gets inside the grocery. Four people are waiting for sandwiches near the deli counter, a guy is making himself coffee at the coffee station, and three people are browsing for groceries. Jaunty opera music blares from a radio attached to the wall, adding to the chaotic vibe.

Nomi squeezes to get through to the shelf racks, seems nonplussed when she realizes Simon is still on her heels. But something in his face clearly makes her take pity on him, because she keeps speaking.

"Okay, listen." She grabs two jars from the shelves—sauerkraut, jelly—and talks as she searches for other items. "There's lots of ways to trace a person, but you need a minimum amount of information. A complete name is the best place to start. Even an alias. Then you try police reports, municipal records of births, deaths, marriages, hospital records. Or if you only have fingerprints, you try fingerprints, known associates, criminal records . . ."

"No fingerprints." Simon hits his head on a fly swatter poking out from a top shelf, pushes it away, takes his sunglasses off. "So without a name, you're nowhere."

"Basically, yeah. Sorry."

She grabs three more cans and a plastic package of sugar, stuffs everything into the tote bag, then maneuvers past him to the counter. Strings of sausage and chilies and garlic hang above the charcuterie display window, and two guys are handling orders, barking out commands to the elderly man on the register. Somewhere behind all this, the whine of a meat slicer.

Nomi waves her tote bag, can't get anyone to add up her groceries.

"Let me get that." Simon takes the bag from her—being over six feet tall is an advantage here—and raises it to attract notice.

Her mouth makes a tight line. "If you must."

"I must." He did just pump her for information, so paying for a few groceries seems like a fair exchange.

Simon pays the man on the register for Nomi's things and also makes purchases for himself: a green tomato, a tub of coleslaw, two ripe figs. Nomi's tote and his own brown paper bag in hand, he struggles his way out of the store behind her. Back outside on the pavement, she turns in the sun, and he hands her the tote.

She seems confused about it. "Thanks for the groceries. You didn't have to do that."

"You just gave me advice, which, as you pointed out, isn't free."

"I didn't help, though." She grimaces. "You've really only got a first name?"

"Yeah."

"Can I ask what you've already tried?"

"A bunch of things . . ." He's got a record of them in his notebook. Thinking about it makes him tired. "But I don't know, maybe I'm chasing my tail on this."

Nomi tilts her head. "This isn't a hypothetical, is it?"

"No."

"Who are you trying to find?"

And this is really the moment when he has to choose. He's been carrying this mission for months—more like years—on his own. Maybe it's time to stop being completely self-reliant. But how much does he tell her?

Simon thinks of a discreet blue card stuck to a wooden door in a grungy building in a dingy neighborhood: This woman might be an investigator, but she's not top of the line. Not someone likely to rat him out, considering his vulnerabilities. He has a lot of vulnerabilities.

He makes a call and hopes it's the right one.

"Me," he says. "I'm trying to find me."

"Pardon?"

"I was pulled out of the Usumacinta River in Guatemala in 1982, with a gunshot wound to the head. They patched me up, but I lost my memory, and I had no ID. I don't know who I am."

Nomi's tote hangs down by one strap. "You lost your memory. Like, what, amnesia?"

"Yes."

"Amnesia." She tests the word.

"Yes."

"Okay. Wow. That's . . ." She steps back, steps forward again. When she's not frowning and trying to seem gruff, her face is quite expressive. Her hard, mink-dark eyes are focused on him and have taken on a new inquisitiveness. "So what do you already know?"

"I know . . ." He hesitates, but they've got to start somewhere. "I know I'm American—or at least, I have American dental work. I have a name, Simon, that was on a label sewn into my clothes."

"So you have new paperwork." She picked that up quickly. She's no fool.

"Yes." It was always going to come out. He continues the litany. "The rest is . . . random. I'm right handed. I'm not color-blind. My first language is English, but I seem to be good at languages. At least, I didn't have much problem picking up Spanish and Maaya t'aan—"

"And Italian," Nomi says.

Simon looks at her. "What?"

"You . . ." Nomi wets her lips. "You just spoke Italian with the deli owner."

"Italian." He can feel how his mouth has fallen open. He doesn't know how to react.

"Yes." Nomi keeps her eyes fixed on his. "You didn't realize? Oh wow."

Simon blinks at Nomi, blinks at the store. Raises a hand to rub at the groove in his skull. His headache is making a numb spot at his temple.

Is it always going to be like this? Living this strange double life, his shadow self always one step ahead, driven by impulses and instincts and appetites he's barely conscious of . . .

There is a deep part of you, something inside, that you do not yet understand. Flores spoke the truth. It's not right. He can't go on like this. He needs to know who he is.

Simon draws his shaking hand over his face, turns back to Nomi, the same hand open toward her. "Now do you see why I need your help?"

Chapter Three

September 1987, Friday

Amnesia.

Let me think about it.

Nomi hits the corner of Gansevoort and turns right onto Washington. She hardly needs her beanie—fall has arrived, but the afternoons refuse to let go of the last heavy summer heat. She keeps it on anyway for anonymity. Sun shoots through the iron rafters above her as she passes under the portico of Centaur beef packaging. Her boots already have that tacky feeling underfoot from walking around on streets and sidewalks that never really lose their residual lip-gloss scum of blood, no matter how well the meat workers hose everything down. She adjusts the tote with her groceries and keeps marching, trying to reach Enrique before he finishes work at three.

Underneath, the awareness that she's also marching to get some distance from Simon Noone and his bizarre, alluring story, too much like a *National Enquirer* headline to be real: Amnesia in the Guatemalan Jungle! Details page 4.

If she hadn't been watching Noone as he explained his problem, she wouldn't have believed it. But she saw his face when she told him he'd been speaking Italian in the grocery: You can't fake that kind of shock. It wasn't just surprise; he was genuinely horrified. Nomi's willing to bet real money he's now standing at the phone kiosk back on Gansevoort, combing his memory for all the times he might've spoken a foreign language without even realizing . . .

But she doesn't have time for this now. Solange Jackson is relying on her to stay focused, and that woman has a metric ton of *actual* problems, not some possibly invented amnesia story. Even if Noone isn't lying, trying to run a line of some kind—to what purpose? Who the hell knows, the world is full of shysters—maybe even the stuff he told her, the stuff he thinks is true, is compromised by his fucked-up brain. Because how do you survive a gunshot wound to the head? In her time on the force, Nomi never saw such a thing.

So Noone's probably lying, and his reaction outside the grocery was a really good fake-out. Also, she just doesn't need to be around the brand of slightly terrifying menace that he exhibited with Malcolm Forest outside her apartment. And that should be the end of it.

Right.

She avoids getting run down by a J.A.W.D. Inc. Poultry Distributors truck as she crosses at the corner of Washington and Little West Twelfth and turns right. A bunch of white vans, some of them tagged with graffiti hieroglyphics, are parked haphazardly off the curb up ahead. The metal shutter of the auto-mechanic shop is open: Nomi can hear someone working an angle grinder, and the background radio noise of Billy Idol mixing with the sound of a pneumatic wrench.

She walks through the wide door, nods at the two other men in the workshop. There are a lot of metal edges and sharp tools in here, which she's mindful not to look at. Skirting the carcass of a utility van, she scouts for legs at floor level, finds them under the body of a diesel one-ton truck jacked up on three tires.

"Enrique, you home?"

He slides out on the crawler board from underneath the truck, a good-looking Puerto Rican guy who seems like a typical grease monkey except for the pierced ears and the eyeliner. "Hey, baby girl—you want to pass me that piece-of-shit socket wrench there? I got your mail, don't worry."

"You're a champ."

"I know it."

Nomi finds the socket wrench; Enrique fishes out a gold envelope from the top pocket of his coveralls; they make the swap.

"Appreciate this," Nomi says.

"No problem, babe. And hey, I heard from my jeweler friend, Marco, about that piece you ordered? He says maybe it's ready today or tomorrow."

"Really?" Nomi feels her palms sweat a little, controls it, redirects. "Okay, that's great. How's your aunt doing?"

Enrique fits a spark plug socket to the wrench. "Irma's good, sends her love. Says she wishes you were still hanging out with her in the RMP."

"Yeah, man, I wish that too." It's the right thing to say, but it's a lie. She loves Irma, her former partner, like she loved her own mother, but there's no power on earth that could make Nomi want to return to radio motor patrol—or any other patrol—with the New York City Police Department. "You give her a hug from me, okay? Tell her I'll try to arrange for us to meet up soon."

"Will do." Enrique slides halfway back under the truck, pops out again. "You coming to the thing tonight?"

"What's that?"

"At the Riverview. Gonna be some party."

"Your girls will be there?"

"You betcha." Enrique taps the wrench head against the metal undercarriage. The radio has switched from Billy Idol to Kim Wilde. "We're onstage about eleven, but I'll be around before then. Come along and I'll comp you."

"Well, that would be fine." Nomi grins, taps his booted foot with her own. "Cool, see you then."

"Bye, hon."

Back out on the street, Nomi retraces her steps toward Washington. A Friday-night party at the Riverview means she can talk with a few district contacts. Irma's envelope hopefully has the information she needs on Eric Lamonte's priors, which will help with Solange Jackson's case, but Nomi still needs more on Lamonte's associates, which is news she might be able to get locally.

She hitches her tote, does a quick head check of the street: A car is cornering farther along near Hector's Café, a song by Georgia Satellites blaring from the speakers. Nomi stays cautious. The last thing either she or Irma needs is to have their continuing connection exposed—bad for Irma, still on the force, and bad for Nomi, whose access to police intel would be crippled. She turns left onto Washington, then left again toward home, staying low.

Before the deli grocery on Gansevoort, she stops. Simon Noone is still making his calls at the pay phone kiosk, his paper bag sitting on the phone housing. His back is to her. To be honest, this is a guy she's barely noticed except for registering his presence on the floor above with the polite disinterest you maintain as an urban courtesy for your immediate neighbors. Now she retreats near a dumpster and its typical whiff of garbage and rotted offal so she can examine him like he's some kind of weird bug.

First, the superficial stuff: He looks to be about mid-twenties. He has height, a lean build, broad shoulders. His peacoat hangs well over his black shirt and jeans—the shirt looks like silk, although she might be mistaken. He's wearing engineer boots, and he's pushed his sunglasses up into his hair. It's a good look on him; the pieces all seem thrifted, but he clearly knows quality. Which is interesting, because living among the artists and drag queens of the West Village, Nomi's learned that personal style is almost always about instinct, what feels good, what looks right. If this guy really has no memory of his past, if he's dressing purely on instinct, she'll bet a dime to a dollar that he once came from money.

And he has no idea. Because he has amnesia.

She chews her lip. Goddammit. Is she really thinking of engaging with this?

That would be stupid, because there's something off about him, no doubt. The way he followed her—that lack of recognition of social cues could signify that he's lived somewhere the cues are different, or it could mean he's a jerk. Hard to call. Although the way he monstered Malcolm in the hallway . . . That's significant. The blankness of Noone's tone during the incident was unnerving—then after it was over, he seemed completely casual, as if he'd flicked some sort of internal switch from "intimidatingly scary" back to "normal."

Noone said he's good at languages: Violence is a language, apparently one he knows well enough to toggle on and off.

Again, living in Central America for five years might have affected his reactions to incidents that seem threatening. But confrontational situations aside, there's something else strange about him, like a flush of fever under his skin, radiating heat when you get too close . . . Nomi's own skin prickles in response, although she can't quite put her finger on why. The strangeness is there, though: amorphous, subliminal.

Unfortunately, she's just messed up enough to find strange people interesting.

And it doesn't dilute her kneejerk reaction to his story. *Amnesia.* To lose your memory is to be cut off from everything you know. All your people. Your understanding of yourself: your lifestyle, your job, your identity. To be pruned away from all the elements that form a picture of yourself that makes sense . . .

She knows what that's like. Knows it fairly intimately, in fact.

Noone turns in profile, taps his pen against the phone housing, talks down into the handset, glances toward the dumpster. Nomi feels his attention land when he sees her. He gives her an acknowledging nod, maybe knowing that she is—right this minute—making up her mind about him.

She thinks of the way his hands shook. *Now do you see why I need your help?*

"You're not doing this," she whispers. "No fucking way. Just cut him loose."

Right.

Nomi marches along the street to the phone kiosk. She makes a small wave, although she's clearly already got his attention. "Hey."

"Okay." Noone's eyes are on her as he finishes his call. "Yes, I appreciate this very much, thank you." He hangs the battered receiver back on the hook. "Hi."

"Hi," Nomi says. "Who are you calling?"

No preamble, no apology for the rude question—Noone's eyebrows rise, but he replies anyway. "A bunch of organizations that may have done missionary fieldwork at the border of southwest Mexico and Guatemala from 1981 to 1983. I want to see if any of them lost any people."

"You think you were a missionary?"

"No." He makes a thin smile. "But . . . I don't know. That's the problem, right? I could have come from anywhere. I could have been a backpacker, or a missionary, or—"

"Look, I can't help you." If she's going to be rude, might as well give it to him with both barrels. "I'm sorry, but I have to be selective about which cases I take, and my slate is too full right now."

"Oh." His expression falls, then firms. "All right, I understand."

"Do you?" She wants to get this straightened out. "Because I don't want you knocking on my door tomorrow with—"

"I said I understand." He tucks a page of notes and his pen into his coat pocket. "I asked, you answered. It's fine. I can be a grown-up about it, you don't need to worry."

He looks stiff, but not petulant. Nomi examines his eyes. He has very blue eyes.

"Fine," she says. "Great. It's just that we live in the same building, so . . ."

"Nomi," he says quietly. "I won't harass you to take me on as a client. Okay?"

"Okay." She's suddenly uncertain: His politeness and use of her first name have given the exchange a solemn intimacy. She shakes it off.

"Thanks for taking it so well. And it was good to meet you, anyway, considering we're neighbors and everything."

She offers her hand. Like with their first introductions, his handshake is warm, firm, professional. It feels like they've come to some kind of gentleman's agreement, and that's a good note to end this on, so she extricates herself and lets him get on with his calls.

On the way back to the tenement, she turns it over in her mind. Noone was civil, almost genteel. Could he originally be from the South? Would he have behaved like that as a client? Was turning him down a mistake?

No point worrying about it now. Nomi navigates the steps, the lobby, the stairs, uses her key in the door of her apartment.

She unpacks her tote onto the counter in the tiny kitchen on the right past the entryway, tucks the jars and cans away in the cupboard. Her apartment is soothing with muted light, with gray and brown colors. She likes to think the decor has a kind of Nordic simplicity, although she has too many plants for that. Green leaves and stems spill from bottles and trail over the ends of shelves, whisper down over the folding screen that divides her sleeping area from the living room, hang from pots suspended near the doors to the bathroom and her office room. Without the plants, things would look too gloomy. Plants also make casual disorder seem elegant, for the times when she can't be bothered tidying up.

Nomi fixes herself coffee, grabs the gold envelope from the countertop, takes mug and envelope into the second-room office. The space is compact and dim; she raises the blind over the long window to the right, takes her seat behind the small desk. The Jackson file is already there in front of her, from Solange's visit. A red light is blinking on her answering machine: It's a short message from Solange, saying that everything is fine with Malcolm. Good to know.

Now, the gold envelope. Nomi unwinds the red thread, opens the flap. Inside, a thick bunch of papers, mostly photocopies but a few faxes as well. Nomi draws them out and unfolds them, a yellow legal pad under her forearm for making notes.

A credit history, an insurance report. Six separate charge sheets, all photocopied. She was hoping for arrest reports—oh wait, Irma's included some of those too. Also, three photocopied photos, so she knows what Lamonte looks like if she sees him in the street. Nomi begins a new file on Lamonte and collates information on the legal pad: a précis of the arrest reports, previous charges, jail time.

It's a complex case. Eric Lamonte, known locally as a club manager, is the slimeball behind Solange's daughter's abduction. That's not a hypothesis—Solange's handler, Malcolm, straight-out told her. They wanted leverage to keep Solange working with an exclusive client, and by grabbing Brittany Jackson, they've sure as hell got it. Lamonte is mob connected, which makes him hard to touch, putting Solange in a tough spot.

And now Nomi's in a tough spot. She should probably have turned Solange down when she first knocked on the door—the case is edging right up on "out of her paygrade." But she's in it now, and no matter how she tries, Nomi can't let it go. First of all, it's about a vulnerable kid. That's a personal weak point. She's got her own history as a vulnerable kid, history that she pushes down hard. History that she refuses to think about, because thinking about it makes her skin prickle and tighten and she doesn't need that distraction—not right this moment, not ever. But it makes her sensitive to this case, to *this* kid, and stiffens her resolve to find Brittany Jackson and get her back home.

And second of all . . . Nomi doesn't know what the second of all is, except she's accepted the case and she's like some kind of pit bull or weasel by nature, one of those tenacious mammals that lock their jaws and refuse to detach.

At the end of the day, she hates slimeballs—and she likes to win.

Nomi spends the next hour compiling data for the file. Unsurprisingly, much of the work she does as a private investigator involves the same tedious paper shuffling she once did as a cop. There's a page in the envelope on Lamonte's known addresses and aliases. Most of them are historical, so she spends another hour on the phone trying to run down a couple of those leads and getting mostly nowhere: It's hard to reach people right before Friday end of business.

Before she examines the last few pages from the envelope, she gets a drink of water and checks the time: just after six.

Okay, final stretch. Three sheets are left in the envelope haul. One of them is a Known Associates list, but it's years old, so it's basically useless. If she chases the names, though, she might find connections to newer names. She did tell Irma to give her everything. The other sheet is a photocopy of a DMV car registration under the name of "Eric Monte" with a picture of Lamonte.

The last sheet in the bunch is . . .

"What the fuck." Nomi squints at the page.

It's a photocopy of a fax, and it's an old fax—she can read the date from six years ago up in the left-hand corner. Unfortunately, that's all she can read, because the rest of the words aren't in English. This is some kind of international arrest warrant, or charge sheet, or some goddamn thing that she doesn't know because she can't read it.

"Dammit." She holds it up to the light from the window, but sunlight is not an aid to translation. She tries sounding out the words near the top. "Cog-nome . . ."

She can't read this page—and she needs to read this page. It might be as useless as the old KA sheet, but she doesn't *know*, because she can't read . . . What even is this language, anyway?

"Per ordi-nan-za del Tri-bun-aal? Tri-bu-nale? Di Pal-ermo . . ." Nomi sits back, astonished.

Italian. It's in Italian.

After a moment, she groans, knowing what this means.

She allows herself a few minutes of loud swearing. Then she gathers up her yellow pad, her pen, the fax copy and sweeps out of her office and apartment, stomps up the stairs to the third floor.

Chapter Four

September 1987, Friday

It's surprisingly nice up on Three. A skylight lets in warm sun; extra windows give a feeling of airiness.

The door on Nomi's left seems to be for the apartment directly above her own. Trying not to think too much, she walks over and knocks.

"One second," a voice says from inside; then the door is pulled open, and Simon Noone is standing in front of her. Again.

"Hi," she says.

"Hi." He's shed some layers and stands at the door barefoot in jeans, black shirt open and brown hair untidy. He looks confused. "Um, didn't you—"

"I need something translated." Nomi refuses to blush. She waves the fax copy. "Look, I know what I said, and that still stands. But I received this sheet of information from a contact, and it's in Italian, which obviously *I* don't speak but you do, so—"

"Yet you recognized spoken Italian in the grocery." His head tilts.

"I mean, I recognize it when I *hear* it. And I know the guy who owns Perrotta's is—obviously—Italian. But it's not like I could understand what you were *saying* when you—"

"Okay," he interrupts. "So you have a sheet of information in Italian, and you want me to translate it for you."

"Yes." She forces herself to shut up.

"You do understand that I didn't realize, before today, that I even *spoke* Italian? I don't know if I'll be able to read any of the words when they're written down—"

"Just . . . try it," she suggests.

There's a long pause, in which Noone tongues his back teeth and Nomi feels the full import of what she's doing.

"Please," she blurts, and she does blush then. "I don't have anyone else to ask."

His expression doesn't change. But he holds the door open wider. "Okay, fine. Come on in and show me what you've got."

Noone's apartment is . . . delightful. Larger than her own, high ceilinged and shockingly sunny, with walls painted the palest creamy yellow, so the room is still gleaming even this late in the afternoon. It's also almost completely open plan, so she can see his staggering lack of furniture: Two chairs, a low double bed, a dresser, a breakfast table—that's it. A chess set on the dresser looks to be mid-game. He has no wall decorations of any kind, just coat hooks near the door. Lots of books, though, both fiction and nonfiction, including what appears to be a complete set of medical encyclopedias. All the tomes are stacked in piles near three tall, narrow windows; the windows, with white muslin curtains, show views all along Gansevoort. It's like a little aerie up here.

"Nice," she says, although she deducts points for the absence of plants. But better to get on with this, so she walks straight over to the round breakfast table, where a copy of *Gray's Anatomy* (twentieth edition) lies open at an illustration of the bones of the human hand. Nomi pushes the book aside and smooths the fax page out on the wooden tabletop. "Here's what I've got. Just one page, but I think it's from the court in Palermo—"

"That's in Sicily." Noone stands beside her, buttoning his shirt, eyes on the fax copy. "That's a pretty terrible copy."

"I know, sorry."

He snags a cigarette from a pack on the table, running the finger of his other hand across the top lines of the fax. "This isn't recent?"

He picked that up quick. “I told my contact I needed whatever she could get. This is what she got.”

“Interesting.” He grimaces at the letters, at her. “Look, I don’t know how this works. I spoke Italian in the grocery without meaning to, it’s very different from reading the words on a page.”

“What if you tried—I don’t know—speaking the words aloud?” This has to work, or she’ll have embarrassed herself for nothing.

He tucks the cigarette behind his ear, grabs the page, and steps back.

“Let me see. Servizio Operativo Centrale . . .” His eyes—blue as a jay—suddenly meet Nomi’s; he’s still patently flabbergasted at how this language falls out of his mouth so smoothly. Then he looks down again and continues. “Servizio Operativo Centrale del Ministero della Giustizia Italiano, per ordinanza del Tribunale di Palermo . . . That’s, the, uh, Central Operational Service of the Ministry of Justice of Italy, by order of the Palermo Court . . .”

They get the bulk of the translation done this way. Noone reads and gives her the basic gist, which Nomi writes down on the legal pad. She gets him to go back and reread some sections, to see if she can get a more accurate sense of certain words.

“So ‘mezzano’ means a pimp.” She makes an underline. Sunlight is fading out the windows. “And ‘fare il mezzano’ means . . .”

“It’s like—the manager of a prostitute?” Noone scratches his temple with the end of his own pen. They’re both sitting at the table now, although he still hasn’t put on any shoes. “I mean, that’s not the exact phrasing, more like if you’re the one arranging how someone *becomes* a prostitute—”

“Pandering. This is a pandering charge.”

He sits back, snorts. “It’s amazing that I understand the word for something in Italian when I wasn’t even aware such a word existed in English.”

“Your messed-up brain.”

“Tell me about it.” He winces, tosses his pen on the tabletop. “Excuse me for a second.”

He gets up and walks to the bathroom. Nomi thinks he might be in pain—he's been squinting over the scratchy fax-copy words for a long time—and sure enough, she hears him open his bathroom cabinet, run the faucet. It's still warm in the apartment; he must have the heating turned up, which makes sense for a guy who's come from Guatemala.

He emerges into the bathroom doorway, wiping his hands with a white towel. "Sorry. Headache."

"You get a lot of those?"

"Only every day." Noone's smile is humorless. He tosses the towel back into the bathroom as he starts for the kitchen, feet padding on the linoleum. "Coffee? I'm very sorry, I should've offered you one before."

"Oh," she demurs, "that's okay . . ."

"Hey, you turned me down as a client, but that doesn't mean you have to turn down my coffee." He flicks on the kitchen light, raises an espresso pot in one hand. "Let me make it easy. I'm making coffee. Do you want one?"

Her pause is only brief enough to preserve her dignity. "Yes. Thank you."

"Great. Hold on."

Nomi watches him go through the process of filling the funnel part with dark, aromatic grounds, adding water, screwing the sections back together. "You even make coffee the Italian way. Have you considered that you might actually *be* Italian?"

He rinses his own mug, gets out another one. "I don't think so. I woke up speaking English, with this accent. And there's my American dental work. Cream?"

He warms half-and-half on the stove. When they both have their mugs back at the table, he finally lights his cigarette, which she suspects he's been wanting to do for nearly an hour. "This guy with the Italian charge sheet, he's someone you're tracking?"

"Something like that." The espresso is rich and delicious; it's a long way from her budget Mr. Coffee brew.

"But he's involved with some case you're working on. Is this for Solange's case?"

"It's for a client," she concedes. But he's been poring over the fax-copy information with her; she can give some ground. "Solange is my only client right now, but the case is . . . challenging."

"So Lamonte is connected to Solange . . ." Noone's eyes are alert, thoughtful; then they turn sharp. "You should be careful with this guy. He appears to be someone who doesn't play nice."

"Oh, he definitely doesn't play nice." As she's already well aware; she's most concerned about Lamonte's pandering charge. But best to put that aside right now. Nomi sips her coffee and decides it doesn't hurt to be a little curious. "So. Guatemala."

"Yes."

"Amnesia."

"Yes." He gets up to fetch a glass ashtray from the windowsill, returns. "I don't quite know why you're hung up on that word."

"Never met anyone with amnesia before." She tidies her notes and crosses one knee over the other. "You said you were pulled from the river."

"Yeah. November, 1982."

"What happened?"

He draws, exhales. "I mean, if you're asking how I got in the river, I can't tell you. A farmer found me on the riverbank. They took me to a village medical clinic."

She cups her mug. "A village doctor treated your gunshot injury?"

"An Anglo-Mexican, Richard Flores." Noone sips his coffee, focuses on the ashtray as he taps into it. "He'd trained in London."

"What the hell is a London-trained doctor doing in the Guatemalan jungle?"

"He was a Marxist." Noone sits back, watches his cigarette burn. "He got booted from the medical establishment in London, ended up back in Mexico, then over the border. Guatemala has been in a state of civil war for a long time, he'd done a lot of battlefield medicine.

He patched me up, and I was in recovery for over a year. I still get headaches, and I sometimes have serious migraines, as well as vision problems."

His eyes dart away when he mentions the migraines. Something off there. Nomi's own eyes narrow. "It's amazing you're still alive."

"At least I got a cool scar," he says brightly.

When he sets down his cigarette on the edge of the ashtray and parts the dark hair near his left temple, it takes a second to work out what she's looking at. Then she realizes it's a thick striation of white, like the vein of a mineral deposit on a cave wall, running over a dent in the bone as if someone once pressed their thumb into the wet clay of his skull. The scar tissue straggles back, dividing behind his ear into a lightning bolt that darts for his crown.

Nomi finds herself reduced to gasping. If there's one thing she knows, it's scars, and that is real; that is absolutely real. "Holy shit."

"There's still bullet pieces inside there somewhere." He lets his hair fall back into place, recovers his cigarette. "I avoid metal detectors when I can."

"Very funny." She's never seen anything like it before, and she's still getting over it. "So when you woke up, you had no idea who you were."

"Correct."

"But you said you're right handed, you're not color blind . . . You've done some testing. So what else do you know about yourself?"

"Well, I can read and write, obviously, and retain information. I seem to be good at math and languages. My motor skills are fine. I can ride a bicycle." His eyes get a faraway look. "One of the kids from the village came to the clinic and showed me cat's cradle, but I already knew how to play . . ." He shakes it off. "Anyway, I wasn't catastrophically brain damaged. I can make new memories okay, I just can't access the old ones."

Her instincts to scrutinize are firing up, as if physical gears are ratcheting in her head. "Did the fact you'd been shot have significance?"

"Hard to say. The URNG were fighting government forces all up and down the country—getting shot was surprisingly easy in Guatemala back then. I might've just gone somewhere I shouldn't have, walked into a bad situation, met the wrong person." Noone stubs out his smoke, stands to go to the kitchen and rinse his empty mug. "Flores said there were basically four options. That I was a student or tourist of some kind, possibly in training with Médecins Sans Frontières . . . that I was a missionary . . . that I worked for one of the petro companies . . . or that I was a smuggler."

Nomi turns in her chair. "So you could be a criminal."

"Maybe. Who knows?"

"You don't need anyone examining your papers too closely."

"Not really, no." He stands sideways, one hand on the metal sink, black shirt loose over his jeans. "I've only been in the country seven weeks, and I'd like to stay a little longer."

"Until you figure this out." Makes sense. "What've you been doing since you arrived?"

"Working, mainly. I've got the early-morning shift at Gennaro's. They pay okay. Sofia Rosa gave me this apartment on no bond and no advance—I've scraped up enough to give her a month extra, so she knows I'm not going to skip out on her."

If he gets along with their landlady, that pushes Nomi's opinion of him closer to the green than the red. She suddenly realizes it's dark outside the apartment windows; she's stayed longer than she anticipated. It's Friday, and her skin is prickling, calling to her—plus there's tonight's Riverview party to consider.

"Okay, that's all good to know. I should really get going." She clicks her pen, collects her notes, and stands. "Thank you for the coffee. I didn't mean to take up so much of your time. But I appreciate you doing the translation for me."

"Right, of course." Noone extends a hand, escorts her to the door. "Come again, for all your translation needs."

"Have you tried with any other languages?"

"No. But I guess I should do that."

Nomi realizes she's already decided, so she stops at the open entrance to Noone's apartment and turns to look at him. "Okay."

"Okay what?"

"Okay, I'll help you."

His blue eyes light. "That would be—"

"There's conditions." She wants to make this clear, before he gets any ideas. "I'm not moonlighting. This is my primary business, and I don't do this work for nothing. I charge a fee. But on the upside, I'm pretty cheap."

"I can pay you," he says immediately.

"Great. It's great to be paid." It's cooler out in the hallway; she cradles her notes and pulls her cardigan closer. "So if I'm trying to look into your identity, your history, you'll need to give me everything you've got. Research, papers, that clothes label, everything. As soon as I can, I'll give it all back."

"Okay."

"I have stuff to do tonight, but I'd like to talk with you again tomorrow."

"I finish at Gennaro's at eleven in the morning. But then I nap after I get home—I don't really get up until about one."

"I can work around your schedule." Nomi feels strangely breathless. There are sharp edges to Simon Noone that make her wary, and she really hopes this isn't a decision she'll regret changing her mind about. "What are you going to do when we find out who you are?"

He stops. "I've got no idea. Figure out a way to make both halves of me join up somehow, I guess."

Good answer. "Okay. See you tomorrow."

She leaves him rubbing the back of his neck, goes to the stairs.

Her apartment seems cluttered after Noone's space; she closes blinds, picks up a little dirty laundry in her sleeping area, waters her plants. Unfolds her notes and the fax copy, slides them into the Lamonte file. Then she finds a clean manila folder and creates a new file, called

Simon Noone. She jots down everything she can remember about her conversations with him, in a series of bullet points. Finally, she sets her pen aside. It's evening.

She took Noone's case because it's intriguing. *He's* intriguing; his injury is real, and there's something pure about it: He just wants to know who he is. There's no "people being awful to one another" aspect to it, which describes a lot of the cases she's taken on over the last two years. Half the time, her typical clients don't really want to know the outcome of her investigation; it's usually a worst-case scenario, because people don't hire a backstreet private investigator when the situation is a happy one, so she's always put into the position of feeling like a carrion crow who delivers terrible news.

But Noone *wants* these answers; Nomi could see it. It's eating him up, not knowing. To him, she's not a black-winged bearer of bad tidings, but someone who will provide him with valuable insight.

And he helped her with the Italian. For a moment, it took her back to her experiences of collegiality while working with a team on a case. It had felt good to sit next to someone, both of you collaborating to dig up information. She used to like working with others—in the NYPD, it was only that she couldn't stomach dealing with the people she was supposed to be on a team with. This was different. Better.

Nomi checks her watch: A little over an hour before she needs to walk to the Riverview. She's antsy—that familiar restlessness under her skin—but she can control herself until she gets home later. She's getting better at this.

She makes a small dinner: omelet with lots of butter, sauerkraut on the side, a handful of tortilla chips. She showers and changes into fresh jeans and a sleeveless Cramps shirt, plus an oversize black leather jacket. Eyeliner, silver earrings, a studded leather cuff, and she's ready to go.

Through the door, downstairs, out in the street—the district is starting to come alive again in the early dark of night: There are more people on Gansevoort now than there were at midday. Nomi heads toward Washington, nods to a girl on a fire escape farther along, nods to a man behind the wheel of a truck near the corner. She's glad for her boots on the cobblestones; most of the hookers around here wear stilettos, and she's always worried about their ankles.

Hands shoved deep into her jacket pockets, she crosses the street and follows the road toward Horatio, watching for headlights, taillights. There are a lot of folks cruising in cars, some on business. Back in the day, she would've dreaded a street-beat detail in the Meatpacking District—too many variables, too many loose units, too much risk. But those same aspects help her now, covering her tracks, disguising her passage. She can stay low to the ground here, which is how she likes it.

The tall pylons of the elevated train overpass are solid blocks of concrete and steel, like walking around under a jetty, as if Pier 51 has spawned a dry-land version of itself here under the streetlamps. Nomi stays out of the really dark pools of shadow. Up ahead, the Riverview's red brick ramparts, genteelly dilapidated. The building has been a local institution since 1908, as much a part of the district as the blood in the streets.

The plan is to get inside, check in with Enrique, watch the show. Between dances and people watching, she can catch up with at least three contacts who might have some information on Lamonte's known associates.

A small crowd is wandering around or toward the hotel on Jane Street, lured by the sound of a pulsing club beat. Nomi does a quick scan, ducks up the steps and between the grand columns at the hotel's entrance. In the lobby, the music is louder, and people are gathering, chatting, laughing. It feels like a party. The black-felt-covered ballroom door opens occasionally, letting out the soaring vocals of the Communards and an exciting flash of sparkling glitter before closing again.

A little entry queue has formed behind a tall Black drag performer in booty shorts and kitten heels, who's getting change from the cashier. Once they walk off, the line moves forward, and eventually Nomi steps up to the grille.

"Hey, Cherie, how you doing?"

"All good, just don't ask me for change." Cherie, currently chewing gum, is twenty-three years old, from Hoboken, and lives at the Riverview as well as working here. "Hey, Nomi, when you gonna learn how to dress, huh? That Cramps shirt . . ."

Nomi grins. "Shut up and give me a ticket. Is Enrique around? He said he'd put my name on the door, but I can pay if he hasn't arrived yet."

"Nah, you're good, he put you on the list. Hold up, let me stamp you." Cherie administers a pad stamp to the back of Nomi's left hand. "There you go, honey. Go crazy. Enjoy the show."

"Thanks."

And she's through the felt-covered door. There's no bouncer, because this is not really a club, in the same way that the Riverview—with so many permanent residents—is not really a hotel. Tonight, the ballroom here is an event space; tomorrow, it could be something else, a market or a sex dungeon or a cinema for a community movie night. Everything is fluid in the Meatpacking District. Nothing is permanent.

Well, some things are permanent. Past the strobes, Nomi takes off her leather jacket for the cloakroom, exposing her tattoos. This is how most people in the West Village know her: by the black ring circling her right bicep, by the flames and thorny vines and roses climbing up her left arm from her wrist, by the two ravens battling across her right shoulder blade, wings feathering the back of her neck. And now, by the—hard-to-make-out—pad stamp of a pair of burning lips on her left hand.

Turning from the cloakroom, she sees Enrique wave nearby; he's laden down with a makeup case, a garment bag for his outfit, a pair of heels dangling from one finger. "Nomi! Hey, girl! I got your thing."

She squeezes through to reach him, grinning. "Another thing?"

He scrounges in the back pocket of his parachute pants, holds up a little clear baggie. "Here you go. Marco says he's sorry the old amethyst one broke, and he hopes you love this new one."

Nomi takes the baggie, swallows hard: inside, a perfect obsidian arrowhead, no bigger than a Kennedy half dollar, wrapped in silver wire at the base and ready to be suspended from a necklace.

"It's gorgeous." She's dry mouthed. "Marco did a great job."

"He said he's got a chain for it, if you want."

"I don't need a chain." She clutches the baggie, tries to keep her hand from shaking as she thanks Enrique, as he air-kisses her cheek and sashays away. Between her fingers, the obsidian's hardness bites through the plastic. Now, the question of what to do. She should wait; she knows that. But there's an incessant hum on her body's entire surface. If she doesn't do something to calm it, she'll be distracted all night.

Okay, fine.

She finds Mischa among the crush of people closest to the corner by the door, with the rest of the dealers whose business model involves being accessible. He's wearing leather pants with a silver velvet shirt, and a Day-Glo headband already dark with perspiration.

He returns her nod. "Hey, what's happening, sugar?"

"Those pants look too hot," she notes.

"Ohmigod, I *know*," Mischa says. "I'm sweating like crazy."

Leo Farina, with one foot propped against the wall, peers around his hangers-on to see her. "Well, lookie here, it's Dirty Harriet."

This gets a few guffaws. Leo's in tight white trousers with a shiny black shirt, open to show off his chest. He has a lot of gel in his hair and looks like he's already got a good buzz on: It's common knowledge that Leo gets high off his own supply.

Nomi usually ignores him; Leo is a tourist at the Riverview. His primary beat is Chachi's, a few blocks south, where the straights are cashed up enough to afford blow, Leo's stock in trade. But tonight, he's in her territory, and she's jazzed by the baggie in her hand, happy to wrestle. "Hey, Leo, the guys from *Saturday Night Fever* called. They want the costume back."

A chorus of "ooohhh"s from the corner boys. Lip twitching, Leo waves a hand to show he can take a joke.

"Don't tease." Mischa play slaps her arm. "You want some party favors?"

"Nah, nothing fancy, Meesh, just the usual." Nomi gives him the money, they make the exchange, then she ducks behind the cloakroom to a small empty bathroom, which is badly lit and smells like moldy drywall.

From Mischa's packet, she takes a single Valium and breaks it with her short thumbnail, swallows one half with water from the faucet. It's less than she needs, but she's super careful with benzos; getting into a bad habit is too easy. She has enough bad habits already.

Out in the ballroom, the Communards have given way to New Order. Nomi holds up the clear baggie from Enrique, with the pendant inside glittering like a black shark's tooth. The arrowhead is surprisingly heavy, nicely weighted. When she takes it out, the silver wire is helpful for grip. She's sweating a little. Normally, she would never do this here—she has rules. But it's Friday, it's past her regular time, and getting her new tool has got her thrumming.

She doesn't want to ritualize it here, and this space isn't private. Better to move fast.

Nomi lifts the hem of her shirt and flicks the sharp edge of the arrowhead against the skin to the right of her belly button. Blood wells, and the humming wasps inside her body still. Her focus returns. She sighs in relief.

Because this is also how people in the Village know her. It's part of who she is, part of her identity, a side of herself that she occasionally lets loose. It's one of the reasons why she's here. Because being in the district isn't an accident.

Nomi stanches the red with a Kleenex, pressing hard.

Chapter Five

September 1987, Saturday

What do you wear to an appointment with your private investigator? Simon stands above his dresser, scratching through his hair, before realizing it doesn't matter. Nomi saw him yesterday with his shirt open. Admittedly, she'd come to his apartment, his space; this meeting will be in her space. But it's not a big deal.

Except he's spent a month and a half being mindful of how he presents, whether he blends in, and now—confronted by an outlier situation, where he's not sure of the rules—he finds himself at something of a loss.

Americans are a paradox, Flores said. *They like to talk about independence and individuality, but they actually love the homogeneous. They prefer things and people to be "regular"—just like them.*

Apart from managing his headaches, Simon's biggest challenge and most constant sensitivity has been around how to stay homogeneous. Choose the correct clothes. Wear your hair the correct way. Speak with the correct rhythms and intonation and casual slang. Blending in is vital if he wants to stay off official radar, of course, but it's also a pathway to figuring out where he might belong—or who he might become—in the absence of a real identity.

He's aware of how easy it might be, when you don't know who you are, to simply fall through the cracks of daily life and become a nobody.

Shapeless, formless nobodies are everywhere in New York: on street corners, in alleyways, beneath overpasses, in dumpsters. Imitation, then, is a guardrail. He can't "be himself" because he doesn't know what that entails, but he can imitate others, and that's usually enough to both give him form and allay suspicion.

So he's accustomed to playing a role. But now he has to figure out what the role of "amnesiac guy on his afternoon off" looks like, and perhaps unsurprisingly, he's coming up blank.

There's a knock at the apartment door.

Dammit. He grabs jeans, a white shirt. "Hold on!"

It's the second time he's opened the door on Nomi while barefoot, but at least this time his shirt isn't unbuttoned.

She's leaning one hand on the doorjamb and doesn't seem to care. "Hi. Look, I know I said two thirty, but I have to do a thing."

"A thing?"

"A thing, yeah, a thing." She drops her hand, half turning and clearly in a hurry. "I've gotta go see a guy. Another guy, I mean. So can we take a rain check?"

He's been agonizing over clothes for nothing. "You have to see another guy."

"Yes, I've gotta catch a train in—" she checks her watch—"in, like, fifteen minutes. I've gotta be there before he takes off at four. So, rain check?"

He realizes suddenly that she's dressed for action: black combat pants, black tank, black leather jacket. The shitkicker boots are still the same. She's taken out some of the metal in her ears.

He narrows his eyes, thinking of the Italian fax sheet from yesterday with its ugly mug shots and intimidating list of prior charges. "Is this something to do with Lamonte?"

"No. Yes." Nomi shifts on her feet, impatient. "Kind of. Look, I don't have time to—"

"I'll come with you." He's already pulling on his boots.

"What? No, you don't need to—"

"Yeah, I do. Lamonte doesn't play nice, remember?"

"Do you think I'm an idiot?" She gives him a hard stare, her urge to move tightly reined and vibrating beneath her skin. "I've been doing this job for two years. I take precautions, okay?"

She opens the side of her jacket. The matte black object tucked into the holster under her armpit is a gun, Simon realizes. *Interesting.*

It still doesn't sway him. Yesterday's glimpse into Nomi's world has intrigued him, and his desire for answers to his personal quest is like a persistent itch. He grabs his trench coat, which holds keys, cash, cigarettes. "Where are you going on the train?"

"What? Flatbush, I'm going to Flatbush. But—"

"That's, what, an hour away? We can talk on the train, then I can jump another train back home while you go about your business." He pulls the door closed behind himself.

"You're crazy," she blurts.

"A little, probably," he admits. "Come on, you'll miss your window."

She throws up her hands, but she's either given up or run out of time.

Downstairs and out on the street, she walks fast enough that he'd be struggling to keep up if he wasn't nearly a foot taller with a longer stride. They've already crossed Greenwich Street, heading for Hudson. Nomi dodges a teenage white girl with a dog on a string lead, ignores the crosswalk sign and strides straight across the Hudson intersection like she's bulletproof.

Simon hauls after her. "Where are we getting on the subway?"

"West Fourteenth and Eighth Avenue—keep up." For a while, the pace is brisk, and he knows she's still annoyed. But after cutting past an art space near the corner of Gansevoort and turning left near Jackson Square, Nomi's lope settles down.

Behind them, Eighth Avenue is afternoon-quiet, enjoying the lull before it revs back up again with its small army of red delivery trucks and white-coated meat workers pushing hand trolleys. Ahead, both the Greco-Roman pomp of the New York County National Bank and the wedding cake tiers of the Bankers Trust Company high-rise seem vaguely insulted to be sharing space with pizza shops, delicatessens, liquor stores, peep show signs. The Port Authority Building looms in the distance.

But they're not going that far up; Nomi clatters down the subway stairs, and Simon follows behind, saying goodbye to the sun.

They buy their tokens and get to the platform about ten seconds before the next train arrives. The carriage isn't too packed, but it has that subway smell of urine, old body odor, and hot steel. Graffiti is everywhere, and the nearest seats glisten with fresh spray paint; Simon chooses to stand.

Nomi holds the pole beside him. Her posture seems more relaxed now they're locomoting, but her face is hard to read.

"What?"

"I'm wondering if you're still mad," he says.

"I just don't need a bodyguard, okay?"

"Fine. No bodyguarding. It's only . . ." He lets his gaze float as he thinks of a way to explain why he's gate-crashed her afternoon activities. "I've been trying to figure this out on my own for a long time, so I'm ready to get started. Call me overeager."

"Overeager, huh?" Her stance softens as the train bumps along.

He shrugs. Farther along the carriage, a guy in a business suit smokes a cigarette; now Simon kind of wants one.

"Okay, I'll buy that." Nomi seems resigned, if not entirely content. "You're still the weirdest client ever."

That almost makes him smile. "You should've seen me when I first regained consciousness."

But it's not really funny. He remembers that time as a transcendental whirl with no discernible pattern: He'd wake up to morning light, wake up again at night, wake up crying, wake up mid-conversation. He could never remember blacking out. His tongue had been dry and fat in his mouth, and he'd been barely lucid, his mind a bouncing roulette ball. He'd asked Flores a million questions—*Where am I? How did I get here? Who are you? What is happening?*—but could never retain the answers.

"What's it like, having no memory?" Nomi is examining his face.

It's the most awful thing you can imagine. Simon doesn't want to say that, doesn't want to scare her. He keeps his expression neutral. "I don't know what it's like any other way, so I can't really tell you."

They get off at Fourth and Washington Square, changing to a B. There's a panhandler in a flat cap in their carriage; Nomi waves him off, finds them both clean seats. But she's also apparently been watching Simon's eyes flick around.

"You don't ride the subway much, huh?"

He's ridden the subway exactly four times, including the time he traveled from Penn Station to the West Side on the day he arrived in the city. It took one train trip for him to figure out he had a problem with it. Now he only uses the train out of absolute necessity.

"I don't like being underground," he admits.

"Claustrophobia, as well as amnesia?"

"Not normally. Just on the subway." He winces. "I really need to buy a bike."

"Bummer about the subway. The train's the best way to get to know New York." Her mouth twitches in an almost smile as she lifts her chin at clumps of other passengers farther down. "You get the whole smorgasbord on the train—goths, geeks, gays, punks, New Romantics, New Wavers, homeys, rappers . . . It's a cliché, but NYC really is a melting pot."

Not as homogeneous as Flores thought. Although there's a kind of homogeneity in everybody dressing in their group's fashion to show their individuality. So are Americans more loyal than individualist? Simon doesn't know, and it's disturbing because he's supposed to be one of them.

"I can only compare it to New Orleans," he says.

"You came in through New Orleans?"

"By way of the Gulf of Mexico. I spent three weeks on a fishing boat from Ciudad del Carmen." It's not a wholly pleasant memory. But Felipe Brava was a patient man, standing on deck to smoke his endless supply of Flor Morada tobacco and talk about what Simon should do once they arrived in the USA. "The boat captain was connected to Sofia Rosa—she keeps the top floor room open for new arrivals. I had my paperwork already, from a contact in Mexico."

"So checking your fingerprints might be complicated." Sallow flashes slide across Nomi's face from the fluorescent droplights outside as they pass through a station.

"I'd like to exhaust other ways of figuring out my identity before we start trying fingerprints and rap sheets," he concedes. "I want to stay under the radar, if possible."

"It's possible. Tough, but possible. You said you'd been in America seven weeks?"

"Yeah. Six weeks on the West Side, plus it took me five days to get from New Orleans to New York." Simon glances at a kid, probably about twelve, sleeping on a seat across the aisle. "I was down to my last dollar when I got the job at Gennaro's."

"They're always looking for staff—high turnover." Her gaze sweeps over him, taking in details. "I think I'm going to start with missing persons from the US East Coast, from November 1982."

"Why the East Coast?" Just as he asks, the sun returns at last as the train emerges from the tunnels at the opencut Prospect Park station. He can breathe slightly better now.

Nomi shrugs. "I don't look at you and think California or West Coast."

This he finds intriguing. She's more well versed in the homogenous groups of this country, in the same way he could probably explain to her the difference between a Guatemalan cardamom farmer and an ORPA fighter, if she cared to ask. "How can you tell?"

"You have a kind of European look. Did you pick those clothes?"

"Yeah, from Goodwill. Why?"

"Your style seems east. Not west, not flyover states. And your skin's very pale. Is that your natural hair color?"

He touches his nape without thinking. "I guess. Flores shaved my head for surgery, and this is how it grew back. Is it important?"

"Well, with your coloring, and if you dress like that instinctively, it makes me think East Coast. Maybe even New England." She glances out the window before standing up. "It's someplace to start anyway. Okay, this is our stop."

They've emerged at Church Avenue, near Prospect Park, and there's a ton of traffic in the street, a lot of trash on the sidewalk. Nomi leads a winding path past locksmiths, T-shirt sellers, hair braiding stores, down one side street, then another.

Steam rises from the drains, and the sun that Simon appreciated on the train is now making him sweat. "Who's this guy you're going to see?"

She throws him a look. "Weren't you going to go back to Manhattan?"

"I'm avoiding getting back on the train. I promise I'll stay out of your way."

"Right," she mutters.

"Seriously, I can behave. So who is he?"

Obviously reluctant, she spills anyway. "His name's Ricki Cevolatti. He's a small-time good guy who does jobs for Lamonte, according to my sources. He's supposed to be at this address until four o'clock, when he leaves to start work at one of Lamonte's clubs in Greenwich Village."

"So you just want to talk to him."

"That's the plan. I have a few questions."

Simon raises his eyebrows. "And he's going to talk to you?"

"I can be very persuasive." Nomi's gaze is flat as she opens the other side of her jacket: A badge hangs from the inside pocket, one he recognizes.

It gives him enough of a jolt that he stops walking. "You're a *cop*?"

"Ex-cop." She doesn't seem excited to be talking about this. "I've been out two years, but I managed to hold onto the tin. Come on, it's nearly three thirty, let's move."

The entrance to Cevolatti's tenement is right next door to a Vietnamese seafood place, and the smell of rotting bass is strong as they take the outside steps. Nomi checks the names on the letter boxes inside the door at right, but most of them have been scratched out and written over too many times to be useful.

"I was told he's on the second floor, apartment twelve." She wrinkles her nose. "God, it smells in here."

They go up the stairs, and Simon avoids touching the banister. Linoleum peels at the edges of the second-floor hallway.

Cevolatti's apartment door is unlatched.

Nomi steps to the side and draws her weapon, goes into a mode that Simon hasn't seen before. "Get back from the door," she whispers, then, louder, "Hey Ricki, you home? What's happening, man?"

No answer.

Nomi meets Simon's eyes briefly, pushes the door open with her elbow, ducks inside.

Abiding by his self-imposed rule to keep out of her way, Simon only sets one foot over the threshold before he hears her say, "Oh *fuck*," through a thickened throat; then he moves faster.

Chapter Six

September 1987, Saturday

The front door opens straight onto the living space of a run-down, untidy apartment. The living room is dominated by a single tableau, and for the briefest moment, Simon sees it all in extraordinary detail, clear as the flare of a camera flash or the black-and-white afterimage of a silver halide photograph.

Cevolatti—or the guy Simon assumes is Cevolatti—is on the living room rug, tied to a chair. He's a solid, slope-shouldered guy of about thirty, hair already thinning a little on top, and he's been dead for some time. A large quantity of blackened blood has soaked into the rug. Someone's left the apartment window open, so flies are involved.

"Oh Jesus." Nomi has staggered a few steps away, arm raised and mouth tucked into the crook of her elbow. "Do not touch *anything*. I mean it—not one goddamn thing."

Simon studies the body, and his own reaction to it. He's not reacting like Nomi—why? He felt discomfort on the subway, but now he's oddly dispassionate about this man's death, and even that awareness comes with a sense of disconnection. Instead, he feels . . . curiosity. A complex interest. Also annoyance? Where is that coming from?

Something dormant inside him has activated, and now his eyes move from detail to detail, compulsive, instinctive. For a moment, with the blood and the bitter smells, he's at work: his hands encased in slithering chainmail, his cleaver chopping through the joints, breaking knife moving smoothly—an extension of his hand and wrist—as he assesses the lines of muscle and tendon and fat, instantly judging the best places to cut.

But the unprofessional mess here in this living room brings him back: This is *not* like work, and the incorrectness of it jags on him like a broken tooth.

"This isn't . . . clean," he says quietly. "But some parts of it are clean. This is wrong."

"What the fuck are you talking about?" Nomi drops her arm, appalled; the gesture disturbs the flies, and she's forced to raise her arm over her mouth again. She looks at the body, her expression contorted. "Oh god, this is gross. I'm gonna puke . . ."

"Don't be sick in here!" Simon whispers.

"You don't have to fucking tell *me* that!" Now she's angry and miserable, not just miserable. "Jesus—I need to look around for a minute, see if there's anything left behind. Just—I don't know, stay the hell away from smooth surfaces!"

He stands there for about one minute, listening to her curse as she checks the rest of the apartment's rooms. Then she returns and holsters her weapon, begins using a pen to poke at the pizza boxes on the coffee table, the loose change in the cookie tin on a bookshelf ledge.

What does it mean that it's not clean? Simon needs to look at something before they leave—it's a compulsion, one he can't contain. He breaks for the kitchen.

"Noone!" Nomi stage-whispers, her cheeks pink with alarm. "What the fuck are you *doing*?"

Simon ignores her and crouches, uses his sleeve to protect his hand as he yanks open the cupboard door beneath the kitchen sink. Everyone keeps their dishwashing gloves under the sink, and Cevolatti is no exception: Simon grabs the gloves, turns them right side out and pulls them on before returning to Nomi and the body.

He leans to get a closer look at what's been done to Cevolatti's face and chest and tongue, waving flies away. Then he steps carefully around to the rear of the body and takes a knee to examine the hands where they're tied at the back.

"That's clean," he mutters to himself. "But the front of him isn't the same. It's inconsistent."

"We need to get out of here," Nomi whispers. "*I* need to get out of here."

"One more second," Simon whispers back. He examines the stubby collection of digits on the floor, picks one up to check, places it back where he found it.

"Noone, for fuck's sake!"

"Okay, okay."

"Noone."

"Okay, let's go."

They go out the same way they came in—Nomi uses her sleeve to close the front door so it's unlatched the way they found it—before they clatter down the stairs. Once they're out, past the seafood shop, Nomi makes serious strides down the block until she reaches the mouth of an alley a little distance away from Cevolatti's tenement. Then she ducks around the corner of the alley entrance.

Simon finds her, one hand against the brick wall, heaving up her most recent meal into the drain near an open dumpster.

"Ah fuck." She spits, wipes her eyes with her forearm. "God."

Simon takes his gloved hands out of his trench coat pockets, peels off the gloves and throws them in the dumpster before taking her elbow. "Are you dizzy?"

"Yes," she groans. "No. Dammit—I'm okay. I'm fine."

"Are you gonna fall? Do you want to sit?"

"No, I don't want to *sit*." She hawks and spits again, yanks her elbow away, rounding on him. Her eyes are very wide, red rimmed. "What the *fuck*, Simon. We just saw a dead body—how are you not fazed by that?"

"I lived with a doctor for five years. I work in a slaughterhouse." Those reasons make the most sense, anyway. "Didn't you get used to seeing dead bodies when you were a cop?"

"Not like *that*. However long you've been on the force, you don't get used to seeing people who've had their tongue and eyelids *hacked off*—Jesus Christ." Her face is ruddy. "And what was the deal with the dishwashing gloves? Were you doing a goddamn *examination*? They fucking tortured him!"

"Yes, they did torture him." Simon puts his hands in his pockets. "*They*. More than one person went to work on him. More than one person was there."

Nomi smears her palms down her jeans, wipes her face with the hem of her T-shirt. "How can you know that?"

"The fingers—they were clean. Clean cuts, right between the middle and proximal phalanges. From the angles, I'd say they used bolt cutters. Whoever did that knew exactly what they were doing, it was professional work."

Her face screws up. "How can you—"

"Again, I work in a slaughterhouse. I know the difference between a hack job and a pro cut." He steps back to give her space. "I didn't see a set of bolt cutters in the apartment, did you? Someone brought that, and the ropes to tie him with. Someone prepared, efficient, professional. They came to question him, like we did, except they were using stronger means of persuasion."

Nomi exhales, regaining composure. "Okay. But if they wanted to ask him questions, why cut out his tongue?"

"That wasn't clean, it wasn't . . . elegant." He shakes his head in distaste. "It was just vindictive."

"It wasn't *elegant*?" Nomi is looking at him like she's never seen him before.

"No. It was messy—angry. The tongue and the eyelids and the chest wounds were done with a knife, a sharp one. Maybe from his own kitchen, which they took away and dumped later—there wasn't a knife in the sink or on the floor nearby. But someone else was in that room, someone who was very unhappy with Ricki Cevolatti."

"Jesus." Nomi puts both hands behind her head, elbows out, before dropping her arms and turning around. "Okay, fine. It's fucked, but it's fine."

"Now what do we do?"

She grimaces, spits once more before walking back toward the street. "Well first, I need to wash my mouth. And we need to move. I want to get as far away from this mess as I can before I call it in."

"You're going to call the police?"

"No, *you're* going to call the police, from a pay phone, with an anonymous tip. I don't want my voice anywhere on record, but they don't know you. But before that, I need a Coke."

That's what they do. Nomi buys a soda from a bodega near the corner of Church Avenue. Simon follows her instructions and calls the cops from a phone kiosk at the subway station, hanging up when the operator asks for his name. They get back on the subway—Simon holds his breath when the train dips and enters the tunnels again. Nomi gives him some of her Coke as a consolation prize.

He tries distracting himself with conversation. "So . . . you were a cop?"

"Keep your voice down." She scans the carriage, but the only other passengers are near the far end. She's sitting facing him across the aisle, knees wide, forearms resting on them as she leans forward. She still looks a little haggard. "Yes. For two years. I quit in '85."

He takes another sip of soda. "Folks in the district, like Solange, will trust an ex-cop?"

"The relevant word is *ex*. And yes, they trust me because I'm one of them."

Her eyes dart around. Something she's hiding there, but he's not going to pry. Once again, she reminds him of a mink, a trickster animal—slippery, predatory, a true survivor.

He diverts. "So what does the business with Cevolatti mean for your case?"

"Nothing good." She shakes her head, reaches into her jacket pocket. "At least I got this."

She's holding a man's wallet, brown leather, bulging with receipts and cash and other detritus.

Simon's eyebrows lift involuntarily. "You told me not to touch anything!"

"I told *you* not to touch anything. And I only touched the stuff I was going to steal." She tucks the wallet back into her pocket. "Looks like Cevolatti never threw anything away, so hopefully there'll be something useful in there."

Simon examines an advertisement for Newport 100s above her head, turning things over. "Solange is mixed up in some bad stuff, then."

"Yeah." Nomi straightens. The silver handrail on her left casts glinting reflections on her skin. "Her daughter has been abducted."

Simon's eyes snap back. "To keep her quiet?"

"To keep her compliant. So she does what Lamonte tells her to do."

"What is he telling her to do?"

Nomi shakes her head again; that's something she won't reveal. But talking about it has given her a brittle, glittering energy—this isn't just a job she's been employed to do; she has some kind of personal stake in this.

"And Solange doesn't want to go to the regular cops?"

"She's been warned by Malcolm that going to the cops would put her daughter's safety at risk. Anyway, why would she go to law enforcement? So she can have her case deprioritized? Even if they got Brittany back, they'd take her away from Solange and give her to social services."

It's starting to come together for him now. "Because Solange is a prostitute. And Malcolm is her pimp."

"Give the man a prize."

Simon hands her the soda bottle. "How old is Brittany?"

"Seven." Nomi screws the cap back on slowly. "She's seven years old."

Simon looks at her flinty expression—a solid tell. She's angry and worried about the kid. "That's heavy. You weren't joking when you said you had a full slate."

The phrase seems to deflate her a little. "I don't mind being busy, but I don't like it when dead bodies are involved."

"At least you don't have to worry about that with my case."

"We'll see." Nomi's look is cool, appraising. "I don't know you very well yet."

"That's funny," he says. "Neither do I."

Chapter Seven

September 1987, Saturday

Back in the sun on the corner of West Fourteenth, Nomi ditches Simon Noone outside the New York Savings Bank building, saying she needs to run some errands.

It's the truth; it's just after five, so if she legs it, she might be able to get a message through to Irma before tomorrow. But it's also a lie by omission. She needs some headspace, some time to process. She's still getting flashes of Noone's disturbingly fascinated expression as he examined Ricki Cevolatti's finger stumps.

She crosses Eighth Avenue, passes the art deco Bankers Trust building, the shamrock-decorated facade of an Irish bar, and a stately Italianate mansion. Finally, the baroque iron grille of Our Lady of Guadalupe looms up, and Nomi pulls open the heavy door and slips inside.

There are two racks of votive candles, one just inside the door on the left and another, smaller rack beside the confessional booth. Nomi crosses herself at the holy water font, goes to the small rack and drops a couple quarters into the donation slot to pay for a candle. Using the small roll from her pocket, she wraps a belt of blue electrical tape around the candle's waxed waist and sets it—unlit—into position on the bottom left-hand corner of the rack.

When Irma comes in later to attend mass, she should see it. It's not a perfect system, but it's safer than calling, and they already have a standing arrangement for where and what time to meet.

A hassock for the devout rests in front of the candle racks. For a moment, Nomi longs for faith; if she could simply kneel and pray and have all her various problems solved by a higher power, life would be a hell of a lot simpler. But this is not her religion and not her church—and if the last few years have taught her anything, it's that she's constitutionally incapable of kneeling down.

She leaves the blue-banded candle in place, walks for the outside air.

Her feet are tired—all of her is tired, and a little hungover from the medication she took last night. She's ready to get home and shed her shoulder holster. But it's only a quick walk along West Fourteenth and down Seventh Avenue to HE Travel. A guy called Beko, who she knows as a leatherman at the clubs, is staffing the agency desk, in front of a giant wall poster for RSVP male-only cruises; as he finishes closing the shop, Beko answers her questions about the possibility of tracking a missing American tourist in Mexico or Guatemala in 1982.

When she gets back to Gansevoort, the day is cooling, and there are long shadows on the cobblestones. It's coming up on six in the evening, and there's one more task to complete.

She takes the central staircase up to her apartment, then keeps going to the third floor. From behind Noone's door, the faint strains of some classical music track she doesn't know. She knocks briskly.

Simon answers in his usual fashion: shoeless, white cotton shirt pulled out of his jeans. A glass of red wine lolls in his hand. He has long fingers, slender, with prominent joints—but Nomi doesn't want to think about fingers now, after seeing Cevolatti.

Dusk light filters through the thin curtains on the other side of Noone's living space. His eyebrows are raised. "You're back."

"I'm back." The air from his apartment is warmer than the air in the hallway. Nomi notices the medical text open again on his breakfast table. She studiously avoids staring at his bare feet. "Errands are run. Have you got that stuff you wanted to give me?"

He blinks for a moment. "Oh, right, the stuff—I'll get it now. Come on in, if you like." He leaves the door open, walks off toward the dresser in the far corner, where a small Sanyo tape deck is playing the music at a low volume. "You want a glass of wine? I needed one, after today."

"Thanks, but no." Nomi feels a sudden urge to walk inside and sit down at his tiny table. She takes a single step over the threshold, makes herself stop. Now is not the time to let down her guard. "You drink a lot of wine in Guatemala?"

"None at all. People across the border make wine punch for special occasions, but if you want a drink in Piedras Negras, it's mainly just corn moonshine." He snorts, glances over his shoulder. "I'm getting a taste for wine, though. This is only a cheap merlot, but it's not bad. I wanted to buy a nice Sangiovese, but I'd have to sublet my apartment to afford it."

Nomi doesn't think he's realized that knowing the differences in flavor between expensive wines is a learned skill. If you've never encountered wine before, you don't typically talk like a sommelier in seven weeks.

He returns, carrying an orange cigar box and a short stack of worn hardcover notebooks stuffed with papers. "Okay, this is everything."

"Does that pile include your current identity papers as well?"

"Yes." He brushes his brown hair off his forehead. He still hasn't handed over the bundle. "You'll return these as soon as possible, right?"

"As soon as I've read through everything, I'll give it all back."

"Okay." He hesitates, his cheeks softly flushed. "These notebooks are like my journals, so there's personal stuff in here. Sensitive stuff. Medical information. So . . ."

"I promise I'll take good care of everything and do my best to respect your privacy," she says.

He finally passes her the collection. She flips the lid of the cigar box on top: nestled in tissue paper like a holy relic, a single scrap of woven cotton label tape. Originally white but now yellowed, either from age or exposure, the label clearly displays the name SIMON stitched in a curling font. On the right, just before the label tapers off into a torn, frayed edge, is the starting curve of another letter.

Nomi pokes the frayed edge with a finger. "Huh. This could be something—maybe a *C* or a *G*?"

"Yeah, I spent a long time trying to figure that out." Simon has retrieved his glass, and now he sips, leans a shoulder against the wall. "Didn't get anywhere. Is it the start of a middle name, an initial, a surname? Maybe it's the start of a phone number, I don't know."

"Right." Nomi flips the box lid closed. Simon's apartment smells of espresso and cigarettes—not unpleasant; she wonders if he keeps his work knives here at home, then pushes the thought of blades firmly away. She still can't identify the classical piece. "Okay, thanks for this. Like I said, I'll return everything as soon as humanly possible."

He straightens, gestures with his glass. "You're sure you don't want to come in?"

"Appreciate it, but I've gotta go make some calls."

"Following up on the stuff in Cevolatti's wallet?"

"A little of that," she acknowledges. "A few calls for your case too."

"I've been thinking about the scene in Flatbush." Simon's stare becomes sharp. "There's really only two questions you need the answers for, right?"

Nomi purses her lips and nods. "They tortured him for information. So what did he know?"

"And who did he tell? That's probably what got them so mad."

Nomi feels her hackles rise. She'd kind of assumed that Cevolatti was mutilated to convince him to give up information, and that the vicious assault on his tongue was the killer getting angry when he wouldn't talk. But Simon's right: Cevolatti would've given up his info after losing the first finger. Whoever killed him was angry about the info being shared elsewhere.

"It was Lamonte, wasn't it?" Simon says quietly. "The hack job, I mean."

"No theories yet. I'll make some calls." Nomi won't commit until she knows more. She clutches her new bundle, heads for the staircase. "Okay, have a good night."

"Yeah. You too."

Simon seems either confused or disappointed that she's not up for socializing, his wineglass drooping in his fingers as he closes the door. But that's not how this works: Nomi doesn't want to get too familiar with clients, especially not clients who live in her building. Not clients who give her advice about other cases she's working on.

Not clients who seem too insightful about murder for their own good.

Once she gets inside her apartment, breathing feels easier. She sets the cigar-box bundle on her desk, sheds her jacket, dumps her weapon in its holster in the dedicated drawer. From the kitchen, she grabs a beer. Schlitz in hand, she turns on the desk lamp and makes two calls—one to an NYC library contact who can maybe help her track East Coast obits and missing person reports from 1981 to 1983, and another to a journalist friend who can help with the same request. It's good to have backup. Nomi writes a note to herself for tomorrow, to see if it's feasible to contact the US State Department about American citizens missing in a foreign country, which was what Beko suggested—considering Noone's fake papers, she's doubtful.

Now, the cigar-box bundle. She takes a swig of beer, burps loudly. Examines the scrap of clothing label again, this time with a magnifying glass. Nothing much to see. Woven labels with custom-embroidered names seem like something only rich people would have, though. Unless this is a brand label—but that would likely be printed, not sewn, right? The label fabric seems to be standard cotton in a tight weave; no clues there.

She pushes the cigar box away and flips through the hardcover notebooks. Simon Noone's spiky, sprawling handwriting is like a jagged mountain range. She removes the loose papers—his ID documents, which appear to be excellent, artfully weathered fakes—and stacks everything together, puts it all to one side. She's going to have to spend some time examining everything and taking notes, but she doesn't have the energy for that right now.

She sets her beer down, walks out of her office to dig Cevolatti's wallet out of her abandoned jacket, returns to her desk, upends the wallet onto her blotter. Receipt, receipt, receipt, receipt . . . Just a shit ton of receipts. At least a dozen business cards. Two or three old sticky notes, folded up. A stub of what looks like a bookie's slip. Cevolatti was a pack rat; if this is the state of his wallet, she'd hate to see the glove compartment of his car.

Nomi digs out the rest: a few lost quarters, a New York driver's license, a credit card in his name, a subway token. A small key, maybe for a post office box. Cevolatti would have had a letter box at the bottom of his apartment building stairs—so why would he need a post box? Something to check out. Forty-three dollars in bills, which she pockets: Cevolatti sure won't be spending it.

She sets aside the post box key, the business cards, the sticky notes, the bookie's slip, and goes through the receipts. Throws out anything marked McDonald's, A&P, Foodtown, D'Agostino, 7-Eleven, or Dunkin' Donuts, keeping three that have phone numbers on the backs. Everything useful she bundles with a rubber band. The driver's license and credit card she adds to the pile; the subway token and quarters she sweeps into her top drawer.

Now it's dark beyond her office window. Faintly, from upstairs, the crisp, poignant lilt of violins. Nomi sits on the corner of the desk with her feet on the chair, finishing the dregs of her Schlitz as she watches the lights of the street outside. Yesterday she told Simon Noone that Solange's case was challenging; now she's got a mutilated body on her hands. This whole thing is shaping up worse and worse.

Lamonte was Ricki's boss—but did Lamonte kill Ricki? The connection makes it seem like an obvious jump, but it's an assumption. Could it have been someone else? So far as she knows, Ricki wasn't involved in anything that would put him in another set of crosshairs. He was Lamonte's man. Maybe Ricki was killed by one of Lamonte's enemies? Lamonte would have plenty of enemies. But being Lamonte's man would also afford you a certain level of respect and protection, and there's been no word on the street about internecine squabbles or planned retaliatory action.

So it comes back to Simon's idea, that Lamonte killed his own guy, which makes more sense than any other theory. Reputationally, Lamonte is a man of volcanic anger, and Nomi knows he's killed people personally before—in fact, today's crime scene bears a distinct resemblance to a homicide near Chachi's two years ago that Lamonte was implicated in. She heard that the detectives from Sixth Precinct were never able to pin it on him, but the similarities are there: the victim tied to a chair, stab wounds from a stiletto knife . . .

Question is, why would Lamonte kill his own guy? It's usually a matter of disloyalty: someone working for another boss on the side, someone with their hand in the till, someone screwing up bad or talking out of school. From what she heard at the Riverview last night, Ricki Cevolatti was strictly small beer: too content in his position to become a dog with two masters, and the kind of guy unlikely to steal from his boss. If she had to wager real money on motive, she'd put it on Ricki talking to someone he shouldn't—or talking *about* something he shouldn't.

It's not what he knew, it's who he told. Again, Simon's probably right. So what did Ricki know, or who did he tell, that got Eric Lamonte riled up enough to go crazy with the knife?

Nomi tries to step it out in her mind. Small-time Ricki is asked by Lamonte to carry out some mundane shitkicker job, because that is the function of small-time Rickis the world over. In the course of this job, Ricki discovers information he's supposed to keep a lid on. But, being the type of guy he is—sloppy, from the looks of both his wallet and his apartment—or maybe under the influence of a few drinks or whatever, he spills the beans. Word gets back to Lamonte that Ricki talked. Shortly after that, Lamonte and his efficient associate with the bolt cutters pay Ricki a visit . . .

It has to be something to do with Brittany Jackson's abduction. *Has* to be. Eric Lamonte runs three clubs in the district, and so far as Nomi's aware, there's nothing going down in any of them that's worth killing for. But the job that Malcolm's got Solange working—the level of secrecy around it—is weird and excessive, and Lamonte set it up. The only way Nomi's going to get Brittany back to her mom is if she follows that trail of secrecy to its source.

All these men—Lamonte, Ricki, Malcolm—and at the center of their web is a seven-year-old girl being used as collateral.

Nomi rubs a hand across her face, trying to unclench her jaw, remembering how Solange had shared a Polaroid of Brittany at her first appointment. The photo showed a sturdy girl maybe a year younger than she is now, her black curls tied up in high pigtail knots, her smooth cheeks tinted bronze as she grinned. A girl who was happy and thriving because her mom had made a bunch of tough, unpleasant sacrifices to ensure she's well cared for.

It makes Nomi catch her breath. Maybe it's not just Brittany herself, but the combination of elements that's getting to her: the daughter and her mom being victimized. Because Nomi's been that girl, she understands those sacrifices, and it burns her to see another mother-daughter pair getting screwed over by a guy like Lamonte, who thinks of women as merchandise and thinks of children—especially little girls—only as useful bargaining chips . . .

If Nomi dwells on it too much, she gets the urge to torch something. But she has to be strategic, not rage-filled. She needs calm.

She's earned a bath—and a little more.

Nomi gets off the desk and pulls the blind down, dumps her empty in the kitchen, walks on for the bathroom. Her apartment may have its deficiencies, but the bathroom is nice—compact, the inside walls golden with brown trim, a big claw-foot tub squeezed in. She pushes aside the trailing ends of a heartleaf philodendron to run the faucets. While the tub is filling, she strips out of her boots and clothes, avoids looking at the damaged skin of her midriff, wraps a towel around herself. She wanders back to the kitchen to put a Grace Jones album on the turntable, get a glass of water with ice.

Nomi sets the glass and a washcloth and a lit candle in a jar on the bath caddy, along with the other half Valium from Mischa. Her bath candle and the votive candles at Our Lady of Guadalupe seem to strike the same note; she pushes the mental comparison aside. Takes her kit bag out of the mirrored cabinet above the pedestal sink—it's a small yellow toiletries bag, and she has strict rules around using only the tools from this bag. Opening the zip, she pushes the new arrowhead tool aside and removes a piercing needle, a tiny bottle of rubbing alcohol, and a small stainless steel barbell earring she's been keeping, wrapped in paper. She arranges everything on a hand towel on the lid of the toilet, balances a shaving mirror on the cistern.

The bathwater is high and steaming. Nomi's mouth is watering. She sits on the edge of the bathtub, removes the needle from its paper sleeve, swipes her upper left earlobe with the alcohol, swipes the mirror to clear off condensation. Without too much buildup, she clamps her upper earlobe with her fingers and shoves the needle through. The pain is bright and cleansing, and endorphins rush through her like lightning: Nomi lets herself rock in place for a moment, lets herself feel it. Then she removes the needle and slides the barbell in to take its place, screws on the securing ball. She turns off the main bathroom light and drops her towel, sets one bare foot and then the other into the bath, sinks down into liquid heat.

Warmth inside her as well as on her skin. Muscles relaxing. Jaw unclenching. She swallows the Valium, which will help her sleep. The candlelight flickers, hypnotic, as Grace Jones sings. Behind Jones's voice, there are still faint violins. Nomi's new piercing throbs, quieting her mind. Last night's cut near her belly button stings, submerged, but it's a good sting. She trails the washcloth through the water, wrings it out and wipes her face, lays her head back on the rim of the bath.

Friday night, Saturday night, those are her only ritual nights. It's allowed—allowable. All her anxiety and tension channeled into a small pierced hole, a small shallow slice. It's freeing—but she has to exercise control: When she first started at fourteen, she did a lot of damage. Now she has her rituals, her rules, and things are more manageable.

She considers her reaction to the homicide scene today, reflects again on the incongruity: What she does to herself is fine . . . What a criminal does to someone else is not. But it's an issue of consent. She *arranges* this; she has very specific guidelines around it; she's made an agreement with herself about it. Ricki Cevolatti sure as hell didn't agree to anything.

Tomorrow, her next step is to find out what Cevolatti said and who he talked to, hopefully before Lamonte catches up with them. But for now, Nomi pushes aside thoughts of Cevolatti, the horrors inflicted on him before his death.

Instead, she closes her eyes and listens to the violins upstairs while thinking about Simon Noone's feet: white and naked, long as the rest of him, toes faintly dusted with hair.

Chapter Eight

September 1987, Sunday

Sunday morning, Florent Diner, regret and coffee. "More."

Jamie looks at Nomi sideways as he pours. "This is your third."

After a restless attempt to sleep last night, Nomi took another half pill, which was definitely a mistake. Her newly pierced ear is pulsing in time with her heart.

She waves a hand. "More."

Jamie tops off the cup. "I'm just saying, I've got a joint in my purse. You could come out back and share it with me, might help take the edge off."

"This'll be fine." Nomi slumps back, squints behind her sunglasses. The music playing in the diner is some kind of 1940s piano-tinkling tune with a soulful female voice. "Jamie, there's a little too much chrome and red vinyl in the decor here for this time of the morning."

"Honey, it's ten thirty in the a.m." He rolls his eyes as he walks away with the coffeepot.

She manages to get three cups of black coffee and a bowl of onion soup into her stomach before she has to go to her first appointment. Back on the street, Nomi discovers that the weather is shockingly gorgeous: full sun, sparse wisps of high cloud. But she's itchy and grumpy and not in the mood to appreciate it.

Her outfit is purposefully out of character: pale acid-washed jeans, a white button-down shirt, a black bolo tie, a houndstooth blazer, a plain tote. She's pulled her hair into a braid that disguises her side cut, and she's wearing a short-brimmed black felt hat. The ensemble is designed to make her look unlike herself. Combined with the comedown, she also *feels* unlike herself, an impostor: a mangy black wolf in sheep's clothing, walking up Ninth Avenue.

But it's a suitable facade for visiting St. Bernard's Church, where Father Anthony Staggs is tidying up hymnals left on the pews after mass. She's hoping that he'll be able to help her dig into the question of who was running missionary fieldwork in southern Mexico and Guatemala five years ago.

He scratches his cheek. "'81 to '83? It was probably us Catholics. Maybe the Baptists. But if you're talking Central America, more likely us."

"Would the archdiocese have records?" Nomi flips her notepad closed, clicks her pen, drops them both back into her tote.

"Probably. When do you need the information?"

"I can come by in a couple days. Say Wednesday?"

"Wednesday's fine. Or I can give you a call if I get something sooner." Father Tony has walked her to the main exit. "You doing okay? I don't see you around much anymore."

"I'm doing good." Feeling guilty for lying to a priest, she slides on her sunglasses as he opens the door for her. "Yeah, I'm doing fine."

"Glad to hear it." He glances out into the street, then back to her, sheepish. "I still sometimes get the urge to call you Officer Pace, you know."

She tries not to bristle. "It's been a long time now, Father—I'm out of it for good. Okay, see you in a couple days."

Walking back along the rows of apartment blocks, Nomi scans the street. But nobody's out of place; no one is watching her pass. She descends the steps to the subway and catches the C train, braces herself for Irma's not being at the meeting spot. It happens sometimes: The votive candle gets moved or burned, or Irma forgets to check, or she misses evening mass because of work. You roll the dice and take your chances. But she really needs to talk to Irma.

In Hell's Kitchen, near the beauty school and a giant billboard for Donnie's Softening Lotion, Nomi turns off West Fiftieth. Kitty-corner is a big vacant lot that kids are using as a basketball court. There are a whole lot of four-story brown row houses with rusting air conditioners half falling out of windows. A bunch of yellow cabs go by, a few delivery vans. She's still tracking people and movement on the street, because anywhere between Chelsea and Hudson Yards is officially enemy territory, but it's very mixed trade: men on the stoop reading the newspaper, pedestrians heading for public transport, workers unloading goods out of trucks, women in their church clothes. Lots of Black and brown faces. Some folks are just outside getting some sun. Plenty of loiterers, but nobody setting off Nomi's alarm bells.

Past a liquor store and a Magic Cue Billiards place, there's a bodega on the corner of West Forty-Ninth—Nomi steps inside. At the counter, she orders a pastrami on rye with Swiss cheese and mustard. It's one o'clock. Benito has the radio going in the store—Robbie Nevil crooning "C'est la Vie" through the speakers. Nomi turns the steel barbell in her ear; the lobe is hot to the touch. She dawdles among the shelves as Benni makes her sandwich, watching as other customers come and go, waiting for the bell above the door to ring for the right person. Just as she's starting to think that this trip has been for nothing, Irma walks in and up to the counter.

"Hey, Benito, how you doing. You wanna make me a chopped cheese on a kaiser roll?" Irma spots Nomi and smiles. "Benni, me and my friend here are going out the back, okay? Jesus, Nomes, what the fuck is going on with that hat."

Irma Rosado is short and tough faced, dark circles around darker eyes, light-brown skin and a crown of springy black hair. She's dressed in civvies—a T-shirt and tight jeans and knee boots, a quilted vest, her ever-present gold hoop earrings—and she's fifteen years Nomi's senior.

Nomi's glad as hell to see her. "It's my cover, dummkopf. Holy shit, look at you—it's been too long. Give me a hug."

They embrace; then Irma grabs a soda from the refrigerator and hustles Nomi toward a door plastered in grocery advertisements that looks like the entry to a walk-in pantry. It *is* a pantry, but past another door at the back, there's the world's tiniest outdoor area: flagstone pavers surrounded by corrugated iron fencing. Beneath a short washing line flapping with dish towels, one of those ugly cast-aluminum patio tables.

Irma grabs one of the side-ended apple crates that Benni's using as chairs, pulls it up to the table, lights a Winston with the Bic she had tucked in her bra. "Okay, look, I would love for this to be a fun reunion, but everyone's stressed about more West Side mob action."

"Yeah, I know." Nomi shakes her head at Irma's offer of a cigarette as she finds her own crate. "I was at Cevolatti's place. I called it in."

"*You* called it in?" Irma's thin, overplucked eyebrows dance; smoke wreathes her face and soaks into the dish towels above them. "They said it was a guy's voice on the recording."

"I got someone to call it in," Nomi clarifies. "Cevolatti had been like that awhile when I got there. It's part of this Lamonte case."

"Sure it's the Lamonte case." Irma ashes her cigarette with a flick. "He's all over it, and eventually he'll leave traces somewhere, for some other crime, and we'll nail him for good. But right now, we're not interested in a soldier like Lamonte. We need his boss, Galetti."

Nomi feels cold ripple into her stomach at the mention of the old mob capo's name. "Galetti runs Lamonte?"

"My next envelope through Enrique, I was gonna tell you." Irma stands to pop the cap off her soda with the wall-mounted bottle opener near the pantry door, reclaims her seat. "We've been looking into it—Galetti's extending his reach north of Leroy Street, and he's bought out the leases on Lamonte's club properties. Lamonte has kissed the ring, but there's been some shuffling for position. I mean, maybe this Cevolatti thing is Lamonte getting pissed that Ricki was trying to muscle in somehow?"

Nomi considers telling Irma about her theory, that Cevolatti blabbed something important. But she has nothing concrete on that yet except her own gut feeling and Simon Noone's speculation. "I don't think so. Ricki was just a grunt, and word is he was loyal to Lamonte. Could be he screwed up somehow, which put Lamonte in a tight spot."

"Makes sense." Irma sips her soda. "But Lamonte must've been pretty pissed off. That murder scene seemed personal. If you're mob, and you're small, you don't need that kind of mess—you don't usually bring your friendly neighborhood finger remover along, for instance."

That sounds like solid confirmation of Noone's crime scene deductions. Nomi shrugs. "Well, the Italians love drama."

"Almost as much as us Puerto Ricans." Irma grins. "Anyway, now you know what you're dealing with, yeah?"

That could mean *So you know this is serious*, or it could mean *So you know how dangerous this is*, or it could mean *So you know the NYPD has its eyes trained in the same direction*. Any of these meanings stand as a warning.

The dish towels flap; higher above them, a cloud drifts through a rhombus of sunny sky. Nomi sighs at the new complication. "Galetti, huh?"

"Yeah." Her former NYPD partner makes a face. "We're getting reports higher up the chain about kickbacks, extortion, intimidation tactics. Bigger ripples—that's what Balter and the other boys are talking about down at the station. How the big fish create ripples in the pond."

"Shit." That puts Solange Jackson between a rock and a hard place. "So the problem I have is that my client is working for Malcolm Forest, who's set her up with an exclusive VIP, some guy called Jeremy. She's not thrilled about the arrangement."

"And Lamonte runs Forest. Right." Irma frowns, takes another sip from her bottle. "Your client should maybe get off that train."

"She would, but Lamonte's got her daughter. Which is why she hired me."

"Oh, that's a problem."

"Tell me about it." Nomi gestures to get a drag off Irma's cigarette. "So you and me are dealing with the same issue."

"Yeah." Irma points a finger. "But I'm investigating it as a member of the force. You're on your own. And Nomes, you were always a good cop—coulda been a great cop—but, girl, you're still a rookie. I've been in this game longer, and even I don't want to go toe to toe with guys like Lamonte and Galetti. Be careful."

"Irm, you know me, I'm careful as I can be." Nomi returns the cigarette, exhaling a thin stream of smoke. "Okay, it's good to get the background on all this. Listen, one more thing—it's unrelated. I'm tracing a guy for another client. Can you find out about missing person reports within these states in this time frame?"

She fishes the memo paper out of her tote, the one that has all the relevant dates and information. Irma balances her cigarette on the edge of the ashtray, takes the memo and reads.

"Huh." Irma swigs soda, her eyebrows doing that dance again. "You got me checking the whole eastern seaboard—wow. You don't want me to—I dunno—turn straw into gold or something too?"

Nomi snorts. "If you figure out how to turn straw into gold, let me know. We could both retire early."

"Damn, wouldn't that be the life, huh?" Irma's eyes soften above her grin. "You look like half-baked shit, Nomes—how you doing?"

The question needs a genuine response, not the lies she told Father Staggs. But Nomi can't reveal everything either. "I'm okay, just a little hungover. And this case is getting hotter than I'd like."

"Look at me, babe." Irma hunkers forward. "Watch your ass with this. Galetti's a businessman, but he's still a snake. And Lamonte's not screwing around—you saw what he did to Cevolatti."

"I'm not doing anything to disrupt Arthur Galetti's business," Nomi demurs.

"No, but you've got a client who wants to disrupt his business. For whatever reason, your client's work is necessary for what Galetti's doing. You said Lamonte's got her daughter as collateral to keep her working?"

"Yeah, and I'm getting the kid back." Nomi feels her stubborn streak levitate right to the surface. "I'm not leaving a seven-year-old girl with a guy who has priors for pandering."

"Well, if you get a clear shot, just take Lamonte out." Irma ashes her smoke and laughs. "It'd save me a whole lot of trouble and paperwork in the long run, you know?"

This is the thing that Nomi has always loved about her ex-partner, and one of the reasons it was so damn hard to let policing go: She'd finally found someone on her wavelength, with the same sense of humor and the same rough brand of ethics.

Irma cocks her head. "You ever miss the station house, hon?"

Guilt was another thing that had made leaving hard. Being a woman cop is a tough row to hoe, and Nomi still feels as bad now about leaving Irma to hoe it alone as she did two years ago.

"I miss you." She steals a sip of soda, shrugs. "Sneaking around like this to stay connected is a pain. And I miss having colleagues. But so long as Balter is still ruling the roost at Tenth Precinct, I've got to steer clear."

"You don't want to lock horns with the commanding officer who kicked you out—I get it." Irma dabs out her cigarette. "Balter can be an asshole."

Irma doesn't know the half of it. But they can't get into it today, because just like that, time's up. She and Irma used to spend hours together in the cruiser, and now all they get is the time it takes Irma to smoke a Winston.

They exchange final news—gossip from the station, brief missives about family, last hugs—then they go collect their sandwiches. Nomi pays for Irma's soda and her chopped cheese.

After giving her ex-partner a five-minute head start, Nomi exits back into the breeze along West Forty-Ninth. It's nearly two in the afternoon. She hitches her tote and does her usual street check, pulls her hat down as she walks past a graffiti mural, a tobacconist, a set of fire escape stairs draped with Old Glory.

In her mind, she turns over the stuff Irma said about Lamonte and Galetti—*He's a snake . . . Lamonte's not screwing around.* Is she getting in too deep? But the NYPD is only interested in nailing Galetti; bit players like Solange Jackson and her daughter get caught in the crossfire. Who's looking out for them? The idea of leaving Brittany Jackson to Lamonte's tender mercies makes Nomi feel sick.

Cars go by. Across the street, a guy pulls a wheeled pallet of carpet rolls in the other direction, toward Ninth Avenue. On Nomi's side, a hunched bum in a dirty jacket and a khaki beanie is on the approach. She prepares to give him a wide berth, but as their paths cross, he reaches out and grabs her by the elbow, swings in beside her.

Nomi jerks, pulls back to give a swing of another kind. *"Hey—"*

"It's me," Simon Noone says. "Please don't punch me."

"Noone?" She feels her facial muscles go slack. "What the *fuck*?"

He's almost unrecognizable in grubby brown drill trousers, a gray sweatshirt with dirty cuffs, a zipped nylon jacket the color of phlegm. The khaki beanie he's wearing makes his hair bunch at the sides and the back. There are sweat stains on his clothes and smears on his face. Even his posture is different.

But when he removes his cheap plastic sunglasses, his eyes come into view, and there's no disguising those. "You're heading for the subway, yes?"

Nomi's squinting, horrified. "What the fuck are you even *doing* here? Did you *follow* me?"

"Yes?" He seems confused by the question, which is ridiculous. "I saw you come out of Florent as I was walking home from work, and—"

"And *what*?" She wrenches her elbow out of his grip, slaps his sunglasses from his hand. They clatter on the sidewalk. "You figured you'd tail me for a while and find out what I'm up to? Do you know how *fucked up* that is? Jesus Christ, Noone!"

His cheeks pink as he glances at the sunglasses, back to her. "There was a guy in the street. He was watching you, when you came out of the café. An older guy, stocky—"

"No." This is something concrete she can refute. She's been doing her street checks; she's not a rank amateur. "I don't believe you. There is no guy."

"There was a guy!" A touch of desperation from Noone, but she's onto him now. His hands spread helplessly. "Look, I'm sorry—"

"Listen to me." She grabs a handful of his disgusting jacket, jerks hard. "I'm going to use small words so you understand. This isn't a game. This is my *job*, and I know what I'm doing—I've been doing it for literally years. I don't need some kind of self-appointed guardian trailing me around."

"Nomi—"

"Get out of my face." She pushes to release him, steps away, turns back. "And stop following me! You're not a fucking detective, and we are not partners. You want something to do after work, get a fucking hobby!"

She spins again and walks away, stomping hard up West Forty-Ninth. The stomping helps, but when she gets to the subway station at the corner of Seventh Avenue, she's still angry. No—she's fucking *furious*. She takes the subway stairs down. Simon Noone and his goddamn stalker behavior . . . Oh, he doesn't "recognize American social cues"? Bullshit to that. He's just a creepy, personal-space-trespassing *asshole*.

An asshole who somehow knows how to tail someone undetected.

She glares across the subway tunnel at the grimy white tile on the other side. How the hell did she not notice him? She's had a tail before, had to lose one. Tailed plenty of suspects in turn. Her guard is always up. *I know what I'm doing*: That's what she said. Well, if she's so goddamn on the ball, how did he slip past her?

How did Noone manage to be so covert? Who the fuck *is* this guy?

A heavily graffitied train arrives, brakes squealing, blowing hot metal air. Inside the carriage, an old man is playing a mouth organ at the far end. Nomi finds a seat, tugs her hat brim down. Should she dump Noone as a client? He crossed a line—more than one—and this whole thing is looking more and more like a bad deal. But how to get rid of him?

She thinks on the problem, eats half her pastrami on rye, rewraps the other half to get out of the subway. She's still thinking at quarter to three, when she reaches the tenement. Sun has warmed the concrete steps. Sofia Rosa is checking her mail in the hallway, her trench coat belted and a collection of plastic shopping bags at her sneaker-clad feet. Nomi nods hello, takes the center stairs up two at a time to her apartment.

On the second floor, a forty-something guy, craggy features, flat cap, black zip jacket with the FedEx logo. He's holding a large yellow document envelope and glancing from a clipboard to the number above her door.

Nomi's not expecting anything by courier, although she sometimes receives mail meant for others in the building. Still, she gets a prickling feeling as the memory of Simon Noone's warning comes back: *There was a guy, older, stocky.* It suddenly occurs to her that Noone had no reason to stop and reveal himself in Hell's Kitchen unless he really *did* see someone on her tail . . .

She keeps her distance. "Help you?"

The courier guy looks over. "Nomi Pace?"

"Yes?"

"Ah, great, this is sign only." He proffers the clipboard, with an attached pen.

Nomi's eyes narrow with suspicion. But this guy has her name and address, the jacket, the clipboard, the impatient courier attitude . . . Everything about him seems legit. How far is she willing to take this paranoia?

She makes the call, moves closer.

Which is when he steps forward and punches her in the stomach.

It all seems to happen in one action: His fist hits, her tote falls, then she's curled over like an anemone. *Be careful,* Irma had said. Too late. Nomi's bunched around the courier guy's fist, her solar plexus made of cement. The clipboard has clattered on the floor and spun away. Her hat has fallen off.

The craggy-featured guy backhands her viciously across the face. Her head snaps sideways, smacks the jamb of the closed door. A blinding explosion of black-edged stars. Stunned, asphyxiating, Nomi slides down the door until her cheek hits the cool, gritty linoleum.

The guy steps closer, his boot near her face. He tosses the yellow document envelope onto the floor beside her. "You got your delivery, understand?"

She can't even nod. Without air, her ribs are hot and empty as the wind through the subway tunnel. Everything is flipped, pink and rubbery. Her eyeballs throb, pressure burning at the back of her throat. The courier guy's shadow recedes. His footsteps echo as he walks away.

"Ai-ai-ai!" Noises somewhere, excited, yammering exclamations. "No-mee! No-mee!"

Wet on her cheek, air whistling. She manages to suck oxygen—it hurts. Slapping for purchase on the linoleum, her arms are limp as spaghetti. Suddenly, in her fish-eye field of vision, a wrinkled, brown, worried face.

"No-mee," Sofia Rosa says, "the man is gone, but you are bleeding. You must get up."

Getting up seems impossible. Nomi finally manages a whole breath; her chest and head both light up with pain.

"Quick now!" Her landlady seems determined. "Downstairs to my apartment, until we are sure he's not coming back."

Nomi scrambles away from the floor. She's going to throw up. No, she's got it. Sofia Rosa's surprisingly tough hands grip her biceps. Nomi leans against hard wood, then soft flesh. Christ, she's leaning on a seventy-year-old woman. Together they stumble down the stairs.

"Inside," Sofia instructs, using her key and pushing open her door. "On the couch, yes. Very good. This—take this dish towel, put it against your head. Against your head, like this. Yes, harder."

Sofia Rosa's apartment is minuscule, poky with too much furniture. Brown floral drapes and a big TV, a particleboard end table. Velour footstool near this saggy couch that smells of gardenias and cigarettes. Nomi concentrates on staying upright, on pressing the dish towel to her face, on not puking.

Her landlady is bustling. "We will need the doctor, yes?"

"No doctor," Nomi rasps. No cops, no doctors, no partners—she's on her own.

"Oh, I must get my groceries! Un momento."

Sofia Rosa steps out the front door to fetch her groceries. Sharpness throbs at Nomi's eyebrow; she tastes salty blood on her lip. Somewhere in the back of her mind, it registers as interesting that when she makes herself bleed, that's good—necessary, even—but when someone else does it, it's a totally different story. Her vision is still spinning, filmed with pink. Voices out in the first-floor hallway are garbled, like she's under the ocean.

No—it's not distance making the words hard to understand. Whoever's out there is speaking Spanish.

Her vision is graying fast. Someone says, "Dónde está ella?" and Sofia Rosa says, "Here, she is here." Then the apartment door opens, and Simon Noone strides through, shoving his beanie into his jacket pocket.

"Christ, what a mess," he mutters, and also what seem like curse words in Spanish as he takes over with the dish towel and braces her head gently. "It's okay, I've got you."

"Oh, perfect," Nomi says, right before she slides into the dark.

Chapter Nine

September 1987, Sunday

Simon realized five years ago, after resurfacing in Richard Flores's village house, that some functions came back automatically, some things he had to relearn, and some things he had to pick up from scratch. With a few of the latter skills, he showed enough aptitude that Flores suspected he'd had some experience with them before; they even became instinctual.

Simon has another skill category, of course, which is "things that seem to have unfolded from inside him, fully formed." He's discovering more of these skills since arriving in America—he discovered a new one today, in fact. A few of them have been disquieting.

But he focuses now on one of his "studied yet instinctual" skills, which is providing medical attention. Amid all the confusion and strangeness here in America, it's good to have a personal competency about which he's entirely confident.

He catches Nomi as she passes out, tips her side-on over a cushion, which prevents her from falling off the couch and keeps her breathing clear. Simultaneously, he keeps pressure on her head wound with the dish towel.

"Too much blood!" Sofia Rosa declares, fluttering behind him.

"Head wounds always bleed a lot." Swapping hands on the dish towel, he shakes out of his jacket, sits down on a footstool. He's considering moving the dish towel to examine Nomi's head when she gasps awake, her bleary eyes flaring open.

"It's me," he says. "Hold still."

With a groan, she pushes herself upright.

He sighs. "Or not. But maybe don't move around too much."

Her face is messy with blood, and she looks disoriented. "This's Sofia Rosa's place."

"Sí," Sofia Rosa replies on automatic, still hovering as she removes her coat.

"Yes," Simon confirms, watching Nomi's gaze regain focus. Her pupils don't seem too blown. "How are you feeling?"

"Like shit," she rasps. Her head droops. "Guess this is where you get to say I told you so."

"Is it?" He's still maintaining pressure with the dish towel. "Seems a little brutal, under the circumstances. Okay, let's have a look at this."

He peels back the reddened cloth. Nomi hisses. Sofia Rosa makes tsking sounds over his shoulder. The wound is a simple one-and-a-half-inch laceration above the right eyebrow extending down to the orbital rim. Not a long cut, but it's gaping. Edema is developing—it'll swell more the longer they leave it. Bleeding has slowed with pressure, still seeping at the lowest edge. The right eyelid is purple.

"Bad?" Nomi's left cheek is fiery where she's clearly been hit.

Simon discovers something else that's new—something cold and black and enraged, growling up inside him at the sight of Nomi's injury. He flashes on the man who followed her: He should've broken his kneecaps. He'd had opportunity. If he'd had his knives from work, he could've made three quick cuts, groin-stomach-neck, and then—

He controls his thoughts, grimaces. "Not bad. Not great. Let me wash my hands."

He asks Sofia Rosa to steady Nomi on the couch as he washes and rinses at the kitchen sink. He makes sure to clean under his nails. Forces himself to fall into a pattern he knows, a skill he's familiar with. Concentrating on the task ahead helps him feel calm, methodical, like he's back in the clinic, or even back at his table at Gennaro's: boots solid on the rubber mats, cimeter knife heavy in his hand, a sense of relaxation settling over him as he makes neat, precise cuts . . . He returns to the footstool.

"I need to touch your face, okay?" When Nomi gives the tiniest nod, he palpates the supraorbital and infraorbital rims. The flesh is tender, but there's no step off or indication of fracture. "Tell me if there's pain."

"It's fine." She looks like she's controlling the urge to wince.

"Double vision? Headache?" No, it seems. "Watch my finger."

He holds up his index finger and traces it left to right, observes her ocular movement. Seems okay. Her eyelid also seems to have normal movement. He presses the dish towel against the blood still leaking from the wound.

"Will she be all right?" Sofia Rosa falls back into Spanish when she's anxious.

Simon replies in kind. "She'll be fine." But he's worried about the loss of consciousness, however momentary. "Did she throw up?"

"Not yet." Sofia Rosa recovers her English. "You want coffee? I need coffee."

"Go make coffee," Simon suggests before turning back to Nomi. "You're going to have a hell of a hangover. I'm concerned about concussion because you passed out. But right now, I think you need stitches on this cut."

"That's a bummer," Nomi replies, voice hoarse. "Because I can't go to the hospital."

Simon thinks for a moment. This presents a certain level of difficulty. The cut is too long and badly positioned to use surgical glue. "I can stitch this. I've stitched plenty of wounds before. But it'll really hurt—faces and hands are the worst places to get sewn up. A local anesthetic would be best."

"That's too bad, I guess," she says wearily.

He's sutured wounds in conditions worse than the ones in this apartment. He turns to Sofia Rosa, switches language. "Auntie, we may have to fix this ourselves. Is that okay?"

"Eh." His landlady isn't thrilled about it. But sometimes people need things they can't get through official channels, which is why she keeps an empty room up on the third floor. She ties on her apron, fishes for a cigarette in the pocket, puts a small saucepan filled with water on the stove. "I don't mind if you do it, but I don't want to watch. Do you need special medical things?"

Sunday afternoon, there's unlikely to be a drugstore open in the area with the necessary supplies. Fortunately, that's something he's accustomed to. He won't have a needle driver, which will be awkward; the rest he can probably cobble together.

"I need a stiff needle, strong thread, boiling water. A pair of metal scissors. Some clean cloth . . ."

"Are you talking in Spanish so I won't get nervous?" Nomi interrupts. [illegible]

Simon ignores her. "Neosporin and Band-Aids. And if you have a metal thimble, that would be good."

"I have those things." Sofia Rosa adds ingredients to the saucepan: dark-brown sugar, ground coffee, a cinnamon stick.

"Is there more boiled water? And dish towels?" Simon waits as his landlady sets her cigarette in an ashtray, ferries those items to the small end table on his right. Then he has a brainwave. "Auntie, does anyone here on the first floor have numbing cream? Like for bedsores or leg ulcers?"

Sofia Rosa brightens. "Mr. Harvey across the hallway has cream for ulcers. He will be home from church by now. As soon as this coffee is boiling, I'll go talk with him."

"What's going on?" Nomi's voice still has a punch-drunk slur. She seems bewildered by the Spanish.

Simon dampens and wrings out a new dishcloth, uses the same mild voice that he'd use for any bewildered patient in the village. "Once

Sofia Rosa has made coffee, she's going to put together everything we'll need to stitch your head. How do you feel?"

"You asked me that already." Her carnivore eyes blink, soften. "You said there was a guy. I didn't believe you."

"Forget about it." He wipes carefully at her cheek, the side of her jaw. The blood on her face is fresh and easy to remove. "How did he get you?"

"He had a jacket and an envelope and a clipboard, like a courier." She seems mildly astonished that she fell for it. "You tried to warn me. You asked me how I feel? I feel like an idiot." She flops a hand toward the damp cloth. "Gimme that, I've gotta wipe my other eye."

"Let her drink this." Sofia Rosa sets a glass of warm water on the end table, switches to English. "No-mee? We will get the things for your head, yes?"

"Thank you." Nomi carefully dabs the inside corners of both eyes. "And thanks for helping me."

Sofia Rosa makes a "fffssshhh" sound that indicates these are the things neighbors do for one another, stubs out her cigarette. "Simon, I go talk with Mr. Harvey, okay?"

"Thank you, Auntie." As his landlady leaves the apartment, Simon turns back and watches Nomi sip the warm water. Her hand isn't shaking too much. He feels some sort of way—he's not sure what—mostly unsettled. "Look, I didn't mean to follow you. I saw you as I was coming home from work. The courier guy was already tracking you, I just . . . tried to keep up with him."

Nomi can't really squint at him, but she's giving it a try. "Have you tailed anyone before?"

"I don't know," Simon admits.

But he was good at it. More than good: It felt natural, comfortable. One of those fully formed skills, rising up unbidden. His reactions and movements were so smooth, following the courier: He knew how to keep his distance, double back, slide into doorways, tracking the man in the flat cap.

Even as he performed the actions, he found it all deeply unnerving. How does he know how to do this stuff? And he's still thinking of slicing up the courier like he'd bone out a beef shoulder. *Concentrate.*

Nomi sets down the glass, more worried about the courier himself. "So the guy saw what I was doing in Hell's Kitchen before he jumped me?"

"No." Simon takes back the cloth, dunks it. "He followed you to the church, then the subway. But when you got out at Hell's Kitchen, he was . . . distracted." Might as well admit it. "I pushed him down the subway stairs."

"You what?"

Simon shrugs, wrings water out of the cloth. "There was a crowd. I tripped him, he fell back. I didn't stick around to see." There was a detached mental arithmetic he'd applied to it. "You were dressed to blend in, be unobserved. I figured you didn't want some sneaky guy checking out what you were doing."

"So you became the sneaky guy."

Oh, the irony. "Sorry about that. But I tried to warn you, when you came out of the bodega."

"And instead of listening, I got angry with you. Great." Her face is cleaner now. She glances away, back; she's about to make a confession. "My ex-partner is still with the NYPD. She feeds me intel, but we have to be careful. The bodega is one of the safe places we can meet."

"I'm really *not* trying to be your guardian, or an amateur detective." Simon winces. "Although you're possibly right that I need to get a hobby."

Sofia Rosa returns then with a small tube of cream, which turns out to be the lidocaine-prilocaine mix he was hoping for; it's typically used for catheter insertion and skin debridement, so it should dull some of the pain he's about to inflict. As his landlady turns off the coffee, Simon helps Nomi to recline facing the ceiling, applies the cream.

As the numbing agent takes effect, he and Sofia Rosa prep the rest of the equipment, transferring everything to a clean towel on the end table. Sofia Rosa switches on the standing lamp before exiting to take coffee to Mr. Harvey. Simon washes his hands in the kitchen again, this time more thoroughly. He has no gloves, but it won't be the first time.

He returns, checks everything over—cooled water, needle and a tough silk thread, scissors, thimble, everything boiled. Dressing materials sit to one side. He has enough light. Medical treatment is like cooking; it's good to have all your ingredients prepared beforehand. He's feeling much calmer now, with something useful to do.

Nomi is stretched across the couch cushions in her odd outfit, a towel under her head and another beside her face. Blood streaks have matted her white shirt collar to her neck, although she's undone the top button and tugged off the string tie. Her hair is unraveling from its braid, and red stains are smeared in the shaved side cut over her right ear.

Her breathing expands and deflates her skinny rib cage in a jagged staccato rhythm: She seems heightened, anxious, with good reason. Simon's tempted to reassure her, but she's the kind of person who views reassurance with suspicion. Better to just go with the reassurance that competence provides.

He moves the scissors so they're more accessible. "You're up to date with your shots?"

"What, like tetanus?" Nomi's eyes swivel, with nothing to focus on but the ceiling. "I had one about three years ago."

"Good enough. Okay, I'm going to rinse the wound now." He cleans everything gently with the cool boiled water, which also tests her level of numbness at the site. Seems all right. Best to do this before it gets more swollen. "The cut isn't too deep, but it won't stay closed on its own. I'm only going to place enough stitches to keep it together, so it can heal."

"Fine."

"Last chance," he says. "Do you trust me to do this? This is your face."

"Just do it." Her voice is rough. She closes her eyes.

He takes up the needle and thread. "Did you get what you needed from your ex-partner?"

"Mostly, yeah. Some of it was useful—" Her breath hisses sharply as the needle goes in, and her cheeks flood with color.

"Keep talking," he suggests.

"Jesus fuck." Nomi's lips tremble, but she's tough. She blows out air. "Okay, so Ricki Cevolatti was a gofer for Eric Lamonte."

"Our friend with the Italian pandering charge," he notes. The thimble is useful for creating counterpressure to achieve skin puncture.

"Lamonte manages three clubs on the West Side." Her face is still furiously flushed, and she's looking at the ceiling, at the lamp, anywhere but at Simon. She also appears to be distracting herself by divulging information. "He coordinates hookers, drugs, booze deliveries, stuff like that. But the club properties are owned by a businessman named Arthur Galetti, who's connected to the Gambino mob."

"That's a criminal organization." Sofia Rosa has told him about the Italian mafia. "Please don't nod your head."

"Sorry. But yeah. So the last few months, Galetti's been buying up waterfront land like crazy—" She exhales as Simon ties off the first stitch. Her fingers clutch her shirt, the fabric pulling over her stomach. "Then he petitions city council to rezone. All above board, all legit—respectable investor in the community . . . You get the drift."

"What's Galetti doing with the real estate and the rezoning?"

"We don't know. And city council must have concerns too, because they've been holding up the rezoning requests."

"Right." Simon snips thread ends with the scissors. "Well, maybe Galetti really *is* investing in the community."

"I don't believe it. Galetti's a crook. But whatever he's doing, he keeps his hands clean by using smaller guys like Lamonte. Ow."

Despite the "ow," she's doing better with the pain than he expected. Maybe it's the numbing cream. "Second stitch. You're doing great."

"Thanks, Mom." With her head immobile, Nomi's eyes dart away as if she's embarrassed. Then she looks back, blinking. "You're good at this."

"I did a lot of assistant work for Flores in the village." Her skin is pouched and tender. It's a little harder with this straight needle, but he's getting the hang of it. "I told you I lived with a doctor."

"And you work in a slaughterhouse." Her gaze is still on him.

Simon pierces her skin again with the needle, has an uncomfortable vision of himself tying up a carcass for spit roasting: trussing the marbled meat with neat stitched lines of twine. But he's not at work now. And he's strangely discomfited by Nomi's flushed, sweaty face, her gasping breaths, her body held at exquisite tension.

"I've sutured injuries plenty of times." He wets his lips. Better to go back to their previous topic. "Okay, so Galetti's at the top, Lamonte's below him, and Ricki Cevolatti was the guy at the bottom who spoke out of turn."

"Yes." She closes her eyes as he ties off the second stitch, her respiration high and unsettled, humming through her closed lips. "Mmm . . ."

"Keep breathing." He snips. The numbing cream really is doing a fine job.

She exhales as the needle goes in for the third stitch, her breath coming out choppy. "So I don't know for sure, but I think Ricki blabbed about Solange Jackson. Lamonte runs contractors, small-time pimps who send hookers through the clubs. Guys, girls, whatever. Solange's pimp, Malcolm Forest—"

"The loud guy outside your door."

"Malcolm works for Lamonte." Nomi braces as Simon pulls the thread through the other side. Her fisted hand butts against his knee, and he tries not to flinch at the contact. "Fuckfuckfuck. Okay, when Solange first hired me, she told me that about ten days ago, Lamonte arranged for Malcolm to send her to party with an exclusive client outside the club. All hush-hush, real shut-your-trap stuff. But Ricki knew about it somehow."

"And Ricki didn't keep his trap shut."

"So that's three questions now—what did Ricki know, who did he talk to, and what did he say?" She chews her bottom lip. "I'm trying to think of anyone *I* know who would've been in Ricki's orbit."

Simon ties the final knot carefully. "You said Ricki was a gofer? Lamonte must have had him doing something to help Solange's assignment—driving her to the client, delivering food . . ."

"Delivering drugs." Her expression is thoughtful. At least the conversation is keeping her distracted.

One last snip, and Simon leans back. He's gotten over his odd discomfort of a moment ago; now he can assess the work. For emergency surgery with improvised equipment, it's not a bad job, and he managed to avoid sticking himself with the needle. He rinses his hands in the bowl of water, dries them on a clean towel. "All done."

"All done?"

"Sit up nice and slow." Once she's sitting, he gives her a hand mirror.

"Holy shit, I look like an extra from a Freddy Krueger film." Nomi grimaces at herself in the glass. "I need to go back to my apartment, clean up, change clothes—"

"I still have to put a dressing on that." Simon sets the suture equipment away to one side, reaches for the Neosporin.

"Wait." Nomi straightens, touches his hand. Her cheeks are still pink, and she seems weirdly energized, but he's seen people affected by postinjury adrenaline react this way. "Wait one second. I'm a mess, but we can use this."

"What do you mean?"

She gives back the mirror. "Let me up. I think I know someone we can talk to about Ricki—"

She stands abruptly, wobbles.

"Hold on." Forced to stand as well, he grabs her by the waist. "You have a head injury. I don't think you should be going anywhere."

Her face is animated, and her hands grip his forearm. "He's one block away. Come *on*, Noone. We've got a real chance here." Now her eyes get stubborn. "I'm going, even if I have to go slow. So you can either come along, or—"

"Are you seriously trying to either-or me?" His tone is disapproving, but it's theater. She's asked him to go with her. A tiny part of him is sparking, victorious. "Forget it, I'm coming along so you don't collapse in the street."

"Ohmigod, I won't collapse in the street—"

"Or get beaten up again."

"I got caught by surprise!"

"If you say so." He glances around. "Wait, I don't want to leave this mess here."

He tidies everything in Sofia Rosa's living room—bloody dish towels, surgical equipment, the tube of cream—and puts the couch to rights. The dressing materials go into his pants pocket for later. He ties his ugly jacket around his waist by the sleeves.

Nomi has been testing her limitations with standing and moving around. Now she's ready, impatient. "Okay, let's go."

Chapter Ten

September 1987, Sunday

Rather than hold his arm as they make their way out of the first floor of the tenement, Nomi holds the couch, the door, the wall. Simon finds this amusing. It reminds him of a saying they have in Piedras Negras about a stubborn person: that they can see the storm clouds coming but refuse to kneel and pray for God's protection.

Nomi is exactly like that. She sees the storm but refuses to kneel. Much as Simon knows the aphorism is supposed to be cautionary, there's something gutsy about her attitude.

They get out the narrow door and down the steps, into the late afternoon on Gansevoort Street. After the cool gloom of Sofia Rosa's apartment, the sidewalk seems to radiate the day's heat. Now there's no furniture to use as support, Nomi's forced to lean on him as they walk.

"Where are we going?" Simon asks.

"One block, to Hector's Café." The bruises around her eye and the gory stitches on her eyebrow pop like neon in the sunlight. Her cheeks are developing a chalky green color. She presses her lips together.

"Nausea?"

"Yes." Grimly determined, she concentrates on her steps. They skirt someone's pushbike, chained up to a street-sign pole. "Talk to me. Distract me."

"We don't have to do this now—"

"Shut up. Yes, we do. Are you gonna talk to me or not?"

He relents, steadies his bracing arm against her weight. "Okay, you said Solange Jackson is seeing an exclusive client for Eric Lamonte. Is that what got her daughter kidnapped?"

"Yes." Nomi swallows, firms her knees. They're almost at Perrotta's deli grocery. "Solange starts spending all her time with this guy. When she asks for more money, Malcolm says yes. Placating, right? Then she tells him the situation is making her uncomfortable—the guy is off his face on drugs all the time, Lamonte keeps loading him up—plus the secrecy around it is weird, and she's losing time with her daughter. Next thing, she goes home and Brittany's gone."

"Who's the client?"

"I've got a name—Jeremy. I'm trying to find out more. I know he's young, white, and an addict. Solange sees him at an apartment here in the village on Perry Street, and she thinks Lamonte is paying the rent on it."

"That seems like a strange arrangement to have with a client."

"No kidding." Passing the grocery, closing on the corner with Washington Street, Nomi straightens her shoulders. "Okay. Okay, I got this."

This whole expedition is ridiculous. But they've come this far, and Simon feels compelled to be encouraging. "You're doing great."

"Yeah, I'm a fucking hero. We turn right here. What's the deal with your clothes?"

"What's wrong with my clothes?" Simon can't believe she's critiquing his outfit when her white shirt is crusted with bloodstains. Other pedestrians stare as they pass by.

"When I saw you in Hell's Kitchen, I hardly recognized you. Is that what you wear to work? They let you dress like a bum at Gennaro's?"

"I'm not dressed like a bum. Everybody dresses like this. I fit in."

"You fit in, right." She winces as they cross Washington and take the curb. "Wonderful. Simon Noone, human chameleon. Just up here, on the left."

They're under a chicken processing plant's portico, but it's not blocking the glare of the sun lowering in the west. The pylons of the High Line vibrate from the ambient rumble of traffic. A red delivery truck rolls around the corner up ahead; then Nomi is shaking him off.

"Let me walk alone. You can lurk behind me, but this guy won't cooperate if I look like I can't stand by myself."

It's a bad idea, but Simon lets her go.

She lists, steadies, spits onto the sidewalk. Now she's got it. "Okay, listen, I'm going to talk to a low-level drug dealer called Leo Farina. He was a friend of Ricki's. I'll be faking him out, so just—I don't know—try not to look surprised at stuff I say."

Pinching her own cheeks for color, she takes the last ten paces to Hector's Café unaided. Simon follows close enough behind that if she drops, he can grab her.

The café is a redbrick box under the elevated rail line, plainer than dirt, but the inside is shaded and cool. Brown linoleum that looks unchanged since the sixties, red stools fixed in place at the counter, tables with granite-look tops and padded metal chairs.

Four men are clustered around one table, having pushed aside coffee cups and plates of egg scraps and sausage fat. They're having postprandial cigarettes and tiny glasses of some clear spirit. Simon finds it easier now to recognize when people are speaking Italian, and that's what these guys are speaking.

"You can tell me what they're whispering behind my back," Nomi mutters.

"And help you stay upright."

"See? You're multifunctional, like a Swiss Army knife." She steps forward with the appearance of confidence, her voice gaining normal volume. "Hey, Leo? You got a minute?"

One of the men at the table—black trousers, gold satin shirt, brown tinted sunglasses—looks over and does a double take. "Harriet? What the fuck happened to you?"

"Bumped into a door," Nomi deadpans. "Can we talk?"

The other men chortle. One of them grins. "You gonna say the magic words, princess?"

Simon straightens involuntarily to his full height.

He keeps his tone jovial. "'If you laugh at her again, I will shove that steak knife in your eye'—how's that for magic words?"

"Don't oversell it," Nomi murmurs to him, before looking back at the men around the table, who have suddenly become much quieter. "Leo, just get the fuck over here, okay?"

Leo extricates himself and slouches closer, pushing his sunglasses up into his hair. Nomi directs him outside to a spot near a trash can on the corner, under the riveted beams of the overhead rail line. Simon shadows her, his arms crossed, watching and curious.

"Okay, I'm here. What's your problem?" Leo pulls a cigarette out from behind one ear, lights it with a gold Zippo, eyes tracking warily between Nomi and Simon. "Who's your friend?"

"Gee, I don't know—my personal valet?" Nomi's lip curls as she points at her injured eyebrow. "Look at my face, Leo. Who the fuck do you think he is? I'm walking around my own goddamn neighborhood with *security* because of your last conversation with Ricki Cevolatti."

She said this would be a fake-out, and now she's playing it to the hilt; Simon makes an effort to follow her lead and appear more coldly menacing. Apparently, it works, because Leo glances over, then takes a step back.

"Whoa. What?" Flustered, Leo squints, his cheeks reddening. "What are you talking about? I didn't have no conversation with Ricki—"

"Do you think I'm stupid, Leo?" Nomi steps into his space, fronting the guy in a way he seems unused to. "Do I look like a stupid person to you? Everyone knows you and Ricki cut from the same source. So what the fuck did you *say*?"

Leo's full lower lip drops. "Nothing! Last time I saw Ricki was, like, Thursday last week, and your name didn't come up!"

"So what were you two chewing the fat about on Thursday?" Hands on hips, she somehow looks more cop-like.

"Nothing, I swear! We were just having some drinks with Janice—"

"Janice?"

"Yeah, Janice." Leo swallows. "She's Ricki's main girl. He says, come over to Janice's place after her shift for some drinks and stuff, so I go."

"This Janice, she's got auburn hair?"

"Nah—Janice D'Addario, with the brown hair."

Nomi frowns, which Simon is sure must hurt. But the way she's manipulating Leo into spilling his guts is both fascinating and masterful.

"Right," Nomi says. "So there you are, having drinks and snorting blow with Ricki and Janice, and my name comes up—"

"No!" Leo's obviously a guy who works hard to maintain a cool image, but right now, his defensive twitchiness is just making him look petulant. "No, I told you, no way. We didn't talk about you or nothing, we just talked work. You know how it is—Ricki's moaning about how he's getting the same amount of gear, but his boss expects him to stretch it. He's got some special delivery that's eating into his cut."

Nomi sucks her teeth and glowers. Considering the state she's in, it's a remarkable performance. But it's working on Leo; his bottom lip is wet, and his eyes keep lowering to his shoes.

"So if it wasn't you and Ricki talking, then why've I got a fucking *black eye*?" Nomi sighs heavily. "I'm getting it from all sides here, Leo—my old PD boss is breathing down my neck, and now I'm dodging Ricki's boss's pals . . . I'm feeling a little like the meat in the sandwich, you know?"

Leo raises his right hand like a Boy Scout. "I swear on my mother's life, Nomi, your name didn't come up."

"All right. Then I gotta ask around some more." She rubs her mouth, scanning the street, then steps in and grasps his shoulder, squeezes. "Look, Leo, we can keep this local—my name stays off your lips, then I don't need to drop *your* name to anyone at Tenth Precinct, okay?"

"Absolutely, sure." This chumminess is apparently more Leo's style. His stiff posture relaxes, and he nods compulsively. "I'd appreciate that, Nomi, I really would."

She lets her hand drop. "Okay, done."

"So we're cool?" He glances between Simon and Nomi again, his eagerness to have this conversation over giving his features a shiny cast.

"We're cool." Nomi snorts, shooing with her hand like he's a naughty kid. "Now go on, go back and finish your drink. Have one for me."

Leo grins, happy to be let off the hook. "You're solid, Harriet."

She rolls her eyes. "Get the fuck outta here. Take it easy, Leo."

As Leo moves back to open the door into Hector's Café, Nomi walks off without looking at Simon. He has to fall in beside her as she crosses the road and stomps down Washington, hands fisted.

Simon glances at her: Her lips are fish-meat white. He keeps his voice lowered. "Are you okay?"

"Don't talk to me. Keep walking." They're nearly at the corner with Gansevoort. She blows out air. "Has he gone back inside Hector's?"

Simon glances back. "Yes."

"Good."

She manages to make it around the corner before her knees buckle and she staggers, clutches the lip of a nearby dumpster.

"Easy . . ." Simon grabs her shoulder, plus a handful of the back of her shirt.

"I'm fine. Seriously, I'm fine, let's just get home. This whole damn street smells like blood." She pushes up, grimacing with nausea.

"I don't even notice anymore," Simon admits. "We don't have far to go. But is it a smart idea to return to your apartment?"

"They're not coming back today." Her eyes are bone weary. "I already got my delivery."

At the tenement, she insists on tackling the stairs to the second floor herself. He holds his jacket loose in one hand as his other hand hovers at her elbow. She bats him away. At her apartment, Simon collects her hat and tote, and a yellow document envelope lying on the linoleum in front of her door. Nomi snatches the envelope, scrounges for her keys.

He frowns. "Is opening that envelope really wise?"

"What's it gonna do, give me a paper cut?" She's already inside, ricocheting gently off the hallway walls. "All right, make yourself at home, I guess."

Simon follows her in. Her apartment is long and thin, a corridor with a bathroom on the left, then a left-side living area. On the right, a galley kitchen, then the door to a tiny office. A large number of plants. Actually, that's an understatement—there are *dozens* of plants, slender and twisting. Leaves spill down, reflect the light, green tones softening the gray-brown space. It's like being back in the jungle, and he suddenly wonders why he's never thought to recreate something so familiar in his own apartment.

Nomi holds the wall, the back of a brown leather sofa, the edge of the kitchen counter, until she gets to the office. She opens the yellow envelope, leaning on the top of a compact desk, before snorting and throwing the envelope toward the waste basket.

Simon's curious. "What was in it?"

"Nothing. Blank piece of paper." Turning carefully, she backtracks, hobbling for the bathroom.

"Do you need me to help you with anything?" he offers.

She gives him a withering look over her shoulder.

Okay then. Simon finds a brown leather lounge chair in the living area that he's happy to settle into. There's a narrow coffee table. The sound of water running in the bathroom. As he dumps his jacket and pulls the dressing materials he needs out of his pocket, Nomi—in her weird baggy jeans, damp hair slicked back, bare shoulders, a towel wrapped around her pale lean torso and tucked under her armpits—shuffles past the sofa and his chair, disappearing behind a Japanese folding screen.

It's not until she's left his line of sight that he registers she was topless under her towel.

Also, that she has a ton of tattoos. He's glimpsed the black flames around her left wrist before, but more flames, plus thorns and rose blossoms, reach all the way to her elbow. She has a circlet around her right upper arm and—most astonishing—two large black birds fighting across her right shoulder. From his observations, most American women don't have tattoos. Maybe here in this country, tattoos for women mean something different than they do in Guatemala. But so far as he knows, it's illegal to get tattooed in New York City.

Simon can hear her fussing with drawers behind the screen as he lays out the dressing supplies on the coffee table.

"Don't look," she calls sternly.

"I literally have my back to you." Maybe that's her bedroom. It feels strangely intimate, this compact space. Not many windows—he would feel claustrophobic, living here. "Do you have soup, or something like that?"

"Soup?" Dressed now in black sweats, she emerges, skirts the coffee table and clambers slowly onto the couch, pulling her bare feet up. Her face is wiped clean, the trauma colors around her right eye cast into rude relief. "I have nothing. There's, like, beer and eggs and sauerkraut in the refrigerator."

"I only mean that it's good to have something warm when your body's still in shock," he suggests gently.

"I had soup for breakfast." She scrapes her dark hair back with her fingers. She seems more relaxed in her own space, at least. The baggy sweats emphasize how petite she is—she usually disguises it with the tough clothes and tougher talk.

"How's your pain level?"

She looks upward. "Hm, well, my face feels like it got slammed into a wall . . ."

"Funny."

"I know." She squeezes her nape. The damp ends of her hair make spots of deeper blackness on the fabric of her sweatshirt. "Look, I have a pretty high pain threshold, so it's hard to judge. My neck and ribs are kinda sore. Headache's coming along. The stitches are stinging, I think that cream is wearing off. Otherwise, I'm okay." She scratches at the pale skin beneath her collar. "I *am* considering that beer, though."

Simon's not sure about alcohol. He moves to sit on the coffee table in front of her, leans forward to examine her face. "Your concussion markers are varied. Your pupils aren't too big, but you passed out. You've got headache, nausea, dizziness, but no blurred vision." He thinks about it. "I'd like to give you a painkiller. I have some Vicodin upstairs that I take for headaches, if you can sit here for five minutes without keeling over."

"Sounds better than a Schlitz."

"Hold on."

Simon exits, takes the stairs two at a time to his apartment, lets himself in. Through his own apartment windows, the dying light; sunset is less than an hour away. In the bathroom, behind the mirror, the pack of Vicodin. He assesses his supply, pops three tablets out of the blister pack.

When he closes the cabinet, his own face in the mirror is a shock. Good grief, he really does look like a bum. He tears off his sweatshirt, leaving only his white waffle weave Henley above his brown pants. Splashes his face at the basin, dries off, tames his hair, returns to Nomi's apartment.

As he lets himself in, everything seems very quiet. "Are you still awake?"

"No, I'm dead." Her droll voice reverberates up the corridor.

"Hilarious." That comment stays under his breath. He gets a glass of water from the kitchen, digs up a pair of scissors from a drawer. He rounds the leather sofa to set the scissors on the coffee table and hand her the glass, along with two pills. "Take these. There's another one in reserve if you need it later. Then let me finish putting the dressing on—I've got to wash my hands first."

After a quick trip to Nomi's bathroom—more plants, of course, endless plants—he returns to perch in front of her on the coffee table, drying his hands on a towel. "If I were a real doctor, I'd suggest you need medical supervision for the next twenty-four hours because you're a concussion risk."

"I'm fine. I took a hit, but I'm okay." She'd be more believable if she didn't look so wiped out. She glances away. "And listen, I'm sorry for calling you an asshole and saying you're fucked up, or whatever the hell I said earlier. I appreciate that you tried to warn me, and now I appreciate you doing triage on my face."

"I said forget it." He keeps his tone casual but firm. "You want to pay me back? Take a head injury seriously. As someone who's experienced a head injury, I'm kind of sensitive about it."

"I'm taking it seriously." But she seems focused on something else as he preps the dressing. "I've got a question. You said you don't know if you've tailed someone before today?"

"That's right."

"Well, I'm paranoid, and I've been trained in this stuff, and I didn't see you." Her dark eyes are intent.

He carefully peels the paper wrapping off the Band-Aids he needs. "Like I said, I just tried to stay out of sight."

"Sure. But how did you know how to do that? And how to do it so well?"

"I've actually got no idea." He pauses. But maybe talking about it will bring some relief. He's going to have to reveal more about his personal quirks eventually—if she hasn't already figured them out from reading his notebooks. "It was like the Italian speaking. I kind of did it without thinking. Before I even noticed it was happening, I was doing it."

And it had felt familiar. He'd recognized it, like muscle memory. Like you'd recognize the swaying steps of a dance you did once, long ago.

But it's worrying. He used to think, whenever new skills and thoughts and behaviors emerged, that it meant his old identity was coming back, that memories would soon follow. The memories never came, though. All he's left with are these disparate, uncontrolled elements of what he can only assume is his former self leaking into his everyday life.

He doesn't like it.

"'Being good at following people' wasn't something I expected to have in my skill set," he admits stiffly.

Nomi seems to be thinking about it. "This is going to sound strange, but could you be, like, ex–Special Forces or something?"

He's considered this already. "When I was nineteen, twenty?"

She chews her lip. "Yeah, I don't know."

He peels open another Band-Aid. "Now I've got a question. Two questions."

"Ask away."

"First, why does Leo call you Harriet?"

"It's a bad joke. You know the Clint Eastwood films? *Magnum Force* and stuff?"

"I really don't."

"Then don't worry about it. Suffice to say that Leo watches too many movies. Next question."

"Why do you have an accent?"

Her body acquires a subtle, all-over tension. "My father is Pennsylvania German. Religious Germans," she explains. "They're American, but some of them keep very old traditions, and they speak a dialect of Palatine German at home."

This country continues to reveal its mysteries to him. He takes up the scissors. "You were one of them?"

"When I was a kid. I got out of it with my mom, but I retained a little of the accent." She shifts on the sofa. "It's kind of boring, and I'd prefer not to talk about it."

He glances up from trimming the Band-Aids he needs. "Hey, I have to tell you about my personal details all the time."

"Yes, and when *I* get amnesia, you can ask me a bunch of questions about myself then."

"Fine. Okay, lean forward a little for me."

The dressing isn't complicated: Neosporin and Band-Aids, with some maneuvering to figure out how to get the Band-Aids to stay in place and not obstruct her eyelid. He uses a fold of Kleenex to dab on the Neosporin. From somewhere outside the apartment, the faint strains of some jangling pop song.

Nomi tilts her head to give him better access. Her skin is warm under his fingers, and her right eye, below his hand, is a flat, unblinking brown. "Tomorrow I'm gonna have to dig out this girl of Ricki's, Janice D'Addario. I'm hoping she'll talk to me. I want to hear more about this special delivery Ricki had to stretch."

"That's tomorrow." Simon works to fix down a corner of sticky plastic. The sutures have dried a little; they scratch against the dressing. "You did well, holding it together to get information out of Leo."

"I'm an opportunist. And I don't know if you noticed, but Leo's not too bright . . ." Her pupils are contracting with the medication, and her voice is getting hazy. "S'that your standard procedure, threatening to put people's eyes out with steak knives?"

"Only when I'm pretending to be somebody's hired thug."

"The outfit made it work, but you're really too pretty to be a thug. You should let me break your nose, so you look more authentic."

He snorts. The dressing is nearly done, and he can allow his focus to relax. "Where the hell is that stupid music coming from?"

"The Duran Duran? That's probably Nelson across the hall. *Rio* is a classic."

Those lyrics are words he knows, which is funny. "That was my name for a while in Guatemala, you know."

"*Rio* means 'river' in Spanish, right?"

"Yes. Except in Maaya t'aan, the word for river is *haw*. So I was called Haw for a couple of years. Then Flores examined my old clothes and found the label . . . so I became Simon. *Simón*." He says it in the Spanish way.

"It suits you better."

"It fits better. And no, I don't know how I know that—it's just a feeling." He fixes the last edge of the dressing. It's not attractive, but it should help protect the wound in the short term. "There you go.

Now if you sit back, I'll wash up, then make us both something warm to drink."

Remarkably, Nomi follows his instructions. He makes hot tea, because it turns out she has loose-leaf tea and milk that's not out of date. She sips the tea, relaxing with the medication. She has no interest in eating, which is probably for the best.

He lights a cigarette—his first in hours—and settles back on the brown lounge chair. When he informs her that he's staying in her living room tonight, to keep an eye on her, she puts up surprisingly little resistance.

"I mean, I haven't done a sleepover since junior high, but fine."

"What's a sleepover?"

"Y'know, you act so normal, and then you say shit that reminds me you don't remember growing up American . . ." She regards him over the lip of her mug. "Don't you have work?"

"Nope. I don't work Monday mornings."

"Convenient." Her tone is dry, but she's almost fully reclined on the leather sofa, a pillow under her head and a gray crocheted rug over her lap. She sighs. "Should've known that fucking guy wasn't a courier."

"Live and learn, right?"

She sets her mug on the coffee table and rolls to face him. "I just figured it out."

"What's that?"

"'Noone'—it's a compound of 'no one.' Your surname means 'no one.'"

"Wordplay in place of wit—that's me," Simon admits. He sips his tea. "And is Pace your real surname?"

"Pacek. But I don't use my father's name." There's a dullness in her eyes when she talks about it. She blinks it away. "What's Guatemala like?"

He ashes his cigarette in the nearest pot plant, then eases back, watching the smoke eddy up. He's never really explained his experience of Guatemala to anyone before. It wasn't the standard tourist encounter.

"Well, at first," he says quietly, "it's just a small, white-washed room with a dark curtain over the window. Then, when you stop drifting in and out of consciousness, it's a gruff old man who brings you maize soup and speaks to you in a variety of languages until you recognize one. He explains that you were found by the edge of the river. That when you arrived at his village clinic, he had to jigsaw your head back together with superglue, and he thought you would probably die."

"But you didn't die." Nomi's voice has a lazy burr, her head cushioned on the pillow. "And there's really nothing from before that you remember?"

"No." Simon tilts his head at her. "What is it about the amnesia that you find so fascinating?"

"Ah, it's just . . ." Her body shifts as she looks away from him, toward the ceiling. "We all have memories we'd like to get rid of, right?"

Do we? Simon wonders which of Nomi's memories she'd like to obliterate.

"I'm afraid that's not how amnesia works—you don't get to choose." He takes a drag, examines his cigarette as he explains further. "I mean, in the beginning, I couldn't even retain basic information. I'd wake up in a panic every morning, not knowing who or where I was. Flores had to reintroduce himself whenever he came into the room, had to explain the same stuff over and over—*I am a doctor. You are in Guatemala. You have a head injury. For the time being, your name is Haw.* That first month, I'd go sit outside on the porch, and neighbors passing by from the village would remind me that we'd met before. It took a while for my brain to remember how to remember."

Simon hears his own voice develop the gentle rolling intonations and cadences of the storytellers in Piedras Negras. He ashes his cigarette once more.

"Amnesia is hard to describe. Physically, it feels as if your head is full of cotton—that was my experience, anyway. Your normal state is a state of confusion. It's like you've lost traction, lost your foothold on the world. Like you're just an outline of a person. Even after the physical symptoms fade, you experience moments when everything around you feels unreal. Or maybe *you* feel unreal. Does that make sense?"

But when he looks over, Nomi's already asleep.

Chapter Eleven

September 1987, Monday

When she opens her eyes, the first thing Nomi sees is Simon Noone in her living room.

He's stretched out in her brown leather lounge chair, knees loose, eyes closed. Hands flopped over his stomach, chest rising and falling with the deep rhythms of sleep. The top of his white Henley has pulled away from his collarbones; he's got a puckered silver scar that she hasn't noticed before in the right-side hollow there. His head is canted at an awkward angle—he's going to wake up with a crick in his neck.

Nomi won't be the one to wake him. Mainly because she's nervous about how he might react.

Which is, thinking about it, a dozen different kinds of fucked up. She's let him into her confidence on the Jackson case. She's let him sew her up—and with the reaction she experienced during the stitching, boy, was *that* awkward. Now the guy's asleep in her living room: She's allowed him into her *home*. But she still can't read him. She hasn't been able to get a read on him from the start. And that's a giant red flag, because with her upbringing and line of work, reading people is supposed to be one of her primary skills.

But Noone is like a goddamn Easter Island statue.

Actually, that's not accurate. He's not impassive—far from it. But he's . . . contained. She thinks about the way he freaked out Leo and his friends with the steak knife comment at Hector's yesterday. Did Noone just say it for effect? Or was he really angry? She can't tell if his behavior and reactions are genuine, can't read the intention behind his eyes, behind his words. Maybe it's the amnesia. Maybe even *he* doesn't know what he's really thinking.

Seeing him like this—asleep, unguarded—is useful. She feels like maybe she's at least getting a base reading.

It also feels a little sneaky. He sat up half the night to make sure she wasn't affected by a concussion. The least she can do is not stare at him like a creeper while he's unconscious.

Nomi gets up and goes to the bathroom.

She takes the Band-Aids off her face, examines everything in the mirror. Ugly, but she's seen worse. The stitches look neat, astonishingly professional; best to keep her mind off the sensations she felt as Simon Noone placed them. She's gonna need makeup for the bruising. There's still a little blood in her hairline; she dampens a washcloth to sponge it away.

Behind the cabinet mirror, the yellow kit bag with her tools hasn't been disturbed. Noone didn't do any snooping last night, or if he did, he's been real subtle about it.

Nomi finishes with the blood, examines and tends to her new ear piercing—it's a little swollen, but doesn't look inflamed. She cleans it carefully, then washes up, goes to make coffee. She's moving slow; the Vicodin last night was strong, and with the added concussion, she still feels dopey. For the first time in a while, she wants a morning cigarette—probably because the smell of Noone's Pall Malls is still hanging around the apartment. She's going to have to open some windows, spritz her plants to clear the air.

A soft whine from Simon Noone, flopped on the lounge chair. His mauve eyelids flicker, and he mutters, repeating an unintelligible word. His hands twitch as if he's dreaming.

Nomi tries to ignore him as she shuffles around in the kitchen between the benchtop and the fridge. She pours two mugs, adds cream and sugar. Makes a few gentle sounds with the spoon on the mugs, the refrigerator door. Next time she looks over, he's awake.

"Hey, you're up."

"I never really lay down." Noone clears his throat, squeezes his nape. Some of his hard edges seem blurred so soon after waking. "How are you?"

"I'm fine." Nomi makes a ghost grin. "Except some jerk woke me up every four hours to check I hadn't slipped into a coma . . ."

"What an asshole."

"Right? Thanks anyway." Now she comes over with the mugs and hands him one.

He rubs his neck, peering up at her face. "You took the dressing off."

She settles back, cross legged, into her nest of blankets and cushions on the sofa, blowing on her coffee. She hopes she's not blushing. "It was itchy, and I wanted to take a look."

"It's not a terrible idea, to give the wound some air."

"I can't believe you sewed me up with stuff from my landlady's mending basket." She takes a sip. The coffee won't be up to Noone's exacting standards, but it's hot and has caffeine in it, and that's all that matters. "You talk in your sleep. Did you know you did that?"

Simon stops in the act of raising his mug to his lips. "No. What did I say?"

"You repeated a word, maybe a name—Chris? Christian? Crystal?" Nomi tilts her head, until she realizes she probably looks like a crow examining something shiny. "Does that mean anything to you?"

"Not at all." He seems genuinely baffled. He sips his coffee and manages to avoid grimacing at the taste. "Have you, uh, read my journals yet?"

"Not yet," she admits. "I've been too busy getting beaten up. Although I've asked my ex-partner and a few other people for information on your leads."

"That's fine." He rubs sleep out of his eyes, focusing on his mug. "It's only that the journals might give you some insight into my condition. I have a few . . . weird symptoms."

"What do you mean by 'weird'?"

He sips his coffee and sidesteps the question. "Well, for one, I have a recurring dream. I've had it ever since I woke up in Flores's house. Every night, at first. Now, maybe a couple times a month. More frequently when I'm under stress."

"Like the stress of moving illegally to a new country," Nomi suggests. "What's the dream?"

Noone tries to look casual about it. "It can vary, but there's always a forest, and a girl, and she leads me to the river, and I drown."

Nomi is intrigued. "Do you recognize anything? The forest—"

"It's not familiar to me. It's not a jungle, is what I mean. It's more European looking."

"And the girl?"

Noone squints and thinks. Tiny wrinkles at the corners of his eyes suggest he might have woken up with a headache. "She has white hair. That's all I know about her. I don't know her name, I don't know who she is. She puts a crown of flowers on my head and takes me to the river, and I just . . . go in. The current gets stronger, until I'm swept away. And I drown. Then I wake up."

Nomi blows on her coffee. "Well, that sounds fucking awful."

"No kidding." Noone stops studying his mug and makes eye contact. "So you're really okay? No vision changes? No ringing in the ears?"

"Nope. I'm really okay. A few aches, but nothing Advil won't fix. The headache and dizziness and nausea are gone."

"Good. The stitches look fine. You should apply some more Neosporin later." He squeezes the back of his neck again. "So what's the plan today?"

Nomi sips. She's been thinking about it. "First, I have to find Janice D'Addario. I'm pretty sure Ricki wasn't tortured to death because he spilled the beans to Janice, but she might know who he did talk to and what he said."

"How does this get you closer to Brittany Jackson?"

"I might hear about a location—the place Ricki had to pick up his drug deliveries, maybe? I don't know. All I want is a location. Where the hell are they holding this kid?"

He's looking at her in a way that makes her think her facial expression might be a little too glowering. "Have you ever met Brittany?"

"No." She glances elsewhere. But she can give him a reason without sounding overly invested. "I just hate the idea of a seven-year-old being held against her will. And her mom is terrified."

"So you track down Janice, get more information . . ."

"Yeah. But not yet." At every stage, process and common sense temper her impatience. It's such a drag, being a stickler. "I've got some business cards and phone numbers from Ricki's wallet that I should follow up on first. I'd also like to find out a little more about Solange's client, this Jeremy guy. And I want to find out the name of the jerk who jumped me. And it's only eight thirty in the morning."

"Right." He smiles faintly at the reminder that they're both still newly awake. "How will you get the courier jerk's name?"

"No clue," she admits. "All I can do is ask around with a physical description. I haven't got a photo, and there's no CCTV here in the building, so no action stills. But I want to know who I'm dealing with."

"What about CCTV at the subway?"

She shakes her head. "There's no way I can get access to that. I'll just write down everything I can remember about him. If you've got any details you can add, that would be—"

"I could draw him." Noone leans to put his mug on the coffee table. "I followed him for a while yesterday—I got a fairly good look at him. I think I could just about draw him from memory."

Is he telling her he can make the equivalent of an Identi-Kit picture? "But can you actually, like, draw? Because that's where I always get tripped up—"

"Yes, I can actually, like, draw." He sounds reasonably confident about it. "Just find me some paper and pencils."

She does. In fact, to make it easier for him, she retrieves his topmost hardcover notebook from the stack on her office desk, so he's working with a familiar format. While she's rooting around in the office, he goes to the bathroom. When he returns, she's set a small pile of materials on the table, including an eraser and a pencil sharpener.

"Will this be okay?"

"This will be fine." Noone has run a wet hand through his hair in the bathroom; damp strands spill over his forehead. He wipes remaining dampness onto his waffle weave shirt, collects the notebook, eraser, examines and selects pencils. Then he sits back in the lounge chair and opens the notebook on his knee. He sticks one of the pencils behind his ear. "He was stocky, wasn't he? Pale, with a kind of blunt nose . . ."

"His face was sort of craggy," Nomi offers.

"That's right. He had those grooves either side of his mouth . . ."

Noone's sketching hand moves with unhurried confidence—broad strokes, firm angles, making corrections with the eraser or smudging with the edge of his thumb. He digs absently into his pants pocket for a cigarette, lights up. She's going to have to talk to him about smoking in her apartment, but not while he's engaged like this.

"That's it." A face is taking shape on the paper, one she recognizes. "Bushier eyebrows, though."

"You saw him close up."

"Unfortunately, yes." She glances between the image and Noone's loose posture in the chair. "That's really good. How are you so good at this?"

"From being in the village." Smoke eddies up from the cigarette stuck in the corner of his mouth as he concentrates on some finer shading. "Before I learned enough Spanish and Maaya t'aan to communicate, I used to sketch the stuff I didn't have words for. I think this is getting close, yes?"

"Yes. Holy shit, that's him. You can really draw. Could you do this before?"

"No idea." His expression is relaxed, guileless. "But it's nice to have a skill that's innocuous for a change."

"All your weird skills . . ." Nomi chews her lip, thinking about it. "But maybe we can use that."

He glances up. "What do you mean?"

She ticks off on her fingers. "Drawing, covert tracking, Italian speaking, even those dreams of yours . . . They're all probably things you could do or were connected to before your head injury, right? It's got to be related to your amnesia. To who you were before. We can add details like this to your missing person profile. It might help us get some hits."

"Really?"

"I told you, I'm an opportunist." She examines the sketch. "His sideburns came a little lower down . . ."

Noone works on the sketch some more, with Nomi providing suggestions or guidance on the details. After a few minutes, it's done.

"There." He stubs out his smoke and sets his pencil down. "That's as close as I can get, I think."

He tears out the page and hands it to her. Nomi holds it at arm's length. "Goddamn, that's him. The courier guy. Wild stuff. Like working with a police sketch artist. This is going to be incredibly useful, thank you."

"No problem."

"I can take this around and ask if anyone's seen him." She notices Noone scrubbing both hands over his face. "You okay?"

"Ah, yeah . . . Just a headache." He sets down the notebook and pencils. "I might go upstairs and get some medication. Unless you need me for something?"

"No way," she says. "I mean, don't worry about it. You should go home, get some rest. You were up half the night with me—you must be exhausted."

"A little exhausted, yes." He laughs shortly, extricates himself from the chair, stiff limbed, and finds his stuff. "Okay, I'll leave you to get your work done—I think I'm going to take my meds and get some more sleep. I'm really glad you're feeling better. And thanks for the coffee."

"Thanks for the sketch. And for staying on coma watch." She can be more generous than that. "Actually, thanks for a lot of things."

"You're welcome. Watch out for strange men in courier jackets."

Nomi tracks him as he heads for the door. Once he's gone, the apartment feels oddly quiet. But the day has just started, and it's not like she doesn't have plenty of shit to do.

After a shower, back in her jeans and a fresh black T-shirt that has a picture of a hand making devil horns and the word *DISOBEY* scrawled across the front, she takes a couple Advil and moves to her office to start the grind. The rubber band–bundled items from Ricki Cevolatti are in the tray on her desk: four business cards, two sticky notes, the bookie's slip, three receipts scrawled with phone numbers. For the next few hours, she uses her time-honored technique for cold-calling, which involves chewing gum while sounding bored and telling the person who answers the phone that they may be eligible for a refund on their car insurance.

Almost all the calls go nowhere. The bookie turns out to be one of the receipt numbers, and he informs her that the slip is only valid to cash out for a month after the date of issue, which turns out to have been in July. One of the other receipt numbers is for an escort service in Crown Heights. Another one rings out unanswered. A business card for a guy called Herschel Sebbitz has the same number as one of the sticky notes, and Sebbitz appears to have a legitimate business as a mechanic. Two other business cards are for a care nurse for Cevolatti's aunt and a pool hall in the Lower East Side. The final sticky note number has been disconnected. Either the disconnected number or the unanswered number could belong to Janice D'Addario—impossible to know.

Nomi puts her gum in the trash, takes a break, makes fresh coffee. As she's waiting for the brew to perk, her eyes are drawn by a sharp, bright edge: The shiny silver key from Cevolatti's wallet is still on her desk. The number *202* is stamped on one side.

It could be a key to any post office box anywhere in the city, and the idea of chasing around for the right box doesn't hold a lot of appeal. But she can at least try the most obvious places: the Flatbush Station post office on Church Avenue, and the Farley Building in Midtown.

On the off chance, she calls Flatbush and discovers that the key, as she describes it over the phone, is definitely for a post box, and—more importantly—that they only have 180 post office boxes at the Flatbush location. *Interesting.* That just leaves the Farley Building.

First, though, she wants to see if one of her hunches is correct. It's just gone noon, which means Teresa will finally be awake; Nomi gives her a call. Teresa is a fifty-three-year-old New Jersey native who used to be a madam; she now functions as a kind of den mother to a lot of the women—hookers and bar staff alike—who work at Chachi's. She's a tough old bird, and Nomi helped her recover some money from a scam artist about eighteen months ago, so she sometimes gives Nomi a line on what's happening at the club.

When Teresa confirms that Janice D'Addario is usually behind the bar at Chachi's three nights a week, Nomi does a fist pump right there in her office.

Bingo. "Teri, I need to go see her. Have you got an address?"

"Hold on, honey; I'm still in my pajamas . . ." Teresa makes a rattling cough, sips something that Nomi can only assume is coffee, but who knows. "Okay, I got it for ya. Janice D.—I got her in my Rolodex as that, so I don't get her mixed up with the other Janice, with the auburn hair. Now listen, Janice D. hasn't shown for work the last few days, so I don't know if you'll find her, but here's the address. Are you ready? You got a pencil or something?"

"I've got a pencil," Nomi confirms. "Go for it."

When she hangs up from the call, she fist-pumps again for good measure because hell yeah, she was due a win. Then she takes another two Advil, shoves on her boots, gathers her tote and jacket and sunglasses.

Before she leaves the apartment, she tucks both Noone's sketch of the courier guy and Cevolatti's silver key into her jeans pockets.

The third floor is, once again, slightly warmer and sunnier, because of the skylight. Nomi raps on Noone's door—no answer. Dammit. Yesterday, she was wondering how to get rid of him, and now when she needs him, he's not around.

She clomps down the stairs to the foyer, slips on her sunglasses before spilling out the narrow door into the noonday heat. There's not much traffic on Gansevoort, just a smattering of delivery trucks and pedestrians; the district meat workers have mostly finished their shifts and gone home. The street smells of bleach and beef fat.

She's about to turn for Greenwich Street when she sees the black metal folding chairs outside Florent, the familiar posture of the guy smoking and reading a newspaper behind gold-framed sunglasses.

Shaking her head, Nomi walks straight over. "Holy shit, you're here. I knocked at your place, but I figured you'd gone to see *Hellraiser* or something."

As she pulls out a chair, Simon folds up his newspaper. "Hello again. What's a hellraiser?"

"Your cultural gaps are showing again, my friend—I'll explain it to you later." He has an espresso demitasse and a small bowl of green grapes on the table beside him. She steals a grape, pops it into her mouth, talks while she chews. "Right now, I got a lead on Janice D'Addario, and I was hoping you might want to come check it out with me. Unless—I don't know—do you still have a headache?"

"Yes." He pushes up his sunglasses, blue eyes scrunched against the glare. "But if I stopped all activity whenever I got a headache, I'd never come out of my apartment, so I've just taken a bunch of drugs."

"Fair."

"You really want me to come along? I seem to remember something you said about us not being partners."

"I changed my mind." She shrugs, eats another grape. "You're growing on me."

"Like mold."

"Exactly. Plus, I told Leo yesterday that I've hired personal security, which is basically like announcing it to the whole neighborhood."

"So now you've got to keep that up."

"You got it."

He snorts, reaches forward and slides down her Wayfarers so he can examine her eyes. "You still have a concussion. How are you so bouncy?"

"Because that's my secret, Noone—every time I take a hit, I come back stronger." Nomi pops another grape and grins. "Come on, have you got anything better to do?"

Chapter Twelve

September 1987, Monday

They've crossed Greenwich Street, and they're about to hit Hudson. Nomi examines the building walls on this side, which sport geological layers of tattered advertising posters for shows, clubs, bands, fundraisers—there's some good gigs coming up. A kid goes by on a bike. Far in the distance, rusted water towers.

Before they left Florent, Nomi scooped the rest of the grapes into her cupped hand. She snacks as they walk. "Okay, I was planning to catch the subway, but given your aversion, and my concussion, we should probably get a cab."

"Probably, yes." Noone is wearing more normal clothes: jeans, a dark chambray shirt, his black peacoat, his engineer boots. It's quite a contrast from his work wear. "Although if I'm pretending to be hired security, I feel like you should be paying me."

"See? Your sense of humor's coming back, you must be feeling better." Traffic is bustling on Hudson Street. As they reach the curb, Nomi finishes the grapes, wipes her hand on her shirt, flings her arm up toward the road. "Hey! Hey, I'm waving here!"

It only takes about three seconds for one of the clunky yellow Checkers to pull up in front of them. Nomi wrenches open the cab's rear door and pushes Noone inside, clambers in after him. "Talking in Your Sleep," by The Romantics, is playing on the radio. The cab smells of old Chinese takeout, and the black vinyl seat is slightly sticky, with a broken spring.

Noone grimaces in distaste. "Delightful."

That he's spent five years in Guatemala and is still such a snob is hilarious. "You don't like the subway, you don't like cabs . . . What's next, bus phobia?"

"I really need to buy that bicycle. Where are we going?"

"South. But we've got to do a Midtown loop first." Nomi leans toward the driver, a weedy Irish guy with a bulbous nose. "Take a left onto Horatio, then go up Eighth Avenue to West Thirty-Third—the Farley Post Office building. Then we're going to Hudson Square. And, sir, it is illegal to mess with the meter, just drive how I told you, okay?"

"So you found Janice D'Addario's address?" Noone asks.

"Yep." As they pull into traffic, she turns back. "I got in touch with someone I know who works at Chachi's, this club off Hudson in Greenwich Village. With the connection to Leo Farina and Ricki Cevolatti, I figured Janice was probably on staff there. It was a hunch, but it played out."

"Nice work."

"I told you, this is my job. I want to get this fixed. Brittany Jackson has been missing for nearly five days, and it's bugging the shit out of me."

Noone cocks his head at her. "You're pretty committed to this case, aren't you?"

"Yes. I mean, I *am* getting paid." She tries to downplay it further. "Plus, I'm personally motivated—if I can avoid getting jumped outside my apartment again, that would be fantastic."

"I do prefer it when I'm not sewing pieces of your face back together." Noone's hair ruffles in the breeze coming through the window. "So why are we going to the post office building?"

"Because I found this in Ricki's wallet." She leans back on the seat to scrape the key out of her front jeans pocket, shows him the number. "I called the post office, and this is definitely for a post box. No boxes marked two-oh-two at the post office near Ricki's place in Flatbush, so the main Manhattan building is my next best guess."

Traffic on Eighth isn't great, but it's not terrible. They pass a Wine & Liquor store, and a Nude Revue Video, then an Irish pub on the corner of West Thirtieth. Things are snarling up ahead, where the Farley building and Madison Square Garden face each other across the street like Scylla and Charybdis, turning Eighth Avenue into the Strait of Messina for cars. Nomi tells the cab driver to ease into the left lane.

"Okay, here's what we're going to do," she says to Noone, her eyes on the road ahead. "We're going to pull over out front, near the steps—"

"It's No Standing out front of the Farley building," the driver says mournfully from the front.

"Shut up, I'm not talking to you. We're going to pull over out front, near the steps. You're going to get out." Nomi shoves the key into Noone's palm, folds his fingers over it. "Go up the steps, stay left, go into the foyer."

"You want me to find the post office boxes?" He looks unsure.

"It's easy—they're immediately to the left once you're through the doors. Go to locker two-oh-two, see if the key fits. If it does, bring me back whatever is inside the locker. Shouldn't take you longer than five minutes."

"And if it *does* take me longer than five minutes?"

"It won't. After this set of lights—are you ready?" They pull up near a hot dog stand and another cart selling fresh-roasted chestnuts. "Okay, *go*."

Noone, to his credit, doesn't hesitate. He flings open the car door and strides up the steps, long legs eating up distance it would've taken twice as long for her to cover, until he gets through the ornate, left-side foyer door.

Nomi sits in the cab, watching the place he entered, willing him to move fast. Car horns sound behind them; the cab driver sighs.

Noone comes back in under five minutes, jogging unhurriedly down the marble steps, a bundle under one arm. The hems of his black coat flare, his profile framed by Corinthian columns like he's royalty.

"The key worked." He slides fully into the cab and slams the door behind himself. "The box was bigger than the normal ones for mail. This was everything inside."

He's deposited a stack of paper in her lap. Nomi frowns at it. "What the hell is this?"

"Looks like a pile of newspapers," he notes.

"Lady, where to?" the cab driver says. "I gotta get off the curb."

"This is bizarre," Nomi says, and then, to the driver, "Okay, pull back onto Eighth, turn left onto West Thirty-Third, then left onto Ninth. Follow it all the way onto Bleecker Street. Seriously, Noone, that was everything in the box?"

"That was everything. Just the newspapers. Maybe there's something important mixed in with them?"

Nomi waves both hands to indicate "maybe?" and then shoves the stack of broadsheets—looks to be all *New York Times*—into her tote for safekeeping. "I'll go through this later."

"You wanted me to check the post box because you thought it might be under surveillance, didn't you?" Noone doesn't seem mad about it, but he'd clearly like a response.

The radio song has changed to "Nothing's Gonna Stop Us Now," which is plenty loud, but Nomi still keeps her voice lowered. "My ex-partner said the cops have Cevolatti's murder on their radar. If they're surveilling any locations connected to Ricki, I'd rather they saw you—who they don't know—than me."

"You're really trying to stay out of sight of the police," Noone notes. "Is there anything I should know?"

"Only that I don't appreciate folks from Tenth Precinct being all up in my business. Apart from my ex-partner, there's nobody from my old job who I want to stay in touch with."

Noone regards her curiously. "So why exactly *did* you leave the NYPD?"

Nomi just shrugs, noncommittal. Noone's brows lift, but there's really no response to his question that she's prepared to give here, in the back of a cab.

Ninth Avenue turns into Hudson; they're almost close enough here to just get out and walk home. But there's still Janice to deal with. The cab barrels past the Meatpacking District, heading farther south. Buildings either side of Hudson Street begin shrinking, begin bristling with fire escapes, begin looking more residential. They pass the playground at the top of Bleecker, and suddenly there are some nice streetlamps and brownstones. The streets become narrower. Their cab gets held up by a yellow school bus.

Past a Hertz garage, they turn onto Seventh Avenue. At the intersection with Carmine, where it turns into Varick, Nomi tells the driver to pull over so she can pay. They get out, the spires of the financial district poking up like hypodermic needles in the distance. A guy in jean shorts goes past on roller skates. Nomi checks the address she wrote on her hand as she and Noone jaywalk across Varick.

He scans the landscape, scraping back his hair. "This is Hudson Square?"

"Yes? Or maybe Greenwich Village. Or Soho. I don't know—folks call it different things depending on how fancy they want to seem." She hitches her tote, nods toward a left turn just after a printshop and a little red corner café. "Okay, this is the address I have."

The street is narrow, with a bodega and signs for an Italian social club. The buildings along here are mixed tenements and industrial businesses: a bakery, a carpentry workshop, two garages. Some of the fire escapes are folded down right onto the sidewalk. But street plantings—including some full-grown trees—make it into a nice neighborhood.

They reach a tenement, indistinguishable from the other tenements on the block. Nomi doesn't try the front door, ducks through an old carriage entrance on the right. It leads through to an ugly communal garden area with concrete pavers, a dried-up fountain, withered shrubs. At left, an open wooden door shows six shallow stairs leading into the tenement.

They arrive at a short, dark landing with two apartments opposite each other. Nomi can smell old drains, cooked vegetables, body odor: the scent of many people living in close proximity. These are the types of apartments where the bathtub is in the kitchen.

"Here goes nothing." Nomi knocks on the left-hand door. No answer. She tries again. Still nada. She tries the door handle. No luck. "Shit."

"If she's not home, is that it?" Noone looks a little frustrated.

Nomi winces. "Okay, I heard that Janice hasn't been at work the last few days, so I have a feeling . . ."

She scrounges in her inside jacket pocket, feeling for pointed sharpness, and comes out with two slender metal filaments. She's practiced a lot with these, mainly on Keil locks. This is a Kwikset, but it doesn't look tough. Now she slips her tension wrench into the keyway, applies some light torque to the plug, rakes the pins gently . . . There's a click. She tries the handle again. This time, it gives.

She glances over her shoulder at Noone, her unstitched eyebrow raised. "Oh wow, looks like the door's open."

"Did you . . . Did you just pick the lock?"

"Shut up, come on."

This is the second time in three days she's snuck into a stranger's living room. Thankfully, there are no dead bodies in this one.

The apartment is three rooms—the living area, one cramped bedroom, and a kitchen with a bath, as predicted. Janice has worked hard to pretty things up: She's hung nice curtains, polished the hardwood floors, kept the shelves and fixtures white to match the walls, added a few ferns. But it's still a fairly down-market place.

"Stay by the door," Nomi says quietly. "I want to look around."

"Not much to see."

"Noone, you're great with corpses, but not so good with domestic details." She points at signs he overlooked as she pulls on a pair of leather gloves. "Some small picture frames are gone from their spots on the walls, no keys on the hook by the door, no coat on the coat stand. And I'm not seeing a handbag anywhere. I think she's split, but keep watch while I check."

Noone returns to the door as Nomi searches the apartment. The bed is unmade, and a bunch of clothes are missing from the dresser. No jewelry, no makeup. Janice D'Addario is in the wind. Nomi checks old mail on the kitchen benchtop, but she only hits the jackpot when she looks through the wastebasket.

She goes back to Noone, holding her prize. "Okay, we're done, let's go."

"We're done?"

She shows him the matchbook and the flyer she found in the trash. Both display the same image: a pair of lips, open wide to show tonsils and teeth, done in a comic book style. "That's the logo for Big Mouth—it's a club up near West Fourteenth and Ninth. One of Lamonte's."

"You think Janice might be there?"

"I think Janice is covering her ass. She's staying somewhere else, because she's not an idiot. But she's probably working shifts at Big Mouth so Lamonte knows she hasn't flown the coop just yet."

Noone examines the flyer. "How can you be sure she hasn't just—"

"Not here," Nomi interrupts. She takes back the flyer, shoves it and the matchbook into her tote. "I'll explain later, but hanging around when you've broken into someone's apartment is never good policy. Let's go."

Nomi locks the door behind them. Once they're down the shallow steps and out of the building, she feels safer.

But as they walk through the courtyard, someone else arrives through the carriage entrance: a guy in his thirties, medium build on the shorter side, curly dark hair and glasses. He's wearing polyester trousers and a turtleneck under a brown corduroy jacket, carrying a large coffee to go, and Nomi recognizes him instantly.

She pinches the elbow of Noone's peacoat and trains her eyes forward, voice low. "Keep walking."

Nomi's never mentioned anything to Noone about the guys she used to work with at Tenth Precinct, but something in her tone must send out alarm bells, because she feels him straighten. When they pass the guy wearing corduroy, and his voice behind them says, "Hey, hold it right there," Noone has already positioned himself in front of her before they turn around.

"Can we help you?" Noone's posture is relaxed, but his words are completely cold.

Nomi can see this going poorly, opts to defuse. "Nah, it's okay, Detective Gaffney was just saying hello, weren't you, Calvin?"

"Nomi Pace?" Detective Calvin Gaffney seems genuinely surprised to see her, which is wild because this is homicide related and they're in her district: They'd *have* to know she'd make inquiries. It doesn't say much for the general level of intelligence at the precinct since her departure if they haven't figured that out. "Ah geez, I thought it was you. Someone finally got ya, huh?"

He nods toward her bruised eye and makes a shit-eating grin, which has always been one of Gaffney's standard facial expressions. God, she hates twerps like him.

"Yeah, they got me all right." Nomi tries to make her tight smile look more normal. Beside her, close enough to maintain contact, Simon Noone seems ominously quiet. "Fancy bumping into you, huh?"

"So, what, are you here on business?" Gaffney removes the lid of his coffee, takes a casual sip as he comes closer. "Did you just try to check Janice D'Addario's apartment?"

"Yeah, I did," Nomi confesses. "I just came by to see Janice, but I guess she's not home."

"Well, yeah. Janice is gone. Whoops, skedaddled." Gaffney swaps hands on the coffee cup, shaking out his burning fingers. "And respectfully, you probably shouldn't be poking your nose into this one, Pace. This is out of your line."

"It's all my line these days, Calvin—you know that." Now Nomi's showing some teeth. "And it's not exactly your line, either, is it? Why's Balter sent you to Greenwich Village from Tenth Precinct? Are the guys from Sixth all washing their hair or something?"

"Hey, I just go where I'm told."

"So here you are, just hanging around, watching the place . . ."

"Yeah, that's what I'm doing." Gaffney nods importantly. "Keeping an eye out for Janice, securing the scene—normal cop stuff. I'm sure you remember that."

"It's not a crime scene, though, is it? There's no tape."

"No tape, but it's out of bounds." Gaffney looks through his glasses and down his nose at her. "And that's all you need to know about it. Police business isn't your concern no more if you ain't police, you know what I'm saying?"

Noone has lost interest in the conversation; he's crouched down to fix the buckle on his boot. Nomi tilts her head to see Calvin Gaffney from a better angle, but he still doesn't look less annoying.

"Calvin, this isn't just police business," she points out. "It's district business. That's why people hire me. I heard about Ricki, so I figured I'd drop in on Janice. But you being here kind of tells me there's more to it. Is this connected to Lamonte? Or maybe Arthur Galetti?"

Gaffney seems flustered, which is satisfying. "Look—"

"What about this guy?" Nomi snaps open the paper folds on Noone's sketch.

Gaffney steps in, squints at the drawing. "Jesus, Pace. What are you doing walking around with a picture of Claude Ameche in your back pocket?"

"Claude Ameche, right . . ." Nomi says. "Well, it's been a pleasure talking with you as always, Calvin."

"Look, respectfully? You don't know what you're doing, and I'm gonna suggest you stay out of it." Gaffney is letting his irritation get the better of him. "When Balter hears you've been bumbling around his crime scene, he's gonna be real unhappy. We're trying to conduct an investigation, and you're—"

"I'm not trying to get in the way of any investigation," Nomi says. "And *respectfully*, Balter needs to calm the hell down."

"Listen, you're out of your depth on this one, Pace." Gaffney swaps hands on his coffee again, sneering at her. "You want to investigate Galetti? You should've sucked dick like a good little girl and stayed on the force—"

Noone rises abruptly from his crouch. His shoulder brushes Gaffney's elbow and somehow knocks the cup he's holding: Sixteen ounces of hot black premium roast spills straight down Gaffney's front.

Gaffney screams, jumps so hard he dislodges his glasses. "Ahhh, *fuck*! *What the fuck?*"

"Oh, I'm sorry," Noone says in a flat voice. "I didn't mean to bump you."

"You didn't mean to . . . What the *fuck*?" Gaffney swipes at his jacket, holds his sodden turtleneck away from his chest with pinching fingers. "Who the fuck are *you*?"

"Nobody." Nomi wants to laugh but she really can't. She tugs on Noone's arm. "He's nobody."

"That was all my fault," Noone says. "I do apologize."

"*Seriously*, man!" Gaffney exclaims.

"Real sorry about that!" Nomi is practically dragging Noone away. "Anyway, hey, thanks for the warning, Detective. We'll get out of your hair, okay? Bye!"

She uses a combination of shoving and pulling to get Noone out of the courtyard and through the shadowed tunnel of the carriage entrance, onto the Downing Street sidewalk. Noone seems to want to keep checking back on Calvin Gaffney, who's still swearing in the courtyard and shaking coffee out of his stupid jacket. Who buys corduroy?

Nomi yanks on Noone's sleeve to bring him around, forcing him to walk fast enough to match her. "*Stand down.* Are you fucking nuts? The last thing we need is you getting arrested!"

"He can't arrest me for spilling his coffee," Noone says stiffly. "And it's his own fault. He was being rude."

"Jesus Christ, Simon, he's a *cop*—being rude is basically an employment requirement." Nomi smothers her snort, pulls Noone forward. "Now come on, we got more than what we came for, and I want to get out of here before Gaffney decides to file some kind of report."

Returning to Gansevoort Street in the back of another cab, Nomi takes a pen from her tote and writes *CLAUDE AMECHE* in big letters at the top of Noone's sketch. Then she examines the Big Mouth flyer.

She's already getting ideas. "I'm thinking we go tomorrow night, see if Janice is there, find out what she knows, have a drink, get out."

"What?" Noone seems somewhat distracted by the lingering satisfaction of dumping hot coffee all over a police detective.

"How would you feel about coming to a nightclub with me?"

"Now?"

"No—tomorrow. Pay attention."

"You're in the middle of an investigation and you want to go clubbing."

"I want to dig up *information*, Noone. There's a difference."

"The difference being that this information is in a nightclub."

She grins at him. "Come on, you know you want to come. Have you been to a club in NYC yet? I'll even pay the cover charge."

Chapter Thirteen

September 1987, Tuesday

So it looks as if he's going to a nightclub tonight.

Simon turns this concept over in his mind as he walks across the dark cobblestones at 2:45 a.m., on his way to work, pulling on his wool cap and smoking a cigarette. Nomi was right; he hasn't been to a nightclub in this city yet—hasn't been to a nightclub before, ever, in fact. He's been busy getting his life set up; he hasn't felt the urge to socialize. Looks like that's about to change, although he's not sure how he feels about it.

He crosses under a streetlamp, where a guy in a fisherman's sweater is manhandling metal barrels through an open cellar door; an older man in a porkpie hat watches the barrel wrangler, smoking a pipe and offering suggestions. Simon smells the pipe smoke, as well as car exhaust and raw meat. Trucks honk, goosing a pair of boys in corsets and high heels and long coats who scream with laughter as they scurry clear of the road.

As Simon comes through the door of Gennaro's and finds his apron, Mike Nell gives him a nod. Nell is recentering a thin blade on a honing steel, and the whisking action sounds like powerline music.

"Nice cuts so far, Noone. Take a hook and a meat saw today—you're on forequarters. Might get you doing some ribs."

The magic of work is that it's so soothing. Huge marbled slabs of beef hanging in rows, ass to ass and shoulder to shoulder, white fat gleaming—something pristine about it, almost holy: Here's warm life transformed into cold carcass, the butcher ready to complete the process of carving, dismembering, feeding the hungry people of this hungry country. Everything that we are is meat—ask the boys at the Manhole near Hudson Street; ask the girls at the Vault; ask the hookers on the West Side Highway; they'll tell you—and now Simon is doing his part, contributing to the great cycle, his knives working in rhythm with it all.

They're down a worker on the production line, and Nell asks him to do an hour's worth of overtime. Back at the tenement after his shift, Simon's climbing the stairs when Nomi pokes her head out her open door.

"Do you have an outfit for the club tonight?"

"I have a suit," he confirms.

"A suit." She bites her lip. "Okay, we'll work with that. Also, I bought a gift for Donna Rosa, to thank her for Sunday."

"If it's chocolate or alcohol, she'll love it."

"It's chocolate liqueur."

"Perfect."

"I have stuff to do this afternoon, but I'll see you at nine, okay?"

In his rooms, he takes a shower and takes his rest. On waking at 2:30 p.m., he does a little light tidying to compensate for the neglect of the weekend. But something is niggling at him—an electric wire touching itself to the back of his neck, a tiny cattle prod. Returning from the laundromat, Simon figures out the problem when he steps into the midafternoon sunshine and sudden, shocking pain strikes him deep in the left temple and behind his left eye.

Shit shit shit. He knows this—prodromal pain. This isn't just a headache, it's the start of a migraine. He needs to get home.

By the time he reaches Gansevoort, the sun is an assault, and the peculiar lights have arrived, distortions and auras that make everyday things seem bizarrely psychedelic. At the narrow door of the tenement, he staggers. Getting to the third floor becomes complicated when the risers under his feet begin to look doubled.

Once inside his apartment, he closes the door with his back, dumps his bag of laundry and his coat, fumbles his way to the bathroom. Gulps four Vicodin and—from another packet—one Valium. It won't stop what's about to happen, but it might alleviate the pain to come. He feels spacey, and time has started jumping around. Slippage is about to occur, and there's nothing he can do to prevent it.

Nomi asked about his amnesia, about his headaches and weird symptoms, but he didn't give her the whole story. He didn't explain how he worries that one day, he'll wake up from a migraine to discover everything gone, his mind once more wiped clean. Rebuilding himself five years ago took almost everything he had: The idea of starting from scratch again fills him with a kind of cosmic dread.

His vision is starting to fracture. He kicks off his boots, puts a towel on the floor near the bed in case he throws up. Crawls onto the mattress with his eye mask, waits for the drugs to take effect. The pills usually take about fifteen minutes to come on. One day, he'll run out of medication, but not today: He has a black market American script pad, all the scripts prewritten and signed by Flores.

Flores had been hopeful. "Maybe when you get to America, you will discover more about your condition, find ways to resolve it. Maybe they will have some new treatment. These medications are drugs of dependence, you understand. You should not take them as often as you do."

Simon doesn't give a shit. Because now his teeth click together as the real pain arrives. Like orgasm, it climbs up his body, gaining strength and heft. Everything above his neck goes numb: his lips, cheeks, eyelids. Tinnitus screams like a buzz saw in his ears. The pain is a chichicaste vine that colonizes his insides, thickening and expanding, extruding wicked thorns. His hips and neck stiffen. His legs prickle, and his hands lose coordination—

The pain crests, slamming into his left temple and the backs of his eyes, and he's gone.

When Simon comes to, he's on the floor.

The apartment is dark; it's night. Moonlight filters through the curtains. Little twitches and tremors are rippling through his body, muscle spasms. His jaw hurts, like he's been clenching his teeth for hours. His mouth tastes disgusting; he must have thrown up. He rolls over and realizes he's been lying on a book. All of his books are on the floor, spread out around him.

But he remembers his name. He remembers who he is. This is his apartment in New York City. It's Tuesday evening.

Getting up is doable, if he moves slowly. His head is throbbing. He's shirtless. There's sticky dampness at his left wrist. He fumbles his way to the bathroom, flicks on the light, winces. His own face in the mirror—eyes, hair, bone structure—looks slightly off kilter. Not unrecognizable, but definitely unfamiliar. This is the postdromal phase, when everything feels strange. The dampness is blood, running down his left arm from a shallow, narrow-edged gash on the pale inner skin between his elbow and his wrist. Dammit.

He runs the sink faucet to rinse off the wound, then gives up and runs a bath. While the tub fills, he inches around the apartment, straightening things, wiping up his mess, restacking his books. The apartment seems a little wonky—some objects appear to have been moved or rearranged. He can't figure out how he cut himself. He's shaking, but it'll pass.

Simon smokes a cigarette in the hot bath and does a personal inventory: His head has a heavy thrum, and he's lost some time. Objects still have a faint aura. He feels slightly stoned: That's not just aftereffects from the migraine; he took a lot of medication. Rubbing at his cheeks, he feels a residual numbness. His emotions feel out of whack. But the firestorm in his brain has banked and cooled.

As he's brushing his teeth, the hammering in his head is superseded by hammering at the door of his apartment. Wonderful. He spits, rinses, pulls on his terry cloth robe and his sunglasses before answering.

"Hey, I was going to suggest—" Nomi suddenly stops and examines his face. She's wearing a tank top, and Simon feels a hot lick of interest from somewhere inside his mind at the sight of her bare shoulders. "What's wrong with you? You look worse than me. You got another headache?"

"A migraine. Yes." There's a difference.

"Fuck. We leave for the club in thirty minutes. Are you going to be okay?"

The nightclub—*goddammit*. Is he going to be okay? What an excellent question.

"I don't know," he says finally.

"Shit. But you're up. Can you function?" She pulls his sunglasses down a little, peers at his eyes. "Oh man, you look baked."

Without the dark lenses in the way, Simon can see she has a purple aura. He watches how it curls around her. His left forearm itches as blood seeps toward his wrist.

"Hold on," Nomi says. "I know what you need. Wait here."

She spins and walks off, leaving the door open. He leans on the wall, listens to the sound of her boots clomping on the wooden stairs.

Is it really nine thirty at night? He's lost nearly five hours. The soft doubling of everything—the banister, the dark skylight, the door across the hall—is still affecting his vision. He pushes his sunglasses back up. He's naked under his robe. This is insane. Is he really going to a nightclub? What is he doing? He picks his way back to the bathroom, applies a Band-Aid to the cut on his arm.

As he emerges, Nomi returns with a bottle of some clear liquid and two shot glasses. She stomps to the kitchen and turns on the light, goes to the breakfast table and fills each glass all the way.

"What is that?" Simon wobbles closer and stares at the liquid, suspicious.

"There weren't many benefits to having an upbringing like mine, but this is one of them." Nomi hands him a shot glass. "It's schnapps."

He sniffs, recoils. "It smells like medicine."

"It is." Nomi raises her own glass at him. "Drink it fast."

She slugs back her shot. Dignity demands that he do the same.

"Holy Jesus Christ," he says, and then some more religious curses in Spanish as he sits down abruptly in the nearest chair. He puts a hand to his mouth.

Nomi grins. "It's disgusting, but it wakes you up."

No, it's just disgusting. The back of his throat is burning. There's an herbal taste. His cheeks are no longer numb.

Nomi snorts at his facial expression. "You look like a cat that drank sour milk."

He hands back the glass, shuddering. "Don't give that to me ever again."

"You feel better, though, right? You've got color. Where are your clothes?" She spots the black suit suspended on a hanger from a wall hook near the door, walks over to inspect it. "Wow, okay. Where did you get this?"

"I can't remember." He still has an acerbic tang in his throat. "A thrift store."

She's shaking her head, side-eyeing him. "You're unbelievable. This is Saint Laurent, you dork. How do you find this stuff? Okay, and here's your shoes."

She brings everything over and lays it on the bed where he was passed out in agony barely an hour ago. He has serious reservations about this plan. "Nomi, listen—"

"It'll be all right." She returns to where he's sitting, puts a hand on his shoulder. "Come on, I believe in you."

He removes his sunglasses, grasps her forearm. There's an electric prickle of static from the contact and a fascinating light show where their auras intermingle. He tears his eyes away; he needs to concentrate to explain this in a way that will make sense. "Listen, you should know. I get loopy when I have a migraine. I'm sensitive to noise and light, I'm bad tempered, I'm—" He drags his memory for Flores's term—"dysregulated."

"Noone," she says firmly, "I don't mean to be insensitive, or unsympathetic, or whatever—I'm sorry to haul you along on this escapade if you're in pain. But dysregulated or not, I really need your help tonight."

He wets his lips; his mouth tastes like he's been chewing aspirin. Because he wants to keep touching Nomi, he releases her. "Okay, fine. I'll get dressed and meet you downstairs."

Nomi has already started backing for the door. "Twenty minutes."

So that's it. Christ, this is such a bad idea.

Simon strips off his robe, gets dressed. In the full-length mirror behind the door, he looks acceptable. But his skin is sensitive to everything: the black trousers cinched at his waist, the snakeskin fabric of the black shirt, the blue tie tight at his neck, the weight of the black jacket. He shoves his feet into Chelsea boots, collects cigarettes, cash, sunglasses. Dry swallows two more Vicodin. Scrapes back his damp hair, closes the apartment door, goes downstairs.

Sofia Rosa is standing with Nomi in the lobby area near the mailboxes—she has a pale gray aura that feels friendly. Nomi is surrounded by an electric purple haze, her energy humming. She's wearing her oversize leather jacket and no pants—wait, she must have a dress underneath the jacket. If there's a dress, it must be astonishingly short. Chunky black boots are buckled high on her white legs. She's twisted silver rings into one decorative braid around her side cut and covered the worst of her facial bruising with makeup. Both she and Sofia Rosa are assessing his outfit as he descends the stairs.

"This is a nice suit. Very handsome." His landlady is smiling approvingly and holding up a small brown bottle. "And you see? No-mee gives me a lovely gift!"

"Congratulations." God, he's really going to have to keep his bad humor in check.

"Yes, very good. You will have a good evening, I think." Sofia Rosa wafts toward her own apartment. "Now I go watch *Matlock* and drink this."

"See you tomorrow, Sofia." Nomi turns back, grabs his lapel and pulls him closer to her level. Her eyes are smoky with kohl, and her mouth is glossy pale; she has a thin silver ring in one side of her bottom lip. "Okay, first of all, ditch the tie. And while we're at it . . ."

She yanks his blue tie off, stuffs it into her pocket. Then she starts unbuttoning his shirt.

"What are you doing?"

"You're going to a club, not a job interview. Here . . ." Digging in her other pocket, she comes out with a black leather cord, reaches up to sling it around his neck. She fastens it with a loop in front. "You're too tall. And how are you so lean?"

Her fast, clever fingers in close proximity to his bare chest are doing strange things to his brain. "You're aware that I'm not twelve. I can dress myself."

"You're aware that you have no birth certificate, so there's no way of knowing how old you are."

"You have a lip piercing."

"It's a fakey." She pushes the ring sideways with her tongue to demonstrate.

"But the one in your left ear is new."

"Aw, you noticed."

His shirt is wide open almost to his navel. "I look underdressed."

"You look just right." Her carnivorous teeth gleam as she grins and steps back. "Okay, that's better. How do you feel?"

He decides to go with honesty. "Like an alien in an ill-fitting human skin."

"You'll be fine. Great, let's go."

She spins and heads outside. Simon follows, his head thumping.

Immediately, the sulfurous light of the streetlamps hits him square in the eyes, sets off tracers in his vision. Nomi has turned left toward

Greenwich, walking fast. Simon works to keep up. The street is dark, but he can hear music at a distance, the swish of cars on the cobblestones, laughter from down the street, everything echoing. People are moving in the black, like lantern fish swimming in the depths of the ocean. There's the smell of frying meat.

Being outside is overstimulating. He should probably have stayed at the apartment. But there's something perversely enjoyable in the experience: A coldness in his nerve endings makes the air feel fresh on his body, makes colors and edges vibrant, distinct. On his right, Nomi strides along, oblivious to the bioluminescence that floats around her and turns her loose dark hair into a swirling oil slick, turns her pale skin into creamy fire.

"Are we getting a cab?"

Nomi snorts at him. "It's two blocks. The walk will sober you up. Now listen, I know you're in a bad mood, but I've got some unfortunate news."

Of course she has. "Just tell me."

"Three of my contacts got back in touch. They've hit dead ends on your case. No missionary workers went missing—I've got confirmation on that—and obituaries for men in your age range during the time period are coming up blank."

They've turned left onto Greenwich, where a Black girl in tight jeans is having a muffled conversation in a lit-up phone booth. Trash blows elegantly against the wire links of a side fence as they cross West Twelfth.

Simon watches a car corner up ahead. "Your missionary contact, that's the Catholic priest from the church you visited on Sunday? Could there have been mission groups from other denominations?"

Nomi shakes her head. "No. Clergy talk to each other, you know, regardless of affiliation, and they keep centralized records. The missionary angle is done." She glances at him, appraising. "I never really saw you as a religious zealot, anyway."

"But . . . no obituary hits, either."

"Nope." Nomi strides past a store that advertises butcher supplies: boots, gloves, knives, scales. "That doesn't necessarily mean anything. I suggested they search East Coast records, but you could be from someplace else. We don't know. Trying East Coast was just a shot in the dark."

It's hard to make his synapses work in concert, but he can extrapolate from what she's saying. "We're unlikely to hit the bull's-eye on this, are we?"

Nomi slows for a car, then crosses West Thirteenth, clearly considering how to phrase her response. "I don't think we're going to suddenly stumble onto your point of origin, no. I think it's going to be a slow process of elimination. We'll narrow down our search to an inevitable moment where we say, 'You are most likely this guy.'"

"That could take years."

"It could."

He's surprised at how desolate that idea makes him feel. "Maybe you should just run my fingerprints."

She pauses their matched steps so she can look him in the face. Her eyes are faintly purple, lit by stars. "Hey, I told you it would be tough. It's only been five days—have a little patience."

Her faith is curiously touching. "You're not put off by any of this, are you? I'm an illegal immigrant with sketchy papers and medical issues who's sent you on this wild-goose chase, and I tell you that I might be a whole different person in my previous life, and you just take it in your stride."

Nomi waves a hand. "Look around, Noone. You're on the West Side. Everyone here is from somewhere else, everyone is pretending to be something they're not—someone cooler, someone better, more sexy, more confident, more cunning. When the sun goes down and the clubs open, we all put on our masks and turn into different people. You're worried about what I think? I think you fit right in here, with the rest of us." She grins at him, silver lip ring flashing. "Now come on—Big Mouth is just across the street."

Chapter Fourteen

September 1987, Tuesday

They cross over Ninth Avenue, and before them stands the five-story pink Triangle Building. Prospective patrons are milling at the black-painted doors at the base of the Triangle, mostly men in jeans, all with generous mustaches. Lights flash in the dark windows; music is thrumming in the sidewalk. Cars cruise around slowly, and a line of yellow cabs stretches away to the right.

Nomi realizes she should probably explain. "We're not going to a gay club. There's a bunch of clubs in this building—Big Mouth is mixed gay and straight. Mainly it's just for people who like to dance. The entry's around the other side, on Hudson."

She ushers Noone through the crowd, where he's getting a lot of appreciative looks, and up to the tip of the Triangle, skirting a tall double streetlamp at the end of the block. On the Hudson side of the building, Nomi spots the door to Big Mouth with the regulation beefy guy standing out front. Dealers mill along the external wall, and a line of people in hybrid fashion—jean shorts and afros, leather and Day-Glo, white suits and teased hair—have gathered nearby on the curb. The security meat is letting people in two at a time.

Nomi turns to see Noone glowering at the club entry area in a way that suggests he's having profound misgivings.

She pulls him to face her. "Listen, just follow my lead. We go in, have a drink, look for Janice—if we talk to her, great, if she's not there, we go home. All good?"

"This seems like a very bad thing to be doing in my current state of altered consciousness."

"Thousands of drug users would beg to differ." She paws in his jacket pocket, pulls out his sunglasses. "Here, put these on if you're worried about the lights. You look great, they're going to let you in."

The whites of his eyes flare. "You weren't sure I'd get in?"

"I knew *I'd* get in—they always let in girls." From her own pocket, she digs out cash. "You'll have a good time. Come on! Baby's first nightclub! It's gonna be great, let's go."

The security guard lets them both through the doors, like she thought he would. She pays the cover charge to the girl in goth makeup behind the wire cashier's cage; she and Noone are given their wrist stamps. People are coming in and out. They climb four flights of wide wooden stairs, lit by a dim green bulb, before reaching a balcony corridor where they find another door, heavy with sound insulation. Nomi pulls on the handle; behind her, Noone takes an audible breath as the full wash of heat and sound and darting lights spills over them.

The entry is black. Most of the interior of the club is black, with exposed pipes near the low ceiling. Music is pounding—maybe not tunes as good as some place like Paradise Garage, but the beat is seductive. Probably close to two hundred people of all races and genders are crammed into the space, dancing, spilling drinks, laughing and waving their arms, making the sprung floor bounce; Nomi is relieved she's not a cop anymore, because this place is a health-and-safety violation nightmare.

Noone seems to be hypnotized by the maelstrom. Even though he needed to be coaxed out of his lair to come along, Nomi's glad he's here. There's a nonzero chance they'll see Lamonte tonight, and if they do cross paths, she wants Noone's brand of crazy on her side. The downside is that she did not anticipate he would look so insanely hot in Saint Laurent, holy shit. It's fucking distracting.

She ignores the disco ball flashes and points-pushes Noone around to the cloakroom window, unzips her jacket and hands it to the guy. Underneath, the shortest dress she owns, bought at Lee's Mardi Gras store last year: a fluttering black slip with string straps and a thigh-skimming slashed hem. It looks indecent but still somehow manages to cover all her midriff scars. Black leather boy shorts in case she falls on her ass. This outfit is perfect with her small tits, and it makes her tattoos look big, which is right for this crowd. She's never been much for glamming up, but she's glad she made the effort tonight, although she keeps bumping the fake lip ring with her teeth.

Noone has been gazing around the club with his sunglasses in place. Now he looks back, pauses, removes the sunglasses to blink at her.

"What?" Nomi half yells.

"You're . . . in a dress." He scans her. "I think."

Nomi rolls her eyes. "Jesus—how much medication did you take, exactly? I shouldn't have given you the schnapps."

Noone breaks into a disarming laugh. "Too late now."

"Stop staring at me and look around. We're looking for Janice—Italian, long brown hair, roughly my height. She'll either be working the floor or behind the bar."

"There's two bars," Noone points out.

Nomi squints, shields her eyes against the laser lights, wishing she could wave the dry ice smoke away. "We might need to split up."

"I'm not letting you out of my sight." Noone leans closer. "You're purple."

Did he just say she's purple? God, the music is ridiculously loud. "What was that? Jesus Christ, I need a drink. Let's go right, start with bar number one, work our way around to the couches on the far left side."

To her surprise, Noone leads the way, carving through the crush of patrons. A minute ago, he seemed disoriented. Now, he's straightened up, his shoulders have broadened, his jacket swings. Is he actually enjoying himself?

At the first bar, most of the bartenders have given up on wearing shirts in the club's pulsing heat. Noone waves a fifty-spot for attention. In the sea of *Miami Vice* pastels and postpunk dance wear, he looks darkly exotic in his black suit, damp hair swept off his face and those blue, sardonic eyes. Nomi pleads for bottled water, and he adds it to the order, finesses his cuffs. When the order arrives, he passes her the water and then turns to give her a tall glass and lean his elbow on the bar, posture relaxed, as he raises his own glass.

"Champagne?" Nomi's never drunk champagne at a club. "What are we celebrating?"

"This." Noone grins at the mess of bodies on the floor—the heaving gyration of harem pants, studded cuffs, mirror shades, black lace. "Mystery of Love," by Mr. Fingers, is spinning, and people are getting into it. "It's bizarre. You can't see the colors, can you?"

"What!" She watches him quaff half his drink in one swallow. "Hey, slow down."

"Why?"

"Just . . . pace yourself."

"I like this. I didn't think I would, but I do." He smiles at the chaos of the club, then back at her, apparently fascinated by her dress. "This is nice too. Is it silk?"

"No idea."

He rubs a corner of her hem between his fingers. "I think it is. It's very soft."

Now he's closer, she can see his pupils are just teensy little pinpricks. "Oookay, my extremely stoned friend . . . Listen, I need you to stay focused for me. Can you do that?"

"I'm *very* focused. And there are no female bartenders here."

"Fine. Then let's do a circuit."

She gathers her bottled water and the rest of her champagne, tugs on Noone's sleeve to encourage him to follow—they have to push through the dancers in front of the DJ decks and mixing boards to go farther in. Noone seems fine, but he touches her occasionally to steady himself, his large hand an ember burning between her bare shoulder blades, or over the silk at her lower back.

Eventually, they reach a point where the crowd thins out enough for Nomi to draw breath. There are some video arcade games along the wall: A few folks are playing Pac-Man and Moon Cresta. Farther ahead, a wall of banquette seats and tables, a handful of freestanding bar tables. People are sitting or leaning, doing their best to flirt, or doing a bit more than that in the corners. Other folks smoke and chat, oblivious. Laughter shrieks nearby.

Nomi spots a face she recognizes at a bar table. "Geri! Good to see you. Where's Shannon and Rob?"

It's not ideal for talking, but it's not much worse than the Riverview. She chats to Geri as Noone lights a cigarette and peruses the scene. Hard to tell where his head is at. He seems alert, engaged, but his attention is floating all over the place, and his skin is gleaming with sweat, although that could be the humidity in the club.

Maybe a half dozen staff members in club tees wind through the throng, collecting glasses, cleaning up spills, doing minor crowd control. Janice could be on the floor, but Nomi needs to get closer.

She finishes her champagne and sets down the glass, pulls on Noone's lapel to bring his ear to her mouth. "I'm going for a dance, to check out staff on the floor."

"Have fun."

She assesses his grin. "Look at me—do *not* leave this table, or I'll never find you again. Stay here."

She spends most of her dance time examining staff or casting back to ensure Noone hasn't wandered off. At least the music is good: "Fascinated" by Company B bleeds into Touch's "Without You," and the heavy bass creates a sensual thump that resonates through the floor and spirals up her legs.

When the track is over, she leaves Geri and returns to Noone at the bar table, takes a long draft of water from her bottle. "It's mad out there. I didn't see Janice."

"I don't think she's on floor detail," he notes.

Nomi caps her water, faces the horde. "Jesus, look at it. I can't believe you've gone from Guatemala to this."

He seems more amused than appalled. "It's like Día de Muertos. Fire and lunacy and lust all mixed together."

"But Día de Muertos is only once a year—this party runs three nights per week. And this is just one club. The Vault and the Hellfire Club are on other floors. There are, like, five or six clubs within a block and a half of where we are now."

"*Hell is empty, and all the devils are here*," he quotes.

"Never took you for a Shakespeare fan, Noone."

"There's a lot you don't know about me." He huffs a laugh. "There's a lot *I* don't know about me . . ." Then his gaze skims over the top of her head, and his energy changes. "Come this way."

"Why?"

Instead of replying, he closes his hands over her shoulders and walks her to another bar table farther right, angles her slightly toward the back of the room—when she sees it, her breath catches.

At a round table circled by a padded leather bench seat, four men sit reclined. Eric Lamonte, fifty years old, smoking a cigar, his cream shirt gleaming with a thin shiny stripe, gold rings on his fingers. With his hair combed back, he looks like a lizard: chin up, affluent, cold, predatory, as he surveys his domain. At his right is the guy who's the reason Nomi currently has three stitches in her eyebrow: Claude Ameche is smoking cigarettes, not cigars, frowning at something in a small notebook; a serious, forty-something man on serious business. He hardly looks at the club—jaded, just focused on work.

Two other men sit either side of Lamonte and Ameche: a guy in his late twenties who looks no-nonsense, practical, in jeans and a T-shirt like an electrician or a carpenter, and another mid-thirties guy dressed like a pimp—loud-print shirt and pale trousers, a girl on his lap. The carpenter guy is drinking a beer. On the pimp's knee, the girl wiggles in a dress that's short and tight enough so you can see where his hand is moving under the fabric. He's laughing, looking back at the others like "Can you believe this chick?"—not a man of sustained intelligent thought.

Nomi feels a sudden hornet buzz on her skin, so intense it's almost painful. For a brief, awful second, she wants to cut more than anything. She clutches her bottled water and sinks back against Noone's chest, keeping her face as hidden as she can, and the feeling passes. "There's the whole gang—wow. Fucking Lamonte and Ameche. The guy getting a lap dance, I've seen him in photos of Lamonte's known associates, but I don't know his name. The guy drinking beer is new to me."

"He'll be the one with the bolt cutters." Noone is staring at the group. "He looks like a tradesman."

"Well, now we know what we're up against."

"What about Galetti?"

It's a sign that Noone's brain is still switched on, which is good. "Galetti wouldn't be caught here in a million years. He's, like, seventy years old, rich as God, house in the Hamptons, boat off Long Island, the whole bit. Being on-site at the club is not his scene."

"The invisible puppeteer."

"Just dealing with the puppets is trouble enough."

She could go over to their table right now and demand Brittany Jackson's location. They'd laugh in her face, but she gets an irrational urge to do it. She wonders how much they'd laugh if she put a gun to Lamonte's head . . . Another irrational urge—she doesn't even have her piece on her—but it's the only language these guys understand. Only violence and anger have meaning for them; saying "You are hurting a vulnerable child and her mom" has no impact at all. Men like Lamonte don't have a soft side to appeal to.

Nomi forces herself to look away. Then she sees Noone; he's staring at Claude Ameche like he's considering the best way to carve him up for a roast.

"Hey." Nomi tugs hard on Noone's lapel. "*Hey*. Whatever you're thinking right now, you need to stop thinking it."

"I had an opportunity last time, and I missed it." He's still staring.

"And you don't get a second shot. I mean it, Noone. The last thing I need is you going off script because of some insult to your sense of chivalry, or whatever the fuck. There's more at stake here. Stay focused, remember?" She tries to divert him. "Oh, look, there's the other bar."

The second bar is longer than the one near the entry, with at least six bartenders working double time to keep up with demand. Laser lights glance off the mirrors and glassware behind the staff, off the fishbowl full of matchbooks in front. Up this end, two young women in Big Mouth T-shirts are pouring shots—

"There's Janice." Nomi straightens. Before she can step forward, she realizes the proximity to Lamonte's table is going to screw everything up. "Shit. If I show my face up there at the bar, I'll get busted by Ameche for sure. And Janice won't want to talk if—"

"I'll go," Noone says.

Nomi stops worrying a nail. "What?"

"I said I'll go. Ameche didn't see me when I followed him."

"How do you know?"

He raises his eyebrows. "I know. And I can be useful for more than just muscle."

She's dubious. "Okay. But if you're gonna be the one talking, we need to know who Ricki spoke to, what he might have said, where he picked up his deliveries—"

Noone stops her. "We won't get all that. But I'll do my best to get two out of three."

"Shit." She rakes at her hair. "What are you gonna say? It's not like you can flash a badge."

"Trust me." Noone smiles, showing a glint of sharp incisor. "Even without a badge, I can be persuasive."

His energy has changed again, his gaze roving lazily over her face, curious and hungry, lingering on her mouth with its enticing ring. He's close enough so she can smell him—clean sweat, tobacco, the oily herbal tang of schnapps—and the smile is pure predator. Trust him? You wouldn't leave him alone in a room with your wife.

Where the hell did this come from? Is he fucking with her? Well, if it's working on her, it'll work on Janice. Goddamn, though, she should never have unbuttoned his shirt.

Nomi wets her lips. "Go on, then. Show me what you've got."

Noone grins, strolls away toward the bar.

Nomi has to move a little closer and blend with another cluster of patrons at a different table to keep both parties—Noone and Janice, Lamonte and his crew—in her line of sight. But Lamonte's group doesn't look like it's going anywhere. Wheedling a cigarette from a girl nearby to keep her hands busy, Nomi focuses her attention on Noone as he does some wheedling of his own.

He calls Janice over to place an order, and his face comes alive. He seems genuinely engaged, touches Janice's hand to get a light for his smoke, initiates what looks like flirting chat as he waits for the pour, knocks back a shot. It's quite a transformation. Nomi's made a performative switch herself on occasion, when she's had to fish for information, but it's disconcerting to see Noone change like this. Standing at the bar, he's all elegant angles in his black suit. He tilts his head, makes a panty-dropping grin. Janice looks dazzled. *"All the devils are here"* is right: He looks like a prince of the underworld.

Even under Noone's spell, though, Janice reveals a few anxious tells. Her gaze flicks toward Lamonte's table. Noone draws her attention back. Janice's smile becomes less certain, but she's still talking. Noone must make a joke—she smiles for real—then she's getting him a second drink, something acid yellow in a martini glass with a white napkin. He pays, leans forward across the bar and whispers something in her ear. Janice blushes, giggles. Nomi feels a flash of sympathetic heat between her legs.

Now Noone turns with his glass, catches Nomi's eye, looks pointedly toward the couches closer to the entry, between the cloakroom and the bathrooms. He walks off in that direction. Nomi clears her throat, feeling like she's just watched a live sex show. She drops her cigarette under her boot and dumps her empty water bottle, starts pushing through bodies.

There are maybe four couches, all of them black and ugly, with wide arms. Space is at a premium, but Noone's somehow found a spot.

Nomi kind of wants to smack him. "Do I get a seat?"

"Right here." He takes her by the wrist, pulls her into his lap, hands her his martini glass. "Here, you should try this, it's good."

The drink tastes of citrus and vodka, an icy-cold blast of sanity against the shocking warmth of Noone's body. Maybe he's having trouble throwing off the bit: His long fingers make glancing touches at her arm, shoulder, waist, hip, soft as the wings of a butterfly. She should slap his hands away when they stray too close to her scars, but something inside her doesn't want to. Oh, she could get into *so* much trouble with this guy tonight. She won't, because she's not a fucking moron, but she can play a little.

She sips again. "Mm, nice—it's a lemon drop. So what did Janice say?"

"She's too scared to talk much. But she gave me this." In Noone's palm, the unfolded white napkin with the words *Daniel Sullivan—Sully—Photos* written in Sharpie.

Nomi examines the napkin. "Score two for Janice. That girl is not a dummy."

"Apparently 'Sully' is a freelance photographer and journalist."

"Ricki was talking to a journalist? No wonder Lamonte was pissed." Nomi takes another sip of the cocktail, twists in place to see if Lamonte and his goons are still around. Too many bodies in the way. "No phone number for this Sully guy?"

Noone scrapes her hair away from her nape. His voice rumbles right against her earlobe. "You'll like this—he's over by the DJ."

"You're kidding. Has he got a death wish?"

"He's got security." Noone steadies her with one firm hand on her thigh, his thumb stroking gently near the groove of her crotch. "So did I do good?"

"You did very good."

"I told you I'm persuasive." Now his nose is sunk against her neck, his breath tickling the sensitive spot behind her ear. The hard ridge of his erection pokes against her butt.

"Noone . . ."

"Hm?" He's preoccupied.

"Noone." Nomi turns in his lap until their faces are aligned. "You look fucking amazing in that suit, but I think you might be getting a little dysregulated." She returns his drink. "Here, you finish this. Fix your pants. I'm gonna go look for the photographer."

She climbs off him and walks away.

Chapter Fifteen

September 1987, Tuesday

For a moment, Simon's not sure how to react.

In close quarters, her ass pressed against him, Nomi's presence was overwhelming. She smelled salty like the ocean, loamy like coupling. Purple stars billowed off her in dark waves. Her skin was slippery with the damp heat of the club, tattoos swirling.

Even departing, she looks regal, mink-sleek in her silky dress, hair swaying. He wants to exult, wants to cheer. Wants to lunge forward and cover her with his body. Wants to wrap his hand around her delicious throat and squeeze.

Except this isn't why you're here. You're here to provide her with backup.

Right. He clenches a fist, makes a monumental effort to reassert control. Temples thumping, he puts down his glass and stands, tracking Nomi as she walks through a crush of people with their arms raised. The landscape of the club is watery, undulating, shifting in his vision, the heavy beat of the music blending from one track to the next. Colors are a neon riot. People dance, their bodies swaying and jerking like they're on hooks at Gennaro's.

Simon presses his thumb against the cut on his left arm to clear his head, works to pull himself together and follow Nomi's path. Shaking off the sensations in his own body is difficult. He's throbbing every time he looks at her. He needs to slap himself. Clearly, if nothing else, tonight has established that combining the postdromal effects of a migraine with meds, alcohol, and the sensory overwhelm of a nightclub is a phenomenally bad idea. Got it.

Nomi has reached the DJ station, a short dais to the left of the first bar. At least three men are standing, bobbing, at large turntable setups, banks of machines behind. One of the men is wearing green running shorts and long white socks and white running shoes and nothing else. All of them are wearing headphones.

Around them, another guy circles, holding a large and extremely expensive-looking camera up to his eye. He's white, maybe early thirties, a little schlubby in a maroon plaid shirt and jeans, with a ginger mop of hair—Daniel Sullivan, Sully. Close by, a stony-faced Black man in coveralls, the approximate size and shape of a house.

Nomi is already chatting with Sullivan, who smiles and raises his camera to take a few shots of her. Simon wants to detach Sullivan's head at the neck, marshals himself as he comes alongside. Nomi doesn't introduce him—Simon's learned, from the visit to Hector's Café, that you don't introduce your security—but continues the conversation she's already started with Sullivan, yelling a little to be heard.

". . . hoping I could ask you about it?"

"Oh, sure, sure." Sullivan cocks a grin at her. "We could go to my place and talk over a drink, if you want. I'm pretty close by."

Simon thinks someone should be giving him some sort of prize for being civilized right now.

"I'd *love* to," Nomi gushes, "but I'm here with friends. Can we maybe go talk outside the door? It's freaking loud in here."

"Absolutely," Sullivan yells back. "Just lemme grab my man Max."

He steps aside to talk with his security; Nomi leans toward Simon. It's all he can do to stop himself from grabbing her by the scruff and rubbing his lips against her neck, but he settles for inclining his head so he can hear her.

"Feeling better?" Nomi's eyes are sparking.

"Somewhat."

"It's been quite a night." Her grin is mordant. She refocuses on Sullivan as he picks up his camera bag and waves her toward the main-entry door. "This guy is kind of a creep, but I might learn something here, so keep your shit together, okay?"

Sully leads them out the big insulated door onto the balcony corridor, the one Simon remembers reaching after they climbed all those stairs on arrival. As soon as the door shuts in their wake, the upper registers of the music disappear; the remaining sound, even the deep thud of the beat in the floorboards, becomes quieter and more manageable. Simon feels it as a slight relief, like someone's poured warm wax into his ears.

They're standing about ten feet along the balcony, under the glow of the emergency lights and one of those weird green bulbs. Max the Security Guy positions himself by Sullivan's shoulder; Simon, hands shoved in his trouser pockets, takes up a similar pose with Nomi.

"Hope I'm not talking too loud." Pushing his camera bag to his back, Sullivan lights a cigarette. "I've been taking snaps in there for nearly two hours, and my hearing has gone to shit."

"Oh no, you're fine," Nomi reassures.

"You're a private investigator, huh? Never met a private investigator in a club before." He smiles, like their meeting is a personal compliment. Simon recognizes Sullivan's type: young men of the Upper East Side who come down to the Meatpacking District on the weekends for a little strange. "How did you get my name?"

"A friend of Ricki Cevolatti's."

"Shit, poor Ricki. I saw in the papers what happened." But Sullivan looks more nervous than sad.

"Is that why you've got security?" Nomi asks politely.

"Oh, nah." Sullivan waves his cigarette perilously close to his ginger fringe. "Not at all. I had a couple rough experiences a while back—I was riding along with the Guardian Angels about three years ago, yeah? Anyway, I ask Max to come with me sometimes when I'm going someplace hairy."

"Lamonte's clubs can get hairy?"

Sullivan just smiles and shrugs. "It's the West Village."

Nomi nods, lets it go. "So, look, I'm not investigating Ricki's death, but I'm trying to find out a little more about Ricki's last few days. Where he went, who he saw, what he said, that kind of thing. It could impact another case I'm working on."

"Ah, Ricki. Well, Ricki was a doofus, you know. Always shooting off his mouth."

"How did you know him?"

Sullivan takes another drag, gestures toward the door of the club from which they've just emerged. "Like this. We met at clubs in the Village, or down in Soho. I mean, he was my dealer, right? But we got friendly. We'd have a few drinks, gossip a little. We weren't super tight or anything, but we got along."

Nomi's kohl-dark eyes have narrowed. "He knew you were a journalist?"

"Oh yeah, sure. But you know—photojournalist. Ricki thought it was just about taking pictures."

"He didn't know you broke stories."

"Long photo essays, mainly, but yeah."

"Can I ask what you and Ricki chatted about, last time you saw him?"

Sullivan scratches the back of his neck, perhaps annoyed that this tête-à-tête with the hot girl has become more interrogation than seduction. "Look, Ricki was an okay guy, but he wasn't the brain-surgeon type, you feel me? We'd talk about the scene, talk about work—that was mainly it. I don't even remember what we talked about last time."

"Bummer." Nomi smiles, trying to be a little more coaxing. "It would really help me if you could remember."

"I mean, we covered some ground." Sullivan waves, noncommittal. "You know—the situation in the district, places shuttering since AIDS, the city cracking down. The future of the clubs, basically. I guess it doesn't matter now."

"I guess not." Sensing Sullivan's impatience and his obvious lack of interest in cooperating, Nomi calls it. "Okay, well, I appreciate you talking to me. I'm sure you've gotta get back to the floor, so let me just . . ."

She moves to grab a Sharpie sticking out of the breast pocket of Sullivan's plaid shirt. Max the Security Guy glares, takes a step.

"It's fine, Max," Sullivan says, handing Nomi the pen.

"Be careful," Max says to his boss in an undertone.

"You know me, Max, I'm always careful."

"It's just a pen," Simon notes.

Max startles, stares at him.

Sullivan blinks at Simon, flustered. "Hey, you speak French? Makes sense—you look kinda like a northerner."

Nomi is gaping, and Simon has to think on his feet, not having realized they were speaking French at all. He hopes Sullivan mistakes his wide eyes for blithe surprise, not stunned shock. "You were raised French speaking?"

"Yeah, I got the US-Canadian thing going on." Sullivan nods amiably. "That's cool, man. Don't meet so many Québécois in NYC."

Nomi has recovered fast and is now just giving Simon side glances as she uses the Sharpie to write on the back of Sullivan's hand. "Okay, so this is my number. If you think of anything else about Ricki or your conversation, give me a call."

Sullivan grins at her, sly. "Can I give you a call anyway?"

Simon has an abrupt vision of himself as a French-speaking cannibal tearing strings of tendon off Daniel Sullivan's bones with his teeth.

"Sure," Nomi says good naturedly.

"Sweet." Sullivan gives her what appears to be his most-practiced smile. "Real sorry to bail on you, but I gotta get the rest of these shots. Good to meet you, though. We'll catch that drink some time."

"I'd love that," Nomi says, managing not to sound insincere. "See you 'round."

Sullivan and Max the Security Guy move past them and back to the heavy door, which lets out a wail of cresting music as it opens. Nomi maintains her smile until the door closes, then lets her expression drop as she turns.

"Sully's bought." She crosses her arms over her chest. "I mean, that guy he's got for security is huge, but I'm telling you right now, it's not Max who's keeping Sully safe in the clubs. Lamonte has got to him."

Simon leans back on the banister. "He was nervous. His hands were shaking while he smoked."

"I saw." She glares accusingly. "Oh, and hello—did you know you could speak French?"

"No," Simon mutters, feeling inexplicably embarrassed.

"You were just standing there exchanging sentences in French, and I had no idea what all three of you were saying. Wow."

"We were just talking about the pen." His lips feel numb. He rubs his face, avoiding glancing over the banister at the four vertiginous flights of stairs below them. "I thought we were speaking in English."

"French, Italian, Spanish, Maya, English . . . You're a regular little United Nations of languages."

"Can we discuss this later?"

"Sure, but—"

Before she can finish, the door of the club opens again, lights and music making a localized spill in the corridor. Max the Security Guy steps out, holding a white business card between thumb and forefinger.

"Sully asks me to give you this." Max's English is heavily accented. The card looks like a flower petal in his large hand. "You give him a phone number, he gives you a phone number."

"Uh, thanks?" Nomi releases her arms, takes the proffered card.

Max glowers, but it doesn't seem directed at Nomi. "And he cannot tell you, but I will tell you. They give him money to be quiet, but also they make threats, you understand? Me, I take no money, I can say what I like."

Nomi exchanges a glance with Simon. "What do you want to say, Max?"

"Sully and Ricki, they are talking about the . . ." Max grimaces as his tolerance of English runs out. He appeals to Simon. "Can I just tell you in French? That would make everything simpler, I think."

Nomi's expression reveals that they've switched languages, but Simon nods anyway. "Of course. Go ahead, I'll translate."

"As you like." Max thrusts his hands into the pockets of his coveralls. "Ricki and Sully discussed the politics of Ricki's business. Ricki was not as stupid as Sully makes him out to be, you understand? They discussed the city council land rezoning, and the woman senator who opposes Mr. Galetti."

Simon is giving Nomi the translation in spurts, but now she lifts a finger to interrupt. "The woman senator—do you mean Gloria Axedale?"

Simon doesn't know that name.

"Yes, this is the woman," Max confirms. "Mr. Galetti wants more properties. He's buying places all along the High Line route. He submits his rezone applications, and this Axedale woman is denying them."

"Did they mention any policies?" Despite the language barrier, Nomi's trying to drill down for details. "Anything to do with monopoly land ownership?"

Max makes a "maybe" face. "There is something about the Cabaret Law. But this is a New York issue I don't understand."

"This is all public information, though," Nomi insists. "It's not something Ricki should have gotten killed for sharing."

Max shakes his head. "No, listen." He turns to Simon. "Tell her this—tell her that Ricki said the Axedale woman can no longer refuse the rezoning. He said that Mr. Galetti has found a way to make her behave."

When Simon is finished, Nomi frowns. "What way?"

"This, I do not know." Max has shifted back to English. "Sully, he wants to report this, but then he learns of Ricki's death. He receives a phone call. Now, of course, he cannot report, not if he wants to keep his tongue in his mouth and his fingers on his hands."

"Or the money in his bank account," Nomi says.

The big man shrugs, his shoulders like two ham hocks. "That is all I can tell you."

"Max, this is incredibly helpful," Nomi says. "Thank you for speaking with me."

"He is a foolish man, my boss—too much powder, you understand? But you should have this information." Before turning to go back into the club, Max looks at Simon. "Look after your lady. And I do not think you are Québécois, my friend. My father is from Rouen, I have been to France many times—you have more Parisian than Canadien in your accent. It was a pleasure to meet you, though."

The security man raises a large palm in farewell, walks back through the door.

Nomi spins around. "Goddamn."

Simon's head is hammering, and he wants to unpack Max's comment about his French-language background, but this puzzle is still tugging at him. "Who's Gloria Axedale?"

"I mean, seriously, god*damn*." Nomi looks rattled and excited at once. "Axedale is a former member of the New York State Senate. She's the current chair of the New York City Planning Commission."

"So Ricki talked with a journalist about clashes between Galetti and Axedale, the chair of the planning commission, over rezoning."

"And how Galetti now has a way to make Axedale approve his rezoning requests," Nomi says. "Don't forget that part. That's the biggest part."

"Then Ricki turned up dead. And now Lamonte has bought the journalist."

Nomi chews at the metal in her bottom lip. "How is Galetti influencing Axedale?"

"Mobsters, state senators, New York City planning . . . This is getting a little complicated, wouldn't you say?"

"Not to mention that you've somehow picked up the ability to speak Parisian French."

"I didn't 'pick it up,' it just . . ." Simon exhales, his head fuzzy. "Is it time to go home now?" He doesn't want to sound plaintive, but it sort of comes out like that.

"I need my jacket," Nomi reminds him.

They return to the club, head for the cloakroom. Nomi hands the guy her ticket, but there's a queue. Simon stands beside her and wonders what her lip ring would feel like on his tongue if they kissed, distracts himself with a final scan of the floor.

He should say something. "I apologize. For—you know, before, on the couch."

Nomi glances at him and snorts. "Don't worry about it."

"I acted like an idiot."

"You're recovering from a migraine, half cut on medication, then I pour schnapps down your throat and drag you along to a nightclub . . ." She shakes her head at her own poor judgment. "You did tell me you get a little loopy."

"I'm sorry."

"Forget about it."

He stares at all the people on the dance floor, doing their thing. "You really think I look good in this suit? Wait, don't answer that."

As he moves his head, he sees something else: Claude Ameche, serious man in a polo shirt and chinos, with a burgundy jacket, is about to walk past them.

Simon touches Nomi's shoulder in warning. *"Ameche."*

She stills, angles to look just as Ameche's path crosses with the cloakroom queue. Ameche catches sight of Nomi: There's a flash of instant recognition. In the same moment, he sees her dress, her loose hair, her bare legs, and makes a lascivious grin.

Simon feels Nomi stiffen, and a kind of red film washes over his vision.

"Stay here," he says, separating from her.

Nomi is having her jacket handed to her at the cloakroom window. "Noone. What are you doing?"

As Ameche reaches the entry door, Simon is already striding toward the first bar. The gods of violence are smiling on him: When he looks over the lip of the benchtop, someone has left a paring knife on a plastic cutting board next to a pile of limes. Simon snatches up the knife, ignores the bartender who calls out, spins into a jog to reach the door.

He yanks it open.

"Noone! *Stop!*"

But the slithering viper inside him isn't listening. He strides out the door about ten steps behind Ameche. The man has jogged down the first set of stairs to the landing. By the time Simon catches up with him, they're halfway down the second set of stairs.

Simon doesn't see the point of announcing himself. He kicks Ameche in the back of the knee, leaving a heel print on the twilled cotton. Ameche stumbles forward onto the second landing, turns with a look of galled shock.

Simon surprises himself by punching Ameche right in the face.

"*Noone!* For fuck's sake!" Nomi has reached the balcony corridor.

Ameche grunts and falls back to the top of the third staircase. Simon's fist is smarting, but the cool alien blood in his veins is just getting started.

The older man, accustomed to swimming with sharks, reaches into the inside of his jacket. Simon discovers his own movements have become explosively fast, or maybe everything is happening in decelerated motion, like the Earth's revolutions have slowed: Ameche drawing the pistol, Simon's own hand slamming into Ameche's wrist, the gun falling over the banister. Green light casts everything in a murky, underwater haze, like they're brawling at the bottom of the Hudson.

But they're on dry land, and people are present in some background shadow play, crying out, scurrying for safety as Simon backhands Ameche's face, shoves him hard in the chest. Ameche tumbles ungracefully down the third set of stairs, sprawling on the final landing.

Simon stalks down, hauling the man up by the lapels of his burgundy jacket. Blood leaks in a soft stream from Ameche's nose as Simon slams him against the landing banister.

"You like beating up women?" Simon hardly recognizes the pitilessness of his own voice.

"*You cocksucker*," Ameche spits. "Do you know who you're dealing with here?"

Simon just laughs. Is this guy really going with *Don't you know who I am*?

As Ameche gropes for leverage on the banister railing, Simon takes the paring knife out of his waistband, rams it hard through the back of Ameche's left hand, into the wood. The paring knife is not as sharp as his work knives, but it stabs through meat and muscle just the same.

Ameche howls, fixed in place. Simon grips his throat.

"Simon, have you lost your fucking mind?" Nomi is on the stairs behind them.

"Go downstairs." Simon speaks mechanically over his shoulder as he squeezes the soft structures of Ameche's windpipe. The man thrashes. "Get outside."

He senses more than sees it when Nomi squeaks past behind him and heads for the exit. Ameche is choking, cursing.

Simon twists the knife in the man's hand, enunciates carefully. "So you know who *you're* dealing with—my name is Simon Noone. If you go near Nomi Pace again, next time we meet, I'll cut out something important."

He slams Ameche's head against the railing, then releases his hold, spins and walks briskly down the final set of stairs. Behind him, Ameche is groaning. Other people are backing away to give Simon space as he exits the building.

Out in front of the entry area, in the cool dark of the street, a yellow cab with Nomi in the back seat. "Simon, *get in the fucking car*!"

He climbs in, shuts the door. "I thought we weren't taking a cab?"

"Do not say ONE GODDAMN WORD." She looks like she wants to kill him.

"Where to, lady?" New York City cab drivers must have to sign some kind of unflappability agreement before they get this job.

"*ANY-FUCKING-WHERE,*" Nomi shouts, before turning to Simon as the cab takes off. "You *absolute fucking fuckhead.* I should push you off the Brooklyn Bridge, I swear to god. I am not even kidding."

"Nomi—"

She pulls the silver ring from her lip, throws it into the rear passenger footwell. Turns and holds up a declamatory finger, her expression wild. "*What* did I say to you? What did I *say*? *Don't go off script.* You fucking *asshole*—do you have *any idea* what you've just done?"

Simon still feels light somehow, as if the brutality on the stairs has lifted a weight. "Nomi, come on—Ameche already knows where you live. At least now he knows you're prepared to fight back."

"Oh, right—I'm going to *fight back.* I'm fighting back against *the fucking Gambino mob.* Christ, do you even *hear* yourself?" Nomi is a lightning storm, her oil-slick hair swirling in the wind of the cab's rapid movement down Hudson Street, her eyes black with fury. "I'm just one person! Ameche can bring down so much more firepower, it's not even a contest—and *this isn't even about Ameche*!" Her voice is raw with accented emotion. She shoves Simon hard in the joint of his shoulder. "How do you not get this? It's *not about Ameche,* and it's not about *you,* and it's not about *me*—although Lamonte will be quite happy to escalate things now, so thank you very much for that . . ."

Simon recognizes the callback to what she said when they first met, like he's returned to square one. The idea dampens the quicksilver in his veins.

Nomi closes her eyes, cups them in her palms. "But it's not about *any of that.* It's about a *seven-year-old kid* trapped in some place she can't leave, with men who think of her as a commodity—"

She throws up her hands, looks away. Simon realizes she's crying.

"Nomi." He straightens, the elation he's feeling draining away as fast as it arrived. "Nomi, hey . . ."

"Goddammit, *shut up*." She looks anywhere but at him, sniffing, swiping her eyes roughly with the back of one hand. After a moment, she turns to him again. "Look, I dragged you out tonight while you're loaded, and that's on me. But I need you to think about the bigger picture. To think about someone other than *yourself*. Because otherwise, what are we? No better than schmucks like Lamonte."

Simon suddenly realizes in his bones: He has made a mistake. Maybe a bad one. If the expression on Nomi's face is any measure, maybe very bad. What can he do?

He opens and closes his mouth, reaching for solutions. "I'll . . . I'll fix it."

"You can't *fix* it," Nomi says sadly. She looks away, waves toward the glittering city out the cab window. "Look at it out there—you think you can fix it? I was a cop. I tried. The big problems don't fix."

He swallows. Doesn't know what to say.

"If I've learned anything the last two years, it's that you can only fix the stuff around you." She turns and slaps her palm against his bare chest, something he'd been silently hoping she'd do all night. "Fix *in here*. Fix *this*."

His heart thumps madly under her hand. "I'm sorry," he gets out at last.

"You're sorry. Well, I'm . . ." She turns away to face the window once more. "I'm tired. I'm really tired, Simon. And I know you've somehow walked into this problem I'm trying to solve, and it's not even your problem, and you've just spent five years in the jungle . . ."

The stark truth of it robs his breath. "I don't even know my real name."

"I get it. You don't know your real name. You don't know the man you were. And listen, I'm not a perfect person. I'm not even a good person. So with that proviso, let me give you some advice, okay?" She's gazing at the city neon with a profound weariness. "Stop worrying about the man you were. Concentrate on being the man you want to become."

There's a long moment of quiet.

They drive around in the cab for nearly forty minutes, until it feels safe enough to return to Gansevoort Street. A big yellow gibbous moon glows among the sharp silhouettes of the Manhattan skyline.

Silver tracks dry on Nomi's cheeks, mixing with streaks of black kohl. Simon lights a cigarette and flicks the ash out the window; the embers spin and sparkle in the cab's slipstream, like the lights of a far-off carousel.

Chapter Sixteen

September 1987, Wednesday

Nomi looks around at the rear courtyard of the bodega, which is gray with damp. Benito has given up on getting his dish towels dry today; instead, a half dozen large plastic food-display tubs are stacked together against the fence, their backs exposed to the rain.

"First of all, what's the big deal with the rezoning?" Irma is in her blues, her NYPD cap resting on the ugly table. She's eating her chopped cheese in big bites, a little lettuce and mayo leaking out the side.

Nomi is pacing on the pavers and smoking one of Irma's Winstons while swigging a soda. She stopped buying cigarettes years ago, when the cherry-red glow of the burning tip began looking too tempting, but sometimes she still needs that nicotine hit. "It's something to do with monopoly land ownership and the Cabaret Law. I'll have to do more research. I'm assuming, if Galetti is fighting so hard over it, it's something that's preventing him from making money."

Irma nods, talking with a mouthful. "It's always about the money."

"If Axedale was opposing Galetti in the planning commission, then she was limiting his ability to cash in."

"But Ricki told this Sullivan guy that Galetti had found a way to put pressure on Axedale, so she sings to his tune?" Irma dabs at her mouth with a paper napkin. “Man, I need a board full of index cards to get all this who’s-who stuff straight.”

“No, you’ve got it right.”

“Galetti wants his rezoning plans approved.” Irma sighs. “And Ricki got knocked because he told all of this to a journalist.”

“Yeah, I think so. But now Lamonte has shut the journalist down.”

“Poor Ricki got his tongue hacked out for nothing.”

“I guess he made a good warning for everyone else—talk, and Lamonte will take your fingers off.”

Irma is nodding, chewing. “But then the million-dollar question is, what leverage has Galetti got over Axedale?”

“And how is this all tied to Brittany Jackson’s abduction?” Nomi blows smoke, gnaws on a fingernail.

It’s started to drizzle again. Nomi moves a little closer to the patio table, as if that provides any more protection from the rain. The city is gray; she’s wearing gray—combat trousers with a dark gray T-shirt. Over it all, a big khaki jacket. Every drab thing reflects how she’s feeling today, and she’s too tired to care.

But Irma is making a rolling gesture with her right hand while holding the remainder of her sandwich in her left. “Go back a little—think about leverage. People have lots of pinch points, right? Do this, or I’ll fuck up your reputation . . . Don’t do that, or I’ll threaten you with violence, or threaten your family, or refuse to give you money . . .”

“Or just refuse to support you politically? Could that be it?” Nomi touches the tip of her tongue to the spot on her bottom lip where she yanked out the ring last night; she scratched it, and it’s smarting. “We need to know where Axedale is vulnerable.”

“I’ll have to look into that.” Irma squints at her. “Now tell me what the hell happened to your eye.”

Nomi tries to wave it off. “I had a run-in outside my apartment with one of Lamonte’s goons, Claude Ameche.”

“Goddamn, girl. I told you—”

"It's fine. It's been sewn up." But she has to give Irma more than that. "My only worry is, there was another run-in last night at the club. Ameche's really pissed off now."

Irma swallows the last bite of sandwich, swigs from her own soda, looking serious. "They know where you live, Nomes. Have you considered moving out of your apartment for a little while, until this whole situation calms down?"

"And leave my plants?" But Nomi knows a joke isn't going to cut it. "Look, there's someplace I can go if I need to."

"Good. I'm thinking that's a good thing, because you *might* need to, just sayin'." Irma wipes her mouth and hands with a napkin before digging around in her purse. "Okay, here's something for you—you asked about Lamonte's known associates. Here's the latest mug sheets."

The papers she drags out are photocopies, much creased, a little rough from sitting in the bottom of her bag. Nomi sticks her cigarette in the corner of her mouth and puts her soda bottle on the table so she can smooth out the sheets and look.

She scans through the first KA sheet, gets a hit on the top row of the second sheet. "This guy—Ray Dinkins. He and some hired company were at the club last night with Lamonte."

Irma picks something out of her teeth with a fingernail. "Dinkins has priors for felony pimping and procurement, did a little time about seven years ago. He's a low-level bozo, but he's extremely loyal."

On the third sheet, Nomi finds another photo she recognizes. "This guy too."

Irma fishes in her bra for a cigarette, narrows her eyes. "Gino Hart. Young guy, old school. Priors for aggravated assault, abuse of a corpse. Seems to be a big Norm Abram fan—anything tool related, he likes it. Bolt cutters, blowtorches, wood chippers, that kind of thing." She lights up, lifts her chin at the photo. "Another guy you should probably avoid."

Nomi butts out her cigarette. She isn't thrilled at this news, but she has another bone to pick. "I gotta know—is Balter following up on

Galetti? Because what the hell was Calvin Gaffney doing outside Janice D'Addario's apartment?"

Irma blows smoke, shrugs. "I don't know about that. Galetti's real estate deals are across Sixth and Tenth Precincts, though—there's a list of his land purchases floating around the station house, I know for a fact—so maybe McKee and Balter are getting their heads together on it. Also, I heard a bunch of guys at Sixth have been out with the flu or something, so Balter could've sent Gaffney out as a loaner. Everyone's short, Nomes—Gabino from Seventieth said the boys in Flatbush are trying to investigate Ricki's murder across three precincts." She makes an amused fish mouth. "Gaffney said you spilled coffee on him."

"First, it was an accident. Second, it wasn't me, it was my . . . research assistant, and third, Gaffney was being an asshole, he earned it." Looking indignant is more effort than Gaffney deserves. "Also, it was pretty funny, so."

"And nobody caught it on camera? Damn." Irma grins outright before remembering more stuff to rummage for in her purse. "Hey, that missing person search you had me do? Here's what I got, but I don't think it'll bring you much joy."

Nomi accepts the additional papers Irma passes over. "Nothing useful?"

"A couple hits, maybe, but see what you think."

Nomi stuffs the papers into her tote, takes a swig of soda. She's been considering something for a while, and on this gloomy, brushed-steel day—after what she witnessed last night at the club—she thinks maybe it's time to do it.

She keeps her tone casual. "While I've got you running around doing chores for me, you wanna check out a print? I picked this up on another thing. It could be a random, some bit of scene contamination, but I want to be sure."

She hands Irma an index card from her tote. Two pieces of clear packing tape are fixed to the card; each piece of tape has a single fingerprint—one is a thumb, the other one is probably a middle finger, she's not sure. The whorls and ridges of Simon Noone's prints are clearly outlined in the tape adhesive.

"Easy." Irma tucks the card away and finishes off the dregs of her own soda. "I can send the results through Enrique, probably by tomorrow?"

"No rush." The act of handing over the prints has made Nomi break into a light sweat. She diverts. "You doing okay at the station? They're not throwing more stuff at you than you can handle? I feel bad for loading you up."

"Nah, you know me—I don't stretch out of shape for nobody." Irma grins, then gets somber. "Nomes, you said you had someplace you can go if things get too hot, right? Lamonte's torturing people, buying off journalists . . . Maybe you want to put some thought into an exit plan, s'all I'm saying. Maybe pack a bag for emergencies. Put your plants on a timer or something."

"I'll think about it." Nomi knows Irma; the woman is not an alarmist. This means something. But she's made commitments, and she's not reneging on them now. "I just want to get this kid back to her mom. The longer Lamonte has her, the easier it gets for him to think of her as a transactional asset—and he already has connections to the sex trade."

"You're scared for her," Irma notes.

"Yes. But I'm also fucking *furious*. This sort of stuff—kids and their moms, you know? It just . . . gets me."

"With what happened to you and your mom, that's understandable." Irma grinds out her smoke, stands, reaches for her hat. "But you get too attached, sweetie. It was always your thing. I applaud it—I do—but you've gotta keep something in the tank."

"I'm trying."

"Just don't burn yourself out. And don't get burned. And keep me posted, okay?" She gives Nomi a hug, a smacking kiss. "Mwah—see ya, babe."

Nomi sits on her side-ended apple crate after her ex-partner leaves, capping and uncapping her soda. Thinking about leverage, about blowtorches, about exit plans . . . about fingerprints. Then she goes through the bodega's pantry storeroom, back into real life. Pays Benni, checks the outside landscape at the door, heads back onto West Forty-Ninth.

The afternoon is waning, and Old Glory, on the fire escape up ahead, is limp and dripping. On the other side of the street, an older man pushes his food cart. People are mostly at work or inside, taking refuge from the first miserable day of fall weather. School hasn't let out yet, and the normal bustle in the street is absent.

Nomi hears her own footsteps echo strangely in the quiet. She glances back over her shoulder. Seeing Lamonte and Ameche at Big Mouth last night shouldn't have been a shock, yet somehow it was. Now she's letting Irma's warning spook her.

"Fuck it," Nomi mutters. But when a cab passes, she flags it down.

Back home, she hangs her jacket, dumps her keys, pulls on her warm black sweatshirt. Going through the mug sheets from Irma, she adds the info to her files: She can dig a little into Dinkins and Hart, find more connections and, hopefully, locations. When she's done updating her Jackson file, she pulls out the sheets with the East Coast missing person info. It takes all of two minutes to establish that none of the cases Irma's highlighted have anything to do with Simon Noone.

She goes to the kitchen and washes out the coffeepot, replaces the filter, refills the machine, turns it on. Waiting for it to brew, she does a little tour of the apartment, wiping leaves here, spritzing with water there, pinching off brown tendrils and petioles. Mainly thinking about Irma's info, but occasionally allowing herself to consider why she handed over Noone's prints.

At least three things changed her mind. First, he seems desperate to find out who he really is, and her foremost responsibility is to Noone as a client. She said she'd help him find out his real identity, and that's what she's going to do.

Secondly, he flipped from normal guy to satanic sex god at the club last night, and it threw her. Maybe he was just putting on a show for Janice—but if Noone is that good an actor, how can she tell which parts of him are real and which are faked? Does *he* even know the difference? She needs some understanding of his actual personality.

Third was the main event: the way he'd gone for Ameche. Noone's movements had had an almost robotic efficiency: fluid, spontaneous, instinctual. Ruthless. Nomi has seen some shit, but she's never seen anyone use a paring knife to stab someone so hard their body part got stuck to the surface underneath.

She can make allowances for Noone being under the influence, sure. And she's no wide-eyed innocent; she's familiar with violence—perpetrated it, on a number of occasions. But even in her angriest, most off-the-leash moments, she's known when she's taken things too far. Noone doesn't seem to have those guardrails.

He hadn't even seemed particularly angry. He'd been completely cold about it. And she'd seen his look of confusion as she'd bawled him out in the cab: He really did not get it. Not only had he ignored her explicit instruction—a prohibition she'd set down, that he'd trampled over without thinking of the consequences to herself or Brittany Jackson or anybody else—but he'd seemed oblivious as to why physically attacking someone at a nightclub was a bad idea.

Her fury was insulating in the cab last night, but now, in the cold gray light of day, Nomi finds herself even more unsettled. Yes, she told Noone that he should stop worrying about the man he'd been. But for her own peace of mind, she'd like as much information on that man as she can get.

There's a knock at the door, and she startles.

Before she takes off the chain, she remembers Irma's words: *Maybe you want to put some thought into an exit plan.* She stops her hand, steps to the side of the door. "Who is it?"

"It's just me, Nomi."

Noone's clipped consonants bring instant recall—and Nomi discovers the worst thing about all this. Because it's not only the confusing, infuriating, frightening parts of last night that are coming back. She's also remembering unbuttoning Noone's shirt in the lobby . . . His lean dark figure at the bar, like a demon on shore leave . . . His breath on her neck, and the way he looked at her, greedy and sensuous . . .

The way he plunged that knife into Claude Ameche's hand, the blade piercing skin and sliding right through, the sight of it exploding inside her mind like an atom bomb—

Simon Noone scares the shit out of her. But being around him also makes her vibrate at some deep, restless frequency. She thinks of his thumb stroking the skin of her inner thigh, like the rough lick of a cat's tongue.

Goddammit, she really needs to get laid.

Nomi sighs, leaves the chain on, opens the door. "What's up?"

Noone is standing in the hallway. Black peacoat, black shirt, navy sweater, blue jeans, boots—entirely normal clothes for a supremely normal person. Rain glitters on the shoulders of his coat and at the ends of his damp hair, and he's got a small spiral-bound notepad in one hand.

He sees the chain on the door, and his posture becomes awkward. "I, um, thought about buying you a plant."

"What?" Nomi frowns.

"But then I thought you might appreciate this more." He raises the notepad, begins reading. "Gloria Axedale, fifty-two years old, born in Queens, attended public high school, graduated valedictorian 1953—"

"Noone . . ."

"Attended Radcliffe College, Harvard Law School, married to Bill Axedale since 1961, three kids. After practicing as a litigator with McMahon, Segal & Holtzman, served as Democratic member of the New York State Senate from 1971 to 1978. Appointed by the mayor to the New York City Planning Commission in 1980—"

"Okay, stop." Nomi takes off the chain and opens the door wider. "Just . . . stop reciting Gloria Axedale's curriculum vitae outside my apartment."

"Are you still angry?"

"I'm not answering that. Where did you get all this information?"

"Public library."

"You caught the subway?"

"Yes."

Nomi considers the significance of that. "Right. Well."

He brings his other hand out from behind his back. He's holding a small soggy potting tube with waxy green leaves spilling over the side. "I . . . also bought you a plant."

She touches her tongue to the scratch inside her lip as she looks between him and the plant. "You're really trying hard, aren't you?"

"I've never bought a plant before."

She waits a beat before relenting. "Fine, come in. Stop cluttering up the corridor."

He looks so grateful, she wants to laugh, but that wouldn't really be appropriate.

In the hallway, he sniffs the air as they get closer to the kitchen. "You made coffee?"

"You don't have to pretend to like my coffee, Noone. You've done enough." She pours them both mugs, but when she hands his over, she pauses. "I'm still angry."

"Okay," he says cautiously.

"But I don't want to rehash it right now."

"Okay." He's more relieved.

"Sit down and show me your Axedale notes."

Once they're situated in their respective spots—Noone on the lounge chair and herself on the sofa—Nomi gestures "gimme" and he hands her the notepad. She sips from her mug and scans through his spiky scrawl. He hasn't done a terrible job as her quote-unquote "research assistant," although there are some gaps she'd like to fill.

"This is a good start, but we might need a little more detail." She sits back and crosses her legs, examining the notes. "I'd like to know who she hangs out with. We should see if she pops up on the society pages."

"Axedale seems very conservative." Noone leans forward with his mug, forearms on his knees. "Very proper etiquette."

"Twinset-and-pearls type, right. Well, she did go to Harvard." Nomi grimaces. She waves the notepad, making the pages flutter. "So what has Galetti got on her that's made her bend over?"

"Maybe he doesn't have anything. Maybe it's a direct threat."

"She's a lawyer and a former senator—I imagine she's been exposed to threats before."

"She's got three kids in their twenties."

Could that be a possibility? "What are their names?"

"Charles, Marion, and David." Noone settles back, finally looking more relaxed. "No Jeremy, sorry. But maybe it's the husband—an affair, a business scandal."

"You bought me a hoya," Nomi says suddenly.

The plant is sitting on the coffee table, where Noone placed it before he sat down. It's a small specimen, clearly propagated from a cutting, but it's already got some nice leaf growth, variegated and glossy. The tube is sitting in a little puddle of Saran wrap, which appears to have been wreathed around the base so Noone could transport it.

"You were upset last night. I'm sorry I upset you. I'm sorry I screwed up." Noone scratches the bridge of his nose. She wouldn't say he looks penitent, but his eyes have gone softer. "I don't know what a hoya is. I don't know anything about houseplants. You want a plant in Piedras Negras, you just step outside the door and—"

"You freak me out." Nomi clutches her mug.

"Okay." He seems to be mentally debating how to phrase his response. His words come out halting. "I don't . . . always have great control over how my condition manifests. But I didn't exactly cover myself in glory last night. Again, I apologize."

"I put you on the spot at the club." Her admission is a peace offering. "And it *was* really good to have backup—I wouldn't have gotten the information from Janice or Max without you."

He opens out his hand. "I'll try to do better?"

Nomi sighs, stands up. "Okay, come on. I got some more stuff from my ex-partner today about Lamonte's guys—let's see if we can figure out which dots connect."

Chapter Seventeen

October 1987, Thursday

Simon is on his 7:00 a.m. break at work. He's already eaten a corned beef sandwich in the employees' room, and he's now drinking coffee out of a thick white ceramic mug while having a cigarette with other workers in the alley beside Gennaro's. The alley is dark, the external walls dripping with slimy condensation. The location is insalubrious, it's noisy with the factory air-conditioning, and there's only milk crate seating, but this is still somehow the most enjoyable cigarette Simon smokes all day.

Mike Nell pushes his mustached face, then his entire stocky self, out through the plastic strips in the staff doorway. "Noone? A word."

Simon doesn't like the sound of that, but he walks over. "Something else you need me for?"

"Not exactly." Nell's face is impassive. "Some fella came around last night asking about you. Said he owed you money, but I didn't believe it."

Simon finds a smooth, cold pit has opened up in the middle of his stomach. "That's good to know."

"Look, I'm not gonna ask if you're in trouble, because I honestly don't give a shit. But if you're planning on skipping town or something, do me a favor and let me know so it doesn't fuck up the roster."

"I'm not skipping town," Simon says immediately. "If I have to take a break, I'll tell you."

"Good," Nell says. "I hate having to deal with new hires. Also, you're the best cutter I've got for the morning slot, and I'll be pissed off to lose you."

"If that guy comes again—"

"Don't worry, I know how to say 'fuck off.'" Nell turns and walks back to whatever he was doing.

Simon strides home after his shift, mulling things over. So here it is: the inevitable consequence of his own stupid actions on Tuesday night. Wonderful. He'd even given Ameche his name. What on earth had he been *thinking*?

There was no thought, *you didn't* think, *you just acted*—Nomi's words from their very first meeting roll back, hammer home. Simon feels like the worst kind of fool.

He checks the lobby of the tenement, and the stairs as he climbs them. There's no one lurking on Nomi's floor or his own. He lets himself into his apartment, closes the door, flips the deadbolt. If Nomi's trick with the lock picking tools is anything to go by, the deadbolt isn't a serious obstacle for someone trying to break in, but unfortunately, it's all he's got.

Simon strips out of his boots and clothes, takes a shower. This situation reminds him so much of his first years of recovery in Guatemala: this impulsivity, the lack of self-control, the urge to lean into his instincts, despite being shown again and again that his instincts could be wrong. So many times, he would come to and find himself standing somewhere—outside at the edge of the forest, inside a room of the clinic house—and Flores would take his elbow gently and say, "Whatever you are seeing, it is not there, my friend. Close your eyes and reach out your hand. Touch the tree trunk. Touch the tabletop. That is solid. That is real."

Simon assumed he'd learned this lesson, but like everything these days, he has to learn it again: that his memories and instincts and thoughts aren't always reliable, that even his senses aren't always reliable. That *he* isn't reliable.

He crawls back into bed, sets his alarm, and in this state of mental agitation, falls asleep and dreams again.

The details might shift, but the dream never changes: A girl with white hair . . . A suffocating whirlpool that sweeps him away . . . His limbs won't move, his whole body heavy . . . He's drowning, a crown of white daisies on his head, water flooding his nose and mouth, blocking his ears, turning his eyes into pearls—

Simon jerks awake.

It's one thirty. He's overslept. He must've slapped off his alarm; he doesn't remember. His head is rattling, but at least he's not in pain. He finds clothes to dress and goes to the kitchen, scratching at his hair. Drinks coffee by the window, peering between the curtains to observe people on the street.

It would be great, Simon reflects, if he could rewind Tuesday night like a video movie and scrub out the part with Ameche on the stairs. The damage to his relationship with Nomi has been repaired, but it's still left both of them exposed, maybe left other tenants in this building exposed as well, including Sofia Rosa. Brittany Jackson is already in danger, but she may also suffer blowback.

Listing all the potential disastrous consequences proves fairly depressing; instead, Simon tries to consider solutions. But unless he includes things like homicide, or fleeing New York City, his options appear to be limited.

If this were Guatemala, things would be more straightforward. The year before he left, a man in a neighboring village had stolen a pig and a dozen chickens from the local market, assaulting the woman who owned the chicken stall. The woman's relatives, as well as their friends and other stallholders, had gathered together, found the man, beaten him half to death, and set his house on fire. That is how you handle matters in Guatemala, but Simon suspects that natural justice may not cut it here in America.

At about two o'clock, he gives up on ruminating and goes downstairs to see his landlady and give her a pound of ground beef.

"Ah, this is good." Sofia Rosa has a cigarette in the side of her mouth as she slaps the paper-wrapped package, testing for firmness. "You are doing good things, Simón—you give me mincemeat, you help No-mee. Many good things."

"I don't know, Auntie." He leans against the doorjamb. "I think I did a very stupid thing on Tuesday night. The man who attacked Nomi here, outside her apartment . . . I saw him at the nightclub."

"You had a fight?" Sofia Rosa's eyes are round; she looks thrilled.

"Yes, I'm afraid so."

His landlady shrugs, walks over to put the package in her refrigerator. "Well, I am glad you fought him. Any man would have this reaction, to defend his people."

"Yes, but this man I fought, he is part of the mafia," Simon admits.

"Ohhh." Sofia Rosa stubs out her cigarette in a tin ashtray on the side table, smooths back her hair. "Yes, this is a problem. Now you are not the hero, yes? You are the young man tener mecha corta, who is quick to anger."

"Yes, this is it. And he knows my name."

"Hm, yes, this requires some discussion." Sofia Rosa frowns and nods, removing her apron and hanging it on a hook, straightening her blouse. She collects her purse and a newspaper folded to the entertainment section. "We will talk about it as we walk."

Simon is confused. "We are walking somewhere, Auntie?"

"Of course! Because I will discuss this problem with you, and you will take me here, to the cinema in this advertisement." She shows him the advertisement in the newspaper, gathers her coat.

Which is how Simon finds himself escorting Sofia Rosa to the Bleecker Street Cinema, to see a 4:00 p.m. showing of a film called *Singin' in the Rain.* The film is a musical, and Simon quite enjoys it. His landlady moves at a steady shuffle, and she also wants to stop at a small delicatessen on the way, so it takes them a while to go and come back. But while he and Sofia Rosa spend time in discussion, much of that time involves covering old ground: His landlady has long-standing concerns about certain tenants in their building and disputes with other residents on Gansevoort Street. Simon's not feeling hugely enlightened about the problem with Claude Ameche when they finally make it back to the tenement.

Nelson is playing pop music again on the second floor, but aside from that, there's still no disturbance in or around the building. Once he's inside his apartment, Simon switches on some lights, puts on the Sibelius cassette, makes himself dinner—steak, coleslaw, a glass of the merlot. After he's eaten, he opens one of his windows to let in some air as he sits by the sill, smoking and finishing his wine.

The sun has set; night has descended. Out the window, light from the streetlamps reflects off a sign and the roofs of parked cars. Across Gansevoort, a pale pink curtain blows from a fire escape on the third floor; hookers call to each other on the street, raucous and risqué.

This weekend will mark the two-month anniversary of Simon's arrival in this country. He should feel comforted by that. He's here, he has a job, he's fitting in. He hasn't been picked up by the immigration police. But he also hasn't found a useful occupation apart from work. His search for himself provided some structure, but now Nomi has taken over that search.

Being at loose ends isn't healthy. It gives him too much time to retreat into his head.

Maybe your soul will remember. Despite Flores's fantasy, Simon tried hard not to have any expectations about America. But part of him still clung to the idea that he'd arrive here and the cogs in his head would align, and everything would return. That he'd find his real home, and slot back into his old life like he was a missing piece of clockwork.

Of course, it was never going to be that simple.

Sick of listening to his own internal monologue and plagued by a fidgety unease, Simon pulls on his boots and grabs his coat to go for a walk. But when he yanks open his apartment door, Nomi is standing on the other side—black jeans, black jacket, black beanie, fist raised.

"Hi." She seems taken aback, as if he interrupted her as she was composing herself. "I was, uh, just about to knock."

"So I see. Hi."

She spies the coat in his hand. "You were going out?"

"No. I mean, yes. But no." Good god. She looks confused, and he can hardly blame her. "I was just going for a walk. What do you need?"

"Look, you probably won't love this idea, but how would you feel about coming to the Riverview with me?"

"What's the Riverview?"

"Another nightclub?" Nomi winces. "I know, you're probably allergic to nightclubs now. But this isn't really a club, it's more of a hangout, and I need to talk to someone there."

"A bartender again?"

"A drug dealer." She tries to sweeten the deal. "You don't have to dress up. But we have to go now, because Mischa doesn't stick around past midnight."

He agrees to accompany her, purely on the reasoning that going to the Riverview can't be worse than staying at home on his own.

Out on the sidewalk, the district nightlife has bloomed into full flower. Nomi greets the two Latine sex workers on the corner as she ushers him into a left turn at Washington and continues explaining her plans for the evening. "Ricki was delivering drugs to Solange and this Jeremy guy, right? So I'm thinking, who's become the supplier since Ricki died? That's what I'm hoping Mischa or someone else will know."

"Presumably Lamonte has more than one gofer," Simon suggests.

"Or he could be hiring. Either way, someone's got to be delivering those drugs. Who are they, and where are they picking up their supply?" She stomps along awhile before glancing his way. "Listen—I read your journals."

"Ah." Simon tries to make the momentary wobble in his gait seem natural.

"The first one was a little rambling."

He keeps his voice bland. "That was my first year of recovery, so my brain was very fuzzy."

Everything was fuzzy. His head hurt constantly. His eyes hurt. He was in a continuous state of low-level misery and anxiety: losing time, losing faces and names, things swimming back, then disappearing again. His thoughts and emotions floated in a haze of medication, like they'd been muffled in layers of spiderweb.

"It did have a kind of Hunter S. Thompson vibe." Nomi glances at him to see if he understands the reference. "It was very stream of consciousness."

"As in, information streaming in and out of my consciousness in no coherent order." He can be dry about it, but it's still stressful to remember.

Nomi waits for a car to pass as they cross Horatio Street. "Things got better your second year. But you still had a few . . . episodes."

He snorts. "That's a very diplomatic way of putting it. Do you mean the convulsions, or—"

"You piled all the stuff together in your room and tried to set it on fire." Nomi ticks things off the list. "You continued to see people and objects that weren't there. You tried to strangle a man who came to Flores's clinic. Isolated incidents. Most of the time you were normal. But every now and again, it would be like your electric circuits malfunctioned."

"That's basically what a brain is—a bunch of electric circuits. And mine were glued back together in some kind of random order." A cab goes by with a length of tinsel dangling from the radio antenna. Simon hates feeling like he's justifying himself, but he wants to give her some context, although she should know this from the journals. "Things have leveled out year on year since then. Flores used to say it would take time, and he was right."

They're approaching Moore's Wholesale Meats, and a number of people on Jane Street are wearing fancy outfits, walking toward the hotel.

There's a strong smell of exhaust and also a whiff of pot. The evening temperature is dropping; Simon realizes he forgot to bring a scarf.

Nomi's dark eyes dart toward him, all the metal in her ears glinting in the night. "But you still don't really know what your normal state looks like."

"Sure." He thinks he should probably just say this without thinking too much about it. "I mean, maybe I'm not malfunctioning. Maybe I was just a really messed-up person in my old life, and now when I get, uh, dysregulated, I'm working as the manufacturer intended."

Nomi, her black beanie jammed down, doesn't answer at first. Then she stops in the street and sighs. "Simon, I've run your prints."

That brings him to a dead halt. "What? Wait, where did you get my fingerprints?" It comes to him, then. "The coffee mug."

"Yeah," she admits. "The coffee mug from the time you slept in my living room."

That was days ago, well before the incident at Big Mouth. Has she been holding onto his prints since then, like some kind of insurance policy? He feels ripped off. "We talked about this. I said I wanted to stay under the radar—"

"And you're still under the radar," Nomi reassures. Her breath is warm enough—and tonight's air is sufficiently cold—to create small clouds when she speaks. "I told my ex-partner that I found fingerprints at a scene and I'm trying to eliminate scene contamination. The channels I use, nobody is going to do follow-up checks or pass information along to immigration. Listen, you want to find out, right? And after Tuesday night . . . I kind of want to find out."

That stings. He's stung. He thought things were okay between them. He looks away down the street. "So if my fingerprints get a hit, it means I'm on some police database?"

Hands shoved into her pockets, Nomi gives a short nod. "Yes. It'll show whether you have an existing criminal record in America, or were arrested and fingerprinted in America prior to being charged with a criminal offense."

"Will I show up in the system if I'm not a criminal?"

"Well, there's a couple reasons you might show up, but I guess being a criminal is the main one." Nomi scuffs at the pavement with the toe of her boot. "If we do get a hit, it'll probably be a double-edged sword."

"We'll have some answers, but we may not like what those answers will be." It's a solemn thought.

She tries to keep things positive. "At least you'll have some certainty. You'll know who you are. And if your prints hit, and you have a criminal charge in your background, you probably want to know what that is, right?"

He wants to say "That depends," but the words stick in his throat.

Nomi goes on. "Look, the criminal database is a pretty broad church. Maybe you boosted a car when you were a teenager. Maybe you got busted for shoplifting or something."

"And if I don't have a criminal charge? I'm not wild about the idea of my prints being added to the system." He wonders if she's forgotten the risks. She's not the one walking around with fake papers.

"Like I said, your prints won't be going to immigration. Either way, the best idea would be to not get arrested anytime in the future—which, you know, I'd probably recommend that as a general life strategy anyway."

"Don't get arrested, huh?" Simon makes a grimace. "Well, Claude Ameche was checking up on me at Gennaro's last night, so I can't make any promises."

Nomi straightens, alarmed. "Ameche went after you at work?"

"My supervisor gave me a heads-up about it. I guess it was inevitable—Ameche knows who I am, he knows where you live, he's seen us together."

They both just hold that in silence for a moment. Yes, it's Simon's fuckup that's brought this judgment down. But maybe Nomi's lines of investigation were always going to draw fire. Either way, they're going to have to figure out a solution together.

Nearby, a group of partygoers breaks into laughter. There are weeds on the sidewalk here, sticking up through gaps in the concrete. Up ahead, a six-story apartment building just before the Riverview Hotel.

"Okay, we should talk about that a bit more," Nomi suggests. "But let's do this first."

"Nomi?" Simon looks at her directly. "Will you get the results of the fingerprint search tonight?"

"I don't know. Maybe." She looks as apprehensive as he does. "As soon as I know, I'll tell you. Are you still okay to come with me?"

The idea that he might find out who he is tonight gives him a seasick feeling. Simon takes a deep breath. *Stop worrying about the man you were. Concentrate on being the man you want to become.* This might not be the big deal he's built it up to be. The search might turn up nothing, right?

"Yeah," he says. "Yeah, of course I'm okay to come with you."

"Good. Thank you. All right, let's go."

Simon's walked past the Riverview a couple times as he's explored the village, but he's never seen the redbrick octagonal tower at night before. The entry facade is lit up, the columns glowing yellow and pink. On the sidewalk, near the wrought iron banister at the foot of the grand front stairs, clusters of men gather, walk off, waving or shouting at friends across the street. A thirtysomething guy in shiny sweatpants, a leopard-spotted shirt, and a Day-Glo headband loiters between a dumpster and a fire hydrant.

"There's Mischa," Nomi says. "Hold still here—give me a second."

She walks over to talk to Day-Glo-headband man. Simon finds a spot to lean his butt against the railing for the external stairs to the basement, where he can watch passersby and smoke a cigarette. Nomi and her drug dealer friend make a subtle exchange, make conversation. There's the sound of a car horn honking farther up the block. Music is faint in the background. A few people ascend the stairs to the Riverview lobby.

Mischa strolls off toward West Street, and Nomi wanders back. "Hey, I have to go inside."

"You didn't get what you needed?"

"I did, but Mischa said my friend Enrique wants to see me. It's a film screening, so it won't be too crazy. Let's go up."

At the top of the Riverview stairs, the lobby area has some nice tiling and decorative lamps and balcony railings. There's faint whooping and tinkling piano behind a heavy door, but it doesn't seem like there's a dance party going on. To the right of the lobby, a reception desk. Nomi explains what's happening to the heavily made-up blond kid behind the counter, who's snapping gum.

"Enrique's already changed into Eureka backstage." The blond receptionist has a strong New Jersey accent. "You just want to dash in and talk?"

"Yeah, I don't want to stay for the whole movie," Nomi says.

"Okay, no problem." But as Nomi and Simon walk for the door, the receptionist waves. "Hold up, honey—you can't go in. It's Ladies' Night."

Simon raises his eyebrows, points at his chest. "You mean me?"

"Oh shit. Sorry, Cherie, I totally forgot." Nomi turns to Simon to explain. "Ladies' Night is just femmes."

"Femmes, femme boys, ladyboys, drag queens, dolls . . ." The receptionist gestures at Simon as she lights her cigarette. "Unless you've got a little black dress tucked somewhere in your jacket pocket that you can change into, I can't let you in."

"I can go in on my own," Nomi says. "Noone, you can just stay here in the lobby. I won't be long."

"Are you sure?" Simon's not entirely comfortable with letting her walk into the place alone.

"It's the Riverview. And come on, you're only pretending to be my security anyway."

"Hey, I take offense at that."

Cherie grins, eyes Simon up and down. "Will you pretend to be *my* security?"

Simon isn't convinced. "Nomi, listen, Ameche's lurking around the district, and you were attacked outside your own apartment—"

"Really?" Cherie turns to Nomi, appalled. "Oh, honey."

"I'm fine," Nomi reassures, before addressing Simon again. "Eureka will be in there, she'll look out for me. I promise it's all good—this is only going to take me, like, literally five minutes. You stay here with Cherie. I'll be right back."

She strides over to the heavy door, yanks it open. The inside of the space beyond is very dark, and Simon sees a glimpse of a big sheet screen lit up with scenes from a colorful film before the door closes again.

"What film are they watching?" he asks, curious.

"*The Wizard of Oz*," Cherie replies. "Everyone likes the classics, you know?"

"I went to see *Singin' in the Rain* today," Simon notes, offhanded.

"Oh, down at Bleecker Street?" Cherie seems delighted. "Wasn't it fabulous? I could watch Gene Kelly dance all day, what a man."

Simon leans on the reception counter, trying to let go of his edginess around Nomi's absence, but Cherie clearly notices his level of distraction.

"You're really Nomi's security? And that thing with her eye—she was beat up outside her apartment?" Cherie gestures with a finger at her own eyebrow. "That's so screwed up. Who would want to do that to Nomi? She's a peach."

"She's in a dangerous line of work." Simon glances through the main lobby doors, looking down the stairs at the street outside.

"Oh, honey, I *know*. I keep telling her. Last week, I was like, 'Sweetie . . .'"

"Do you get a lot of police around here?" Simon interrupts. "Because a squad car just pulled up on the other side of Jane Street, near the West Street corner."

"Oh fuuuck." Cherie throws back her head and groans. "Not again!"

"'Not again' what?"

But Cherie has already opened the little door on the side of the reception office and emerged into the lobby. She goes to the lobby doors and closes them, locks them at the bottom with a sliding bolt.

"We get a raid here, like, every couple months or so . . . Honey, can you get that top bolt for me? Anyway, it's boring, but you know how it is."

Simon assists with the top bolt. "You just lock the main doors?"

"That's only to give us some time. Can you maybe go and poke your head into the ballroom, let Marilyn at the door know that there's a raid? Thank you so much."

Simon can see uniformed police officers approaching, crossing the street to reach the hotel. Nomi's words—*The best idea would be to not get arrested anytime in the future*—ring urgently in his ears, but he does as requested and strides over to the ballroom entry. The heavy door is covered in black felt. Inside the doorway, there's a woman in a crop top and a tight skirt—presumably this is Marilyn.

"Hi," he says. "Sorry to intrude, but Cherie at reception said to tell you there's about to be a raid."

"Oh great," Marilyn sighs.

Across the other side of the room, Simon spots Nomi, her figure lit in profile by a flash of green smoke on-screen. She's talking to a statuesque drag queen in a long black wig, with a feathered mermaid bra and a fishnet skirt and long purple gloves. Nomi's holding a document envelope of some kind.

He needs to get her attention; they need to get out of here. "Nomi!"

"*RAIIIIIID!*" Marilyn yells to the whole room.

Nomi turns and sees him at the exact moment four dozen femmes and drag queens erupt into startled chaos in a darkened room against a background of dramatic *Wizard of Oz* music and unkind lens flare. There's squeals and screams, and a mass exodus toward the doorway Simon's standing in.

"Oh shit," he mutters.

He steps farther into the entry, only to be pushed back by Marilyn. "Oh my god, you can't *come in*. We need to be getting *out*."

"But I only want to—" He loses Nomi for a second. "Nomi!"

People converge on the entryway. Simon ducks to the side, separated from Nomi by a flooding river of glamorously dressed patrons. Across the divide, he sees Nomi hold up the document envelope and mouth something at him: It looks like "You're fine." The drag queen in the mermaid bra is pulling on Nomi's arm; Nomi mimes that she'll exit through the back of the ballroom.

Pushed and shoved from six different directions, Simon lets himself be swept back into the lobby, where he finds Cherie over in the corner. She's opened one side of the lobby door. Now she's watching the wave of people dressed in feather boas and bouffant wigs and corsets and some truly amazing earrings spill down the hotel's stairs, overwhelming the four police officers trying to come up.

It's madness; Simon almost wants to laugh. And he's remembering his glimpses of Nomi in the ballroom, holding up the document envelope. *You're fine.* Is that it? The results of the fingerprint search? Does that mean . . . Does that mean everything's okay? Maybe he has no criminal record. Or maybe he's got a record, but it's for something innocuous. Boosting cars. Shoplifting.

Either way, Nomi's got his file. She's got his name—his real name.

"Hey! Hey!" Cherie waves at him to get his attention. She's standing at a skinny side door, opened to show dimness beyond. "Come out this way!"

In the absence of other options, Simon chooses Mystery Door A.

Chapter Eighteen

October 1987, Thursday

Eureka—Enrique, in daily life—grabs Nomi's hand and pulls her toward the backstage of the ballroom, bypassing the pile of abandoned couches and chairs set up for the movie night. The room is in uproar, and people are moving everywhere.

"Come on—the cops'll search at least as far as the kitchen because they're such *busybodies*," Eureka groans, rolling her eyes.

Behind the white sheet hung as a temporary screen, there's a proscenium stage with narrow doors on each side. They hustle through the one on the left, up a short set of stairs, then down again on the other side, through the Riverview's rabbit warren access halls. Fluorescent bar lights overhead make the green paint and beige linoleum look dingy. A cat near the baseboard in the hall scurries away as Eureka rushes Nomi onward.

The echoing sound of chaos filters from the ballroom, but they've reached the Riverview's kitchen, which has a **FIRE EXIT** sign over the door and a tangle of metal and Formica benchtops. Eureka leads a winding route through the room. A half dozen giant stainless steel pots are suspended near the industrial stoves, where a shirtless guy in California beach shorts and flip-flops is stirring a small pot of noodles over a gas flame.

He looks over, curious. "What's happening out there?"

"Another raid!" Eureka exclaims.

"Fucking great," the guy groans.

Eureka beckons toward a door to a corridor. Nomi follows, clutching the document envelope, feeling like she's holding a hot coal in her hand.

Mischa said that Enrique wanted to see her, which could only mean info from Irma. They met up at the side of the ballroom as the movie played, their conversation largely drowned out by the chorus of *Wizard of Oz* dialogue recital going on.

"Okay, here's your thing from Irma." Eureka swung her long hair back to access an oversize plastic tote slung at her shoulder. "She said it was a dead file. Do you know what that means?"

"Yeah, I know." Nomi felt a worm of misgiving in her gut. A dead file is an inactive file—a closed case kept for historic, legal, or administrative reasons, or a police investigation closed because the perpetrator died.

"Well, it sounds kinda morbid," Eureka pointed out. "But anyway, it's all yours."

"Thanks." Nomi took the plain brown document envelope: not thick, but not a single sheet of paper either.

Then the raid happened, and there was no time to think. But now, Nomi feels slightly sick. Noone knows she has the document; she saw his eyes widen from across the room when she held up the envelope and yelled, *"Your file!"* She's just not sure he's ready for what these pages might reveal.

What will he do with this information she has in her hand? Not having an identity, not having a home, is the mystery at the center of his life. Maybe he's a felon. Maybe he's a cop; it's not out of the realm of possibility. Maybe he has a past she can't even imagine—parents and siblings who've been searching for him, a fiancée who loves him.

Maybe *she's* not ready for what these pages will reveal either.

They've navigated the tight, grimy corridor and reached a door, once painted white, that's secured with a dead bolt. Eureka roots in her tote, pulls out a bundle of fabric. "Hold my bag while I put this on?"

"Sure." Nomi manhandles the tote and the envelope. "Thanks for getting me out."

"Can't leave you behind for the Keystone Kops, amirite?" Eureka winks, straightens her arms through the sleeves of a lightweight denim coat. She ties the belt, takes back her bag. "Nomi, you did your time in the Tenth Precinct—you don't need to be dealing with those guys now you're free. Okay, here we go."

She flips the dead bolt, pulls hard to encourage the damp-warped wood to yank out of its frame, and suddenly they're at the top of a short staircase that leads to the back alley between the Riverview and Horatio Street. It's briskly cold, after their sweaty escape; they've walked back into the night. At ground level, there's the smell of garbage and standing water, and a metallic scent like old radiators. In the distance, Nomi hears the whoop of a siren.

She shakes her head. "Why do they keep up these busts? Captain McKee from the Sixth must know it's a waste of time."

Eureka shrugs. "Mayor Koch said clean up the gays, so McKee's gotta show he's ticking the boxes, right?"

"Crazy."

"It is what it is. And Nomi, look, I know Irma misses you, but I'm glad you're on our side now. It feels like you've made a place here in the Village. Word on the street is that you're helping one of the working girls get her kid back—no, don't ask me how I know, I just do. But it's a good thing, honey. You're doing good work. I don't know if you hear that much, but it's true."

"Thank you for saying that. I mean, I try." Nomi hardly knows how to respond when, half the time, she feels like an ineffectual fraud. But if she can reunite Brittany and Solange, at least that'll count for something. She shoves that worry aside, holds up the envelope. "Are you sure Irma didn't give you anything else with this?"

"That was it. Hey, I'm gonna circle around and see if I can find Destiny and Skye and Georgina. Will you be okay to walk home by yourself from here?"

"Of course." Nomi shoos with her free hand. "Get outta here. Go find your girls. Sorry the movie night got ruined."

"Who said it's ruined?" Eureka grins, swoops in for an air-kiss. "Bye, baby girl. See you next time."

Eureka walks off toward Washington, kitten heels clicking on the cobblestones. Nomi looks around; they came out on the West Street side. She could walk back to Florent, get a coffee, read the file there. She could find Noone. They could read it together.

But she wants to know what the file contains. If it's bad, she wants to be prepared so she can manage Noone's reaction.

She heads for West Street, then turns left and walks as quickly as she can, crossing Jane Street and skirting the parking lot chain-link fence as she moves toward West Twelfth. The commotion outside the main entrance of the Riverview has attracted a small crowd; some of the taxi drivers and hookers from the highway have even wandered over. Nomi is walking in the other direction, and she makes it past the Superior Ink building, turns left again, finally reaches her destination: the bagel shop on Bethune Street.

It's nearly ten thirty, but the store never seems to close, and it's warm inside. Her nose is running a little from the cold. She orders a bagel and coffee, claims one of the tiny tables, uses a paper napkin from the dispenser on her nose.

Then she looks at the brown envelope on the table in front of her. Her mouth has flooded with an acidic taste, just like the moment before she unzips her yellow kit bag and reaches for her tools. She rubs her tongue over her teeth.

Okay, time to do this.

Nomi opens the flap and takes out the contents: a gray document wallet of a kind she's seen on law enforcement desks a million times. There's a yellow sticky note affixed to the front of the flimsy cardboard, the writing in Irma's curly cursive: *"Scene contamination for sure! Where did you get these prints?? Crazy."*

Oh shit, that's not good.

Nomi almost jumps when the server delivers her bagel and coffee. She somehow manages to both thank the guy and not bump the table and spill everything. Once the server's gone, she looks down at the gray wallet again. Her breathing has heightened. Her fingers feel cold.

She shakes them out, exhales. Opens up the wallet and removes the pages inside.

There are three pages. Prominently, on the uppermost page, pictures of Simon Noone's face from the front and in profile. He looks younger in the mug shots, his full lips tender, fringe flopping over one eye. And that's the first thing she learns—that he used to have white-blond hair.

The second thing she learns is that his name isn't Simon Noone.

Chapter Nineteen

October 1987, Friday

It's not until after his work shift ends—nearly midday on Friday—that Simon realizes Nomi is avoiding him.

After he and Cherie shared coffee and cigarettes in her cramped apartment, waiting out the police, he spent literally hours last night trying to find Nomi: walking home, knocking at her apartment, checking at Florent, returning to the Riverview to try again there . . . He even walked up to Hector's to see if she was at the counter. But she was nowhere. It was maddening.

Nomi had his file. The answers were right there, in her hands. Not to mention that he was worried about her: Cherie reassured him that Eureka/Enrique was not a wuss and would do a good job as substitute protection detail, but Simon still felt a responsibility.

By the time he finally made it back to his apartment, he'd run out of ideas for places to search and felt a dragging exhaustion. It was after midnight; he had work in three hours. Giving up didn't feel like a choice. Simon smoked one last cigarette at the window, then undressed and went to bed, hoping Nomi wasn't in serious trouble or—potentially worse—really pissed at him.

During his shift at Gennaro's, he tried to sink into the orderly precision of the cutting, the cool, clean smell of the meat, the calming piped music; it worked for a while. He discovered there'd been no reports of strangers lurking and throwing his name around, so at least that was something.

But back home at midday, Sofia Rosa stands waiting for him outside her door on the ground floor.

"Simón?" She waves him over. "I have a message for you from No-mee. She visits me this morning."

"Really?" He wipes his face with the sleeve of his jacket. "You saw her? Is she okay? I tried to—"

"No-mee says to tell you that she is all right." Sofia Rosa wipes her hands and fishes a handful of peanuts out of the pocket of her apron. She begins cracking peanut shells. "She said she has errands to run and she will see you soon. She will visit with you soon."

"She . . ." He's at sea. "She has errands to run?"

"Sí, yes, this is what she tells me." His landlady nibbles a few peanuts. "Do you want some peanuts? I have a pound of peanuts. Do you want coffee?"

"I don't—" He stops himself. "Sofia Rosa, when did you see Nomi? When did she give you this message?"

"Oh, I don't know, maybe eight or nine o'clock?"

"This morning?"

"Sí, this morning." Sofia Rosa finishes with the peanuts, puts the shells in her apron pocket and dusts off her palms. "She has come to me herself, and told me she—"

"You saw her in person? She looked all right?"

"Yes, of course," his landlady confirms. "Of course she is all right. She is looking fine."

"Okay," he says, and that's when he realizes.

Nomi has not been abducted by Claude Ameche. Nomi is fine. She has his file. But she has not knocked on his door to talk with him about it. She has not slipped him a note. She has not given him reassurance of any kind. She has not tried to seek him out in any way. In fact, all the evidence seems to point toward the idea that she is actively avoiding him.

None of these signs are good.

Simon goes to his apartment, showers, takes two Vicodin for a low-but-ramping headache, lies on his bed.

His file must be bad.

He tries to get his head around this. But then why did Nomi mouth "You're fine!" at him last night? None of this makes sense. His file is bad. Like, how bad? How bad can a file for a good-with-knives, good-at-tailing-people, multiple-language-speaking, prone-to-violence person be? Okay, maybe it can be pretty bad.

What did I do? What did I do? He must have asked Flores that question a hundred times during his recovery, imagining the doctor thought his mind too fragile to handle the truth. Every time, Flores would answer, "You've done nothing, my friend. You've simply had an accident. You will get better soon, and all this confusion will fade."

Flores thought Simon was a medical trainee—but maybe he's something less altruistic. Maybe he's a drug smuggler. Maybe he's an assassin. Honestly, with his skill set, "trained professional assassin" might be a best-case outcome, right? So is Nomi avoiding him because she's nervous about telling him what's in the file, or nervous about being around him?

There are other lingering concerns. Nomi is walking around the district unescorted—although she's not an idiot, she has a weapon, and she has, in any case, been doing this job for a long time before Simon's faux-security arrival, a point she's tried to make with him on a number of previous occasions. There's also been no further movement from Ameche. Simon tries to factor that as a net good but can't help thinking of it as an ominous quiet.

He wonders if he should be going out once more to knock at Nomi's apartment door, search around for her again. Because that worked so well last night. Goddammit.

In the end, the Vicodin and his raw tiredness work on him, and he falls asleep. By the time he wakes, at two in the afternoon, the uncertainty is twisting him inside out.

He pulls on his boots and coat, tries Nomi at her apartment again—no dice. Could she just be not answering for *him*? That's quite a concept. Then he thinks of a potential strategy when he sees the small blue card taped to her door. He digs a pen from his coat pocket, writes Nomi's phone number on the back of his hand, goes downstairs and out, and walks to the pay phone outside Perrotta's deli grocery.

Simon tries calling the number. No answer. Gets his change back, tries once more.

Nothing, nothing, nothing.

So she's really not at home. Now what?

He walks back to Florent and gets a coffee, sits outside on the metal chairs to think. Could his file be in her apartment? He can almost visualize it: that brown document envelope she was holding last night, just lying there on the desk in her tiny office . . .

He taps his spoon on the side of his demitasse, angles his chair. Squints up, examining the side of their tenement. If he used the fire escape to break into Nomi's apartment, would anyone see him from the street? Does he even care if he's seen?

Simon finishes his coffee and his cigarette, walks back to the tenement and takes the stairs to the third floor, lets himself in. There are three windows in his apartment; the one farthest left, near his bed, has the attached fire escape. He hangs up his coat and goes to the bathroom for some more medication, then to the kitchen, where he finds the tools he thinks he'll need and puts them in his back pocket.

Then he walks over, unlocks the window and opens it, climbs out.

He hasn't been outside on the fire escape before. The metal grille clangs under his boots, and the pavement seems a long way down. Rusted paint is coagulated on the metal bolts. The hardware securing the fire escape to the external wall of the tenement is loose, and the whole thing seems fairly flimsy. But he's committed now, and if he's going to do this, he needs to just move fast and not think about it.

Is he going to do this? It's a profound invasion of Nomi's space and privacy.

And yet.

Simon squeezes around the fire escape rail and goes backward down the metal stairs. Ducks under the brackets welded to the rampway he's just descended. Nobody seems to be watching him at ground level from the sidewalk; it's almost like people in NYC try to ignore what's going on with their neighbors. Incredible.

Now he's facing the window that sees into Nomi's office. And there it is, almost exactly like he imagined: The document envelope lies to one side of her desk, discarded. On the blotter, a gray cardboard wallet with a yellow sticky note on top. That's got to be his file.

His file. His name, his past, his identity.

There's rust on his hands; Simon wipes it on his jeans without thinking. Looking at the window, it seems like the same double-hung arrangement as the windows in his own apartment. He'd use the same technique to break into either of them: Rather than disable the latch, Simon uses the butter knife he took from his kitchen drawer and removes the beading around one of the small glass panels in the upper window. With so much weather damage, the beading breaks away from the wooden casement quite easily. Then he only has to pull out a few nails with his pliers and remove some old putty, and he's got the bottom left panel loose.

Now he can just remove the glass, reach inside and undo the latch, push up the window, and step over the frame into her apartment. The whole exercise takes him about five minutes.

Nomi's office is cramped and dark. Simon props the glass window panel on the floor against the wall, pulls down the blind, which makes the room darker still. He sets his housebreaking tools to one side.

There's a reading lamp on the corner of the desk, and he switches it on. Wipes the sweat off his palms onto his shirt. Picks up the gray document wallet.

He starts reading the file standing up, but as soon as he sees the mug shots, he sits down.

Chapter Twenty

October 1987, Friday

It's after sundown by the time Nomi makes it back to her apartment. Being at the tenement makes her nervous, but she's really sick of feeling like she hasn't got a home to go to. Fuck it—if Claude Ameche comes, let him come. If Simon Noone knocks at her door, let the cards fall where they may.

It's Friday, and she has other priorities.

She lets herself in, walks down the hall, dumps her tote and her leather jacket in the living room, backtracks to the bathroom. Grabs her kit bag and returns via the kitchen, where she collects a beer from the fridge. She's still got her holster on, and she's too impatient right now to take it off. Her whole body feels fragile. Her skin is tight, itching and humming, like she's a glass balloon stuffed full of angry bees.

The apartment is still dark, which suits her mood, but she needs a light to do this. Nomi moves a strand of spider plant aside, switches on the mellow standing lamp in the living room, sets up on the coffee table. Her skin feels grimy with sweat, but she'll feel better soon.

The Valium she bought from Mischa last night is still in the key pocket of her jeans, but again, it's not her priority right now. Her hands are shaking slightly. Preparing her tools—arrowhead, Kleenex, alcohol, dressing—only takes a minute, seems to take forever; this is the economy of time when you're about to perform the ritual. Once she's got everything laid out, she unbuckles her belt and tucks the hem of her T-shirt under the bottom edge of her bra, uncaps the rubbing alcohol; the acrid smell immediately brings a metallic-tasting wash into her mouth.

She's always tempted by her left arm, but those days are over. When the scarring got too bad, too noticeable, she got her first tattoo cover-up: Now inky flames and thorns and roses protect that space, warning her not to create further damage. Instead, she finds a piece of soft, unblemished skin near her belly button, just above the place from last Friday. She wipes it down, feels herself shiver, takes up the obsidian arrowhead's reassuring weight. Shoves her hair out of the way, holds her breath, makes two swift cuts—*yes* and *yes* . . .

As the blood springs out and a glittering euphoria slides through her body, she exhales deeper than she ever has in her life. Okay, now she feels better. Now she feels human.

Nomi lays her tool on the table and puts her head back. She's allowed to enjoy the rush of cutting but not rely on it. It's tempting to say, "I've had a hard day, I deserve this," but it's a trap she refuses to fall into. Cutting logic is to feel deserving every day, because every day is hard. That's a downward spiral to nowhere. She has appetites; she controls them. Otherwise, the appetites control you, and it'll be a cold day in hell before she lets herself be controlled again. She's fine about feeling relief, though: The last twenty hours have been a fucking nightmare.

Blood dribbles down into the waistband of her jeans in a warm leak, and it's absurdly peaceful. The buzzing inside her has settled. She feels focused, clear, with a kind of satisfied tiredness, like she's just gone for a long run. There's a mild sting, and she folds a Kleenex, presses it over the wound to settle it, pulls down her shirt.

As she leans forward to do the cleanup, a voice to her right says, "Were you ever going to tell me?"

Nomi jerks around and draws her Smith & Wesson in one motion.

In the gloomy living room light, Simon Noone stares along the barrel of her gun, along the taut length of her arm, right into her eyes. The suspension of sound and movement seems to stretch out to infinity.

Nomi remembers to breathe. She doesn't lower her weapon. "You broke in."

"Yes." He's in the doorway of her office. Dark chambray shirt, blue jeans, blue eyes, full lips just like the mug shots in the file. He's older now, but is he wiser? She's seen how fast he can move, but she doesn't think he can move faster than a bullet.

"It's impolite to sneak up on people."

"It's impolite to withhold personal information from a client."

"So we're both rude."

"Yes, we are." Noone blinks and repeats his question. "Were you ever going to tell me?"

Nomi holds for a few beats longer. But this confrontation was inevitable, and in the end, none of this matters. She releases the tension in her arm, uncocks the revolver, lowers it. Lets it thunk on the coffee table.

"Tell you what?" She continues cleaning up: wipes and dries her tool, shoves arrowhead, Kleenex, the bottle of rubbing alcohol into her kit bag with practiced rapidity, zips up. Her stomach is still bleeding; she licks a finger and jams it over the wound. "That I cut? It's really none of your—"

"That I'm a mass murderer."

He's washed out, his cheeks hollowed, posture stiff; it's not the loose, easy way he usually occupies space. He looks like he's in shock. But how can she tell what's real with him? She thinks of his panty-dropping grin at the bar, thinks of his face contorted in a snarl as he confronted Ameche on the stairs. She slaps a dressing on her cut, rearranges her shirt.

"You're not a mass murderer." Nomi realizes she needs to clarify. "That's more like when someone kills a whole lot of people in a spree event—"

"Jesus Christ." Noone scrubs his hair back with one hand.

"You killed a lot of people over about five years." There's no good way to say it.

"Simon Gutmunsson—" He stops, presses his lips together until they're white. "*Me.* I was a serial killer."

"Yes."

"Twenty-one people. I murdered twenty-one people."

"Including six law enforcement officers. Yes."

"That's why you've been avoiding me. Because I'm a serial killer."

"Yes." She pauses. "Also because I didn't know how to tell you."

"Okay, I need to sit down." He finds the brown lounge chair and drops into it.

The coffee table is clean now, but hanging above it, in the air between them, are all the words Nomi remembers from the file: "multiple victims" and "evisceration" and "dangerous" and "statewide search" and "most wanted" and . . .

There are a lot of words. None of them are good.

Still feeling the sting on her stomach and a mild high, she pushes her Schlitz toward him across the table. "You have this. I'll get another."

She knows he doesn't like beer, but apart from schnapps, that's all she's got. She stands and goes to the kitchen, fetches a second bottle of Schlitz from the refrigerator, sits back down on the sofa just as Noone takes a swig from his own bottle, shudders.

His voice comes out hoarse. "So where have you been hiding?"

"I waited until you went to work before I came back here," she admits. "I left you a message with Sofia Rosa so you wouldn't chase around after me."

"I got the message," he notes. "And I still chased around."

She's not going to apologize. "Today, I've mostly been at the library, getting verification and doing additional research."

"What other details did you find out?" His tone is dry, but the words are halting.

Nomi uses the edge of the coffee table to pop the cap on her beer. She doesn't need to consult her notes to give him a broad outline. "You came from a wealthy Massachusetts family—privileged life, educated in Europe . . . That's how you're fluent in the Romance languages. You started young. Eleven homicides before you were caught and tried as an adult in 1980. Insanity defense got you incarcerated in a hospital."

"I've been declared legally insane?" With each new revelation, he pales further.

She nods, short and once. "You participated in a juvenile-offender interview program run by the FBI in 1982. As a result, you were transferred to—and then escaped from—a Pennsylvania jail."

"Right."

She takes a swig from her beer. "You killed another ten people following your escape. Fled toward nonextradition Cuba, pursued by law enforcement. You were presumed dead after a confrontation near the Mexico-Guatemala border in November of that year."

He grips his bottle on his thigh. His other elbow is on the arm of the lounge chair, his fingers against his lips. "I did all this by the time I was twenty?"

There's only one explanation she can give him. "While imprisoned, you were diagnosed as a pure sociopath."

He blinks. "What does that mean?"

"It's a personality disorder. It usually manifests in early adolescence."

"What are the symptoms?"

"High impulsivity. Heightened sense of superiority. Propensity for violence." Each dot point sounds like a coffin nail being hammered in. "Deceptive and manipulative behavior. Disregard for morals and social norms. A fundamental lack of empathy."

There's another pause, longer and more weighted.

"Working as the manufacturer intended, huh?" His hopeless snort seems self-directed. Noone sips from his beer, clears his throat. "All that stuff you described—the murders, the imprisonment. I don't remember any of it. Not one bit."

"Your body seems to remember, though. The languages you speak are Gutmunsson's languages. The dreams you have of the girl with white hair—Gutmunsson had a sister, Kristin. There's a lot of his instincts in you. The way you dress, the way you . . . change."

"Being good at following people—it's a hunting pattern." He meets her eyes, stunned at the realization.

"Yes."

"The medical proficiency. And I have a job in a slaughterhouse, I know how flesh works." It's all coming together for him now. "Are you scared of me?"

"Should I be?" But she holds herself very still when she says that.

"I don't even know." He makes a short, desperate laugh. "Most people would say yes."

"I'm a little scared of you," she admits. Her body is tense. "I've seen you menace people. Examine a corpse. Manipulate a witness. I've seen you lose your shit."

"You haven't really seen me lose my shit." His eyes are dark, and the shadows from the lamp give him a peculiar gothic silhouette.

Nomi swallows. "Well, I don't know if I necessarily want to be beside you when it finally happens."

Noone looks around like he's lost. Then he raises the beer bottle to his lips and drinks, keeps drinking, until almost all the beer is gone. He leans forward and claps the bottle onto the coffee table; Nomi awards herself points for not flinching.

"You cut yourself on purpose?" he asks.

So now they're getting into this. "Only in certain ways, on certain days. I have rules."

"Only on weekends?"

"Fridays and Saturdays, yes."

"Why do you do it?"

She tries not to stiffen. Like everyone else, he's asking the wrong question. "Why do you take Vicodin?"

"For pain relief."

"It's the same thing."

"Is it?" His head tilts. "When did you start?"

That's the *right* question, which is surprising enough that she's jolted into a truthful answer. "Eleven years ago. After my mother passed."

"She was killed, wasn't she?" He pauses. "Was she killed by your father?"

His accuracy makes Nomi's hackles rise immediately. "Why do you say that?"

"You said your mother died. You said you escaped your father's religious community when you were a child. You refuse to use his surname."

Now she does feel herself stiffen. "So you're going to psychoanalyze me about it?"

He sighs, shoves at his hair. "Nomi, I don't even understand the contents of my own head—I'm hardly qualified to examine the contents of someone else's." He squints. "But cutting yourself . . . Where's the benefit in it? Do you get a high from it?"

She's not answering that. "I feel better afterward—calmer, more focused. You're a cutter, too, you should understand."

"I cut different things."

"Apparently so." Her voice is dry.

But now he's thought about it, his eyes narrow. "And I take a lot of Vicodin."

"Well, I have a lot of scars. So we both have something we need to deal with." She glances away, back. "You just have this . . . other something."

"The other something—right." He rubs his face with both hands. "Jesus Christ. I feel sick. So now what? Are you going to turn me in?"

As Irma would say, that's the million-dollar question.

"I've been trying to figure that out." Nomi leans and puts her own beer on the table. "You've done some helpful things. And apart from wailing on Claude Ameche, and a little light breaking and entering, you've been mostly law abiding."

"But you don't trust me."

How can he even *say* that? She wants to laugh, but this is his life, and her safety, and neither of those things is actually funny. Not to mention that there's so much other shit going on—an abducted girl she needs to find, mafia on her doorstep, local cops determined to make her life miserable. Taken in context, his statement is almost like parody. Once again, she's acutely aware that she can't read him, doesn't know him. That he's not the person she was starting to find tolerable, companionable even.

"Simon, you literally just broke into my apartment. On Tuesday, I saw you stab a guy. And I barely *know* you—you introduced yourself to me on the stairs out there just last week." She waves toward the world beyond her door, trying to make him see sense, before gesturing back at herself. "I mean, do you trust *me*? I'm a fucked-up ex-cop, making a living investigating the most sordid shit imaginable—"

"And you don't trust anybody," he says flatly. "Let alone an amnesiac serial killer."

"Can you *blame* me?" She stands abruptly, grabs their bottles and takes them to the kitchen to dump them on the benchtop, buckles her belt over the wound dressing on her stomach.

This whole thing feels bizarrely unfair—she's uncovered all these horrifying details about Simon Noone's life; now she's supposed to make a call on it? Condemn a guy to life in prison, when he can't remember anything about his existence before his catastrophic head injury? She didn't sign up to be judge and jury.

But the uncertainty is pressing on her. Is he safe to leave in the community? She knows about his past, but how much does she understand about his state of mind now? If his behavior at Big Mouth is any indication, that switch inside him can flip with very little provocation.

And on a purely selfish note, what's been biting her all day is how she's back to going solo. Part of her feels resigned, because that's the way it's supposed to be, but another part of her smarts. This isn't his fault; it's her own fault for letting her guard down. She still feels weirdly ripped off.

Her new wound chafes under the belt buckle; she presses a hand over the dressing as she turns to face him. "Look, when I first agreed to help you, you said you were hoping to find a way to make both halves of you join up."

His expression is arid. "Well, obviously that's not what I'm hoping *now*—"

"I kept my side of the bargain. I helped you figure out who you are."

"Do you think I'm dangerous?" he asks.

For god's sake. "What kind of fucking stupid question is that?"

Now his eyes are electric. "I think it's a very pertinent question, so I'll ask it again—do you think I'm dangerous?"

"Yes!" Her hands are fisted by her sides, and she's yelled the word. Now it echoes in the room around them. Simon's face is tight, but she can't put her reply back in her throat, shouldn't feel like she wants to. "Maybe not consciously—I don't know. But you have all these violent skills. You have no guardrails. And so far as I can see, you don't have any control over which fragments of your old life come back—"

"So now you're going to educate me on self-control." He glances toward her yellow kit bag as he stands up stiffly from the lounge chair.

"Fuck. You." The temptation to throw a bottle at him is almost overwhelming. "It's *not my job*, by the way, to help you figure out how to keep this serial-killer side of you on a leash. I don't know if you've noticed, but I have enough problems of my own."

"I don't—"

"You should leave now." It's enough—she's said enough, they've argued enough, and this is an impasse.

"Nomi—"

"Please just go." She crosses her arms.

For a moment, she's not sure if he'll obey. She's very careful not to look at the Smith & Wesson on the coffee table, no matter how her eyes pull toward it. But then Simon wets his lips and walks toward the hall. She holds position as he goes to the door, unlocks it, tugs it open—

He stops. "There's a—"

"What?" Is this some sort of stupid last-word guy thing?

He looks back at her, frowning. "Someone has left a parcel at your door."

Is this a joke? Nomi follows to where Simon is standing. Sees the cardboard box—about the size of a shoebox—that wasn't there before, now sitting on the linoleum outside, and feels all her senses come alert.

"Get back." Something about her face must command attention because he immediately backs away as she crouches down and examines the box. It's plain, sealed with packing tape, and there's no address marked anywhere, just her name on the top. "There's a box cutter in the top drawer of my desk. Could you—"

"Got it," he says, and jogs off.

Nomi leans forward, listens above the box. No ticking, whirring, hissing, or ratcheting sounds. Nothing at all, in fact. She gets down at floor level and examines the place where the box meets the linoleum: no wires she can see. There could be a pressure plate, but that seems complicated.

Simon returns with the box cutter, hesitates, looking between the blade and her outstretched hand. "Um, are you sure you're—"

"Oh, for fuck's sake." She rolls her eyes. "Just give it."

He hands it to her, intelligence returning. "Does Lamonte or anyone in that crew seem like they'd rig up an explosive?"

"I'm not seeing any wires. There's no sounds." She winces. This is really not her area, and she's feeling the lack. She puts the box cutter in her back pocket. "I'm going to pick it up."

"Nomi—"

She picks up the box: Nothing explodes. She exhales through her teeth, brings the box inside.

Simon closes the door, follows her and the box to the kitchen. "Is it heavy?"

"It's not heavy. It's really light. No weight imbalance. I don't know, maybe it's full of spiders or something." She waits for Simon to clear the beer bottles away before placing the box on the benchtop, retrieving the box cutter from her pocket. She snicks the blade out to slice the packing tape.

"Wait." Simon gestures for the box cutter. "Let me open it."

"Why?"

He looks impatient. "Because you've got people relying on you for the PI work you do, and you've got no more experience with explosives or spider-filled packages than me—just let me open it. You go in the bathroom and close the door."

She's not sure what's prompting this, but he makes a salient point. Although if he gets his arms blown off because of her, she'll feel really bad. "Simon—"

"Come on, give me the box cutter."

Biting her lip, she hands it over. He shoos her until she retreats to the bathroom. She doesn't close the door entirely, though.

She can hear the rustle as he opens the parcel. "What's happening?"

"It's filled with . . . packing peanuts. Wait, there's . . . there's another smaller box inside."

"What?"

"It's not heavy." More rustling. "It isn't . . . Oh shit."

She shoves the bathroom door open and strides to the kitchen, where, over the open lid and packing peanuts of the first box, Simon is holding an even smaller box, about the size of her fist.

His face is ashen. "Nomi, I don't think you want to—"

She grabs the small box off him and looks. Immediately drops the whole thing onto the floor as she gasps, involuntary, horrified, her hand flying to her mouth.

The small box spills onto the linoleum in a burst of reddened tissue paper; the objects inside bounce onto the floor and settle at her feet. Nomi can see, with shocking clarity even at this distance, the tiny white chips like pale kernels of corn, the neat, clotted stumps.

They're teeth.

They're Brittany Jackson's teeth.

Chapter Twenty-One

October 1987, Friday

Simon can hear that Nomi has finished puking in the bathroom, and she's now running the faucet to rinse her mouth and wash her face.

He picked the teeth up off the floor and returned them to the small box. They sit innocuously, malevolently, in the middle of the coffee table between Nomi's bag of cutting paraphernalia and her gun, making quite a grim tableau.

Leaning forward on the lounge chair, forearms on his knees, he looks up as Nomi returns to the living room, holding her stomach. "Are you all right?"

"What do *you* think?" Her eyes are red rimmed—from crying, or throwing up, or a combination of both—and her hair at the front is stringy with damp.

He thinks his continued presence in her apartment is only a matter of expedience, so he's going to ignore her tone and stick to professional observations.

"I can't tell if the teeth were pulled or fell out by themselves, but the blood on the root ends is very fresh—they were probably, uh, gathered in the last few hours." He's not sure how he knows this. Normally he'd attribute it to working at Gennaro's, but now he's wondering if the knowledge was already there, part of an uncomfortably innate bundle of skills related to his history of homicide. Although looking at the teeth makes him feel a weird mix of guilt and anger and sadness: Is a sociopath with a total lack of empathy supposed to feel such things? "This happened because of me, didn't it? If Lamonte's pulling out Brittany's teeth, it's because of what I did to Ameche at Big Mouth."

"Probably, yes." Nomi seems to have decided she's not here to make him feel better about himself. Then she sighs, shakes her head. "But they were delivered to me, so it's a double whammy—makes me stop kicking over rocks, makes you feel like shit."

"I *do* feel like shit."

"Good." But she can't quite meet his eyes like she means it. She collects the small box with its horrifying surprise, transfers it to her refrigerator. Trudges past the sofa, around the folding screen, to the dresser near her unmade bed. "Look, I need to go, so you need to leave."

He squints at her over his shoulder. "Where are you going?"

"Well, Simon, let me think—first, I have to go see Solange Jackson and tell her that I have her daughter's *teeth*." She yanks open a drawer, drags her current black T-shirt up and off, stands in her black bra as she hunts for and pulls on another identical black T-shirt. She said she has scars from her strange cutting activities; they're not visible on her back—maybe she can't reach there?—but the huge ravens on her shoulder are an angry flurry of inky feathers. "Second, I have to explain to Solange that it's time to go to the cops, because this is . . . This is out of my league."

Simon stands. "You're giving up."

"Yes, I'm giving up!" When Nomi turns, she's glowering. She grabs a black sweater off her bed and stalks back, pulling on the sweater, tugging her hair out of the collar. "Gaffney was right—I'm fumbling around here, doing this investigation on my own . . . and I'm fucking it up. I'd rather chew off my own arm than pass this kid's welfare over to the cops, especially a slimeball like Balter, but all I'm going to do is get Brittany killed."

"But you said Solange might lose Brittany to social services if you—"

"Better she stays alive and goes in the system than gets *dead* and goes *nowhere*." Nomi shoves her arms into the sleeves of her leather jacket. "And now we have evidence she's in immediate danger, maybe Balter and the Tenth crew will get off their asses and actually do something . . . I mean, I can dream. Okay, get out, I have to go."

"I want my file." Simon's aware he's pressing his luck, but it's *his* file.

Nomi doesn't seem to care as she finds her scarf, collects her shit. "Everything's on my desk, as you're no doubt aware. Just take it. Here—" She pulls her beanie and some random junk out of the tote on the sofa, thrusts it at him. "Put it all in here. This is all my library research notes too."

He takes the tote and goes into her office, gathers up the gray document wallet, the brown envelope it came in, shoves it in with a seemingly random collection of paper notes. There's also his pile of stuff—notebooks, cigar box, identification papers—and another file folder marked with his name on top of a pile of newspapers. He gathers everything, slides it in with the rest.

When he emerges back into the living room, Nomi's chugging a glass of water in the kitchen. She dumps the empty glass in the sink and looks around, preparing to lock the place back up. "Okay, come on, time to go."

Simon holds up the now-almost-overflowing tote. Everything is in here: his backstory, his past, the man he was. Part of him can't believe he was so eager to find all this out. "Thank you."

"I don't know why you're thanking me, but sure." Nomi tugs her beanie on, walks ahead down the hallway for the door. Once they're both out in the gloomy corridor, she pulls the door closed, uses her key. At the point where they're about to separate—Simon for the upstairs, Nomi going down—she turns and looks at him. "Simon . . ."

"Yeah?" For a second, he feels a stuttering flame of hope.

"Break into my apartment again, and I'll shoot you and say it was a home invasion. Are we clear?"

His jaw clenches as hope is extinguished. "Crystal."

"Good."

She turns around and leaves. Simon feels like a fool standing at the bottom of the stairs, watching her go. But for some reason, pivoting on his heel and climbing to the third floor takes all his energy.

It's nearly eight in the evening. He lets himself into his apartment. It's freezing, which isn't customary, and he realizes he left the window near his bed wide open—he walks over and closes it, before going to the breakfast table and dumping the tote. The apartment feels quiet and empty, which is stupid because it's a studio apartment and he's the only occupant, so it's always quiet and empty.

It's taking a while for the air to warm, so he tidies a little, very aware that putting the small details of his life in order when all the big details are a fucking mess is like rearranging deck chairs on the *Titanic*. His head is aching; he takes another Vicodin, can't help flashing on Nomi's steely question: *Why do you take Vicodin?* The memory of her wielding the tiny, glassy blade in the darkened living room of her apartment produces a complex swirl of emotions.

But now his fingers are cold, and he needs something warm. He can't handle more coffee, though; he's already drunk about a dozen coffees today. Instead, with a pang of homesickness, he makes ponche navideño out of raisins and fruit and cinnamon sugar and the rest of the merlot. As the mulled wine mix simmers, he returns to the table and unloads the tote, setting everything to one side.

Pouring himself a glass of ponche, he collects the glass ashtray, sits down at the table, lights a cigarette. Then—with a visceral reluctance bordering on nausea—he begins going through all the paperwork.

The orange cigar box and his journals are something he can just put on the floor immediately, because what use are they now? He focuses on the file pages, Nomi's notes from the library, and a series of news articles that she's photocopied and included. There are pictures of crime scenes. Transcribed witness statements. A comprehensive psychological review. The names and lives of the people he killed. After a while, it starts to feel academic, and he has to keep reminding himself that it's real. He realizes there's a schism in his awareness, which the language of the reports contributes to, which allows him to think, *"Gutmunsson did this, and also this"*—and then, with a sudden, piercing jolt, he remembers that Gutmunsson is not a separate person. This isn't some doppelgänger: *He* is Gutmunsson.

Gutmunsson is him.

By his second glass of ponche and his third cigarette, Simon pushes the papers away. As Gutmunsson, he killed people for pleasure. He killed *creatively*, often posing his victims for display in some sadistic fantasy. How can he live with this? In a just society, he'd be put to death, and maybe that wouldn't be a bad thing. He *should* be absent from the world—it might be safer for himself and for everyone around him.

Maybe he should go back to Guatemala. But the idea of exposing friends and neighbors in Piedras Negras to what he is . . . Explaining it to Flores . . .

How can he do that?

When the cognitive dissonance gets too loud, and his headache turns into a pain like a grinding of bone, and the big box of Vicodin in his bathroom cabinet—enough to just blank everything out and fall asleep forever—becomes too tempting, Simon grabs his coat and leaves the apartment again.

He needs to go somewhere, only he's not sure where to go. Somewhere he's not surrounded by people, who die much too easily, their blood spilling all over the report pages like claret. Somewhere nobody will expect him to talk and pretend to be human, because he's obviously too good at that already. He needs a place where he can sit in the dark and lick his wounds, and maybe—*maybe*—come to some kind of resolution about what to do with himself.

He ends up walking to the Bleecker Street Cinema.

The girl in the booth sells him a ticket for the show that's just about to start; to Simon's surprise, the film is called *Hellraiser*. So now it seems as if he's finally going to find out what a hellraiser is.

It turns out that a hellraiser is an interdimensional sadomasochistic murderer, and the film is just one gory scene of brutal dismemberment after another.

After thirty minutes, Simon stumbles out through the theater doors followed by a chorus of screams and clanging black chains. A kid running a carpet sweeper up and down a patch of spilled popcorn in the hall notices him and grins.

"Bit too much for ya?" The kid pauses, rests the sweeper handle against the wall as he digs a pack of gum out of the pocket of his usher's waistcoat. He peels the paper off a stick and pops it into his mouth, starts chewing. "Yeah, we get a couple people every session who come out looking green. You wanna go to the other movie?"

"I can't afford to buy another ticket," Simon admits.

"Don't worry about it. Nobody's gonna care. I'm the one who's supposed to be checking tickets, and I couldn't give a shit." The kid pops his gum, lifts his chin at the next door down the hall. "There's some old musical on in there. Sounds like it might be more your speed."

Singin' in the Rain has already been going for a while, but it doesn't matter, because Simon has already seen it. He sits in the dark in the almost-empty theater, watches Gene Kelly and Debbie Reynolds and Donald O'Connor dance their way through life as if being happy isn't the saddest, most out-of-reach dream that humanity has ever been sold.

By the time Simon gets back to his apartment at eleven, his mood is bleak. He has work in four hours. Should he quit at Gennaro's? Will carving up meat—the smell, the blood, that smooth, satisfying texture under his knife—trigger a resurgence of all his old predilections for carving up people? Simon splashes water on his face in the bathroom, leans over the basin and wonders how he's ever going to reconcile any of this.

He wipes his face on a towel, walks back out to the breakfast table. At least he can pack up all the horror pages so he doesn't have to look at them.

Under the file from Nomi's office marked with his name, Simon discovers a half dozen copies of *The New York Times*, and he assumes they're part of Nomi's research materials until he knocks one off the stack—as it spills forward, he sees the headline below the fold, which reads Former Senator To Helm Commission. Beside the headline, a black-and-white picture of a stern-looking older blond woman wearing a jacket with big shoulder pads.

Simon remembers opening the post office box in the Farley building with the small silver key. He thinks of Max the Security Guy saying, *Ricki was not as stupid as Sully makes him out to be, you understand?* He remembers Nomi's suggestion that they check the society pages as well as the headlines about local and state government, so that's what he does.

In the fourth copy of the *Times*, he finds something that makes him stand up from his chair.

Simon goes through all the newspapers to confirm, then packs them all into one portable pile, checks the time. It's close to midnight—will Nomi be home yet? More relevantly, will she be willing to listen? Maybe the thought of a seven-year-old girl's teeth in her refrigerator will be sufficient encouragement.

He leaves his apartment. He's trying hard—so very hard—not to think about the image of Nomi on her sofa, shirt rucked, head thrown back in abandon, a delicate runnel of blood leaking down her pale stomach into her jeans. Halfway down the stairs, he sees her: newly arrived, key in her door, a lean black animal returning to her den. Alert to movement, she snaps a look up and spots him.

She relaxes a tiny fraction. "I think I got something."

"I definitely got something," he says. "What's your thing?"

"A list of Galetti's properties, including the ones he wants rezoned. What's your thing?"

He holds up the May edition of the society page of *The New York Times*, which has a group photo of the Axedale family at a gala benefit concert. "Jeremy is Gloria Axedale's youngest son."

Chapter Twenty-Two

October 1987, Friday

Nomi wishes Simon were more annoying so she'd feel more justified being irritated and angry, but the truth is that he's only annoying occasionally, so she can't sustain it. She curses herself for becoming too accustomed to him: her goddamn serial-killer neighbor.

Now he's here with useful information, and it's not as if she can afford to throw it back in his face. She's like a shrimp lured in by a deep-sea anglerfish, compelled by the tiny light . . .

She leaves her key in the door to come closer, grab the newspaper. "Well, shit."

"David Jeremy Axedale." Simon nods toward the picture she's examining. "It's right there, in the caption."

"Well, *shit*."

"Did you visit Solange?"

Nomi pulls off her beanie and shoves it in her jacket pocket, still peering at the photo in the dim yellow light of the tenement corridor. "Her roommate said she hasn't been home for three days, that she's at Jeremy's apartment. How did you find this?"

"Cevolatti's newspapers, from the post office box. I took them with me by mistake when I grabbed my file." Simon takes another step down the stairs; she appreciates that he's no longer towering over her. "You said you got a list of Galetti's properties?"

"I went to Tenth to make a report, and Captain Balter made himself feel good by giving me a nice bawling out in his office."

Simon frowns. "Doesn't sound great."

"Show me the other articles," Nomi says, and she sits down on the second-bottom riser. Simon sits to match her, hands over another news article. She squints at it as she talks. "Yeah, Balter—what a jerk. He called me a bunch of names, then directed me to Calvin Gaffney to file the report. Calvin wasn't at his desk when I rocked up, but he had a pile of paperwork just sitting there, including a photocopied list of Galetti's properties—I mean, my ex-partner said there was a list floating around. Anyway, I took it and walked out of the station."

"You stole from a *police station*."

"I stole from *Calvin*." Nomi closes the broadsheet momentarily and dips into her inside jacket pocket, flashes Noone a glimpse of a folded photocopy, before opening the newspaper again. "If he even realizes it's missing, he'll just go get another copy. He really shouldn't leave shit lying around."

Simon looks like he's trying very hard to keep a straight face. "Should I feel bad about pouring coffee down Calvin Gaffney's shirt?"

"You should not. Calvin's an asshole."

"And disorganized with his paperwork."

"Every now and then, you get a win." Nomi finishes with the newspaper and sets it in her lap. "All I had to do for this one was to humiliate myself in front of my old police captain for twenty minutes. As far as cost-benefit ratios go, it was worth it. So now we have a list of potential locations, *and* we know who Jeremy is."

"'We'?" Simon is being painfully nonchalant.

"I said what I said." She stands up—she's not going to clarify beyond that, she doesn't have time—and gestures for the newspapers he's still holding. "Give me that stuff."

"What do we do now?"

"We get moving on everything first thing tomorrow. I'm just putting it all inside before I go out again." She returns to the key she left in the door, opens up enough to dump the pile of newspapers and the photocopy from her jacket pocket inside the entryway to her apartment, closes up the door and relocks it.

"You're going out again?" Simon has stood up as well.

"Just to the Riverview. Mischa will be there, and he said he'd look for info for me on the dealer delivery angle. If we can find out the name of the new dealer, and where they're collecting their supplies from, it might help narrow those properties down."

"Do you want me to come with you?"

"Nope." She softens the refusal. "You have a shift at Gennaro's in a few hours."

"Yes, but—"

"I'll be fine."

Simon's brows knit. "Be careful."

"I'm always careful." Nomi retrieves her beanie, jams it back on her head, studying his face. It hasn't escaped her attention, how haggard he looks. "You should get some sleep before work. You look like shit."

"Wow, thanks." But this interaction has been less antagonistic than when they last spoke, a few hours ago, and he seems faintly relieved. He turns to head upstairs, turns back. "I finish at eleven. Don't go exploring Galetti's properties without me."

"You got it." She checks her watch. "I've gotta go. It's nearly midnight."

"Nomi?"

"What?" She's at the top of the stairs to the ground floor.

He gestures toward his own head. "You, uh, need your stitches out. They've been in nearly six days."

"Tomorrow," she promises, and then she's gone.

There's nothing like Gansevoort Street in all its chaotic, nasty, lewd, bustling glory in the middle of the night. Refrigerated trucks are humming, traffic and people trundle around, lights cut through the dark. The scents of meat and diesel strike up through her nose, and there's a breeze starting to whip up the sidewalk. Huddled deep in her jacket, Nomi marches briskly past puddles of standing water near the drains. The temperature is crisp, and the cobblestones are slippery. She's feeling good, and it's not just because she's cut recently: Tonight has been a seesaw of disaster and triumph, but it looks like things might actually be tipping toward triumph, and when does that ever happen?

When she gets to the Riverview and Mischa's not there, it still doesn't spoil Nomi's mood.

"You just missed him, hon," Cherie calls out. "He's gone up to the corner."

"Thanks, Cherie." Nomi reverses course.

The corner is the Triangle building. She follows Greenwich until it turns into Ninth Avenue, finally arrives at the pink slice of nightclub heaven. Friday night, the outside curb is absolutely pumping, and it takes her a minute to weave between patrons and pimps and dealers and tourists before she finds Mischa near the entrance to Hellfire.

"Well, hello!" He's in leather pants again, which now makes more sense on this cold night, and a voluminous purple parka along with his regular Day-Glo headband. "How are you, sweetie?"

"Good," Nomi says. "Great. Any word on that thing I asked you about?"

"No-thing," Mischa enunciates. "No damn thing at all. I'm real sorry. I asked everyone I know."

"That's okay, man. Don't worry about it. You did your best." She can't help being disappointed, though.

Mischa makes a face. "Ugh, I feel bad about it. Is there anything else you need, maybe?"

She considers. She still hasn't taken any Valium, and she's only got the one tab left—but perhaps tonight she can stand to relax a little. "Actually, yeah. You wanna help me out with my usual?"

"Of course!"

Mischa has secret pockets everywhere for his various products—he roots inside his jacket. They make the exchange. High above, a quiet grumble of thunder, maybe some bad weather coming in. Nomi's about to thank Mischa and walk off when she sees it.

Farther ahead, outside the entrance to Big Mouth, Lamonte's flunky Ray Dinkins is making a performative farewell with one of the hookers from the club. She's hanging on his arm. He's laughing and waving her off. He looks pretty drunk—he's having trouble pouring himself into the back seat of a cab—and he's alone; Nomi clocked that immediately. No Gino, no Claude, no Eric Lamonte, just Ray in his orange satin shirt and ugly pants and leather tie.

And here she is, without a ticket to the ball.

Nomi keeps her eyes on Dinkins as she speaks in an undertone to Mischa. "Meesh, are you carrying right now?"

Mischa shakes his head. "Baby, you know that's not my scene."

Dinkins finally manages to get himself into a cab, closes the door.

"Okay, no problem," Nomi says. "Thanks for the help tonight."

"Anytime!"

Dinkins's cab drives off. Nomi makes a call.

She jogs over to the next cab in the rank, pushing aside a young guy with George Michael hair, who calls out, "Fucking bitch!"—Nomi takes it as a compliment. Her cab driver is a twentysomething Black guy with a high forehead, and when she tells him to follow the other cab, he looks over with his eyebrows raised almost into his hairline.

"Really? Like something out of a movie?"

"Really. Stay close, but not too close."

He's not too bad at tailing, actually. They follow Dinkins's circuitous route, make it all the way to West Seventeenth and Tenth Avenue before Dinkins's cab makes a turn into a street that Nomi thinks might be a dead end, so she tells her guy to turn right onto Tenth near a closed parking lot and let her out farther down the block.

"Okay, here—drop me here." Nomi points, and he pulls up near a street sign for West Nineteenth.

"You sure?" The cab driver peers through the window at the shadowed corners and listing street poles. Wind blows trash along the line of a wall on the other side of the street. "This place looks sketchy as hell."

"Just drop me. It'll be fine."

"Okay." He clearly thinks this is dubious. "I hope I don't hear about no white lady getting murdered here on the news tomorrow."

But he takes her money just the same, drives away. Nomi zips her jacket against the cold, checks around the corner: The red glow of the taillights from Dinkins's cab recedes up ahead. She turns and quicksteps down the street, trying to stick to patches of dark.

The cab driver was right; the whole area is sketchy as hell and largely deserted. She can smell brine and rust; they're near the Chelsea Piers and the West Side Highway, and wind is blowing in off the bay. There's an Anywheels car and van repair place, closed for the night. Rats scurry along the side of a curling chain-link fence; most of the industrial buildings are crumbling, with chipped bricks and flaking paint. If this is the area that Galetti wants to buy up and refurbish, it might actually be an improvement? All she knows is that she's out here in the dark in the middle of nowhere with no weapon. Not ideal.

But that's not her problem right now: Dinkins's cab has slowed to a crawl and stopped near a decommissioned mariners' hotel. Hanging back, she watches as Dinkins somehow manages to totter his way out of the cab, which takes off like it's glad to get out. Nomi creeps to match Dinkins as he makes his way along a brick wall with a series of garage doors. Then he turns left into an alley, and she nearly loses him.

Shit shit shit. Nomi jogs closer, trying not to break an ankle on the cracked, weedy sidewalk, or accidentally kick a brick and alert Dinkins to her presence. Okay, she's got him again. He's nearly at West Nineteenth and he's coming up on an old two-story warehouse behind a tall plywood fence smeared with graffiti. Beside a rolling garage shutter, there's a door in the fence; Dinkins uses a key, staggers through, locks up behind himself.

Nomi grimaces: It's a place she probably can't access without blowing that she's here. She does a little recon, but the plywood turns into brick fence farther on the left, and a horribly exposed chain-link arrangement on the right. She's not climbing that. Is that it? Looks like that's it.

Unless she's prepared to wait.

Nomi finds a dark place with an overhang, between a broken-down car with melted tires and a burned-out streetlamp. It's not the greatest spot, and now the wind is sweeping a fine mist into the street, but it'll have to do. She pulls her beanie down low, hunkers into her jacket and scarf, settles in.

The first half hour, she catalogs all the features of the street and the building; the second half hour is when the wind picks up and the cold starts to creep into her legs. It's a lot easier doing surveillance when you're sitting in an unmarked with a hot coffee, she's willing to admit. But this cold is something she signed up for, and like she told Simon once, she has a high pain threshold.

A storm's coming in, wind gusting like it's being exhaled by a giant; at least the buildings around her provide some protection. What if this warehouse is the place where they're holding Brittany? Nomi chews a nail, thinking about it. She feels the pull of the idea like a strong magnet. The girl could be in there, awaiting rescue . . . But plunging in without proper reconnaissance would be incredibly stupid. Nomi has to remind herself of this over and over.

A tomcat prowls by the plywood fence she's watching, and Nomi gets a hankering for a cigarette; but even if she had one, she wouldn't be able to smoke it without the red ember giving her away. She's also itchingly aware of the Valium she just bought, sitting inside the key pocket of her jeans, and has to turn her mind toward something else. Something not Simon Noone and all his accompanying mess.

By the end of the second hour, just as she's almost solidified into a block of ice and is ready to call it, there's a rattle from the garage shutter. Nomi scooches deeper into her hiding place.

The shutter rolls up with a complaining clatter, and a car drifts out. When the headlights flick on, Nomi has to duck: She's way more exposed here than she thought. But nobody shoots at her, or calls out, and the car doesn't stop, just revs a little and slides up the street.

Nomi registers the people inside when the driver lights his smoke: Dinkins and Gino Hart are illuminated by the flame of Hart's Bic. Then the car picks up speed and guns away.

It's nearly 2:20 a.m. by her watch; another growl of incoming thunder sounds in the distance. Nomi makes her way out of the dark streets toward a more populated area, and hopefully a cab. Her fingers feel ready to snap off, her nose is numb, her toes have ceased to exist, and her knees are creaking, but all she can think is, *Now I got you, Lamonte, you sick son of a bitch*, and that pilot flame keeps her warm all the way home.

Chapter Twenty-Three

October 1987, Saturday

It's 2:45 a.m., and there's a storm building in the night air outside. Simon puts on dark-brown trousers, tugs a black Henley over his head, adds a pilled burgundy wool vest—even if it doesn't rain, it's getting much colder in the mornings—then sits down on his bed and shifts his cigarette to the corner of his mouth to pull on his socks and boots.

He's feeling better. He's groggy from lack of sleep, and he probably needs a shave, but overall, he's somewhat improved. Working through tiredness is doable; the first week of work at Gennaro's, he was basically a zombie for every shift. What matters is that his state of mind has leveled out, and somehow that seems to count for way more.

Simon's just swigging the rest of his espresso when there's a quiet knock on his door, which is not something that typically happens at this time of day. It's Nomi: She's shivering, but she looks happy.

He keeps his voice low in deference to other residents. "It's quarter to three in the morning."

"No shit—let me in, dummkopf. I'm freezing my ass off out here." She's already pushing her way through the door. "I had another win."

"What happened?" She's leaving soggy footprints on the linoleum. "You're dripping. Let me get you a towel."

"I told you, it's freezing. Going to rain any minute." She accepts the towel he fetched from the bathroom, wipes her face and chafes her hands with it. "I've been standing outside in the cold for the last two hours. I feel like one of those slabs of beef at Gennaro's."

"You're white." He frowns, goes to the kitchen to put a flame under the ponche in the pot on the stove. "You need something warm to drink."

"Sounds great. I'm gonna use your bathroom, okay?" When she returns, she finds a chair, shakes out her fingers to recover feeling. Squints at the glass of hot punch he's set down. "What's this?"

"Mulled wine." Simon's fixed on her eyebrow stitches, at the way they're starting to pucker.

"Awesome." She sips. "Mm, not bad. So I went to the Riverview, but—"

"Keep talking. I'm going to remove your stitches while you tell me." May as well kill two birds with one stone. He walks away to fetch sharp nail scissors and tweezers and a washcloth.

"You don't want to do that later?"

"If you leave them too long, the skin grows together wrong," he calls from the bathroom, before walking back. "And I can listen and do this at the same time."

"Multifunctional, right." She continues sipping, her cheeks gradually pinking. It's a good sign; when she'd arrived, her face had been almost translucent. "Okay, so I went to the Riverview, but Mischa was up at the Triangle, and when I got there, I saw Ray Dinkins."

"One of Lamonte's men." He keeps his tone neutral, but he doesn't feel neutral. He pats at her eyebrow with the dampened washcloth. "Tilt your head this way. Do you trust me to use scissors?"

"What? Sure. And yes, Dinkins is Lamonte's guy. We saw him at Big Mouth."

Simon sighs. "You followed Dinkins, didn't you?"

"Hell yes."

He snips a stitch, teases the thread out with the tweezers. "As your security specialist, I'd like to raise some objections."

"You know, for a serial killer, you've got a real sense of civic responsibility going on there," Nomi says.

She's so nonchalant about it, they both pause for a second.

Simon breaks the moment by snorting. "All right, tell me what happened."

"It was pretty straightforward—he jumped in a cab, I jumped in a cab. I tailed him out to Chelsea Piers and watched him go into some warehouse off West Nineteenth Street. Then I waited around in the freezing cold like a bum for two hours until he came out." Nomi holds still as Simon cuts and slides out another stitch.

"A warehouse."

"Yep. I don't want to get too excited—I want to cross-reference with the property list and see if I can find a match. But even if it's not listed, that warehouse could be the place they're holding Brittany. We've got the Jeremy connection, we've got Galetti's property list, and now this."

"Okay, last one." Simon snips the final stitch at her eyebrow, eases out the thread.

Nomi drains her glass. "Three wins in one night. Does that mean my streak's over?"

"Well, your stitches are over at any rate." He smooths the washcloth over her knitted skin. The line is distinct but neat.

"Good, they were getting itchy." She gets up and goes into his bathroom to check her face, calls out from there. "Looks okay?"

"For a rough job, it's okay," he concedes, as he disposes of the trash.

She appears again in the bathroom doorway. "There's another joke in there about getting medical treatment from a serial killer, but I don't want to push it."

He wants to say, "Why not?" But now he's the one feeling unsure. Maybe she's still scared of him—hard to say. He shrugs and settles for an awkward "It's fine."

"Thank you." Nomi comes closer, her dark hair still beaded with late-night mist. "For the stitch removal, and for the wine. And . . ." She glances away, back. "When I had another win, I wanted to tell you about it. I guess I'm not ready to kick you to the curb just yet."

"Does that mean you won't shoot me?" Simon blurts.

"Oh, if you break into my apartment again, I'll definitely shoot you." Nomi grins. "And you have to replace the window glass in my office, by the way. I'm not letting you off the hook on that." She looks behind him at the clock on top of his fridge. "Shit, I'd better let you get to work."

"Probably." Simon checks the time himself: It's already 3:00 a.m. "Damn, yes, I have to leave. Look, don't take off searching any warehouses without me, okay? You shouldn't go without backup."

"But what if she's there?" Nomi blurts, standing and fidgeting in place.

"Listen to me—you're no use to Brittany if Lamonte catches you while you're sniffing around. Wait for me to come with you."

"Okay, okay, I'll wait." Nomi makes a face, almost whining with impatience.

"Go home," Simon insists. "Get some sleep—your eyes are hanging out of your head. I'll see you at eleven."

"Eleven," she agrees, backing for the door. "Is Ameche still sniffing around Gennaro's?"

"My supervisor says no." He's following her out, grabbing his peacoat and blue scarf, making sure he's got everything he needs in his pockets, switching off the light, locking the door behind them.

"Be careful anyway." They're on the stairs down to her place now.

"Noted. And remember what I said—wait for me, okay?"

"Okay." At the second-floor hallway, they separate so Nomi can go to her apartment and he can take the onward route. Before turning the key in her door lock, she pivots back. "Simon?"

"Yes?" He looks up from the top riser of the descending stairs, holding the banister.

Nomi opens her mouth to say something, as a strong wind outside rattles the hinges on the door of the downstairs lobby. She shakes her head. "Nothing. See you at eleven."

He takes the rest of the stairs down, to the background soundtrack of Nomi unlocking her apartment, then closing up after herself. Out on the street, other sounds intrude: a truck revving, someone's transistor radio, men calling to each other, a handcart bumping along the cobblestones. The wind is really picking up, smelling of cold rain. Simon muffles his face in his scarf and strides faster because he's late. But there's also a spring in his step, and he's not such an idiot that he doesn't know why: He's a murderer, but if Nomi still finds him tolerable, maybe there's hope for him yet?

The lights of Gennaro's pierce the night up ahead, and Simon dodges a van as he jogs across Washington. Inside the slaughterhouse, Mike Nell is mid-conversation with another employee, but he looks over and raises an eyebrow; Simon makes an apologetic gesture, hangs his stuff, grabs his gear.

It's not until he's through the doors and his knives are in his hands that he remembers the concerns he had about whether this job was something he may have to let go. But could butchering here, in an official capacity, be a peculiar kind of release valve? For him, cutting is almost a form of therapy—certainly the only therapy he can afford, and maybe the only way he can reconcile his old life and his new one.

But throughout his shift, he's wondering whether Nomi has thrown caution to the wind and gone to the warehouse without him. Maybe she lost patience; maybe her concern for Brittany Jackson weakened her resolve to wait. Or maybe she decided that a guy with Simon's history doesn't make the best backup.

Thinking about it, he has trouble focusing on work. It's the first time he hasn't found calm in the movement of his blade, the neatness of red flesh exposed, ordered, refined. His eight hours seem to drag. But finally, his shift is over and he's outside on Washington again as the rain that was only spitting earlier really starts coming down. It doesn't feel like eleven in the morning; the sky above is dark as predawn. Simon rewraps his scarf and pulls his coat collar up, watches his footing on the slippery pavement as he hurries back home.

When he returns to the tenement, the lobby is chilly. There are small parcels of ground beef and steak in his coat pocket for Sofia Rosa. He knocks gently at his landlady's door: no answer. She's either not home, or she's napping. He'll come back later, once he and Nomi have checked the warehouse, or if Brittany's not there, after they've gone through the property list that Nomi stole last night.

They could find this kid today; it's a distinct possibility. Then it really will be time to drink champagne. Simon takes the stairs and uses his key to let himself into his apartment, almost whistling. He shuts the door and turns—

Claude Ameche's ugly sneer takes up all of Simon's vision for about one second before he's hit in the head with a two-by-four.

Chapter Twenty-Four

October 1987, Saturday

Nomi rolls over in bed, only wakes up properly when a brilliant crackle of lightning outside brightens the room like a flashbulb and penetrates the fog of sleep. What sounds like handfuls of gravel being thrown at her window is actually rain. Goddamn, it's really coming down out there.

She sits up, swaddled in blankets, scratches through her hair. After leaving Simon to descend the stairs and go to work, she indulged herself with one more session and a double dose of Valium before finally getting to bed at close to four in the morning. It's now . . . She checks the clock—oh crap, it's just gone midday. The dark skies and her benzo hangover have shoved her wakeup time into the afternoon. She clambers out of bed and pads to the kitchen in her sleep tee and socks, drinks water. She told Simon she'd meet him at eleven; hopefully he'll be cool about a minor delay.

Tidiness was kind of beaten into her at an early age, so her kit bag is already put away, and there's no debris from last night in her living area—except for the cardboard box full of packing peanuts still sitting on her kitchen benchtop. Nomi dumps that in her office and, with the reminder of Brittany's teeth now ricocheting in her mind, goes straight for a hot shower. If the warehouse location pays dividends, today may be the day she gets Brittany back.

Today is also going to be wet and dark and miserable—the first shitty storm of fall—so once she's changed the dressing on her stomach, Nomi drags on warm combat pants and a black sweater that's slightly thicker than the one she got damp last night. In her office, she opens the drawer with her service weapon and holster and old police badge. She clips on her holster, adds her weapon, puts the tin in the inside pocket of her jacket. Pulling her jacket on, and with beanie and scarf in place, she grabs cash, keys, and the list of Galetti's properties that she left on the newspaper pile in the hall; then she's out the door.

There's a little bead of worry lodged in her throat as she heads for the stairs. Was she right to grant Simon Noone some measure of absolution last night? It's nonsensical: He breaks into her apartment, freaks her out, argues with her about his relative trustworthiness—seriously, what the fuck—then only a few hours later, she's letting herself be won over by a little productive case research and a glass of mulled wine.

But what she said to him is also true: She has a knee-jerk desire to share the victories with him, when they occasionally come. She thinks of him sewing up her eyebrow in Sofia Rosa's apartment . . . The way he checked on her overnight . . . The little hoya in its soggy plant tube on her coffee table. Can a serial murderer also be a decent human being? Noone's past life is a horror show—she's just not sure whether he should be condemned for that stuff when he can't even remember it. It's not like he was trying to conceal his past either; he hired her to find out the truth, for god's sake.

But whether he's a danger—to herself, or to other people in the community—she honestly doesn't know. She's not sure where she stands on it all.

Still turning the problem over, she reaches the third-floor landing and realizes that the door to Noone's apartment is wide open.

Nomi's skin prickles instantly. Slipping into cop mode, she moves on swift feet to flatten herself at the wall by the side of the doorway.

Pushes the door fully open with one hand so she can see inside. Nobody's home. Nobody's hiding behind the door. She can see a spill of blue fabric—Simon's cashmere scarf—on the floor. Outside the apartment's windows, rain spatters against the metal fire escape.

"Simon?" she calls into the apartment while maintaining position by the door. "Noone, you here?"

No answer. When she steps inside, she sees Simon's keys on the linoleum, and also blood spatter. *Shit.* She looks in the kitchen and bathroom, then the fire escape. No dice. The blood on the floor isn't copious, and the drops haven't dried yet; she's probably only missed this by an hour or so. If she'd been here on time, it wouldn't have happened.

Dread rises up, black dye seeping through the fabric of her brain. This is bad. If Ameche has dragged Simon away to exact a little payback for the incident at Big Mouth, Simon may be in serious trouble.

Where could they have taken him? She chews at a nail. The most obvious location is the warehouse she scoped out last night, where she thinks Lamonte has stashed Brittany. But that could be all wrong—there could be another place on the list of Galetti's properties where they take their abductees and potential torture victims . . .

Goddammit. It's impossible to be sure, but all she can do is start with the likeliest option and work from there. Looks like she's hitting the warehouse on her own after all. She's not in love with the idea—storming the barricades solo seems ill-advised. But what choice does she have?

Nomi grabs Noone's keys, exits the room and pulls the door closed, jogs back down to her own apartment. Inside, she strides to her office. Another burst of lightning above the tenement. It's not until the office blind blows back, exposing the puddle of rainwater on the floor, that she remembers the glass is still gone from the window. *Dammit.* No time for this. She hurries to the bathroom, grabs a towel, returns and stuffs it carefully into the hole—best she can do for now. Then she grabs the phone and calls a number she hasn't rung in person for nearly two years.

The call picks up as she's scrounging for more ammunition in her drawer.

"Hey, Dez Rosado speaking." A male voice, warm and casual.

Nomi tucks the phone between her ear and her shoulder as she unholsters her weapon and opens the chamber. "Dezi, good to hear your voice. It's Nomi Pace."

"Nomi? Oh man, it's been way too long! So good to hear you. What you doing now?"

"Lots of stuff, but I can't get into it this minute." Nomi tips out and reloads the .35 Magnum shells, confirming that she won't have a problem with misfires. "Can you do me a solid and put Irma on? I'm kinda racin' here, Dez."

"Ah shit, okay, one sec." But Dezi understands emergencies, both because his wife is a cop and because he himself is a firefighter. Nomi hears him calling, "Irma! Irma—phone!" in a muffled way, like he's got the receiver against his shirt.

Irma takes about ten seconds to arrive on the line. "Nomes, is that you? What the hell you doing, calling me at home? I thought we said—"

"Irma, listen. I'm about to do something really stupid, and I wanted to tell someone I trust about it." Nomi finishes the reload, clicks the chamber back into position, reholsters the gun under her armpit. Explain to Irma about Simon Noone? Now may not be the time. "Lamonte has a warehouse off West Nineteenth—I think he's stashed my client's daughter there, and I'm gonna go get her back."

"Nomi—"

"The warehouse should be on the list of properties that Galetti is trying to have rezoned." Nomi's holding the receiver in her hand again as she opens another drawer and scratches for her can of Mace. "Ask Calvin Gaffney to check. And listen, Galetti's leverage over Gloria Axedale is her son, David Jeremy Axedale. Lamonte's keeping the kid thoroughly doped and holed up in one of those cheap apartments on the West Street side of Perry Street, where my client is supposed to be keeping tabs on him."

"Jesus, Nomes—did you tell Balter about all this?"

"I tried," Nomi admits, "but I only found out about the warehouse last night, and either way, nothing I say carries weight. You probably have more pull with Balter than me. So if you want to alert the cavalry, that would be fantastic, but I'm running out of time here—I gotta go. Wish me luck."

"Wait! Hold on a second!" Irma sounds worried. "Nomi, don't you run off on this alone—"

"Sorry, hon—you're breaking up in this storm!" Nomi hangs up, grabs a knuckle-duster along with the Mace, bundles everything into her pockets and herself back out the door.

Out on the street, rain is flying into her face. She squints and endures as she jogs to Greenwich—but she only needs to do one quick scan to decide there's no point trying to flag a cab here, so she jogs onward to Hudson. It takes more than five minutes of frantic waving to get a Checker that'll stop for her. Finally, she gets lucky.

She gives the driver directions for West Nineteenth.

Chapter Twenty-Five

October 1987, Saturday

So here he is, in this tiny storage room with the gray metal shelving and brown walls and thirty-gallon-drum Tic Tacs, and the sound of Lamonte's men in the area beyond the door. He's patting Brittany on the shoulder—this girl whose missing baby teeth are in a small box in Nomi's refrigerator—and telling the most appalling lies about how there's no need to worry, that he has a plan, when the reality is that there's no plan, and he and Brittany are both most probably going to die in painful, creatively horrible ways thought up by losers like Gino Hart and Claude Ameche, and there's very little they can do about it . . .

I am a fraud. I am a fraud and a serial murderer, and I lie to children. Simon rubs at his temple like he can rub guilt away, rub his headache away, make his vision focus and stop wobbling. Around them, the storm beats against the brick of the warehouse. Brittany is looking up at him, her big eyes wide, short braids trembling, her small hands clutched in the fabric of his coat.

"Have you got a gun?" Brittany whispers.

"No."

"Have you got a knife?"

"No."

"I think you should beat those guys up that beat you."

"I don't have any weapons," Simon confesses quietly.

Her lips make a little pursed line. "Well, what *have* you got? You're not small like me, you can fight 'em."

Simon squeezes his head with one hand: He's locked in a warehouse storage room with a bloodthirsty seven-year-old. Unfortunately, she's got a point. There's no way they're getting out of here without violence.

And what exactly *has* he got? Simon moves to the desk and goes through his pockets. Cash, no. Sunglasses, no. Cigarettes and lighter, possible—or, at the very least, he can have a cigarette and make himself feel better. A squishy bundle of paper—he's still carrying around the ground beef and steak for Sofia Rosa. Wonderful, eminently practical. He can't find his keys, which would've at least had sharp points. His inside coat pockets hold lint, and . . .

Yes—the box cutter he used to open the package at Nomi's apartment yesterday.

He snicks out the blade. "Here's a start."

"Aw *yeah*," Brittany hisses.

But then Simon thinks about it. He's one guy with a box cutter against four mafia men who are all probably armed. With limited resources, he has to be smart about this. Overwhelming force, he is not, and even if he tries attacking with the white barrels or throwing the desk, the space in here is cramped, with limited maneuverability. Brittany could get hurt, and Lamonte's men will fall on top of him.

What can he do with what he's got?

Ohmigod, if his head wasn't pounding like this, he could think better . . . *Concentrate.*

His biggest vulnerability is actually Brittany. If Ameche or any of the others get hold of her, she'll be the ultimate leverage—Simon will be forced to back down immediately. What can he do to remove her from play?

There's nowhere in here she can truly hide, and he's sure she's tried it. What's the best thing to do if fight, flight, and hide are all out of the question?

"Play dead," Simon whispers.

Brittany is looking at him worriedly. "What?"

"Okay, I have an idea," he says, crouching to her level. "But you'll need to help me with it."

"I can do that." She looks so optimistic, it almost kills him.

"Good. Because if I'm going to fight, I have to know that you're safe or it won't work." He stands, head pulsing, and looks around again. Rain lashes the roof in waves, and they may not have much time. "All right, maybe in this corner? This is what we're going to do. You're going to sit here, flopped over with your head down. I'm going to make you look dead."

She grimaces. "That's not gonna work—"

"It will, because I'm a good actor and we have a disguise. Only thing is, it'll be kind of gross." He shows her the paper-wrapped parcel he'd intended to give his landlady.

Brittany gets it straight away, makes a face. "Oh yuck."

"Yeah. But it's fresh, and a little yuck won't hurt you."

He gives instructions, and she cooperates pretty fast. He likes this kid, which will only make things worse if this all goes belly up. *Put that thinking away.*

Once Brittany's slumped against the wall in the corner, by the door, he quickly gets to work on the set dressing. Ground beef clumped on her Care Bear tee, yellow staining to red from her throat to her stomach . . . Beef juices dripped to create gore . . . Chunks and strips of steak, judiciously placed . . . Floor dirt to darken everything . . .

It's not quite enough.

"Okay, we need some authenticity," he mutters, and rolls up his left sleeve.

"What're you doing?" Brittany whispers, peering from beneath her front braids with her head flopped as instructed.

"We need some real blood—this is going to be kind of unpleasant, maybe look away."

Simon removes the Band-Aid; the wound on his left forearm from Tuesday is nearly scabbed over. He grits his teeth and snicks the box cutter—doesn't think too much, just slices through the already-tender skin.

"Ew," Brittany says.

Blood wells up. At least the box cutter isn't too blunt.

Simon hisses all the same. "Hold still."

The blood runs down his forearm in two thick runnels, falling for the side or coursing into his palm. A high-pitched whine kicks off in his brain at the sight of all that red. He ignores it, distributes as much blood as he can over Brittany's disguise—spatters on her face, her jeans, the front of her shirt, her resting arms, her upturned open hands.

"That looks better," he mutters.

"This is like, the nastiest Halloween costume," she whispers. "There wasn't this much blood when my teeth fell out."

Simon pauses. "Your teeth *fell* out?"

"Yeah. They'd been loose, then they fell out both at once. The man in the coat took 'em. I didn't get money from the Tooth Fairy or anything."

She seems put out about it. Simon doesn't want to tell her how relieved her explanation makes him; he'd been worried about much nastier scenarios.

"Okay," he says. "I think we're done."

He does an assessment: It's not as good as the makeup in *Hellraiser*, but it's not the worst camouflage. Convincing in the short term is all they need. Brittany's going to have to put on a performance. Is she capable of it? Simon's not sure. But she's highly invested and reasonably bright. If it doesn't work, at least they gave it a shot.

"Brittany, listen," Simon says quietly, as he puts the leftover paper in his pocket, pinches the wound on his arm. He makes sure the girl meets his eyes. "I'm going to have to say a lot of crazy stuff to convince them that you're dead. Whatever you hear, just remember I don't mean it."

"Okay."

"And if this all goes badly, I'll try to keep the door open to this room, so if you get a chance, you should run."

"What about you?"

Another gut punch. But he keeps his voice low and firm. "Don't worry about me. I can take care of myself. You just get out, you understand?"

"Okay."

He wants to tell her she's a good kid, the best kid, but he can't afford for either of them to lose focus. "So, go over it for me—what are you going to do?"

"Play dead," she whispers. "Run if I get a chance."

"You got it. You ready?"

"Yeah."

He stands up, blinking against the rush in his head, and faces the door. Out in the warehouse, the sounds of individual voices getting closer: Simon takes some deep breaths, because this was how it was always going to be. His arm is stinging, and his headache is ratcheting inside his skull. A sharp, serrated pain stabs behind his left eye, but he can't think about that now. He tries to let go, like the doctor suggested, tries to release the tension from his muscles, but his body feels stiff, his hearing has a tinnitus whine, his blood is crystallizing into ice . . .

"Good luck," Brittany whispers.

"You too," he mutters back. They're as ready as they're going to be.

Bring on the storm.

Chapter Twenty-Six

October 1987, Saturday

Nomi spends nearly ten minutes crouched behind a junker in the rain, wondering if she's making a mistake. Maybe no one's here at the warehouse; maybe they've taken Simon and Brittany elsewhere. She'll have to go through the list in her pocket, one property at a time, in a laborious—

There's a flash of headlights. She ducks lower.

A white Ford Escort enters the alley, parks by the graffitied plywood fence on the West Nineteenth side; Gino Hart gets out, a raincoat over his head. Hart collects a black toolbox out of the car's back seat, locks up. He walks past the rolling garage shutter to the door in the fence, uses his key, closes the door behind him.

Okay, she's definitely in the right place. And thinking about that toolbox, Nomi knows she needs to be inside.

She exhales, stands and walks forward with a casual confidence she doesn't feel until she's at the door. Her lockpicks are already in her hands. The door lock is garbage, about as secure as a bathroom stall; it takes her less than five seconds to get the lock open. She unholsters her gun and swaps it to her left hand, twists the doorknob with her right; then she's inside, moving low.

This is just an apron of frontage before the main facade of the warehouse: Stacked pallets are to the right, then clear driveway space, then barrels and other detritus near the left brick fence. The warehouse itself is vintage and has an arched front entry—two giant riveted doors are pulled open on either side. The entry is dark as the inside of a mouth.

Nomi holds her weapon with both hands in a low-ready position and creeps quickly past the pallet stacks until she's pressed up against the right-hand door. Rain is sheeting down, and she's soaked; she alternates hands and wipes her palms on her combat pants, which doesn't really help much. Then she firms her grip on the gun and slips through the entry to the inside.

No more rain, which is good. Hella gloomy in here though; Nomi takes off her beanie and uses it to wipe her eyes, lets them adjust as she stuffs the beanie in her pocket. It's a garage, this front section. A couple partitioned offices on this side. Two cars are parked here under cover; she's willing to bet money that one of them is Lamonte's, probably the Audi Quattro.

There's a small forklift, maybe broken, over against the left-side wall. This garage anteroom is backed by another wall, with a large metal door on rollers, all ready for someone to grip the iron handle and slide it sideways to enter the warehouse.

Beside that door on the left, above a stack of wooden crates, is an extremely dirty multipaneled window.

In the lull of the rain, Nomi can hear voices coming from inside the warehouse. The metal door could be slid open at any moment. But she's exposed either way, and she needs to see what's going on—and it's better to move as soon as you've decided on a course of action. So she moves, running fast at a diagonal over the concrete floor of the garage. Reaching the crates, eyeballing the wood, pressing hard on the top of the nearest crate to test whether it'll hold her weight. Should be okay.

Staying low, low, she scrambles up and off an old bag of cement onto the first crate, then the next. The third crate is about a foot below the bottom sill of the window—she hunkers down. The gloom of the garage is helping her here, and the storm gusts are muffling the sounds she's making.

Her jacket is dripping, making the knees of her combat pants soggy. Under her layers, she's all over with sweat; her bra feels like two clammy hands cupping her boobs. Pressed up against the topmost crate, she takes off her scarf, swipes it along the top of the wooden sill, clearing dirt off the bottom inch of the window so she can peer inside.

Through cloudy glass, she sees down into a large brick room, big as a theater, high ceilinged. Partitioned storage areas or offices at both left and right, and the whole place is dotted with thick roof pylons. The center of the room is open. Furniture is sparse: a couple wooden tables, a workbench, a bunch of metal chairs. Near a right-hand pylon, a card table.

Four men caught mid-action: Eric Lamonte, in chinos and a white shirt and brown sweater, wool coat, is smoking a cigarette and leaning against a table. Ray Dinkins is yelling, gray coat shifting at his shoulders as he talks with large hand gestures, his face active beneath gel-smoothed hair. Gino Hart, in a Henley and jeans, raincoat abandoned and looking as if cold means nothing to him, is unpacking his toolbox onto the workbench.

And Claude Ameche, craggy and workmanlike, is pulling Simon Noone out of a left-side storage office, into the room's empty center.

Nomi hears her breathing hitch. *Fuck.* This is bad; this is so very, very bad.

Ameche's bandaged hand grips Simon's right wrist, and Ameche's pistol—a dark, snub-nosed Colt Special—is close by Simon's temple. Simon has to crouch to accommodate the height difference as he stumbles reluctantly forward. Nomi can't see Simon's face, but she imagines he's feeling pretty alive to the fact that the metal mouth of Ameche's gun is pressing against the scar where he was last shot in the head.

Thunder booms outside, making the warehouse shake. Nomi's heart is hammering, clogging up her throat, and her skin feels hypersensitive.

How is she going to work this? Five players on the floor, herself on the outside. Maybe Irma will get the guys from the Tenth here, but how long will that take? Will they arrive before or after Simon's had his head blown off? And where's Brittany? They're going to need a distraction, but Nomi can't do shit until she knows where the girl is. Is she even here? Maybe she's not here.

Ameche raises his bandaged hand to show off the damage, talks to Lamonte over his shoulder, keeping his weapon trained on Simon. Muffled words, and a muffled reply from Lamonte. Nomi winces—goddammit, she can't hear a fucking thing from here, with the thick brick walls and the buffeting rain.

But she can watch facial expressions, actions. Ameche looks displeased. He makes Simon sit in a chair, makes him take off his black peacoat and toss it away. Nomi can see splotches of red on Simon's face. A hot bright thread of fear pulls her nerve endings tight. She needs to get Simon and Brittany out of there. But Simon is exposed. *Think, think.*

Ray returns to the door that Simon was dragged out of, pokes his head into the storage room, reemerges looking pained. More muffled shouting and gesticulation. Ameche seems rattled. What the hell is going on down there?

Lamonte looks up at the ceiling and takes a drag of his cigarette. Gino Hart seems unbothered as he continues to methodically unpack whatever nasty shit he's carried in from the toolbox.

Ameche, watching Simon like you'd watch a black mamba curled on your front doormat, suddenly stands back and aims the gun at Simon's forehead. Lamonte barks an order. Nomi finds her heart is trying to slam its way right out of her rib cage, and she has the same feeling as when she started her first year of policing: the sense that whatever insane scenario you've found yourself in—domestic arguments, dog fights, porno-theater altercations, car accidents—it can't possibly be real. But it was real then, and it's real now, and there are armed men in the room below her who are preparing to kill in a brutal fashion to get what they want.

It's not until the metal door nearby starts shifting sideways that she realizes she's lost sight of Dinkins.

". . . fucking *cut me*—I mean, he's fucking *crazy*," Dinkins is grousing to himself, his voice making a chorus with the sliding door's iron grind as it opens. He steps through into the garage; he's got one hand wrapped around his other forearm, and Nomi can see bloodstains on his shirt, which jump out from the loud pattern.

As Dinkins turns to close the door, he spots her.

Dinkins squints. "What the fuck?"

Nomi shoots him.

She knows straightaway it's an error of judgment, and she also knows it's a bad shot. Even as the boom echoes, she's cataloging the reasons why it's bad: high angle, poor light, moving target, her hand wobbling with adrenaline. The bullet has only clipped Dinkins, but she's got no choice now; she's committed—the shot has given her away.

This is turning into a mess. Four on one is terrible odds. She's tilting at windmills. But it's time to act, and worry about the perfect course of action later, in the aftermath—if they get an aftermath.

Nomi jumps down from crate to crate until her boots hit concrete, ignores Dinkins stumbling back, strides through the door with her gun up, sighting her targets.

"What the *fuck*?" Ameche says.

"This isn't the police," Nomi says, and puts one round in his direction.

Ameche ducks. She sends another round toward Lamonte, but he's already dived. Nomi swivels to take in Hart with his hands raised, swivels back in time to see Ameche haul Simon up as a human shield.

Which is right about the moment her whole strategy starts to fall apart.

"Nomi—" Simon starts.

"Come any closer and I'll put a bullet through his *goddamn throat,*" Ameche yells.

Nomi ignores him, ignores the fluttering of hopeless fear in her chest, pivots right, sights on Hart, fires off a shot. But she's telegraphed too much, and Hart has ducked behind a roof pylon.

Ameche's stoic face is red. "Would somebody *shoot* this stupid bitch?"

That's when Nomi feels a crunch in her lower back as someone hits her with what feels like a hot skillet.

She cries out, staggers forward. Her gun goes off wild as she falls to her knees. It's like a charley horse in her back. But she can't stay still—she twists sideways and snaps up her weapon two handed.

Ray Dinkins whacks her gun with the shovel in his hands, and Nomi screams as one of her fingers snaps—a bright, shocking pain. Her gun goes flying.

Dinkins tries another swing, but his reflexes are off—probably from being shot—and Nomi rolls away. But by then Hart has come close enough to kick her in the stomach. She gasps, and he kicks her again; then she's curled up in the fetal position, groaning and coughing on the cold floor.

That's it; it's over. Too easy.

Lamonte has recovered his cigarette from where he dropped it when he dove out of range. Now he takes a drag and blinks his hooded eyes as he looks at what Nomi has been reduced to.

"Put her in a chair," he says, in a deep baritone that cuts through the room.

Is this real? Again, Nomi feels like she has to wonder. But pain brings her back: the throb of her broken finger, the scrapes on her knees, the ache in her spine, the splintery feeling in her ribs. She gets to appreciate the particular textures of each injury as she's hauled up by Hart and dumped unceremoniously on the padded seat of a metal folding chair.

Ameche yanks her leather jacket roughly off her shoulders—goodbye to her knuckle-duster and her Mace. Then, as she's processing that loss, Dinkins grabs her by the hair and yanks back hard enough to make her shriek. It's all the distraction that Hart needs to simply gather both her wrists and duct-tape them together. Now here she is, like a skein of tangled black wool dumped on a chair in the middle of the warehouse.

Wonderful. She hasn't rescued anybody. In fact, she's made it all worse.

Nomi's been sat down directly across from Simon. His face is impassive, and the collar of his black Henley is torn above his knitted vest. This close, the bruises around his eye and nose, the blood on his neck and hands, all stand out much more. She tries to meet his eyes.

"This was probably a terrible idea," she croaks.

"Probably." He doesn't seem perturbed, though.

Is he matching her gallows humor with his own? Or maybe he's in shock. If they knocked him out to get him here, he's probably got a concussion. As she watches, Ameche starts taping him to a chair. It's a crummy tape job, but it doesn't seem to matter: Simon just sits there, letting them push him around. Nomi finds this disturbing. He seems to have gone into some quiet, reserved space behind his eyes where emotions and external activity don't even register. Maybe he hasn't got a concussion; maybe he's got brain damage.

But she gets a tremor of recognition and alarm: This is Simon's Easter Island face, the same blinkered impassivity as when he attacked Ameche at Big Mouth. Is this his sociopath face? Has something flipped in him? *You haven't really seen me lose my shit.* If being hit in the head has realigned the serial-killer circuits in Simon's brain, could this be the first sign?

Then he speaks. "You shouldn't have come."

"Shut up, you piece of shit," Ameche growls, before turning to her. "Little Miss PI girl, huh? You got your delivery, and you still couldn't keep your nose out of it—"

"Fuck off and die," she snaps back.

Gino Hart clips her over the ear. Nomi sees stars.

Ray Dinkins is somewhere behind her, whimpering. "The fucking bitch shot me!"

"*Everybody shut up*," Lamonte says as he steps forward.

In the quiet, wind crashes on the roof like waves on the shore. The air in here is tundra cold, which Nomi's grateful for because it's keeping her alert. She's trying not to panic, so breathing cold air through her nose helps. Her skin feels like it's been sandpapered, and her taped hands pulse with constricted blood. She thinks it's quite likely that she and Simon will die here, and she's trying not to take it personally.

"Now," Lamonte says in forbearing tones, "we were discussing what happened to the kid."

"Fucking dipshit there killed her!" Ray moans, gesturing at Simon. "Then he slashed me with the goddamn box cutter—"

"What?" Nomi says.

"Shut up," Lamonte says, whether to her or to Dinkins, she's not quite sure. "Claude, did you check if the kid is really dead?"

"Not yet," Ameche says.

"You can check if you want," Simon says quietly, "but I cut her pretty good."

"You did *not*," Nomi says. But she's looking at the blood on his face and hands, looking at his detached expression. Oh god, this is not good.

"I had to." He's looking stonily at the floor.

"No." She swallows hard. "No, I don't believe you."

"Believe me, don't believe me—it doesn't really matter."

This is a joke. A trick. "Tell me you didn't kill Brittany."

"'*Tell me you didn't kill Brittany . . .*'" Ray Dinkins makes the words sound whiny as he screws up his face. "Did you not listen? He fucking killed her! I saw it with my own eyes!"

"Shut up, Ray," Lamonte says. "Claude?"

"Sure, boss," Ameche says, and leaves Simon to start toward the office door.

Simon looks at Nomi and sighs, as if this is all very tedious. "Nomi, listen to me. I want you to think back."

"What?"

"All the way back, to when we first met."

"What?" she repeats, blinking. A choking feeling is bubbling up, like rising damp.

"'I've just come from Guatemala. I have amnesia.'" Simon is impersonating himself. "'I need to find myself, but you can't run my fingerprints. Now do you see why I need your help?'"

"No." The damp is in her throat, clotted and foul.

"What the fuck is he talking about?" Dinkins says.

But Simon's eyes are fixed on hers. "It was fun, following you around. I got to see Cevolatti's body. You let me sew you up—you let me into your home. I got to join in the game. It's a good game."

"A *good game*?" Nomi feels heat in her cheeks. "What do you—"

"The very best game of all." Simon grins at her discomposure.

"No," Nomi whispers. "No, no, no . . ."

"It took a long time to get you to trust me, but once I won you over . . ." Simon smiles, blood on his teeth. "Don't you remember what the report said, in my file? *Deceptive and manipulative behavior.*"

Her throat is very dry. "Stop talking. Please stop talking now—"

"Oh, and there was another one, wasn't there?" Simon looks upward, pretending to think about it. "That's right—*a fundamental lack of empathy*. Remember that one?"

Now Ameche backs out of the storage room and says, "I don't know, boss—the kid looks dead to me. It's messy as fuck in there."

To see a man of Ameche's nature grimacing at bloodshed is so bizarre, it's enough to cause Nomi's world to tilt on its axis. Ameche knows death; if he says that Brittany is dead, she must be dead.

Simon is still looking at her. "I killed Brittany because I want to get out of here alive. A seven-year-old kid is weight, and I don't need extra weight. And what does it matter? They were going to kill her anyway."

"Don't say that." Nomi's head is spinning.

Simon looks at her pityingly, his eyes like twin sapphires, hard and cold. This can't be happening. Once again, she can't read him, doesn't know him—has she ever really known him? This can't be real. But what is real? Simon Noone isn't real. He's just a cipher, a made-up name, a guy with no memories and a past full of blood . . .

"Who the hell is this guy?" Ameche asks Lamonte, gesturing at Simon with the gun. "Could he be with the Westies?"

It's a name that Nomi knows, a rival gang in Hell's Kitchen that she dealt with in the Tenth.

"Ask her," Lamonte says, and he lifts his chin at Nomi.

She looks away. Her body is hurting, her mental landscape is fracturing, and she doesn't want this man to look at her—just being perceived by him is repugnant.

"Who's Simon Noone?" Gino Hart says by her shoulder. "Come on, baby, you can tell us." His voice is surprising, mellow, warm as a foot rub. It's unbelievable that a mob torturer should have a voice like a late-night radio DJ.

"I have no idea," Nomi replies, wooden.

Hart shifts position, and now they're all lined up in front of her at varying distances: Ameche with the gun, Simon in his chair, Lamonte at greater distance, Hart at his workbench. Ray Dinkins startles her as he limps into view, holding his shoulder, his coat blotched carmine as he scrapes his ass up onto a table. This is the worst-case scenario if you're a cop: falling into the hands of the enemy, like falling into a pit of vipers.

Now they're arrayed, and she's being looked at by all of them. Her skin prickles like it's been electrified. Being under the microscope like this, knowing each man is examining her and wondering what use he can put her to, is a horribleness so extreme she almost cracks. And Simon? His eyes are the worst: amused, cruel, detached. Nomi swallows hard, feels her gut tighten and cramp. Every particle of her being wants to break into tears, beg for mercy, plead for her life.

But she'll be damned if she'll give these guys anything. No tears. No pleading. No compliance. Kneeling down is against her religion. They can all go to hell.

"Just tell us," Lamonte sighs.

"How about I tell you to eat a pile of dicks," she says.

Her voice is wobbling, but it's there. *You get too attached, sweetie.* Irma's critique. *That was always your thing.* Irma was right. But there's something else that was always Nomi's thing: being a stubborn-assed bitch. It's gotten her in trouble for years. But now, at last, it's found a purpose.

Nomi recovers her steel, breathes through her nose.

And when she looks over, Simon gives her a wink.

Chapter Twenty-Seven

October 1987, Saturday

Did Nomi see him wink? Simon's not sure of anything, having reached the point where colors are starting to coalesce around every person and object in the room.

He had to play it very straight with her to sound convincing in front of Lamonte. Persuading Nomi that he's killed Brittany was always going to be tricky—he had to lean hard into her natural suspicion. It was tough, though. He kept wanting to break character, to grin or snort or make a joke that would ruin the act. Would've done it, too, if his head hadn't felt like it was being squeezed in a vise.

His brain is too big for his skull and is about to start leaking out the sides. His skin is throbbing. This migraine is about to crash into him like a freight train, and he's never handled a migraine without medication before. He has no idea what the repercussions will be.

He wonders if Nomi saw his wink, if she understood what it meant. She's purple again now, though it's a deep black-purple, like squid ink. Her eyes are still pure carnivore. He hopes she got it—the wink, that is. Maybe he accidentally winked both eyes. Or winked multiple times. God, he can't hold it together. It's impossible to know if his acting is cartoonishly obvious or impenetrably subtle.

"If the kid's dead," Lamonte says to Ameche, from someplace behind Simon at left, "we'll have to hold on to the body awhile, maybe stick it someplace cold. We can string the mom along if we send her bits and pieces."

Ameche scratches his neck with his bandaged hand, a green haze all around him. "We don't need the Axedale dude past the tenth, is that right?"

"I can check with Galetti," Lamonte says, but then his tone turns speculative. "I still want to know who this guy is. If he's not local, he could be with some other family, or even from the West Coast. The last thing I need is the Milano boys or those LA Israeli punks breathing down my neck."

Simon wonders which guy they're referring to, then makes the connection: "This guy" is him. They're talking about him. He's going to be questioned, and he'd better brace for it.

"Could he be a pig?" Dinkins asks, his face swirled an oily yellow.

"Ray, use your brain," Gino Hart says. Hart's aura is a violent magenta, a color only seen in nature in things like poisonous bugs or toxic plants. "If he killed the kid, he's not law enforcement."

"Feds can shoot up in front of you," Dinkins whines, "so who the hell knows? Maybe he's deep cover. How the fuck can you tell?"

"Who are you, dipshit?" Ameche pokes Simon in the shoulder before turning back to his boss. "I only got a few details—he's like a ghost. He works at Gennaro's, lives at that dump on Gansevoort . . . Maybe he's fucking the PI girl." Ameche turns to Nomi then, a big grin stretched across his blunt face. "Is he fucking you, sweetheart? Is that what this is? Did you drag your little boyfriend into this mess because you needed a big strong man at your back? Fucking feminist bitches, it's always the same."

"I don't know who he is," Nomi says blankly, and she actually doesn't look sure, so she's really convincing. Simon wonders if maybe he was *too* persuasive when he talked to her?

"What if he *is* with the Westies?" Hart suggests.

"Does it matter?" Lamonte says, shrugging. "Did you ask him?"

"Hey, box cutter man," Hart says. "Are you with Jimmy Coonan's crew?" He makes a face as he looks at Ameche. "Claude, what did I tell you? You hit him too hard."

"I hit him just enough," Ameche counters, and he slaps Simon's shoulder again. "Hey! I'm talking to you, fuckface. What's your deal? Who are you?"

"I'm no one." Simon keeps his eyes on Nomi when he says it. This is going to end badly, but at least these guys aren't focused on her anymore.

"Ah, Jesus," Ray Dinkins laments.

"Let him have it," Lamonte says.

Simon feels a sudden snap in his neck, and he's looking at the other side of the room, which—even before the explosion in his cheek and head—is the first thing that registers when Ameche hits him across the face with the hand holding his gun. Pain radiates out like a burst of white light, filling up Simon's eyeballs, lifting his brainpan.

"Are you a fed?" Ameche pistol-whips him again. "Are you LA?"

"I'm not either of those things." Simon's mouth is bleeding, and the sting feels fuzzy and warm, makes his voice mumbly. "I'm no one."

Ameche shakes his head.

Lamonte says, "Gino?" in a world-weary tone, and Gino Hart steps in close to Simon and says, "You're mine now, baby," and the expression on Hart's face is as happy as a kid on his birthday.

Simon tries to ignore this. He works at moving his wrists around inside the duct tape securing him to the chair.

What seems like eons ago, Captain Felipe Brava berated a crew member in Simon's presence for using duct tape for some chore. Brava had turned to Simon and waved the roll and said, "I hate this stuff. It's stupid stuff. Who would use duct tape on a boat?" which Simon took to mean that moisture acts on tape like it acts on everything you use at sea, that is to say, deleteriously. Metal and rubber and hemp endure, but duct tape is about as useful as paper and probably more annoying, as you think you've done a job, but then the job you did with it breaks again.

Simon's not sure why he's thinking about Brava, or about boats, except that he'd like to be on one right now, and not here in this warehouse. But the captain was right; duct tape will loosen when it's moist, and the blood covering Simon's left wrist is helping the work.

"Okay," Gino Harts says, as he leans with his hands on his knees, regarding Simon. "I'm gonna make you hurt now. If you want it to stop, just tell us who you are."

He uses scissors to cut off Simon's vest, then yanks down the collar of his Henley, and Simon wonders why, until Hart goes to the workbench and collects a cordless drill.

Nomi makes a strangled noise, says, "Oh *god* . . ."

Simon takes a number of deep breaths.

The sound, when Hart uses the drill on Simon's left pectoral, is like nothing he's heard before, except in the slaughterhouse in an amplified version; it's the screech of the electric meat saw as it cuts through a haunch. It's not quite the same sound, but it's in the same family, and Simon would scream just as loud if it were the meat saw cutting him.

"I'm *no one*," he gasps, when Hart pauses. "I'm *no one*."

But he can hardly breathe, the pain in his head like an eclipse, the pain in his chest like a brand. He's going to throw up.

"Heh, then I guess we try again," Hart says, smiling, as he lifts the drill.

"Stop!" Nomi yells. "Fucking *stop*, oh Jesus *Christ*—"

But now Hart is drilling the other side of Simon's chest. Simon shudders in his chair like he's convulsing, pain bursting inside his head like an exploding star. His jaw locks, his legs turn to water. Nomi is crying.

"Are we having fun yet?" Hart asks, grinning like a magenta demon as he turns to Nomi. "Don't worry, sweetheart—you're next."

Simon is drenched in sweat. Strings of saliva and blood spill out of his mouth and onto the floor between his knees. He looks up blearily through his hair as Hart returns the drill to the workbench, pokes around and collects two roofing nails and a portable battery charger with attached jumper cables. Simon is reminded that this man cut off all ten of Ricki Cevolatti's fingers, one by one.

"Man, Gino, you are one nasty sumbitch," Ray Dinkins groans. "I been shot here, by the way!"

"Shut up, Ray," Ameche says. "Gino, is this gonna take long?"

"Not long at all," Hart replies, and before Simon can catch his breath, Hart positions the nails and attaches the battery charger's cable clamps and flicks the switch.

Simon smells meat charring, hears Nomi screaming, and his teeth click together as he has an out-of-body experience.

In his mind, Richard Flores is bending over him, shining a penlight in his eyes, repeating, *"Who are you? Hello? Who are you, my friend . . ."* and Simon wants to bat the light away. It's piercing him, stabbing into his brain, sharp and hot as a laser. Blue electricity is zapping quickly around his teeth, like the blue lightning in *Hellraiser*, and time is moving slow as molasses, fast as a gunshot.

He is floating; he is in a river of time. The colors behind his eyelids explode into fractals and break apart. There's a girl with white hair putting a crown of flowers on his head—he would do anything for her. Now she's ushering him toward the river, and he goes under the water, is washed away. A torrent of images and sensations and impressions flood over him, things appearing and disappearing with such rapidity that he can't keep up: blood, fire, smoke, metal . . . death, meat, ink, sex . . . the stink of incense and the taste of wine. A blade in his hand and a smile on his lips . . .

And he *knows* this, he knows it—he remembers how to slice a roast, how to make a fine cut, how to make someone cry. For a moment, he's lost in a vast ocean of memories related to a past he barely understands. The sense of loss and nostalgia is almost overwhelming, but there's a sense of power too.

This is who he is.

This is his birthright and his legacy. He is a beast of cold blood, a snake on two legs, an alien in an ill-fitting human skin . . .

Simon gasps awake when Hart throws cold water on him.

"Hi there." Hart's pleased with himself. Simon imagines what he'd look like with his eyelids removed. "I think we might try something a little different. What do you say?"

Hart moves aside, and behind him, Nomi is sitting in a chair with her wrists taped together. Her posture is rigid, and if you didn't know her well, you wouldn't realize she's terrified. She's white faced and stiff, silver on her cheeks.

She's been crying for him, Simon realizes with wonder. Despite what he is, she's been shedding tears for him, this girl made of adamantine with a heart full of glass and predatory, mink-dark eyes . . .

Dinkins and Ameche stand at her shoulders. Simon wants to kill them. He wants to kill all of these men, and now he knows how to do it. He remembers asking Nomi, *Do you think I'm dangerous?* She'd been honest with him then, and she's being honest with him now, because her face is clearly saying that she doesn't recognize him, that there's been a change in his internal chemistry, one maybe only she can read.

That chemical change has back-burnered his pain from the torture, brought different sensations and feelings to the fore. Simon remembers the long-ago incident with Malcom Forest in the hallway of the tenement—the sense of uncoiling, of being released from confinement. That feeling has returned to him now. It's all of him.

Hart is holding the bolt cutters. "Look, you seem like a reasonably tough guy? But there's someone who isn't tough, and that's your little girlfriend over here. So I'm going to take off one of her fingers, and then I'll ask you again—"

"Who is he?" Lamonte's deep baritone reverberates from behind Simon somewhere.

Nomi looks at Lamonte over Simon's shoulder, her lips trembling. "He's no one, I swear to god—"

"Tell them," Simon rasps softly.

"Ah, no, don't do this," Nomi whispers as Hart approaches her. Her eyes are frantic white, fixed on the bolt cutters with a combination of horror and hypnotized fascination. "You shouldn't do this—"

"Nomi, tell them," Simon repeats. *Warn them* is what he means, because the tape on both his hands is loose now, and things are about to get interesting.

"Yeah, tell us," Dinkins goofs, grinning despite his injury.

"See these bolt cutters?" Hart says, brandishing them in front of her. "They used to belong to my father. Do you know why they still look like new? Because I maintain my tools, that's why. I clean off the blood and mess after every session—"

"*He's a killer*," Nomi blurts.

There's a moment of quiet. Then Ameche and Dinkins both look at each other and burst out laughing.

"Oh, so he's a *killer*," Ameche says in a mincing voice, twisting the word like he doesn't understand what it means.

"'Killer' my ass." Dinkins sneers.

Hart is still advancing, and Nomi is babbling. "Simon Noone is a sociopathic serial murderer, you're making a big mistake—"

"Enough!" Lamonte bellows.

The man comes forward, so now he's squarely in Simon's field of vision. Lamonte has an aura the same deep brown as a grizzly bear, and he looks as if he'd like to hit everyone in the room over the head with a baseball bat just so he can get a little peace and quiet.

"Miss Pace," he rumbles, "I have been very patient, and I am not a patient man. I recommend that you stop lying to me, because if you continue to waste my time . . ."

But Simon isn't listening anymore.

He knows who he is, and what he can do. He could do this for his own sake, for revenge or for pleasure, but what he'd really like to do is to offer it like a service. As a gift. If Nomi can shed tears for him, the least he can do is give her this gift in return . . .

But is Nomi prepared to wield such a weapon, if someone puts it in her hands?

"Nomi." He tastes blood on his lip as he speaks—he must have bitten his tongue. "Nomi, look at me."

Her eyes drag away from Lamonte, find Simon's. Her voice comes out a whisper. "You killed Brittany."

Simon shakes his head. "Forget . . . forget that now. Just tell me. Do you want this over?"

He ignores Hart, capering with the bolt cutters. Ignores Lamonte, still droning, and Ameche and Dinkins, laughing. There's a bubble in the room, and he and Nomi are enclosed in it, and the only sounds Simon can hear are his own voice and hers.

"Yes," Nomi breathes.

"You have to say it," Simon says.

He can see her mind casting back to that day they first met, the incident in the hall, Simon's clumsy attempt to force Malcolm to get lost.

Don't hurt him, Nomi said then.

That's not what she's saying now.

She looks directly into Simon's eyes. "Do it. Fuck them up."

Simon sighs, and smiles, and stands from his chair.

Chapter Twenty-Eight

October 1987, Saturday

Thunder booms in the warehouse, and Simon stands, and Nomi thinks it's possible that she may have miscalculated.

She's seen evil; she's familiar with it. But when she witnessed Gino Hart at work with the drill and the battery cables, something inside her broke a little. She knows what Simon Noone is, but watching him writhe in pain flipped her perspective—because how is Simon any worse than these guys? Is a sociopath worse than garden-variety evil, if you're the victim of it? All she could think was *It'll be me next; it'll be me*, and maybe when this is over, Simon will make it quick, because god knows Lamonte and his crew won't be showing her any mercy.

But now Simon's standing, she's having serious misgivings.

He winked at her—she's got no way to interpret that—and right now he's too tall and still, there in his filthy jeans and boots and sweat-loose black Henley, like he's poised to take flight; if he suddenly sprouted sharp-bladed wings and mowed down every person in the room with them, she wouldn't be surprised. He looks calm as an ocean, but she can see the way his blue eyes are lit like torches.

She asked for this—*Fuck them up*—but now she's not sure what she's unleashed.

He told her about the experience of his migraine auras at the club; he told her she looked purple, yet in this moment, Nomi thinks Simon's haloed in black: black as the underworld, black as a nightfire, black as the furious cosmos Nomi sees when she cuts her skin and closes her eyes.

She was scared of him before? Now she's fucking *terrified.*

And she's not fast enough to look away as he steps forward and grabs Gino Hart's hair from behind, wraps long fingers around the handle of the bolt cutters, wrenches Hart's head to the side and bites down on his neck. Nomi hears the *crunch*, flinches. Blood spurts, Hart screams. His arm lifts automatically with the tool, and Simon uses the weight of momentum to yank the bolt cutters' closest blade into Hart's right eye.

Hart shrieks, Dinkins screams. Lamonte jerks away.

Ameche lifts his gun.

Fuck that. This is Simon's time now. Nomi smacks both her tied hands up, into Ameche's arm. His aim flies north, and the Colt goes off at the ceiling with a crack like a whip. Ameche snarls, backhands Nomi off her chair. As the chair tips, she tumbles onto the concrete with a yell; hitting the concrete fucking *hurts*, but she kicks out as she falls, manages to shove the legs of her chair into Ameche's crotch. He curls over, moaning.

Above her, like he's releasing a dance partner, Simon lets Hart tumble down. Simon's still holding the handle of the bolt cutters, so the blade comes free with a ghastly pop. Nomi's distracted by that, and by the sight of Hart choking on his own blood on the floor in front of her.

And now Simon's started, he will not stop.

Nomi sees him adjust his grip on the bolt cutters, then quickstep to Ameche and swing the bolt cutters into the side of Ameche's head like a bat.

Ameche goes down. Hart is down. Simon's closing; he's knocking over all the pins. His face is relaxed, elated. Part of Nomi is horrified to see that there's an engine inside Simon that runs on people's pain, that's greased by their humiliation and hurt. But when it comes to Lamonte's crew, she's somehow all out of sympathy.

Behind her, Ray Dinkins is babbling. "Oh shiiit, I didn't do *nothing*, I didn't do *nothing*—"

Lightning flashes, interrupting whatever Ray's saying he didn't do, as Simon walks past Nomi's tipped-sideways chair, advances on Dinkins with light steps. Nomi doesn't turn her head: Her cheek is hurting from her collision with the floor, and she wants to stay low, doesn't want to see. There's a cut-off scream that becomes a gurgling whistle, then a sound like kitchen scissors on a chicken leg, then a thump, and Nomi knows that Dinkins is dead, or nearly dead, or about to be dead, and that bolt cutters were involved, so she chooses not to look.

The most important thing right now is her gun: She has to find it. There's no way to predict what will happen here now, or how far Simon will take it—pretty fucking far, from what she's already seen—and she has an ominous feeling that maybe he'll be impossible to switch off. Like, maybe this is it: Whether he's been a sociopath from the start, like he just told her, or whether the torture jogged those circuits in his brain back into an order they're more familiar with, now he's been unleashed in his original form, the black prince of murder. And she couldn't give a shit what happens to Lamonte's guys, but without her gun, she's got no chance at all.

Ignoring Hart gargling on his own blood, ignoring her broken finger, she army crawls toward the left. To her right, another ruckus—she glances over. Lamonte is roaring like a bull, his heavy-lidded eyes wide open as he lunges toward Simon, who's moved to the workbench. Nomi flinches as Simon sidesteps, slaps his hand on Lamonte's shoulder; the bigger man howls as he stumbles forward into nothing. Simon has stabbed a screwdriver into the top of his shoulder.

Nomi hears her breath panting, redirects her eyes. She's only three more crawling steps away from something glinting on the floor near the base of a roof pylon. She crawls harder, grabs for it, it's her . . . box cutter. Fuck. But yay? She's found the box cutter that apparently Simon used to wound Dinkins. As in predead Dinkins. Dinkins when he was still animate. Nomi huffs laughter and wonders if she's succumbing to hysterics. She controls it, clambers up, puts her back against the pylon. For a moment, her mind takes refuge in the box cutter's glinting blade, then she snaps out of it and starts awkwardly sawing at the tape on her wrists.

Simon is moving, crouching down. He's got a chisel and a mallet, and he's finishing off Hart. Nomi gags a little at the sound of the man's screams, at the sight of the blood—Jesus Christ, there is blood everywhere.

She's got the tape off, but her hands are shaking. She tries to recover her firmness, the iron certainty that adrenaline gave her as Simon makes the last strike that finally puts Hart to sleep forever. Nomi braces her knees. She's got a support pylon, she's got a box cutter, and if she can find her gun—

There's a garbled cry, and on her right, a rush of movement. Nomi's surprised when Claude Ameche runs at her, is even more surprised when his tackle bowls her over—she lands on her shoulder and cracks the side of her head against concrete, and for a moment, all she can see are black sparkles, fizzy rockets, fireworks. When her vision recovers, Claude Ameche is on top of her, crushing her, hammering with his hands.

"Buckin' bish!" He's screaming, and the damage to his face is terrible: mashed ear, swollen lip, bloodshot eye, probably a broken cheekbone. *"You buckin' bish!"*

"Fuck you!" Nomi screams, and she ducks her head before remembering she has a goddamn *box cutter*—she stabs and slashes as best she can.

Ameche yells; blood streams down his facial crags and crevasses onto his shirt. But he's strong, and when his hands find her neck and squeeze, Nomi can't think of anything but *Can't . . . breathe . . .* and she drops the box cutter as her arms turn to jelly, there's a red film over her eyes, darkening rapidly from the edges . . .

Then the pressure is gone and air rushes in with a whoop. She coughs, coughs again, rolls over—

Claude Ameche is lying on his back beside her; nearby, the battery charger. Ameche's body is jolting. Simon is looking on, fascinated. He turns the dial on the charger up as high as it will go. Nomi hears an electric whine, smells smoke.

She yells, hoarse voiced, and scrambles away on her ass. Bumps into Gino Hart's body, yells again, flips onto her hands and knees to scramble elsewhere, keeps her eyes down and focused on the concrete because everywhere she looks, some unbelievably horrifying *shit* is happening. She keeps scrambling until she runs into a pair of brown leather loafers, and then there's a hand in her hair, someone's hauling her up, and suddenly she's face to face with Eric Lamonte.

"Where're you going, Miss Pace?" Lamonte rumbles, and even when Nomi screams and brings up an elbow, he seems to anticipate her, pulling back her head and smacking her in the throat.

Nomi goes down, retching, and then it's too late. Lamonte has her by the hair again, she's on her knees, and warm metal is kissing her cheek.

"I am not a *tradesman*," Lamonte hisses. "I don't need garbage tools. I am a *professional*, and if you don't call off your dog, I'm gonna put a bullet through your jaw, do you understand? Nod if you understand."

Lamonte's normally swarthy face is white, only flushed around his deep-set eyes. He's sweating. He still has a screwdriver half-embedded in his shoulder. He looks desperate.

Nomi nods.

"Now *get up*," Lamonte commands, "before that fucking crazy motherfucker loses interest in Ameche and—"

He hauls at her again, and Nomi does the thing she was taught by Irma the first week she was on the force: She goes limp, like a bag of sand, all her weight shifting to the lowest part of her body.

Lamonte, like most attackers, isn't expecting it. He overbalances, stumbles forward, the metal barrel of her own Smith & Wesson skidding off her cheek. Nomi grabs his wrist and *bites* as hard as she can—she's seen what's possible now—until Lamonte yells, and blood floods into her mouth, and the gun fires so close to her face that for a second, she's worried that her eyelashes are on fire. She feels gunpowder sear her cheekbone as she's deafened.

When she falls backward, tinnitus screaming in her ears, Lamonte roars, enraged. She can hardly hear him, but she sees the blood dripping down his wrist and hand as he turns the gun toward her and pulls the trigger—

Nothing happens. His eyes go wide.

That's why you always count your shots, asshole. So much for Lamonte being a professional.

On Lamonte's next pull, she hears the empty click; her hearing is still muffled like she's underwater. But he's not out of surprises yet: He dives for his coat pocket, yanks out a blue pearl handle, pops out the switchblade, takes a step—

"Hello, friend," Simon Noone says.

Nomi startles almost as hard as Lamonte—but Lamonte is the one who looks most afraid. Simon, by contrast, looks like the Angel of Death: His boots and hands are covered in blood; the knees of his trousers are smeared dark with it. Below the torn collar of his black Henley, the wounds from the drill are red-black and weeping. His injuries make him look like he's stepped straight off a battlefield, but his blue eyes glow against the bruises on his face, the wet ink of his hair.

He's a body length away, still advancing. His movements have a sinister grace, and Nomi thinks she can feel something like static electricity crackling all around him.

Lamonte backs up, appalled, slashing the knife in a wide arc. "Stay the *fuck* away from me, you fucking *psycho*!"

Nomi almost feels sorry for him. Here's a man who's senior, who's fought his way up through the cesspool of mafia politics to make it to the position of general, now confronting someone completely outside his worldview. For people like Lamonte, murder is business. For people like Simon, murder is fun.

"You're going to die here in this warehouse," Simon says conversationally as he walks steadily, inexorably closer, heedless of the knife's danger. He holds out his hands, which are dripping with red but completely empty. "If it makes you feel better, though—look, no weapons."

Nomi gets a sickening feeling that Simon's playing with his food.

"You want to make me feel better?" Lamonte is still backing up, jowls wobbling, slicing the air in front of himself. "Go set yourself on fire, you fucking *freak*—"

"I would," Simon says, grinning, "but Hart didn't bring the blowtorch."

And he finally walks close enough that Lamonte's blade finds its target: The knife shears through the fabric of Simon's shirt. Nomi sees the white skin below his breastbone peel open, bleeding fast.

"*Simon*!" she screams.

Lamonte makes an ugly grin.

But that's all he gets to do, as Simon grabs the box cutter out of the back waistband of his trousers and makes a quick, ferocious slash that draws a crimson line straight across Lamonte's throat.

The line starts leaking. Lamonte drops to his knees.

When he keels sideways, Simon sinks over him with the blade raised, and that's when Nomi finally looks away.

Chapter Twenty-Nine

October 1987, Saturday

He's lost in a red fugue, and it's like music.

On the cutting-room floor at Gennaro's, nobody wants to lose concentration because with the tools they're using, that could be dangerous. Piping in radio tunes to pass the time is no good—there's always arguments over the station—but quite often, Mike Nell will play classical music through the speakers, so Simon finds himself cutting steaks or boning out a shoulder to the strains of Dvořák, or Vivaldi, or Nell's favorite, Erskine.

This is how Simon discovered the music of Jean Sibelius. He's listening to Sibelius now as he does a similar job: peeling and carving, slicing the best cuts. He's unlikely to get through the brisket as this knife is simply not sufficient to the task, but he's making good progress until he hears someone calling his name.

"Simon," Nomi says. Her voice is hoarse; she sounds a little like she's choking and a little like she's crying. "Simon, *stop*."

"What?" He turns on his knees.

Where before Nomi was roiling like a violet maelstrom, now her colors are fading to a dusky mauve. She's still trembling, pulsing like a heart, but now he can see how washed out she is, pale and exhausted in her combat pants and the black sweater that's falling off her shoulder. Somewhere above them, the white noise sound of rain.

"They're dead, Simon. They're all dead. And you need to stop . . . doing that." She glances at the knife in his hand, glances away.

"I'm just finishing this last—" he starts. But when he turns back to his work, he sees what it really involves.

It's shocking enough that he drops the blade.

He staggers up off his knees, turns to face her, and the thing he just saw is mercifully gone. Was it ever there? The line between reality and hallucination is wavering. Where is he? He puts a hand to his head—god, the ache there is unbearable. "I need to finish work."

"No," she says. "You need to stop."

"But there won't be a—"

"Simon, look at me." Nomi steps close, almost close enough to touch. She has a dark mark—a kind of long streak, like she's been hit with the edge of a ruler—across her left cheekbone, and she's cradling her right hand. "It's over. You've done enough."

What did I do? What did I do? He's not sure he wants to know. He wants someone to take his elbow, tell him everything is all right, that there's simply been an accident. He wants someone to tell him what's real.

Somewhere far away, the strains of Sibelius, like he's still at Gennaro's. "Should I . . . take a break?"

"That sounds like a good idea," Nomi says evenly.

But for some reason, he needs it spelled out. "You have to say it."

She looks directly into his eyes. "Simon, stop now. Take a break. It's done."

"Okay." When he blinks, the room shifts, returns, shifts. His thoughts are spinning, and there are images of beef carcasses on the backs of his eyelids. Or are they bloody corpses? "I think . . . I think I really need a cigarette."

"Come on," Nomi says, voice quiet. "Let's get your cigarettes. They're probably in your coat."

She walks toward the roof pylon near the storage-room door. Simon tries to follow. He manages to take four or five steps before his headache rocks him, and pain starts spreading like a slow fire throughout his entire body as he tips, collapses down, everything happening in slow motion, and then he's lying flat.

"Simon?" Nomi says.

"Simon!" another voice shrieks, and it's a voice he recognizes. He recognizes the girl, too, as she bolts from the storage room like a streak of burning coral, dives onto him and hugs him around the neck. "Simon, *don't die*!"

"I'm not dying," he says weakly, "I'm just resting on the floor."

But she's strangling him a little in her enthusiasm, and the high pitch of her squeals feels a bit like having iron spikes driven into his brain, so dying isn't out of the question.

"Brittany?" Nomi drops to her knees beside him, her eyes wide with amazement.

"I played dead, just like we worked out!" Brittany crows. She's bloody, covered in gore; her yellow tee is half-dyed red. But she looks jubilant, the gap of her missing teeth prominent as she turns to Nomi. "I played dead. Simon put this blood on me, it's ground beef. It's kinda nasty, and he had to use some of his own blood? But we tricked them pretty good."

"*Brittany?* Oh my *god*." Nomi seems to be in shock. "Oh my god, let me look at you—Brittany, holy shit . . ." She's holding the girl at arm's length, hugging her tight, holding her out again.

"Did you see Simon go crazy? He's like a robot," Brittany whispers. "Like the Terminator or something."

"What the hell—when did you see *The Terminator*?" Nomi whispers back, but now she's glancing between the kid and him. "No injuries. Nothing except the damage to her mouth."

"You mean my teeth? Those fell out a couple days ago—Mom says that's what they do, 'cause they're for babies." Brittany's grinning to high heaven. The migraine auras are leaving Simon's vision, but for the moment he can still see that the girl is the color of bubblegum, or those pink-and-yellow candies that Sofia Rosa likes. "I'm not a baby anymore. I'm a kid."

"She's a good kid," Simon murmurs, looking up at the high ceiling. "The best kid."

"*You* have more injuries than she does," Nomi points out.

He's becoming aware of that.

"Let me look at you," Nomi says, but this time, she's talking to him. Her cold fingers touch the skin below his collarbones, fold up the wet fabric at his waist, and she hisses. "That's . . . Oh Jesus. I mean, it's shallow, but it's not a cat scratch."

"Time to go to the hospital," Brittany intones solemnly.

"No hospitals," Simon says, almost at the exact same time Nomi does.

But now Nomi is leaning over him again. "Simon, can you hear that? I can hear sirens."

He can hear them, too—the "brrp brrp" of police cars in the far distance, the tones clashing and mixing somehow. The sounds don't bring a welling sense of relief, the way they clearly do for Nomi. It takes him a second to remember why, but then it comes back. His fake papers . . . his old identity . . . the things he did as Simon Gutmunsson . . . the things he's done now . . .

"*The best idea would be to not get arrested*," he whispers. Then he takes hold of Nomi's arm. "Help me up."

"What?" She looks taken aback that he would even suggest it.

"I can't be here when the police arrive," he reminds her. "Help me up."

"You can't just *leave*!" Her hands are raised and fluttering, even as he rolls onto his side, pushes himself toward upright. "Simon, you've been *stabbed*, you're bleeding all over the place—"

"Nomi," he says earnestly. "Think about it." It takes her a minute, because she's in shock, but he can see in her eyes when she gets it. "I can go out the way you and everyone else came in, right? I'll just walk outside and keep walking."

"*Wait*," she says, then some sort of mechanism rights itself in her brain, and she gets up and runs over to some place he can't see behind him. By the time he's struggled awkwardly into a sitting position—ow—she's back with a set of keys, which she shoves into his hand. "Gino Hart parked outside on the street. It's a white Ford Escort with a busted side window. We're near West Nineteenth and Tenth Avenue—oh shit, can you even drive?"

He starts to laugh at that, but it's too painful, so he stops. "I guess we'll find out." Then, as Nomi's helping him to stand up—fuck, that *hurts*—he thinks of something else. "The cops will ask what happened."

Nomi puts a hand to her forehead; it seems as if she might have a headache too. Brittany looks up at Nomi and pats her knee; then Nomi gets another flash of common sense. "Lock me in the storage room with Brittany."

"What?"

"I mean it—lock us both in the storage room."

It's smart, a level of smart he's only just able to keep up with at the moment. "Good idea. And look, I won't go to the tenement, in case the police go there with you to do follow-up. Meet me at the Riverview?"

Nomi is passing him his coat. "Will you be all right?"

Pulling on his coat involves moving too many parts of him that sting or ache, but he accomplishes it somehow. "I survived a headshot, I'm pretty sure I'll survive this. Okay, let's go."

Nomi picks up Brittany in her arms, walks over to the storage-room door. She's reassuring the girl that next time the door opens, Brittany's mom will be there, but it's still a hard sell—Simon understands why. But the sirens are closing, and there's not much time.

Before he shuts the door on them both, he squeezes Brittany's shoulder and says goodbye, gives Nomi her jacket. "Good luck with the police."

"Good luck on the road." Her dark eyes are a little vulnerable, for what he thinks might be the first time. "See you soon."

Then the solid door has sealed them in, and he flips the hasp and clicks the padlock, walks away.

Simon has no memory of arriving at the warehouse, because of unconsciousness, and now he's got to navigate his way out. He staggers to a large metal sliding door, walks through and discovers a garage. Straight ahead, a large warehouse door is open: Wind blows in, and it's cold, and he can see the outside. He has no idea where he is, but this is the direction he's moving in, and hopefully, he'll be gone before the police arrive.

He pulls his peacoat tighter, limps through this garage area past an old forklift; then he's in a front yard which is open to the gray sky. Rain is still coming down, a light drizzle now, and the cold breeze sneaks in behind his collar; the nape of his neck is damp, and he shivers. There's a plywood fence, and on the left, an entry door, which is swinging a little in the breeze; it bumps him gently as he totters out onto the street.

Sirens are getting louder. He looks around: On his right, parked on the curb, is a white car with a spiderweb of cracks in the rear passenger window. He walks over to it, uses the keys in his hand to unlock the driver's side door.

Getting into the car is tricky and somewhat painful. But once he's in, and the door is shut, he's warmer. Now what? He exhales, lets his hands move: They function confidently of their own volition, putting the blood-slippery key in the car's ignition, starting the engine, remembering headlights and wipers and seat belt. He even knows how to put the seat back to accommodate his legs, which are longer than Gino Hart's were.

I know how to drive. How about that.

Simon puts the car in gear, works the hand brake, and rolls off the curb. He still hasn't had a cigarette, and he has a strong desire for one, but determines that—on balance—destabilizing his newly discovered driving skills and jolting his body's various wounds for the sake of a nicotine hit probably isn't worth it. He's mostly numb right now, and he'd like to keep it that way for a while.

His brain is still whirring, though, and it's currently showing him a map of New York City streets from West Nineteenth to Eleventh Avenue and onward—he even remembers which streets are one way only.

Turn left onto West Nineteenth, left again onto Eleventh, left onto West Fifteenth, right onto Ninth, right onto Jane . . .

He'll be at the Riverview in no time.

Chapter Thirty

October 1987, Saturday

The hardest part, for completely understandable reasons, was convincing Brittany to go back with her into the storage room. But it was worth it, just to see the look on the little girl's face when the door is cracked open by a couple of the guys from Tenth Precinct and Solange is on the other side.

Both Solange and Brittany burst into tears. Nomi gets a bit choked up, before reminding herself that she has to have her shit *vaguely* together in front of Felix Balter and her former colleagues—although she does get a solid hug from Irma, still in her civvies, so that kind of helps. It also helps that Irma assures her she's following up personally to guarantee Brittany and Solange won't be separated by social services; Nomi was worried about that.

Brittany is checked over by the EMT, who says she's completely fine, although he notes that she seems a little underfed, and slightly groggy with shock. Nomi has to wave both hands to get them to check *her* over. The EMT guy says the grains of gunpowder in her cheek will work out on their own, and he examines her finger, finally saying, "Well, it's broken"—so helpful. He doesn't even give her drugs, just suggests she take ibuprofen, before giving her one of those stupid metal finger splints, which she immediately gives back in favor of simply taping her pinkie to her ring finger. Altogether, the EMT's a real dud, but Nomi feels pretty proud of herself that she didn't give the scalpel blades in his medical kit more than a single glance.

Balter wants to question her; then after he's looked around the warehouse, he wants to question her some more. But the beauty of being a civilian is that she can simply say, "I'm feeling crummy now, and I want to go home," and they can't make her stay. There isn't much she has to lie about—apparently, being locked in a storage room for the duration of the incident provides you with a Get Out of Jail Free card—and she's not doing the cleanup, thank Christ: A job of that magnitude is best left to the professionals.

About an hour after the blues arrive, Irma comes over and says, "Are you sick of being here?"

"Yeah, actually, I am." Nomi's feeling that postadrenaline exhaustion now, but she's still amused by Irma's T-shirt, which has a big Daffy Duck on it. "Can you give me a ride?"

"Have you been checked by medical?"

"Sure, for whatever that's worth."

"All right," Irma says, "let me just tell them I'm taking you."

Balter puts up some resistance, but tough shit. The only thing Nomi makes sure to do before she leaves is to wave at Solange and Brittany in the back of the EMT van. Solange gives her a thumbs-up and a mouthed "*Thank you*," and Nomi thinks this feeling may actually be better than cutting.

They walk through the drizzling rain to Irma's shitbox blue Honda Civic, parked a half block away because of all the unit response vehicles, and Nomi pours herself into the front passenger seat. She finally feels like she can exhale. "I really appreciate this, Irm."

"No problem." Irma buckles her seat belt. "Oh, and I heard back about Jeremy Axedale. Gaffney and the other response unit broke into the Perry Street apartment—apparently, the kid was pretty strung out, but he wasn't hurt. They put him in an ambulance with a couple uniforms, and his mom was going to meet them at the hospital."

"Glad to hear that story had a happy ending." But Nomi doesn't actually care much, now Brittany's safety is assured. It's over.

Irma starts the car, puts on the wipers, and pulls out. "Pretty crazy scene back there."

"Uh-huh." Nomi has her head back on the rest.

"Never seen a mess quite like it." Irma seems determined to give her a little side-eye. "Nomes, can you level with me? You're not going rogue on me, are you? Because I know I said you should take Lamonte out if you have a chance, but that was more of a *joke*—"

"It wasn't me, Irma." Nomi can say it with total honesty because it's pretty much the truth.

"Okay. Then good." Irma's face and shoulders soften with relief. She snorts and gives Nomi a grin. "I mean, I never really pegged you as the 'carve 'em up' type, you know?"

"Tell you the truth," Nomi says, "I'm coming around to the idea," and Irma guffaws.

Nomi almost falls asleep on the way back to Gansevoort, but when Irma pulls up at the tenement, she rouses enough to remember something. "Oh shit, my piece."

"I'll get it back to you once ballistics is done with it," Irma says. "Babe, I'm really glad you're okay. Please don't go chasing after mobsters on your own anymore. You nearly gave me a heart attack."

They hug, and Nomi takes a lot of comfort from Irma's soft, tobacco-smelling warmth. "Thanks for the cavalry rescue. Give my love to Dez. And, you know—thank you for everything. I couldn't have worked this one out without you."

Irma sniffs and smiles. "I'm still your partner in all the ways that count."

"I know you are. Get out of here."

Nomi makes a tired wave as Irma drives away. But as soon as the Civic is out of sight, she walks into the tenement, climbs—painfully—upstairs to Simon's apartment and uses his keys, grabs the things she needs from his place before returning to the lobby area and knocking on Sofia Rosa's door.

Her landlady answers, wiping her hands on her apron. "No-mee! You are looking very tired today, yes? Do you want coffee?"

"No coffee today," Nomi says. "But Sofia Rosa, do you still have all the stuff that Simon used to sew me up? Can I maybe borrow it?"

Her landlady puts everything in a big Ziploc bag, and Nomi stuffs it into her jacket pocket before going back outside and limping toward the Riverview. On the way, a few people ask if she's okay; Jamie from Florent gives her half a plain bagel. The drizzle is clearing, a minor miracle. Nomi chews on the bagel, finishes it as she finally arrives at the hotel on Jane Street.

Cherie is in the lobby and appears to have been waiting for her. "He's through the ballroom door, in the side bathroom. I already got him a soda, and some hot water and clean towels. He was real fussy about the 'clean' part, even though he looks like he's about to keel over. I said, 'Sweetie—

"Thanks, Cherie, let me go check."

In the side bathroom—which is much bigger and nicer than the one Nomi used last Friday, with a lot of white tile—Simon is sitting on the countertop, bracing his booted foot against one of the pipes along the wall. A cigarette, almost ash down to the butt, is eddying smoke from its spot in the corner of his mouth. He's shirtless, using a damp towel to wipe blood off his neck and chest; as she arrives, he presses the towel firmly against the shallow slash wound that extends from just under his breastbone over to the ribs on his left.

"That's not going to stop bleeding until it's stitched up," Nomi pronounces. She's talking from experience.

"Or glued," Simon agrees. He tosses the rest of the cigarette into the nearest sink, sighs deeply. "You made it."

"Holy shit, look at you," Nomi says.

He smiles, wan, clearly exhausted, his eyes ringed by brown circles. Beaten up, but still alive. "Hey—I can drive."

"Congratulations." Nomi unpacks her supplies onto the countertop. "This stuff is from Sofia Rosa. I'm going to lay it out here on a towel, and you can tell me what to do."

Simon looks at her hands, which are still shaking slightly, the right one taped up on one side. "Actually, I think what I'd like you to do is assist."

"Rude. Okay, fine—let me wash up." She remembers, scrounges in another pocket. "Oh, and here, I brought you a clean shirt and some Vicodin."

"Thank you," he says fervently, and he puts the shirt aside, swallows two pills with a slug from a bottle of Mountain Dew.

He uses the numbing cream again, this time on himself, and sends her out to the drugstore on Jane between Eighth Avenue and Hudson to look for some larger dressings. But she suspects it's to get her out of the way while he starts the stitching, and sure enough, by the time she returns, he's already completed six of the stitches he'll need.

Nomi walks into the bathroom again just as he's drawing the needle through for the next one, the top edge of skin stretched and gaping red. She turns her face away, cheeks hot like she's walked in while he's getting dressed. "Jesus, Simon."

"You're right about this numbing cream. It's not really adequate." Sweat is beaded on his forehead. "Talk to me? Distract me."

Nomi draws over a plastic chair that someone stacked in the corner of the bathroom, takes a seat. "Okay, so Balter and the guys from Tenth think Lamonte and his men were attacked by a rival mob group. The Westies and the Gambino family both operate in Chelsea and Hell's Kitchen, and there's been a lot of shifting alliances. People get killed—it happens."

"Wow." He ties off a stitch.

"Yeah." Her voice echoes strangely in here, with all the tile. She examines her own face in the bathroom mirror, winces at the streak of gunpowder on her cheek: It looks like bad club makeup. "Gaffney said, with the amount of damage inflicted on the four bodies, it was probably the work of a few guys. I mean, speaking personally, I heard a couple different voices when I was locked in the storage room with Brittany, but it was hard to clearly identify anyone . . ."

"Uh-huh." Simon rinses blood off his fingers in a bowl of boiled water, goes back to work. "Did Brittany get home to her mother?"

"Yeah," Nomi says softly. "That was really good."

"So it was worth it."

He looks like he's in a considerable amount of pain, although his pupils are shrinking, which means the Vicodin's kicking in. Nomi wonders how it works, with head-injury amnesia. Does Simon's persona from the last five years just float away or go to sleep when his serial-killer side comes out? Is it a Jekyll-and-Hyde thing? Is there a trick she can employ to call him back, like ringing a bell at the end of a hypnosis session?

Or maybe it's nothing like that. Maybe they're a gestalt now, the two halves of him finally joined up: the sociopath in him becoming ascendant whenever it's needed, fading when the crisis is over.

But aren't we all like that? She isn't a stubborn-assed bitch all the time, is she? Geez, maybe she is. Whoops.

However Simon's psychology works, it served its purpose: Brittany needed rescuing, Simon rescued her. He even lied through his teeth to Nomi to make it happen. She's not thrilled about that part, but she can appreciate why he did it. And once again, she realizes that she's decided: She's not going to turn him in. She's not going to say anything. She can't dredge up any guilt over the murders of a bunch of mafia creeps—not after what she's lived through today—and she knows from her own experience that sometimes there's a chasm between justice and the law. So if Simon is going to restrict his murderous urges to the creeps of the world, then . . .

Then maybe she's just messed up enough to be okay with that.

She watches Simon snip the ends of another stitch: one more to go. "Brittany remembers you. She remembers what you did—some of what you did. But while we were in the storage room together, before Balter and his guys arrived, I told her it would be best for you if we didn't mention anything about you to anyone. She's her mother's daughter, she gets it."

"I mean, she's just a kid. I guess we'll see if she's able to stay quiet." He glances over. "One of these days, I'll be caught on the radar, though."

"And that will be a problem, one of these days," Nomi says. "But not today."

His hands have a fine tremor as he ties off the final stitch, and he blows out air once it's all done. Nomi helps him to get clean and to apply Neosporin and dressings to the stitched cut, plus his torture injuries and the slash on his left inner forearm. She does, after all, have some personal experience with wound treatment.

Getting Simon's arms through the sleeves of his black button-up is complicated, but then he can fasten the front himself. When he slides off the countertop, he sways; Nomi steadies him at his waist, as he puts a warm hand on her shoulder. He seems vaguely surprised that she's comfortable enough to get this close.

"Are you still scared of me?" He drops his hand, leans on the edge of the countertop, giving her space. His blue eyes are slightly glassy, slightly wary. "You've seen what I am now. You didn't lie to Lamonte—I'm a killer. It's in my blood somehow."

"But when I told you to stop, you did," Nomi points out. "I don't think you have a split personality, Simon. There's no 'other you'—you're just you. And you chose to stop."

"I only stopped when Lamonte was dead."

"Listen, I was *glad* you killed Lamonte." She feels strangely compelled to shake him out of any lingering funk. "D'you really believe Lamonte, or any of those guys, would've given us a single thought after they killed us? No. And instead, we killed them. We do the things we need to do to survive. I mean, you know what I do. What I am. Does that revolt you?"

"No." His gaze is scanning over her face. "We're both . . . creatures of appetite."

"That's right. And I set rules for my appetite. I exercise control over it. I've learned to deal with it. If I can live with myself, so can you."

His expression goes soft. "Concentrate on being the man I want to become, huh?"

"Yes." Nomi moves to lean beside him, takes a swig of his soda. "And, I don't know . . . Keep busy. Work with me."

"What?"

"Yeah—work with me." She's not sure why she's suggesting this now, but it feels right. "I mean, still do your other job, obviously. But also, hey, let me exploit some of those skills and freaky insights and whatever that you've got, in a way that will actually *help* people—like you helped Brittany. Think about it. For the last five years, you didn't know where all that stuff came from. Well, now you know. Now you can *harness* it."

He bites his bottom lip. "But . . . what if the me I was starts to reemerge?"

Nomi stands to face him, caps the soda and sets it down. "Like I said, I give advice with provisos. But you want my advice? Don't overthink it."

"Don't overthink it? Okay." He looks grateful, relieved even, for this strange absolution.

"Yeah." Nomi hands him his coat. "Now come on. Let's get you home."

Chapter Thirty-One

October 1987, Saturday

The walk home is slow going, and Simon feels a twinge someplace on his body with every single step, but at last they're on Gansevoort and back at the tenement. Incredibly, it's nearly five thirty in the afternoon; the day's storm has blown itself out, leaving the district's streets cool and clean smelling, which is certainly a novelty.

Nomi helps him on the stairs, which are a challenge. Then he's back inside his warm, golden apartment—how he's missed it!—and she's steering him to sink into a chair, bringing him a glass of water.

"Here you go." She sets the glass and the bag of medical supplies on his breakfast table. "And hey, I have to get some groceries before I flake out, so I might as well walk down to Gennaro's and tell your supervisor guy that you're out of action for tonight, yeah?"

Simon winces at the thought of screwing up Mike Nell's roster. "Give him my apologies and tell him I'll be back on board in a couple days."

"I'm sure he'll be fine about it. Get some rest. I'll knock on your door later and make sure you're still alive."

He raises his eyebrows. "Coma watch?"

Nomi grins. “I mean, you’ve probably got a concussion, right? Seems only fair that I get to return the favor and wake *you* up every four hours. Okay, last chance—do you need anything from Perrotta’s?”

“Thanks, but no. I’m good.”

She turns for the door, hesitates. “One thing before I go . . .”

“What is it?”

“‘It’s a good game’?” She tilts her head, like the inquisitive little mammal she is.

He sighs. He’d been wondering if she would bring this up, and now, when his energy is at its lowest, she’s hitting him with it. “I didn’t mean it, Nomi. I didn’t want Lamonte and the others examining Brittany too closely, and I had to say something to convince you she was dead, so I picked the worst thing I could think of.”

“*Deceptive and manipulative behavior*, huh?” If they were arguing, or if this were more of an interrogation, she’d be crossing her arms.

“I’m sorry,” he says simply.

She relaxes her shoulders, lets it go. “Ah, forget it. But next time we’re being tortured by mobsters, try not to be such a dick about it, yeah?”

“I’ll do my best.”

She nods and turns, mollified. “Okay, I’m outta here. See you in four hours.”

Once Nomi’s gone, Simon looks around. There’s still a little blood spatter on the floor, and the saucepan of ponche remains sitting on the stove. He drinks the water Nomi left for him and contemplates moving. His bed seems mighty appealing right now, but there are a number of actions he needs to perform to get there. He has to take off his coat, his boots, close his curtains. He also wouldn’t mind a coffee—a proper coffee—and a cigarette.

But before that, even, he needs food: He’s starving. Apparently, being abducted, and concussed, and tortured, and fighting for your life gives you an appetite—who knew?

Simon pushes himself upright by leaning on the breakfast table, hissing sharply when he straightens. But once he's up, it's easier. He putters about slowly in the kitchen, puts on coffee, rinses out the dirty saucepan, finds himself a plate, cutlery.

While the coffee is brewing, he goes to the bathroom and checks himself in the mirror. There he is, all right: a white man in his mid-twenties with a longish face, blue eyes. A fairly standard configuration for a face. He rubs two fingers over the ridged white scar where his neck meets his shoulder on the right. There are parts of him that are fixed, set, branded into him like this scar, like the scar beneath his hair. Other parts of him are life-changingly altered, or still in flux, and maybe—for the first time in five years—he can feel some peace about that. Not everything that was lost had value. Not everything that was lost was worth saving.

In the mirror, there's a raft of new bruises; he looks peaky and pale, and very much like he's been beaten up. But he looks normal. His features are stable, and he recognizes himself—he *knows* himself. He's still him.

Perhaps in this new country and new community, without the pressure of wondering if he'll be able to make the disparate elements of his identity line up, he can rewrite the story of who he is. Not *Haw*, not *Simon Gutmunsson*: just Simon Noone. A man of his own invention. A man who is trying—so very hard—to be good.

Simon gets coleslaw and a nice tomato from the refrigerator, cooks himself a steak. The steak is from his coat pocket, and it's—astonishingly—still fresh, still wrapped in paper from Gennaro's. It should fry up nicely.

As his meal is cooking, there's a knock on the door.

Sofia Rosa is puffed from climbing the stairs, and she's holding a bottle in one hand. "This wine? I do not like it. I have opened it at the top, see, just to try. But I tried, and I do not like it. I know you are drinking wine sometimes, so I bring it to you—maybe you will find some use for it."

“Thank you, Auntie.” He takes the bottle, examines the label. “Auntie, this is a Sangiovese. Where did you get this? Did you buy it?”

“It was given to me as a gift by Mr. Harvey. I think he is trying to ‘get into my pants,’ as the young people say.”

Simon coughs out a laugh, which hurts quite a bit, so he braces a palm on his stomach and holds further laughs in. “Right. Well, at least Mr. Harvey is buying you nice gifts. This is quite an expensive wine. Are you sure you don’t want to keep it?”

“Eh—expensive or cheap, it makes no difference if I do not like it, no?” Sofia Rosa peers at his face. “What has happened to you? You have bruises. Did you have another fight?”

“Something like that, Auntie, yes.”

“Well, I hope you won this time . . . All right, I am going back downstairs now to prepare my own food. That steak smells very good!”

He smiles as she retreats back toward the stairs. “Enjoy your dinner, Auntie. Thanks for the wine.”

Once he’s closed the door, Simon looks again at the bottle he’s been given: Goddamn, a Brunello di Montalcino . . . He’d be scrimping for weeks to buy a wine this good. He sets it on the breakfast table, finds himself a glass in the kitchen, ferries over his plate with the coleslaw and tomato and steak.

Cautiously, he sits down at the table, pours from the bottle, examines the color: gorgeous. What a gift. The aroma is like black cherries, full bodied and rich. The word *Sangiovese* is derived from the Latin, meaning “the blood of Jupiter”—it will pair beautifully with this cut of meat on his plate, which is small and tender, dripping with juices.

Simon takes a long swallow of wine, picks up his knife and fork, and begins to carve.

Acknowledgments

This is my thirteenth published novel, and I'm sorry to say it actually never gets easier to write a book. What keeps me going is the support of fans and friends and family, and my own chronic nosiness—I'm endlessly fascinated by the details I uncover while researching things like how serial killers think, the experiences of people with amnesia, and life in the Meatpacking District in the 1980s.

While researching *No One Is Safe*, some resources were invaluable. *The Answer to the Riddle Is Me* by David Stuart MacLean was my best reference on the subject of amnesia. For life in the Meatpacking District before its recent gentrification, I'm indebted to the NYC Department of Records, which owns the NYC Municipal Archives' Department of Finance Collection photorecord, now digitized as 80s.nyc online. I'd also like to acknowledge the online archive of street documentarian Nelson Sullivan, who recorded hours of amateur video that revealed the landscape, personalities, nightlife, and community of the district during the 1980s. I listened to the mixes of legendary DJ Larry Levan, from his time at the Paradise Garage. I also read through dozens of websites and blogs from queer community members who are working so hard to preserve documents, photos, and recollections about an area that's a significant part of NYC queer history.

As far as how serial killers think . . . Well, I still don't know if I've worked that out. But I must be doing something right, because readers who loved Simon Gutmunsson in the *None Shall Sleep* series keep telling me he's their favorite character—and it was a genuine delight to give Simon a new name and a new story in this book, and pair him up with Nomi to watch sparks fly. Thank you to every reader, especially fans and friends who've supported my work through my newsletters, *The Black Hand* and *Nailbiters*.

I'd like to thank my agent, Josh Adams, and my acquiring editor, Jessica Tribble-Wells, and my developmental editor, Charlotte Herscher, as well as everyone on the Thomas & Mercer team who's helped usher Simon and Nomi into the limelight. Love and thanks to CS Pacat, whose friendship and professional support have made all the difference. Special thanks also to my House of Progress buds, my Sisters in Crime friends, and longtime writing pals.

Finally, I wouldn't make it past page one without the love and support of my kids—Ben, Alex, Will, and Ned—who give me pep talks and hugs and help me game out action scenes. And I'd be lost without my partner, Geoff, who carries the can while I'm grinding away in my writing cave, and who makes all this effort worth it. Thank you, babes—love you guys a lot.

xxEllie

About the Author

Photo © 2019 Christopher Tovo

Ellie Marney is an internationally bestselling author of thrillers. Her titles include *New York Times* bestseller *None Shall Sleep*, *Kirkus Reviews*–starred sequel *Some Shall Break*, and fan-favorite finale *All Shall Mourn*, as well as ARA Historical Novel Prize–nominated *The Killing Code*, and many more. Published worldwide, her work has been optioned for the screen. Ellie has spent a lifetime researching in mortuaries, interviewing law enforcement and autopsy specialists, and asking former spies how to make explosives from household items. Now she lives quite sedately in southeastern Australia with her family as she writes her next book. Find out more about Ellie on social media, at her website, or through her newsletter, *The Black Hand*.